Gordon Stables

Stanley Grahame, Boy and Man

A tale of the dark continent

Gordon Stables

Stanley Grahame, Boy and Man
A tale of the dark continent

ISBN/EAN: 9783337027179

Printed in Europe, USA, Canada, Australia, Japan

Cover: Foto ©Andreas Hilbeck / pixelio.de

More available books at **www.hansebooks.com**

"FINE FUN FOR BOY GREEN."

STANLEY GRAHAME

BOY AND MAN.

A Tale of the Dark Continent.

BY

GORDON STABLES, M.D., R.N.

AUTHOR OF
"WILD ADVENTURES ROUND THE POLE," "THE CRUISE OF THE SNOWBIRD," ETC.

WITH EIGHTEEN ILLUSTRATIONS.

NEW YORK:
A. C. ARMSTRONG & SON,
714, BROADWAY.
1886

TO MY BOLD BOY,

DONALD GORDON,

THIS BOOK IS INSCRIBED.

CONTENTS.

Contents.

Contents.

LIFE IN THE GREAT FOREST BROTHER AND SISTER—THE PARTING

CHAPTER I.

THE great forest.

The forest of Cairntrie.

Far away in the very centre of the Scottish Highlands
it lies; so broad and wide is it, that you might journey for
days and days on its outskirts, yet not be able to find your
way around it. Lost in its depths and you would be lost
indeed. For unless some friendly keeper found you and
became your guide, the dreary winds would sing your
dirge, and your bones, unburied, might bleach for months.

In this great forest are hills and lakes and streams, and
it is the home *par excellence* of the red deer of Scotland.
Wild and free are they as the unchangeable mountains
from which they gaze proudly down on their woody
domains. It was of some such place as this that Professor
Wilson, poet and angler, penned these lines:

> "How lonesome and wild! yet the wildness is rife
> With the stir of enjoyment—the spirit of life.
> The glad fish leaps up in the heart of the lake,
> Whose depths at the sudden plunge sullenly quake.
> Elate on the fern-bush the grasshopper sings,
> And away in the midst of his roundelay springs;
> While up on yon hill, in silence remote,
> The cuckoo unseen is repeating his note."

They tell me that the forest of Cairntrie is also the home
of a race of beings still more interesting than red deer.
That banished by civilization from the woody dells and

dingles of merrie England, the fairies have migrated to this romantic region. That here in straths and glens, in many a ferny glade, in many a birchen hollow, they still may be seen holding their revels under the midnight stars, or dancing by the light of the glowworm's torch.

Leaving braes that are green with the rustling foliage of the silvery birch, or purple with the heather's bloom, a river plunges into the gloom of the pine forest and disappears. And if you follow its winding course, you will find it at times flowing onwards dark and dreamily beneath the lofty trees, as if loth to leave their leafy shade ; at times rushing along with heedless speed among rocks and over boulders, as if in sudden fear of the lonesome gloom around it, and anon dashing in pearly foam through a narrow chasm, then falling down, down, down for hundreds of feet into a dark pool, the black depth of which one shudders even to think of. But sweetest flowerets, born of the forest's balmy breath, and nurtured by the rainbowed spray of the cascade, nod over the rocky walls of the abyss, and gladden even that.

Come with me into the forest, for here we shall find our hero, young Stanley Grahame, and his little sister Ailie.

Here is many a pleasant spot, many a ferny flowery nook, many a leafy labyrinth green-carpeted with moss and odorous with the scent of pines. We may miss the song of the nightingale, but our ears will drink in the ringing notes of the speckled mavis and the plaintive piping of the blackbird, and we may listen to the mournful croodle of the cushat, deep hid in the thicket of spruce, and the wild scream of the curlew hovering in mid air. We may see the nests of the hoody crow, the brown owl, the hawk, and the solitary capercailzie, and at times, far up in heaven's blue, we may catch glimpses of an immense bird slowly circling round—the great golden-headed eagle. Our footsteps shall startle the bounding red deer, but the leveret and coney will scarcely scurry away at our approach ; and as we push our way through the branching breckans, from its little den cautiously shall peer forth the pole-cat and eye us curiously as we pass.

Oh! the world of life that is to be found in this beautiful forest, on its mountains and hills, in its tarns and streams, on every branch and twig and leaf, beneath the ferns, and in the very flower-bells themselves. If you wandered here as often as I do, and if you wandered but to wonder and admire and worship the Creator through His creatures, then, instead of fearing and fleeing from you, every animal, from the gentle dormouse to the mountain deer, would love you and look upon you as, like themselves, a denizen of the woods.

But where is our hero? Where are Stanley Grahame and his sister Ailie.

Let us shout for him until the forest resounds again.

"Stanley! Stanley! Stanley Grahame, where are you?"

But Stanley answers not. For, to tell you the truth, Stanley Grahame is nowhere on the face of the earth. Nor his sister either.

Let us look for them elsewhere.

Hullo! what is this leaning against the tree? A gun, I declare!

And what is this lying on the mossy sward? Why, it is a hat!

And to whom do the gun and the hat belong? To our hero and Ailie, if I am not much mistaken. But where in the name of mystery have they got to? Well, I can tell you. It was a Saturday, you must know, and so Stanley had not to go to school, and as he always spent his holidays in the great forest of Cairntrie, his sister and he left their mother's humble cottage quite early in the morning, he with his gun, she with her little fishing-rod and basket, and they had been wandering about all the day, and a lovely summer's day it was. They had caught not a few trout, they had found many a sweetly pretty fern, and

caplurea some of the rarest butterflies and moths. They
had dined in the forest too ; they had built a fire in a rocky
corner, and fried their fish gipsy-fashion, and their dessert
was wild strawberries, which they enjoyed very much.
But they had grown tired at last of roaming about, and felt
very glad to throw themselves down to rest by the banks
of a clear purling brooklet, which, for the most part, went

singing along over its pebbly bed, but subsided every here
and there into a quiet sandy-bottomed pool. It was near
such a pool that they had sat down, and for a time they
had watched with interest the antics of a whole crowd
of minnows, who were mobbing a big water-beetle, and
apparently laughing at his ungainly efforts to escape, until
at long last a large round-nosed red-speckled trout came
sailing into the very centre of them, like a man-o'-war

frigate among a fleet of fishing smacks, and they darted off in all directions.

Then,

"I say, Ailie," Stanley had said.

"Yes, Stan," Ailie had answered.

"Let us climb away up into the topmost branches of that green beech-tree."

"Come on, then, Stan!" Ailie had cried; "I'll go first."

What a world of foliage was there! What a sea of sighing leaves, glistening in the sunshine, fanned by the summer air, and musical with the hum of wild bees! They had soon lost sight of the earth altogether, but had continued to climb and climb as long as they thought the branches would bear them; and then, side by side, the brother's arm around his sister's waist, they had sat them down on a bough.

My hero and Ailie are there, then, when I first introduce them to your notice. They have quite lost sight of the earth long ago, and, indeed, they have forgotten all about it. They know, I daresay, that it is away down there, somewhere beneath those clouds of living green; but what is the lower world, with all its cares and its sorrows, to them? They are in a little leafy heaven of their own, and as happy and contented as any of the great drowsy-looking velvety bees that are droning around them.

I wonder that the hum of the myriad bees, mingling with the whispering of the summer breeze, does not send them both to sleep. But I think they are quite alive to the fact that dropping off to sleep would mean dropping off the branch, and so they are wide enough awake.

And well they may be, for Stanley is telling his little sister, who is gazing up into his face with round, wondering eyes, an oft-repeated tale, but one she is never tired of listening to.

"And you know, Ailie," the boy is saying, "you were

only a baby then; you're seven now, you know, and I am nearly a man—I'm twelve. But oh, Sissie! I will never forget that terrible night as long as I live! What a lovely farm ours was! even its ruins are lovely still! We used to have ten pairs of horses working together in one field, Ailie. Then father was so big and strong and beautiful. But people often said the steading was built too close to the river. Well, Ailie dear, I was in the harvest-field, when suddenly it grew all dark, and the thunder began to

roll and the lightning to flash, and then it came on to rain and hail. Oh! such awful, awful rain! And all the afternoon it rained and poured, and the night closed in all black and dismal. I had gone to bed, but I was awakened at midnight with the shout, 'The river is coming down! I think I must have been washed out of bed, but my mother caught me—and she had you, too, Ailie—and then she fled with us up on to higher ground, and there we stood all the livelong night in the torrents of rain and in the darkness, and mother praying for poor father, who was not with us, and whom we never, never saw again. He is in heaven, Ailie, and maybe he sees us here at this very moment. Well, Sissie, in the morning we could see nothing of the farm, nothing at all anywhere but the great rolling river that had risen higher than the houses and higher than the tallest trees, Ailie. Oh! it was fearsome, Sissie—fearsome!"

The boy shudders, and clasps his sister closer to his side.

"But," says his little comforter, "we are very happy now in our cottage, aren't we, Stan? And we have mother and Collie and pussy and the two·cows. And father *is* in heaven, isn't he, Stan?"

"Yes, Sissie, I'm sure of that," says Stan.

Then there is a silence for a time, and the children watch the bees.

Presently the sweet, clear voice of Ailie breaks it. "What will you do when you are a man, Stanley?"

"Oh!" says Stanley, "I mean to do something long, long before I am a man. Indeed, I ought to do something now, for I am very, very tall for my age."

"You are very, very handsome," adds his sister.

"I am going to be a sailor, Sissie, and travel all over the world and see strange countries, and have such fun—just the same as Tom Cringle had, you know; and wild adventures like Stanley and Livingstone and Robinson Crusoe!"

"Oh, but not the island, Stan!" says Ailie.

"Well," replies Stan, thoughtfully, "perhaps not the island, although that would be very nice too."

"But then, Stan," persists Ailie, "of course you won't go away to leave us for a long, long, *long* time yet. Say ' of course not!' Stan."

"Well, Sissie, I don't know; it might be sooner than we think, because there is Uncle Mackinlay out in America, and he is so good and kind, and he has promised to ' make a man of me,' Ailie; and if he were to send for me would have to go at once."

Ailie creeps close to him and shudders.

" Look ! look !" she cries. " Look at the evil bird !"

" Craik—craik—craik ! " screams a magpie on a bough close beside them. " Craik—craik—craik—craik !"

Stanley pitches his hat at it, and the bird disappears. So does the hat.

" I should die, Stanley, if you were going away soon."

" Providence will protect me, Ailie, wherever I go," says Stanley, stoutly. " And I'll come back rich, Ailie. Then we will take another big farm like dear father's, and mother and you and I will be *so* happy, won't we, Sissie ?"

But Sissie did not answer.

From the language in which they speak the reader will perceive that these two children were a stamp above the ordinary boys and girls one meets in a Highland glen. They were. For, poor though their widowed mother was, she spared no pains with their education. Mrs. Grahame had married young. She was the daughter of a clergyman, and wedded a wealthy farmer. They prospered in life, and their existence was a very happy one, until the awful night when the river rose and swept away servants and master, cattle and harvest, leaving only desolation and ruin where peace and plenty had smiled before

By the help of kindly neighbours the widow had been enabled to take the small cottage by the forest edge which they now occupied, and by the help of their cows and croft they managed to eke out a humble existence.

The great lord who owned the wide forest of Cairntrie promised to take Stanley Grahame as a keeper, but the boy's proud spirit rebelled against the idea. · He dearly loved a free life, it is true. And he loved nature in all her varied moods. There was not a flower, there was not a weed he was not familiar with ; there was not a creeping thing he could not have told you all about, nor an animal in brae-land, field, or forest, nor a fish in lake or stream, which he knew not the habits of. And as for birds, he knew them all individually and minutely. Firstly, he could tell you the name of any bird from listening a few seconds to its notes ; secondly, he could tell any bird from its eggs ; and, thirdly, he could tell any bird from the build of its nest without seeing either eggs or owner.

He was, indeed, a roving boy, but withal a good boy, although somewhat dreamy and poetic; he never stirred abroad without a book.

I wish I could linger here a little longer, and tell you more about Stanley Grahame's peaceful life at home, for wild and stormy are the scenes through which he has to pass in the future that lies before him.

Suffice it to say that Stanley loved his home, his mother and sister, oh ! *so* dearly.

And what would a sailor be who had no home to think of ? What would he be worth ? Worth ! Why, simply the value of a reckless, careless man, without a stake in life. But a boy at sea or in a foreign land will be apt to be brave and good and true if he has a home for his thoughts to revert to, if he knows that kind hearts far away love and pray for him. Would a boy who has such a home fear to do his duty ? No. "What would they say in England ?" Would he show the white feather ? or would his cheeks blanch with terror on the stormiest day at sea that ever blew ? No; his comrades would notice it, and "What would they say in England ?"

Evening was creeping o'er the glen when hand in hand Stanley and his sister walked up through the garden and entered their mother's cottage.

They found her in tears.

There was a letter lying on the table, to which she merely pointed, and Ailie's wee heart seemed to stand still as Stanley read it. It was from Captain Mackinlay, the uncle in America

The time for parting had come, then. Stanley was almost ordered to get ready at once and leave home to join his uncle. What could he do but obey ? What could his widowed mother do ? It was very hard to part with her boy, but then parting had to come sooner or later, and she would not, dared not, spoil his prospects.

"No," she said to herself; "love is no love at all that cannot make a sacrifice. My boy must go."

We will pass over the week or two that followed ere Stanley Grahame's departure. Probably the bitterest part of the poor mother's grief lay in the sad fact that she could not accompany her son even as far as Aberdeen. But poverty and home duties forbade. He must go all alone.

It was early dawn on a lovely morning—the morning of Stanley Grahame's departure to begin the battle of life in earnest. The blackbirds had not long begun to pipe, the chaffinches were trilling their bold, bright songs, the cushats croodling in the spruce-fir coppice. For through the widely-opened casement of our young hero's bedroom came the gentle sighing of the wind among the pine-trees ; that and the song of birds mingled with the distant bleating of sheep were all the sounds to be heard.

Early though it was the boy lay wide awake, although his eyes were closed and he seemed to sleep.

Half an hour passes away, then the door which had been a little ajar slowly opens, and there stands a figure one might have taken for Stanley's guardian angel.

It is Ailie.

All draped in white is the winsome wee lassie, with naked feet, and hair floating over her shoulders. Her mournful big blue eyes look none the less lovely because there are signs of recent tears about them. She stands for a moment as if undecided, then with her eyes fixed on the boy's face she timidly advances, and then Stanley opens his eyes and their glances meet. One look at that sad pale face tells the brother all. She has never closed an eye, she has been weeping, she has been thinking only of him—thinking and praying; and now she has come to be near him for a portion of the short time that is before them.

She thought he was asleep, but seeing he is awake the child sister advances rapidly, and sinks into the chair by his pillow, and over this pillow both arms are flung in the wild abandonment of grief; her head sinks on her arms, and she sobs as if her heart would break. The brother does not attempt in words to stem this torrent of sorrow. How could he? Poor lad, he is nearly breaking down himself. All the day before he had been trying to keep up her heart by imaginary tales of all the fine countries he would see, and all the fine things he would bring home, and how often he would write, and how happy they would be when he returned; but all this is past now, so he does not strive to stay her tears. He only draws one of her arms round his neck and gently pats her on the shoulder as a mother does her baby. Her sobs, by-and-by, get less violent, the heart has been somewhat relieved; but short, quick sighs still testify to the violence of her grief.

Without moving from his position, or disturbing the little arm entwined about his neck, the boy with his right hand pulls off from his own bed the big Scotch plaid—it was their father's—and draws it round his sister's form.

The blackbird flutes, the cushat croodles in the spruce thicket, then the sun glints down the glen and floods it all with beauty, gilding the green of the lofty firs, and silvering the bosom of the swiftly-flowing river; more birds awake and join their voices to swell the morning melody, and the wind still sighs softly through the pine-trees with a sound like falling water, but the brother and sister sleep.

And when the mother comes at last to the room to see if her boy be stirring, she finds them so, and steals away on quietest tiptoe to prepare the morning meal.

THE "EIRDE" HOUSE ON THE MOOR—DAFT JEAN WEIR—THE SMUGGLERS—MURDOCH'S POOL.

CHAPTER II.

THE summer's day was wearing rapidly to a close, for
though it had been warm and sunny, with every
prospect of a long twilight, no sooner had the sun sunk
behind the western mountains than great grey clouds had
arisen and quite obscured the sky. No moon or stars could
shine to-night; that leaden canopy boded only an inky
darkness—a darkness, too, that would be felt; for as Stanley Grahame, all by himself in the midst of that wild
hobgoblin moorland, turned his face upwards a drop or
two of rain fell on his warm cheek and brow.

"Only heat drops," he said to himself; "it won't be rain,
and the village can't be far off now; I shall soon reach it."

But had he been a sailor he would have thought differently; he would have seen signs in the clouds of a
coming storm; for wicked wee water-dogs were scudding
across the sky, and out from the level blackness near the
horizon came ever and anon many a little puff of greyish
mist, for all the world as if someone were firing a rifle out
of the cloud and speedily retiring after every shot.

How came Stanley here all by himself in the middle of
this dreary moorland? This is a question that is easily
answered.

A walk of ten miles from his own door would have taken
him to the mouth of the glen, where the mail coach passed,

and hence his journey to Aberdeen, called the granite city, would have been both easy and pleasant. But Stanley was not burdened with overmuch money, so he had determined to send his box on with the carrier and walk. He was very young, and for his age as supple and strong as one of the red deer in the forest of Cairntrie. It was only a journey after all of sixty miles; and before he started, stick in hand, he got all the directions his memory could retain from old

Ewen McPhee, once his father's shepherd. Indeed that worthy had accompanied him for five long miles over the hills, and then with his crook he had pointed out to him the way the young pilgrim should take.

They were on the very summit of the brae-land at the time. It was early morning, and taking one last lingering look behind him, Stanley could see all the charming glen spread out before him like some beautiful scene in a phant ismagoria. Woods, and wilds, and meadows green, and the bonnie bright river wimpling through it all, and his mother's cottage among the broom, and the blue smoke curling up from it and floating away over the pine-trees. Was it any wonder that a big lump rose up in his throat and well-nigh choked him ? Was it any wonder that the directions old Ewen was trying so earnestly to instil into him were for the most part lost upon the boy ?

Only the thought that he was going away into the world to make his fortune sustained him. The words of his mother's blessing still rang in his ears, and he knew that she and his sister Ailie would always, always pray for him, so he gulped down the lump in his throat, dashed his sleeve only once across his eyes, then caught Ewen by his horny hand and bade him adieu.

The tears were trickling down the old man's furrowed face, he made no attempt to hide them or to wipe them away. He just let them fall. But his parting advice to Stanley was a queer jumble, though quite characteristic of men of his class in the Scottish Highlands.

He pressed Stanley's soft hand between his own two hard ones as he said,—

" And it's och ! and och ! may the Lord sustain and keep you, my dear boy—and it's down through Glenbucket you'll go, Stanley —and you'll pray to Him morning and night—till you come to the castle o' Towie and see the big hill o' Coreen. And it's och ! but this life is short at the best—and at last you'll come to Paradise,* and if you call there and see old Nanny Watson, she'll give you the best bit o' bread and cheese ever you tasted, Stanley. Och, my *bronan*, my *chree*, it's poor old Ewen's heart that will surely break this bitter night."

And so on, and more to the same effect, spoke the shepherd, till Stanley clutched his stick and fled, and was soon hidden from view by the silver birch-trees.

* Paradise, a beautiful place near Monymusk

But Stanley had made one very great mistake. For after journeying on all day till far into the afternoon in the main road, he had forsaken it for what he felt sure was a near cut, and now he was here alone, not a hut nor house in sight, only heathy moorland with ne'er a stock nor stone peeping through the heather's green, wheresoever he turned his gaze.

" I wish," he said, half aloud, for the silence was irksome, and broken only now and then by whirr of wild duck's wing, mournful whistle of whaup [curlew], or plaintive bleating of mire-snipe—" I wish I had taken Ewen's advice, and kept to the road, I might have been half-way to Paradise by this time. But who's afraid ? I'll stick to this road now I am on it."

He gave one more quick glance at the sky, then hurried on. More than once he had to go off the narrow path to avoid great snakes, that although the day was closing, still lay in sleeping coils here and there. They were not poisonous, but he was not to know that.

And the shadows kept falling. He pulled out a book—it was the Bible his sister had put in his pocket—and found to his dismay it was so dark already he could hardly decipher a word. He walked all the more quickly after that, with many an anxious glance ahead.

Where *could* she have come from ? She stood all at once right in his path, she appeared to have sprung from the very ground on which she stood. An old weazened hag. Surely a witch ? What could she be but a witch, with that stern set face, hooked nose, and glaring eyes— with those elfin locks escaping from beneath her flapping mutch, the long pole in her right hand, and the mantle down-drooping from her raised arm ?

Stanley was afraid now ; he stopped and stared, but he could not speak, and he could hear his heart thudding against his ribs. But her first words reassured him some- what.

"How you scared me!" she cried, in an earnest pathetic voice; "and I daresay I scared you. Whaur are ye goin', poor lost laddie, at this untimeous hour of the night? I'm only daft Jean o' Fondlan' Glen, dinna be feared."

"I'm not afraid," said Stanley, stoutly. "But tell me, am I on the straight road to Glenbucket?"

"Poor lost laddie!" said Jean, sadly; "you're on the straight road to ruin if daft Jean takes not care o' you. There's no' a house within ten miles o' here but Jean's. Dinna be feared, this is not ane o' my mad nights; and if it were I wadna injure you. Dear lost laddie, I knew your faither weel, and you've got your faither's een [eyes]. I'll take care o' you. But if the smugglin' billies were to meet you here they'd——"

"What?" asked Stanley, his teeth beginning to chatter.

"Rob, and perhaps slay ye!" said daft Jean, "and bury your body in a pool so deep that ne'er a bubble would rise to tell a tale. No, Jean's no' mad to-night; sometimes I am. Sometimes at the dark hour o' midnight strange things come to Jean's lanely hut, and they keep speak, speak, speaking, and chatter, chatter, chattering to one another in a corner; then they come to the bed and say, ' Rise, Jean! rise, Jean, rise!' and I have to go with them, away o'er the lonesome moorland, far awa' to the haunted quarry o' Pitfreem, and there I see such sights—such fearsome, fearsome sights! But Jean is sane and wise to-night," she continued, "and, if he'll only let her, she'll save Grahame's poor lost laddie from the smugglers o' Glen Fondlan'. Come!"

Stanley glanced at her face for one quick moment. All the madness seemed clean gone out of it, pity alone was all he could read in that now womanly countenance. He still hesitated, however: but just then a horizontal stream of lightning seemed to cut the sky in two, and blinding darkness followed.

Stanley pressed his hand to his eyes; he saw only bloodied and blue. " I'll go with you," he said, " as you knew my faith——"

The rest of the sentence was lost in the hurtling roar of thunder, and big drops of hail began to patter on the ground before them.

" Let us go quick, then," said Jean ; " it's no' the storm I fear, nor care a pin-head for ; but if the lads come up and see us th'gither they'd suspect treason, and mayhap it's in the black bottom o' Murdoch's Pool we'd have to seek our supper."

Young and strong though he was, it was all he could do to keep pace with this strange wild woman. She forsook the path entirely and took to the hill, the heather sometimes up as high as their waists. They soon came to a little foot-path, and this they followed, and ere long Stanley found himself in what had, many hundreds of years ago, been a field, for the fence that was still round it had sunk almost to a level with the earth. In the middle of this enclosure was a long, low, flat-roofed building, probably not more than eight feet high, and entirely built of flat stones, with pebbles filling up the interstices, but neither lime nor mortar had ever come nigh it.

"This is daft Jean's dwellin'," said his strange guide ; "'twas never built by mortal hands. It's dark and dismal inside, but Jean's lamps will soon mak' it as bricht as day."

The door or entrance to this curious building was at one end. This led to a small ante-chamber, through which you passed into the principal room, some twenty feet long by eight wide, and eight high, stone roof, stone floor, and bare stone walls. At the farther end of this an opening, a few feet from the ground, but not much bigger than a small window, led to an inner chamber, not quite so large as the other, but of the same shape, and built all round of stone like the other.

Stanley had never seen so strange a dwelling before, but he had read of the *cirde* houses of the north, and rightly judged that this was one of them. Well might daft Jean have come to the conclusion that this place was built by no mortal hands, for so old are these buildings, that tradition itself gives no account of the wild beings who once made them their homes.

In the centre of the principal room a fire of peats smouldered on a hearth built around a stone, and this Jean soon fanned into a flame with her mouth. She then lit oil lamps that hung on the walls, both in this room and in the ante-chamber, and Stanley could then see that the few articles of furniture, table, chairs, and a daïs, were all of the rudest description.

"In there is your bedroom, poor lost laddie," said Jean, pointing to the inner apartment; "you'll find a bed o' rushes, but ne'er a light you'll have, for the lads will be here ere long, and if they found you——"

As she spoke she hoisted a great pot from a corner, and hung it on a crook over the fire.

"Soup, laddie, soup," she said, "soup o' the best, soup o' pairtrich, young grouse, eggs, and hare. You'll have the first pannikin, and nice you'll find it. The boys 'll no be here, I reckon, for an hour or more to come. So mak' yoursel' at hame in the meanwhile."

Stanley was both tired and hungry, and therefore not averse to do justice to the good fare daft Jean placed before him. Rude though the hut was, it was a shelter, and the storm that now raged outside made the fire look quite like a friend. Many a strange story of her life in the moorland did Jean tell him, and of the terrible gang of smugglers that made the *eirde* house their headquarters, and Jean herself their spy on pain of death.

"I'm but a witch, they tell me," said the poor creature, "and the bottom o' Murdoch's Pool is only my deserts if I dinna do as I'm told."

"Were you always——" began Stanley, but hesitated, reddening.

"Was I aye daft, aye mad, you were going to say," said Jean. "No, laddie, no; and oh! if ever you meet my Archie, Archie Weir, tell him, oh! tell him to come back and close his auld mither's een, and I'll forgive him for the heart he has broken. He was my only stay and comfort, but wild and hasty like his father before him; one angry word, and Archie went away, and I've never seen him more. They turned me oot o' house and holdin', and this cold bield is all I have to shelter me; but if Archie were back I'd never be daft or wud (mad) again."

"But where am I likely to meet him?" asked Stanley, innocently.

"Somewhere in the wide, wide world," said the old dame, speaking as if to herself, and looking not at Stanley, but into the fire; "somewhere in the wide, wide world Stanley Grahame will meet wi' Archie Weir. His ship was wrecked on African shores, but Archie didna die. I've seen his face in the fire. I see him now; there are savages around him, he is their slave, as I am the slave o' the smugglers. He is trying to escape. Look, look! They chase him, they fell him to the earth with their fearsome clubs; they raise their clubs to finish their work, but sword in hand another rushes in, and stands triumphant over him. That one is Stanley Grahame!

"Oh, Stanley!" she continued, turning to the boy, "I've saved your life this blessed night. Promise me, then, that if ever you meet my boy you'll bring him back to his poor auld mither. Promise."

"I promise," said Stanley, hardly knowing what words he uttered, for there was a wondrous fascination in the woman's voice and eyes.

"Listen," she said. "In this house there is gold buried beneath these stones. We'll dig it up when Archie—but, hush, hush! In with you to your room! Quick, Quick! the smugglers are coming."

In a moment Stanley had disappeared—had leapt through

the opening into the inner apartment with all the agility of a cat.

None too soon. Dripping wet, but singing snatches of old bacchanalian songs, and evidently cheerful withal, five men in all filed into the apartment.

"Ha! Jean, old girl," cried one, laying his hand not unkindly on the old woman's shoulder. "Here is a night."

"Just such a night as we like," said another.

"Yes, lass," said the former, who seemed to be leader, "and a rare piece of luck we've had. But bustle about, old girl, and get us supper. Duncan, give us a dram. Out wi' the bottle, man."

"I'll have the bottle," cried Jean, suddenly springing forward and catching it. "No' a drop do one o' ye taste until you've had your meal. Jean Weir has spoken; thwart her if ye can or dare."

"Weel, weel, Jean, so be it," said the leader; "but you're in a queer temper to-night. Are you goin' mad on our hands again?"

"Never a mad," replied daft Jean. "I've been thinkin', that's all. But sit down, laddies. You'll never have to say that Jean starved you."

The smugglers ate like men who had not seen meat since morning, and the conversation was limited indeed until the banquet was cleared away. Then—

"Now, Jean, the whiskey."

It is not my intention to relate all that passed or was said in the *eirde* house that night. Suffice it to say that these men began by relating their exploits, and some of these relations made the blood of our hero run cold. Then songs were sung, and ranting choruses. Then they must dance, and old Jean, with quavering voice, must lilt to them while they capered and reeled. Towards morning they quarrelled, and fierce blows were given and returned.

"Where are you going?" cried Jean, suddenly, when

peace was restored, seeing the leader of the party staggering towards the room where Stanley lay concealed.

" In there," roared the man, "there is a spy in the house. I know it, men, I know."

" A spy !" was the excited chorous. "Out with him. Off with him to the deepest spot in Murdoch's Pool.

" Out with the spy ! Quick, men, quick !"

For a moment, though but a moment, it seemed that young Stanley was doomed. But Jean was equal to the occasion. She made no attempt to prevent the smugglers from rushing to the inner apartment, but she blew out the lights. Stanley took the hint. He dropped down among his would-be captors, and slipping along the wall, was out and away from the house ere it was possible for the rioters to strike a match.

Out and away from the terrible *eirde* house ran our boy, and never stopped to breathe until he had placed a good mile between himself and his would-be murderers.

He knew not, nor cared, in which direction he was running. All he cared for was to get away ; and, oh that he could find some means of helping poor Jean ! Morning was breaking, though—that was some comfort to him.

In the west the bright stars were still aglow, but away in the east an ever-broadening belt of light appeared and paled the planets in its upward course. He turned his face towards it and hurried on.

Morning broke raw and somewhat cheerless, but with every appearance of a glorious summer's day. Linnets came out of the heathery banks, shook the dew from their wings, and after giving vent to a peevish chirp or two, broke fully into song.

On and on for miles, then he found himself at the end of the wide moorland, and on the edge of a hill, with far beneath him a beautiful and fertile glen, and the glorious Don—it could be no other river—meandering through its midst.

Stanley was glad to remember he had food in his wallet. He made a hearty breakfast. Then he crept in under a bush, where, though sheltered from the sun's rays, he had a view of all the bonnie glen. He did not see it long, however. There was the odour of the golden gorse all around him, the song of the linnet on the thorn, and the drowsy hum of summer insects. His eyes twinkled. He tried hard to keep them open, but the lids were heavy—heavy—heav——. Why, I do declare our hero has gone to sleep.

III.

STANLEY CONTINUES HIS JOURNEY—AND FINDS A FRIEND—THE GOOD SHIP "TANTALLAN CASTLE."

CHAPTER III.

STANLEY CONTINUES HIS JOURNEY—AND FINDS A FRIEND—
THE GOOD SHIP "TANTALLAN CASTLE."

WHEN Stanley Grahame awoke at last from his slumbers under the thorn-tree the sun was a goodly way up in the sky. Smoke was ascending from every cottage and house in the glen below, going straight up into the air, spreading out, and dissolving into ether, for there was not a breath of wind, nor was there a cloud in all the blue firmament. He sat up and rubbed his eyes, closed them and rubbed them, and then looked again. Then he sat for a time with a sort of a puzzled expression on his handsome young face that was quite comical to behold. He could not remember where he was, or why and wherefore he came to be sitting there. He called to mind the events of the previous night, but thought they must be only part and parcel of a frightful dream.

Then he happened to put his hand to his breast pocket, and there he found THE BOOK. Ah! that recalled him to his senses. He remembered everything now—where he was, and whither he was going. His thoughts were thoughts of thankfulness, and although there was a weight as of lead at his heart when his mind reverted to his cottage · home and the dear ones he left behind him, as well as to poor wild Jean, he did not forget to pray.

Just one word about the Bible that Ailie had given to her brother before he started from home. It was a small pocket edition, and, though clear in type. was very old. It had belonged to Stanley's father. There were leaves turned down here and there, evidently marking passages from which a former reader had obtained comfort—perhaps in sorrow. One of these marked the 91st Psalm. Stanley read it all through, and thought it very, very beautiful, as indeed it is.

"Heigho!" sighed the boy. "I do wish, though, I had not to leave home and go wandering away over this world. What do I want of riches? Couldn't I stay at home and be a farmer? But no; I couldn't be a farmer."

He had placed the Bible beside him on the grass, and it had opened by chance, as it were—if, indeed, anything can happen by chance in a world over which God rules; but when next he glanced down his eye fell upon the nineteenth verse of the 77th Psalm, and these words: "Thy way is in the sea, and thy path in the great waters."

Young Stanley got up, very quietly but determinedly, as if full of a great purpose. He restored the Bible to his breast-pocket, then he turned his face in the direction of his home. He spoke, half-unconsciously, aloud, and the words he said were brave words, but there was not one single atom of excitability or theatrical display about the boy as he uttered them.

"Good-bye, mother dear; good-bye, Ailie. I did not feel until this very moment that we had parted. I'm not sure I had not meant to have come back again within a week. But *now* farewell. The boy you love will *not* return until he can do so with houour, if not with riches. Good-bye."

Then Stanley started down the glen. There was a lark high up in air, fanning the clouds with its wings as it trilled its song. Oh, how blithely the birdie sang! It was so filled with joy and hope that I verily believe its little heart would have burst, had it not been able to find vent for its feelings in music. But I doubt if that lark's song was a bit more gleesome than that of our hero's as he marched along the road on that lovely summer's morning all by himself. His thoughts were not with the present, but away somewhere in the golden future, and I am not at all certain that he was conscious that he was singing. Nevertheless, many a passer-by turned round to look after him, and many a country "goodwife" looked out at her cottage door and muttered, with a smile, "God bless the dear laddie! Isn't it light-hearted and merry he is?"

Five miles an hour, if an inch, walked Stanley, twirling his stick in the air as he went, and now and then playing terrible havoc among the nettles and docks by the roadside, but never touching a thistle.

"Will you have a ride, my boy?" said a kind and cheerful voice.

He looked up and found there was a dogcart close alongside him, with a spirited horse and a spirited-looking though elderly gentleman fingering the ribbons.

"Thank you, sir," said Stanley, and next moment he was seated beside his new friend.

"You seem light-hearted, lad," said the gentleman; "you were singing."

"Was I?" replied Stanley.

"Well, yes; I should think you knew, and a beautiful voice you'll have—when it is broken."

"Oh, dear!" said Stanley, "isn't it broken yet? Indeed, I forgot for the moment it wasn't. But I feel quite old."

The gentleman laughed, and even the horse shook his head till his gilt bradoons glittered and rattled, as if even he appreciated so good a joke. "Old? Ha! ha! ha! What makes you feel old, boy, eh?"

"I don't know, sir," said Stanley Grahame, "but I seem to have grown a man since yesterday."

"Dear me!" said the gentleman, gazing at him with smiles chasing each other all round his lips and eyes. "Why, where did you sleep last night? I heard of a boy once who went to bed on top of a b g of guano, and when he awoke in the morning his own mother didn't know him, he had grown so tall during the night."

"But," replied Stanley, laughing, "I didn't sleep on top of a guano-bag."

Then he told him his adventures since he left home, pleading on poor Jean's behalf, and finishing up with these words: "And indeed, sir, it seems quite ten years since I bade old Ewen good-bye on the brae-head, and if I go on like this, you know, I shall be seventy before Saturday."

The gentleman laughed again, then,

"Sing me a song," he said.

This was very abrupt, but Stanley was not taken aback in the slightest. He was one of those boys who always seem prepared for a shift of wind, so off he went into the gold-diggers' chorus, quite as naturally as though he had had twenty-four hours, twenty minutes, and nineteen seconds' notice that a song was to be required of him.

> " Pull away cheerily,
>   Not slow and wearily,
> Rocking the cradle, boys, swift to and fro ;
>   Working the hand about,
>   Sifting the sand about,
> Looking for treasures that lie in below."

A rattling song to a rattling tune, and the rattle of wheels made splendid accompaniment.

" Bravo!" cried the gentleman, clapping his gloved hands. " Well done! I never saw my old mare go like that before. Why, boy, you're a trump."

"I don't know what a 'trump' is, though," replied Stanley. " I was a tramp before you kindly picked me up, and I am twelve years of age."

"Twelve? only twelve?" was the remark.

Twelve last birthday," added Stanley.

" Well, well, well, I never," said the gentleman; " but, don't you tell me, you *have* been sleeping on a guano-bag."

Stanley laughed, and so did the gentleman, and the mare whisked at imaginary flies with her tail, and sped swiftly along the road, keeping her ears back, not in anger, but apparently to find out if Stanley were going to sing again. And much more pleasant conversation followed. The gentleman was full of fun, and seemed to take a delight in drawing Stanley out, while he, on his part, was as merry as May morning when it doesn't rain, and made such curious remarks and quaint retorts that his companion was fain at last to dub him " quite an original."

You see it was hope that was making Stanley feel so bright and gay and happy. All the world was before him. He felt not only that there were hopes of a future for him, but he even enjoyed it in anticipation.

" What a beautiful horse you have, sir!" said Stanley.

" Come now, youngster," replied the gentleman; " all my cattle do twelve miles an hour, and this old mare says she can do fifteen if you sing again. I'll give you a bass, and let us have something that will quiet us both down a bit, for what with the beauty of the scenery and the bright sunshine, and what with talking and laughing, I feel quite elevated."

" ' Ye banks and braes ' ? " suggested Stanley.

" ' Ye banks and braes o' bonnie Doon,' be it then."

" By the way," said the gentleman, when Stanley had finished, " who is going to meet you at New York ? "

" My uncle, Captain Mackinlay, is going to send a man all the way from Virginia to meet me."

" Your uncle, Captain Mackinlay ? " repeated the gentleman. " Why, surely that cannot be the same who owned the estate of The Faulds in Glenkindy ? "

" The same, sir," said Stanley.

" Whew ! " the gentleman whistled in astonishment. " Let me shake hands, my dear boy ; your uncle and I are the oldest of friends. We were schoolmates, and for the first year of our school life we fought every night of our lives, and twice on Saturday because it was a half-holiday. Captain Mackinlay—Sandie McKail, as we used to call him. Don't I remember that day I had him down under, and he drew the big pin out of his kilt and stuck it into me right up to the head—four inches of it, my boy—and I lay a-bed for a month! Now, I hadn't meant going farther than Kintore, but circumstances alter cases; I'll tool you right in to the granite city after we dine. Well, well; wonders never cease."

"To whom have I the pleasure of talking?" asked Stanley.

"Major Kinnaird," was the reply: "but just you ask your uncle if he remembers his old schoolfellow 'Carrots' whom he used the pin to. My hair was red then, so they called me 'Carrots.'"

What a pleasant, happy evening Stanley spent with the major! They did not go on to town until next day, just in time for Stanley to join the steamer for Edinburgh.

The major saw his box on board, and walked on foot to the end of the pier, and waved his hand in farewell as the great ship went over the bar.

Now, dear reader, the heroes of most tales hardly ever eat or drink, and as for getting sea-sick, why such a thing would be out of the question; but truth constrains me to inform you that the good ship *Tantallan Castle* was no sooner well at sea, and beginning to beck and bow to the advancing waves, than Stanley Grahame felt queerer than ever he had felt before in his life. Not that he was noisily sick, though—no, it was worse than that; the perspiration poured off him, all the blood forsook his face, his stomach seemed to be away up among the clouds somewhere, and his heart in the heels of his boots. Poor fellow! he *was* ill, though there wasn't a capful of wind blowing. But the wind was dead in her eye, and she pitched a bit and took a bucket or two of green water on board, to say nothing of any amount of spray.

"Go below, my lad," said the steward, kindly.

Stanley tried, and well-nigh fainted. He was only a steerage passenger, and the warm sickly air of the fore saloon, as it was grandly called, would almost have killed a cobra. Stanley lay down on top of the grating of one of the hatchways, with a coil of rope for a pillow, and there slumber found him, and relieved him for a time of his wretchedness.

It came on to blow a bit during the night, and the *Tantallan* being only a " dug," big as she was, could not make headway, so that when Stanley awoke in the morning they were still at sea, but the Bass Rock was in sight ; she had shifted her course, and was standing in towards the Frith, rolling now instead of pitching, by way of a change.

How very sore Stanley did feel, to be sure ! A grating is a hard bed at the best, and the pattern of the one on which the boy had slept seemed to be printed all over his body. There was the mark of the rope on his cheek and brow too, and to add to this he was drenched to the skin, and *so* cold. He crawled up on to the bridge and stood by the flaming funnel, and when one side of his clothes was dry, he turned the other till that was dry likewise. Very imprudent conduct, I grant you, but then Stanley had been reared among the Highland heather. No hothouse plant was he, so he did not very readily succumb to cold.

And the *Tantallan Castle* bore steadily in towards the land, but a deal of fuss she made about it. She fretted and fumed, and pitched and rolled, and thrashed the advancing waves with her bows, as a whale does with its great tail. She seemed trying to make believe she was the *Great Eastern* buffeted by an Atlantic gale, or some mighty man-o'-war in the chops of the Channel. She seemed bent on making every one on board as uncomfortable as possible, so that even ancient mariners longed for the land, and talked despairingly about the vessel.

Whenever a bit of a sea struck her she kicked like a converted Enfield, and felt as sulky all over as a jibbing horse.

But no wonder, for nobody on board had a good word to say about her.

The passengers who had taken return tickets openly averred that rather than go back in her they would pay the extra fare and go by train. And you could have heard such remarks among the seamen as " Wretched old tub ! " " Shakes and quivers like a superannuated clothes-basket ! " " Time *she* was broken up, Bill ! "

" That it be, Jack ; and I wouldn't mind if she were in Davy Jones, so be that I got safely out of her."

This certainly was not giving the poor old *Tantallan Castle* much encouragement to do the right thing, even if she had wished to. But at long last Edinburgh, " our own romantic town," was not far distant, the city of monuments and mountains, and frowning through the morning haze was the ancient castle,

> " Whose pond'rous wall and massy bar,
>   Grim rising o'er the rugged rock,
> Have oft withstood the force of war,
>   And oft repelled the invader's shock."

Even when the vessel got abreast of the pier she would not behave prettily, but needed all sorts of encouragement and coaxing, and backing astern, and going ahead a little ; and when the hawser was thrown on shore and belayed she attempted suicide in the most determined manner by trying to break her ribs against the granite.

Verily, I feel half ashamed that my hero should have made his *début* as a mariner in so ancient and unseaworthy a dug as the *Tantallan Castle.*

IV.

STANLEY'S GLASGOW COUSIN—"CHILDREN, LOVE ONE ANOTHER"—ON THE WIDE ATLANTIC—AN IDYLLIC LIFE AT SEA.

CHAPTER IV.

TOM REYNOLDS was a good specimen of a class of young men that, so far as my experience goes, you meet with in no city of the British Empire save Glasgow. If you cross the broad Atlantic, as Stanley will soon do, you fail to find such men in New York; but if you take the cars and rattle away southwards to Philadelphia—city of tree-shaded streets and spacious squares—you may find them there; and again in many of the towns, and even villages, in Germany, but hardly, I think, in volatile France.

Tom Reynolds was a young tradesman; his craft was that of a printer. He was only a journeyman, being barely twenty-one. His dress was plain and respectable on a Sunday, but without affectation, and if he did wear a bouquet in his button-hole it was because he dearly loved God's flowers. On week-days he dressed like his work, as the saying is, and had you met him hurrying home of an evening, you might have noticed that his hands were considerably blacker than yours, and that there was even a dark smudge or two on his brow—evidence that he had wiped the sweat drops away more than once during his hours of toil.

A dark, thoughtful, calm eye had Tom Reynolds, and a manly, well-chiselled face withal. Had he been dressed in rags, and you yourself "rigged out" by Poole, you could not have called the man a cad. Had you been lounging in a *cafe* doorway, and Tom Reynolds, in his work-a-day clothes, wished to pass in, you would have stepped aside urbanely and permitted him to do so.

For men like Tom Reynolds the richest in the land cannot afford to despise, while the wise do them homage.

Tom, when quite a boy, had come from the country, where he had herded his father's sheep on the quiet hill-side, with no other companion than a well-thumbed copy of Burns's poems.

Apprenticed to a firm in Glasgow, he was delighted to find that in the city there were not only mechanics' institutes, where he could listen to lectures on scientific subjects, but free libraries!

So Tom worked all day, and read in the evening. Not that he was a bookworm by any means; bookworms are, in my opinion, a nuisance to themselves and everybody around them. For the most part they are mere dreamers, puny in body, flabby in biceps, and feeble in digestion. They may lie in the sunshine and think, it is true, but they seldom act. There is as much difference between a book-worm of this kind and a reading, cogitating, acting man like Tom Reynolds, as there is between a lizard and a beaver. But Tom could take his turn in the cricket-field as well as any one, and he was a member of that splendid body of men yclept the Lanarkshire Volunteers. Nor was he averse to healthy pleasure. You might have met him on the ice in winter, or on board the bustling *Iona* far down the wide, romantic Clyde—

> "When summer days were fine."

Tom was content with his lot, and he worked to the very best of his ability in the station of life to which it had pleased Providence to appoint him.

He was a revolutionist, however. Now, reader, pray do not start, but listen. Tom was a revolutionist, but no revolutionary fidget. He had no French feelings in his nature—feelings that, begotten of ire, can only be quenched in blood. Tom was a law-loving and law-abiding young man. But, nevertheless, he believed in a happy time to come—

> " When man to man, the world o'er,
> Shall brothers be, and a' that."

He was content to wait and work for this good time coming —work as the earthworms work, that, seldom seen but ever quietly busy, revolutionise the very earth on which we tread.

"God forbid, gentlemen," Tom had once said at a debating meeting, "that any of us should attempt to level society by pulling down; let us rather build up. Away with envy and malice, away with dirk and pistol for ever and ever, unless for use against a foreign invader. Let us try to elevate ourselves to the rank of all that is great and good by education—by reading and strict adherence to duty. There is tyranny in the land, you say—there is oppression. We have three glorious weapons of lawful warfare wherewith to fight them—parliament, the pulpit, and the pen. Believe me this: the good that dwells in high places is founded on a rock; the evil is as unsubstantial as the baseless fabric of a dream, and possesses no surer lease of existence than a towering iceberg floating southwards to a summer sea.

Tom Reynolds came to meet Stanley and take him in charge at Edinburgh, for Tom was Stanley's cousin, though they had never seen each other before. I do not know how it was, but our hero knew his cousin before he landed. Something seemed to tell him that that tall, handsome young man in Sunday clothes, and with a tall hat—well, just a trifle too large for him—was nobody else but Tom Reynolds; so from his station beside the funnel, where he was drying off and about half-baked, he waved his pocket-handkerchief, and Tom returned the salute by waving his hand, and showing a set of alabaster teeth which, combined with the smiles that went rippling away all over his face, made him look very pleasant indeed.

Stanley took to him at once.

They were soon as good friends, and as frank and free with each other, as if they had been acquainted for years.

"And I *am* so hungry," said Stanley, with decided emphasis on the "am."

"Ye dinna look very hungry," replied Tom, laughing at his cousin's energy, "but it's the sea-sickness that has done it. Ho! ho! here is a dining-saloon. We'll soon cure your complaint."

"My mother told me," said Stanley, laying a friendly hand on Tom's arm as he pulled out his purse, "that I wasn't to allow you to pay for anything."

The thinking Scot showed well out in Tom's quaint reply.

"Man! Stanley," he said, "I canna conceive in what way your mother—my auntie—can prevent it, nor a' the mothers and aunties in creation. But keep your mind easy, cousin. I'm goin' to run through and see your mother in autumn, and if she insists on refunding me, then I'll insist on paying for every bite and sup I have in your glen."

On their way to the station they came upon two boys fighting, and hitting viciously hard blows. Tom stopped, and using his right hand and left, seized them both, and laughingly pulled them asunder. Still holding them, he held a court of inquiry on the spot, scolded one a little, and reasoned with the other, next preached them both a little tiny sermon, then said something that made them both laugh and shake hands, and finally gave them a "bawbee" apiece, and away went the urchins arm-in-arm to buy black-; Jack.

"Peace restored," said Tom; "peace restored, Stanley price one penny."

As Stanley looked up into his cousin's laughing face, he could not help thinking how good a heart he must have, and that Tom might, at some future day, get more than the worth of that penny.

Stanley stayed a whole week with his cousin in Glasgow, and never a night passed that he did not write home. Stanley had his outfit to get, and gladly availed himself of Tom's assistance in procuring it, for Tom knew all the best shops, and knew as well as anyone how to spend a pound to the best advantage.

Tom's house was a very humble one. There was not a carpet in it, only bare, clean boards, but there was a well-swept hearth, a bright fireside, and quite a flower-garden on the window-sill. His mother was the presiding genius. With the exception of his own parent Stanley had never met so happy and cheerful a little body. And how proud of Tom she was, too ! as well she might be.

Tom, by the way, gave his cousin much good advice. He had, moreover, a way with him of preaching little bits of sermons, that lost nothing in effect from being couched in homely, everyday language. Only one example.

To wit : he found the old Bible in Stanley's pocket.

"You'll do well," he said, "to stick to that and its teaching."

Then, after a pause,

"You're too young yet to do aught else but believe, but I've had to grope my way through doubting darkness. What do you think I've done? Why, man, I've read all the French books—and shallow enough they are—and many of the deep-thinking German works ; I've listened patiently to all sceptics have to say, and my mother avers I can see as far through a stone as a miller ; and I've come to the happy conclusion that there is no book like The Book, Stanley ; no guide through life *like* that, no comfort in death *but* that ; and oh ! cousin, I'm so happy you've started right away on the right road. Shake hands, Stanley."

'Do you know what I think of you ?" said Stanley, with

all the innocent frankness of a young boy's nature; "I
think you are a very good man, and I'm sure I love you,
and I'll never forget you nor all the things you've tried to
teach me."

"If you measure the amount of your love," replied Tom,
"by the standard of my goodness, it is precious little I'll
deserve from you. But I'm willing to accept your professed
love and friendship, only don't let your love stop there.
Here, Stanley, is a book-marker for you; I suggested the
words, and my mother sewed them. Obedience to the
commandment thereon contained will one day revolutionise
the peoples of the world, and make this earth a smiling
paradise."

Stanley, thanking him, took the little gift, and read
thereon the words:

"CHILDREN, LOVE ONE ANOTHER."

*   *   *   *   *

To say that Stanley Grahame was not sorry to leave his
native land would be incorrect. He did not like to appear
quite a child before his aunt and honest Tom Reynolds;
but as he bade them adieu he dared hardly trust himself to
speak, and he had to bite his lips till they bled, in order to
suppress the rising tears. And when the vessel had fairly
cast off, amid much noise and shouting, and was being
tugged down stream, then his thoughts reverted to his own
far off glen and his mother and sister, and he would have
given worlds—if he had had any worlds to give—only to
see them for one short hour longer.

For hours and hours he stood leaning over the bulwarks
like one in a dream—towns and villages went past, and all
the scenery of the romantic Clyde flitted by him like scenes
in a diorama, but he hardly seemed to notice them—their
beauty was all lost on Stanley Grahame.

At last the river broadened out into the wide, rolling
frith, and the frith widened into the sea. The tug-boat

cast them adrift; farewells were said, or rather shouted; the little fussy steamer went puffing and churning away up-stream again; and sail was set on the gallant barque that had to cross the wide Atlantic ere ever she came into harbour again.

Then night began to fall; the stars played hide-and-seek among the fleecy clouds; the wind freshened, and the sails bellied out to it; there was the sound of the watch tramping quickly up and down the deck; an occasional word of command from the officer on duty; and the wish-wash of the wavelets against the vessel's side, and that was all. Presently it grew so dark that Stanley could see nothing but the stars and the glimmering light of a distant lighthouse. Then he turned his attention in-board, and as there was a broad gleam issuing from the cabin in the poop, he bent his steps in that direction.

"Why," said the captain, as Stanley entered, hat in hand, "where have you been, my lad? I had sent the steward to look for you; he couldn't find you, so we both came to the conclusion that you had crept in under something and gone off to sleep."

"I don't feel a bit sick," said Stanley, proudly; "but then I've been to sea before, you know, sir. I made one voyage."

The captain laughed right heartily when Stanley told him that the one voyage had been between Aberdeen and Grantown Pier in the *Tantallan Castle.* The *Ocean Bride* was a barque of some five hundred tons. She looked all over a foreigner, and I dare say at one time had belonged to some Danish or German firm. But in Stanley's eyes she was everything that was noble and romantic, just the sort of ship he had always thought he would like to sail in. She was all painted green, with sham ports, which were black; she had a tall, moonraking kind of a bowsprit, tall, thinnish spars, and long yards. Then she had a real forecastle, and a real complete poop with doors that went into it straight off the deck without going a single step down-stairs. And the ports of the poop were perfect windows in size. So you see she was altogether foreign-looking in appearance. But so comfortable and so jolly every way; quite like a ship you would see in a picture. The men, too, were picturesque enough. They were young, supple fellows, and, with the exception of the officers, they all wore blue worsted Guernsey shirts, like fishermen, and red night-caps.

The captain was big, burly, brown-bearded, and fat, and never spoke without smiling.

"Your uncle has given me entire charge of you," he said, "so do as you like; but if I were you I would join the mate's watch, and learn the ropes, and how to splice and reef and steer. We'll take three months, maybe, to go out, and you are a deal better on an honest sailing-ship than you'd be on board one of those dirty, new-fangled puffing-billies. Eh! lad, don't you think so?"

Stanley did think so. This was his beau-ideal of a ship.

And well it might be so. His whole life during that long voyage was, so to speak, quite idyllic. He did do as he liked, but that was to join the mate's watch, and to learn everything from that kind, good-natured man that he possibly could.

The captain certainly did not hurry his vessel, and if the truth must be told, the *Ocean Bride* was a ship that would not be hurried. So far as speed went, she was nowhere; so far as strength and comfort went, she was everything.

They really did take nearly three months to complete the voyage, but Stanley would not have minded had it been six. Everything went on in this good, lazy old soul of a ship with the regularity of clockwork. The sailors, day or night, never neglected to strike the bells at the proper time, and the steward was never one minute late with breakfast or dinner. When becalmed in mid-Atlantic the captain neither fretted nor fumed. Were the wind astern, abeam, ahead, or a hurricane, it did not trouble anybody; things went on much the same under all conditions. I verily believe that had she been taken aback—and that is a terrible danger—the captain would have eased her in five minutes, and I feel sure he would not have taken that big meerschaum—that suited his complexion so well—out of his mouth all the time.

Stanley Grahame did all he could during this long, happy voyage to make himself a thorough sailor, or as perfect as any one could be in the time.

" Oh ! captain," he said, enthusiastically, the night before they arrived at New York, " I've been so happy here. And if ever I have a chance, I'll sail again in the dear old *Ocean Bride.*"

" Ah ! boy," replied the captain, as he sat beside the stove in his big arm-chair, sipping his coffee, " you won't find many ships like this. She is my own, you know, and I never do anything to put her out. But, dear lad, if you are bound to be a sailor, your hardships are all before you."

And so they were, reader.

STANLEY FINDS A NEW FRIEND—THE JOURNEY
SOUTH— PHILADELPHIA — BALTIMORE —ARRIVAL
AT THE OLD PLANTATION.

CHAPTER V.

OUR hero's introduction to his uncle—in the flesh, I mean—was somewhat original, to say the very least of it. True to his promise, Captain Mackinlay had dispatched a trusty servant to meet the boy, as soon as he had telegraphed his arrival in New York city. It was a day or two before honest Sambo—for that was the negro's name—arrived, and during that time Stanley located himself—to use a Yankee expression—at the Westminster Hotel, and forthwith set about seeing all the sights he could.

There were plenty of fellows willing to "tout" him around, but he very wisely treated all such with distrust. Whatever he wanted to know he sought information about at the office, and the landlord was exceedingly kind to him. So Stanley roamed all by himself in the beautiful park, and through the spacious streets, and in the open tree-clad squares.

It was the Indian summer, and the weather was genially warm and delightful.

In the evenings there were galleries to visit, and lecture rooms, so that, on the whole, Stanley did not think the time long.

But one morning the waiter tapped at his door and brought in his hot water and a great jug of ice, and then coughed and said, "There is a coloured 'gentleman,' sir, down below who has just called on you. I reckon you

don't want to see any one of that sort.   Shall I tell him to
go about his business ? "

"Oh, no ! " cried Stanley Grahame, springing out of bed ;
"that is my uncle's chief servant, and he has called to take
me away.   Get breakfast for us both in twenty minutes."

The waiter smiled.   "I guess, sir," he said, "the guv'nor
wouldn't care to have a coloured gentleman in the saloon
among white folks, unless it were to wait at the table."

Stanley, young as he was, felt angry.   Was he actually
in New York ?   Was he positively among the people who
fought and bled for the abolition of slavery ?

"Bring the breakfast here," he said, with decision ; "and
tell the gentleman to come up."

The waiter shrugged his shoulders and retired.

Shortly after, with a premonitory tap at the door, Sambo
himself entered.

Now Stanley had seen plenty of niggers since his arrival
in New York, but so tall and sturdy a black man as this it
had never before been his lot to witness.

He stooped low as he came in, more from habit probably
than anything else, for the bedroom door was over seven
feet high.

He was by no means repulsive-looking, however.
What a cheerful jolly face he had to be sure !   And when
he smiled, which he did very often, almost whenever he
talked, he showed a mouthful of ivory that a young elephant
might have envied.

Sambo was on particularly good terms with himself; the
fact is, he was the pet servant of old Captain Mackinlay, his
master.

"I'se Sambo," he said, as soon as his head was through
the doorway, "and I'se come to fetch you."

Then he burst out laughing and walked right round Stanley,
and looked at him up and down and all over, just as if our
young hero had been a horse, and he was trying to find out
whether or not he were fault free previous to purchase

"Ah ! Yah !" he laughed. "Yah ! yah ! yah ! Am you de leetle boy I'se sent to fetch ? Yah ! yah ! Why, you am nearly as big as dis child hisself, and massa say I'se going to meet a leetle boy. 'Only twelve,' he say, 'take care ob de poor leetle chile, Sambo, take care ob him.' Yah ! yah ! yah !"

Stanley was half angry, but for the life of him he could not help smiling, because Sambo laughed so heartily.

Sambo was well dressed in a suit of black, and wore rings on his fingers as big as knuckle-dusters, and a gold watch and a chain of gold that might have done for a cable of a small yacht—figuratively speaking. Except the fact that he more than once burst out laughing during breakfast, he behaved himself in a most exemplary way. In fact Stanley and he were soon fast friends. The breakfast was a wonderful one. You do not get such breakfasts anywhere out of America. The waiter brought delicious fruit and iced milk for them first, and with these they trifled until the tea and coffee and cooked dishes came. Stanley had never seen such a beefsteak before, and the boiled shad would have delighted the heart of an epicure. The vegetables too were perfection, and so were the eggs, done in many different ways. When Stanley thought it was all over the waiter entered with hot buckwheat cakes and maple syrup, and of course they had to do their duty by that.

They lingered over this meal, for Sambo was in fine form, and quite delighted the boy with tales about his master and stories about "de dear ole plantation among de woods cf Virginny."

Sambo, although a black man, was just as brave as he was powerful and strong, but he never used either quality in a bad cause. He was also, like many other negroes in the Southern States, deeply imbued with a sense of religion, albeit he was most humorous and funny in nearly every-thing secular he said or did. With this description of Sambo the reader must be content for the present, as there will be plenty of opportunities of judging his character from his actions.

Stanley and he were to start together for the sunny south ; meanwhile our hero invited the negro to take a walk with him through the city, and to attend a concert with him in the evening.

Sambo hesitated and looked serious.

" You see, sah," he said, " I'se black ; as black, sah, as de ace of spades ; and you am white. What you tink de New York Yankees say suppose dey see me walking with a young gentleman like you ? Why, dey would shudder in dey shoes."

" Let them shudder, Sambo friend," said Stanley, boldly. "Give me your arm; now, right foot foremost, quick march!"

Sambo laughed now right heartily, and many a supercilious eyeglass was directed towards the couple as they went strolling up the Fifth Avenue. This did not hurt Sambo in the slightest, and I'm sure it did not affect Stanley.

The pair dined together in the evening, as they had breakfasted in the morning, and next day, having crossed the water in one of those wonderful boats for which New York is famed, they took tickets for the south.

To Philadelphia.   No farther the first day.

" Because," Sambo explained, " old massa, he gib me 'spress orders to show you de cities of Philadelphia, Baltimore, and Washington afore you goes home to de ole plantation."

To Stanley, only recently arrived in this great country, all things he saw combined to make him feel as if he had begun a new life, or been suddenly dropped down into some strange new planet. The great cars in which they rode were immense saloons, more like ships' cabins, with splendid windows and cushioned lounges covered with cloth of crimson.   Then there was the lovely panorama that went flitting past them, no wild mountains and dark lowering glens like those of his native land, but green fields and broad-bosomed rivers, shimmering in the sunlight, peaceful little villages, with quaintly-built cottages, so mixed up with trees that Stanley couldn't help wondering whether these pretty wee towns had been built in the woods, or whether the trees had grown up around them after they were built.

There were long stretches of wild swamps too, where beautiful birds were to be seen in the water, on the bushes, and among the reeds, and here many trees grew in copses, with bright flowers on them as broad as Stanley's hat, and wild creepers clinging around their stems. Then came miles on miles of forest land, through which the train went puffing and ploughing, winding here and winding there, with the trees close to the rails and no fence of any kind between them, and then wonderful bridges, and more villages, and bigger towns, and somewhat wilder scenery ; then Philadelphia herself—queen of cities.

It would take me weeks to tell you all that Stanley saw and did in this splendid city, in its streets and spacious squares, in its wide and beautiful park, and on the Schuylkill and the Delaware, called by the Indians in times long gone past the Arasapha or Coaquanock.

The romantic Wissatrickon flows silently along through a valley, mountain-guarded and densely studded with splendid forest trees, that render the winding road dark even at noontide.

By the banks of this strange weird river Stanley wandered all by himself, amidst the mighty oaks, the tall and tapering poplars, and far-spreading chestnuts, until the rays of the setting sun, shimmering in crimson through the ocean of foliage, warned him that the gloaming shadows would soon give place to night. Then he retraced his steps homewards to the distant city. But he could not help, whilst lingering by the edge of the quiet stream, remembering many things he had read about this country and its earlier history, when sitting by his mother's cottage fire far away in bonnie Scotland. Of the dark, impenetrable forest that once waved where now the houses stood ; of the unbroken stillness that reigned in its depths, save in sunny glades where wild Indians built their wigwams ; of the brave pioneers who first landed on Delaware shores, of their sufferings and their deeds of daring, of the homes they made in the caves of the rocks, and of their wild adventures among the red men,—all these things and a hundred others came crowding into his mind as he slowly returned to the city through noble Fairmont Park.

Ah ! but in the blaze of gaslight such thoughts were soon dispelled, and when he entered the hotel he found Sambo anxiously awaiting his arrival in the hall, for he had quite given up his charge as lost. After their reunion, if there were any shadows of the long-forgotten past still hovering over the soul of our hero, they fled far away at the sight of the dinner that the busy bustling waiter placed before them.

Next day they continued their journey southwards to Baltimore. Stanley, young as he was, was charmed with this quaint but beautiful old city. He must needs roam abroad all by himself and see the sights and seek for adventures. These latter, however, were of a very mild description, for his wilder adventures—" his moving accidents by flood and field and hair-breadth 'scapes "—were all to come. But the sights he saw were pleasant in the extreme. After he had wandered all over the town he must needs climb to the top of the Washington monument and see the city and country all around from that great altitude. This is, allowing for the simplicity of its shape, one of the finest monuments I have ever seen. The eminence on which it stands is in the centre of a beautiful square, and is one hundred feet above tide level. On this hill the square base of the monument has been erected, fifty feet square and nearly forty feet high. From the centre of this towers the great white marble Doric column, twenty feet in diameter at the base, fifteen feet at the top, and one hundred and sixty-five feet high. It is surmounted by a splendid gallery,

with seats, the roof being the vaulted sky, and high above
this gallery stands, on its immense pedestal, the statue of
the immortal Washington.

The dark staircase winds up the centre of the monument,
and up this, lantern in hand,
like some young Guy Fawkes,
crawled Stanley Grahame.
Mountaineer as he was, he
was breathless ere he came
out at the top into the fresh
air and glorious sunshine.

The day had been fiercely
hot, but up aloft here a cool
delicious breeze was blowing, a bright blue sky was
overhead, and, asleep in the
blue, one or two little snow-
white clouds; but the grandeur and beauty of the

scenery that lay far, far down beneath him on every side
defies description. He was in the centre of a star of streets,
so to speak, each one of which, broad and tree-lined,
stretched away and away through the lovely town into the
charming country beyond, where :—

> " Through many a wild and woodland scene,
>   Meandered the streams with waters of green,
>   As if the bright fringe of herbs on the brink
>   Had given their stain to the waters they drink."

The tall steeples and innumerable public buildings of the
city stood well out from the red of the brick houses.
Greener trees Stanley had never seen, redder houses never.
And no smoke was there at all to disfigure or blur the
view. Yonder lies the city hall with marble walls and
giant cupola, yonder the great cathedral with mosque-like
roof and gilded domes and minarets, and still farther away
the long white lines of Fort Henry clear against the blue

of the sail-dotted bay beyond, and all around on the land side a glamour of rocks and woods and cliffs and fields of green stretching northwards as far as eye can reach, and eastwards into the invisible.

Stanley, ere he returned to his hotel, paused by the side of a beautiful monument erected to the memory of one of America's noblest sons, John McDonogh, who dying old and well-stricken in years, left his immense wealth to found an institution for the education of poor children. Stanley could not help transcribing in his note-book a portion of the inscriptions on the marble tablets. They read as follows, and are well worthy of being remembered:—

Rules for my guidance in life: Remember that labour is one
of the conditions of our existence.　Time is gold;
throw not one minute away, but place each one to
account. Do unto all men as you would be done
by. Never put off till to-morrow that which
you can do to-day.　Never bid another
do what you can do yourself. Never
covet what is not your own.　Never
think any matter so trivial as not to deserve
notice.　Never give out that which does not
first come in.　Never spend but to produce.　Let the
greatest order regulate the transactions of your life. Study
in the course of your life to do the greatest possible amount of good.
Deprive yourself of
nothing necessary to your
comfort, but live in an honourable simplicity and frugality. Labour
then to the last moment of your existence.　Pursue strictly the above rules,
and the Divine blessing and riches of every
kind will flow upon you to your heart's content;
but first of all remember that the chief and great
study of your life should be to tend by all the means
in your power to the honour and glory of the Divine Creator.
The conclusion to which I have arrived is
that without temperance there is no health, without virtue no order,
without religion no happiness, and the
sum of our being is to live wisely, soberly, and righteously.

Two days after the hero of our tale had left Baltimore with his sable friend Sambo, they found themselves on the old plantation. It was a beautiful sunny forenoon, and the estate never looked to better advantage. No wonder that Stanley stood amazed at the beauty and the evidences of wealth he saw everywhere around him.

"Now," said Sambo, "we will have some fun. Dat tall ole gentleman walking on de lawn is Captain Mackinlay. Now you come up behind dis snake-fence wid me, I hide behind, den you jump ober and make believe to cross de lawn widout eber lookin' de road of Captain Mackinlay, and we shall see what we shall see. Ah! Yah! it will be fun."

Stanley carried out Sambo's instructions to the very letter, with the following interesting result.

"Hi! hi! hullo, you sir!" This from Captain Mackinlay, as Stanley essayed to cross the lawn. "Interloper, scoundrel, trespasser, how dare you come on my grounds, without permission?"

"Well, sir——" began Stanley.

"Don't 'well, sir' me, sir! Hi! hullo there, Be-Joyful Johnson; run here, will you. Bundle this young scoundrel out of the grounds, and drop him into the pond."

Be-Joyful was a powerful-looking but rather thin-skinned negro, who now came bounding up to do his master's bidding.

"Look here, Captain Mackinlay," cried Stanley, throwing himself into an attitude, "call off your nigger, or I'll hit him—and properly, too. Old Ewen told me never to hit a man except in self-defence, but when I did hit to—ah! would you? Hands off!—there, then!"

Next moment the big negro was sprawling on his back, kicking the sky with his heels, rubbing his nose and shins, and hallooing like a Houdan cock. But high above his hallooing rose the merry "Yah! yah! yah!" of honest Sambo hid behind the snake-fence.

"Now then, sir," cried young Stanley, "will you call off

your nigger before I repeat the dose *cum grano salis,* as we
say at school ? "

It was very mischievous of Stanley, but you must forgive
him ; for he couldn't for the life of him help adding, as he
saw his uncle making a pretence of fumbling for his
revolver,—

"Don't trouble yourself, Sandy McKail—don't bother
drawing your kilt-pin upon me.   I'm not Carrots."

"Carrots ! Kilt-pin ! Sandy McKail ? " exclaimed the
old gentleman, aghast.   " Why, young sir, who are you, in
the name of all that is mysterious ? "

" Why, just little Stanley Grahame, your nephew ! " said
our hero, laughing.

It would have done you good to have seen the captain's
face just then.   A full moon breaking clear away from the
clouds, and shining out bright and serene from the blue
sky, was nothing to it.

He grasped Stanley's hand.   Stanley thought of the time
when he got his fingers into the threshing-machine.

"Welcome to Beaumont Park ! " he cried; "thrice
welcome, my best of boys—my brave boy ! "

" Get up, you lazy, lubberly lout ! "   This to Be-Joyful,
who, by the way, was joyful no longer.

" You doubled him up in first-rate style," he continued ;
"and the touch you gave him on the shins with your toe
was truly artistic—ha ! ha ! ha ! I couldn't have done it
better myself.   But come on to the house."

He pulled Stanley's arm through his own as he spoke,
and with Sambo coming grinning up behind, and Be-Joyful
limping and wincing, off marched the sailor uncle and the
young nephew for the manor house.

VI.

BEAUMONT PARK—DOWN THE RIVER—CRUISING ON AN INLAND SEA—THE DARK CONTINENT.

CHAPTER VI.

IT was Captain Mackinlay's habit to linger long over his
dessert.   He retained old-fashioned English customs,
and one of these was dinner at six.   Stanley did not mind
how long he lingered at dessert, for the fruit was more
varied and delicious than he ever could have dreamt of,
and the tiny cups of black coffee that the negro servant
placed before them must have been identically similar—so
thought Stanley—to that which graced the board of the
author of the "Arabian Nights."

"Yes," said Captain Mackinlay one evening as he pared
a pineapple, "that is what I propose.   I don't say you are
too young to go to sea, and, really, you're big enough, but
a year here at home won't hurt you.   You'll cheer the old
man's life a bit, and it is pretty near worried out of him
with these rascally niggers, for, bar Sambo there, who is as
good as nuggets, never a one of them will do as I want
them.   So I say stop with the old man for a year or two;
you already know a jib-sail from a *gigot* o' mutton.   Well,
I'll try and teach you something else, and so will Sambo.
He was my steward in the old *Nonpareil*; ay, lad, and
could take his turn at the wheel, too, with the best hand on
board.   We'll make a man of you, and then we'll drum you
off to sea."

Captain Mackinlay, who was just a year on the shady
side of sixty, had been at sea nearly all his life in all kinds

of trades and in all kinds of countries, had made his fortune, and the plantation, the manor, and estate of Beaumont Park had been left to him by an old lady whose life he had saved in the Andaman Islands. She had been carefully fed and fattened by the cannibals, who had been so extra-ordinarily polite to her that until the very last moment she had not the faintest notion they meant to spit and cook and eat her. But brave Captain Mackinlay, hearing there was a white captive on an island, and that a great festival was about to take place, with the beating of tomtoms, much ululation, and a vast deal of conchation, landed with an armed boat's-crew, made short work of the savages, spoiled their fun, ruined their hopes of a glorious feast, and delivered the old lady from the imminent peril of becoming a cold side-dish.

So this bluff and hearty old sailor settled down at Beaumont; and a splendid place it was. I cannot tell you exactly in what style of architecture the house was built. I dare say it was a kind of mixture, partly English (if that is anything) and partly Italian. It was built of solid stone —greystone; but you could not have told that easily, it was so bedraped in creepers and clinging fruit-trees. The mauve-blossomed gigantic wisterias clustered high around the tall chimneys, Virginia's glory almost hid the windows, and the numerous verandahs and queer old-fashioned gables were all a smother of roses nearly half the year round.

Then there were terraces, rose-lawns, and shrubberies and lakes, and the glorious wooded park itself, where oaks and hickory and elm, and chestnut and pine trees grew; besides groves and grottoes, and ferneries and fountains, and what not. No wonder that, listening to Stanley Grahame's sincere outspoken admiration, the captain laughed and said,—

"Ay, dear boy, it is a sweetly pretty place, I grant you. I dare say you wouldn't mind saving an old wife from cannibals for such a snug little estate—eh?"

" Oh !" cried Stanley, doubling his fist ; " I'd save fifty old wives for half such a nice place as this."

The plantation proper, where the sugar-mills were, and where the cotton-sheds were built, and where hundreds of dark-skinned, white-garmented negroes worked and sang in the sunlight, was fully a mile from the park, and to the east of it. To the north were wild mountain peaks, the home of the black bear, the python, and the puma ; to the west the dark forest-lands where the red men still roamed at will ; while down to the south flowed the great river.

A country like this, it need hardly be said, possessed an indescribable charm for a boy of Stanley's nature and disposition. The novels and poems of the great Sir Walter were especial favourites of his, and so, too, were the tales of the best American writers, especially those that told of the warlike doings of the Indians of the forest-lands of the Far West. And here he was among them. Stay a year with his uncle ? Indeed, indeed, he thought he could well spend ten, in this country of poetry and romance.

But his uncle gave him distinctly to understand that, much though he valued his company, and willingly though he would have him with him always—even to the end, which in the common course of nature could not be so very far away—he must go out into the world and work, as he, his uncle, had done before him. Then—this was only a mere hint—if he should prove himself a worthy young man, there was no saying what good fortune might or might not accrue to him when Captain Mackinlay rested from all the toils of life in the green churchyard, and under the shadow of the little kirk in the adjoining village he now worshipped in Sunday after Sunday.

One day Captain Mackinlay roused Stanley out of bed at three o'clock in the morning.

Stanley sat up rubbing his eyes and wondering if the house was on fire.

" Get up, my boy," cried his uncle patting him on the

shoulder; "get up, if you really are awake   We are going on a long journey down stream, and we'll have some rare fun, you can stake your shoes on that."

Stanley did not want to stake his shoes, but he was up and dressed and had them on just a quarter of an hour after this. And downstairs into the breakfast-parlour, where salmon cutlets, beef-steaks, and turkeys' eggs awaited patiently the coming onslaught. And there, too, was the old captain, flanked by a pot of fragrant tea, and looking radiant, hungry, and happy. After breakfast they both felt fit for the long row down stream. Sambo was the oarsman, and how he did make that little skiff bound along, to be sure.

The woods looked gorgeous in their autumn tints, and twenty miles of panorama passed them by in no time. It seemed all one beautiful dream.

Then they came to a bonnie wee village, with white-painted wooden houses, and windows with bright green jalousies. And here there was a pier, where a great steamer was puffing and snorting just like a hunter impatient to be off.

"Come along, Captain Mackinlay!" cried the ship-master, extending a friendly hand, and half pulling our hero on board. "I was waiting for you; but, bless your beaming face! I wouldn't have dropped down stream without you for all the world! Are you ready for breakfast?"

"For breakfast number two, yes," said Stanley's uncle, laughing. "We've had a snack already, haven't we, Stan, my boy?"

Stanley laughed when he thought of the steaks and salmon cutlets, but his row had made him hungry—he was only a boy.

It was quite night, although not very dark, when they at length reached the glancing lights of a bustling town. Stanley did not see much of it that evening, but he slept so soundly that when he awoke at last the sun was streaming

into his bedroom, and, everything around him being strange, it was some time before he could remember where he was.

Now Stanley considered himself a good walker, but he thought before sunset that day that he had never really known what walking was till then. There seemed to be no such thing as "tire" in Captain Mackinlay. Then it was *so* hot! When they returned to the hotel his uncle laughingly asked him how he felt.

"Let me see," said Stanley, laughing in turn.

"Tell the whole truth, now," said his uncle.

"Well, then, I will," continued Stanley. "I'm as limp as a salmon out of season. I'm as tired as if I'd been up and down Ben Nevis half-a-dozen times at least. My feet are too big for my boots, the sun has taken all the skin off the point of my nose, my eyes feel like roasted onions, and there is a collection of cinders or something in the corners of them, and I've been sweating so much that my clothes feel like linseed-meal poultices, and my handkerchief—look at it!—is as grimy and wet as an engine rag!"

"Capital description!" cried his uncle. "And now, my boy, go and have a bath and a dry shirt, and then come down to dinner."

"I feel as fresh as a daisy!" said Stanley, bursting into the room about half-an-hour after.

He put one arm lovingly round his uncle's broad neck. "Dear uncle," he said, "you are so kind! What a day I have had of it! and that repeating rifle you bought me is simply perfection. Won't I bag the bears!"

"Always providing," his uncle put in, "the bears don't bag you, Stan! They are wonderfully affectionate, and when they do get their paws round a man or a boy they never know when to leave off hugging and clawing him!"

Six months after this visit summer had once more visited the old plantation. Although he was very far indeed from forgetting his mother's humble co.tage on the verge of the great forest of Cairntrie, Stanley Grahame was much too brave a boy to suffer the pangs of home-sickness, albeit he looked forward to the happy time when he should once more meet in joy those he loved and held so dear. He wrote home regularly twice a week such delightfully descriptive letters, telling of the strange romantic life he led on the banks of the Mississippi, of his exploits in the forest, of wanderings over the prairie lands, and pleasant evenings spent rowing on the river beneath the light of the pale moon.

But the last six months had flown away wonderfully fast. What had he done ?—what had he learned ? Had his time been all spent in one round of pleasure, with every duty banished therefrom, or had he been making preparations for the serious battle of life upon which he was so soon to enter ?

Let us see.

Captain Mackinlay was a very pleasant man, but he had a terribly strict notion of the sacredness of duty.

"I'll superintend your studies, my lad," he told Stanley, about a month after he had settled down. "Now," he continued, "your forenoons must be all work, work, work ; and after that until bedtime it can be all play, play, play ; and I don't think we'll make Jack a dull boy if we go on in that style."

Stanley was, like most Scotch boys of the middle class of life, a fair scholar, both classical and mathematical. He had never studied navigation, however. But that now formed part of his forenoon work, and in a few months he was a good sailor, theoretically speaking. But was this all ? No, for Mackinlay owned a yacht. It had lain unused for years at the distant town of D——, but as soon as he had made up his mind to "make a man of Stanley Grahame," he had her rigged out and refitted from stem to stern ; and one day, much to Stanley's joy, she came gracefully gliding up the stream, and was moored off Beaumont Park. There was a tributary of the great river not many miles distant. It was navigable to a clever sailor, and ere long it led to an immense mountain-bounded lake of water—quite an inland sea, in fact. And wild and rough enough in all conscience this lake used to be at times, swept by winds that few yachts could beat against, and roughened by white combing waves houses high, which it required both tact and skill to prevent pouring their solid waters inboard, or mayhap sweeping the decks.

On the inland sea Mackinlay often went cruising for a whole week or more at a time. Very pleasant little outings for Stanley those were when the weather was fine; when it was not he bore his hardships manfully, and did not even grumble in thought. His uncle knew every cove and creek and natural harbour all about and around the lake; and when the wind freshened to a regular gale that it would have been sheer folly or madness to battle against—well, then the yacht was borne up or run for one of these, and they lay snug enough until such time as the weather moderated.

To land in the silence and solitude of those primeval forests was not always judicious nor safe, for they were oftentimes scoured by roving parties of treacherous tribes of Indians—red men—who, although they had in reality left their distant villages and homes in the mountain fastnesses of the West on hunting expeditions, would at any moment declare themselves to be on the war-path, in order to gloss over with a semblance of rude justice deeds of murder and rapine.

There were bears in those backwoods as well as wild men, and in the swamps hideous alligators, that often made night hideous with their bellowings.

Before they had made many cruises in their saucy yacht, and many expeditions on the hunting-grounds that lay to the north and west of the great lake, Stanley met several parties of these wandering red men, and he found them not quite the same class of individuals he was wont to read of in books at home.   They could be friendly or the reverse, just as it suited them.

"I would never trust a redskin farther than I could fling him." That was how Captain Mackinlay summed up the character of these "braves," and before long Stanley Grahame had an adventure—to be detailed in next chapter— that taught him how true were his uncle's words.   It

taught him something else which in after life he never forgot—namely, caution in all his dealings with savages.

Mackinlay's yacht was a forty-tonner.   Her name was the *Saucy,* and saucy she was in every way.   The crew all told consisted of Stanley's uncle, Stanley himself, bold Sambo, and a mulatto man.   Sambo was very clever in many ways, but especially as a sailor.   He was worth a deck-load of Lascars or Kroomen.   Perhaps he had Mackinlay to thank for his tuition, and he (Sambo) became Stanley's tutor in turn.

But he not only taught our young hero the manual labour of the upper deck, he taught him something else—namely, the languages of the Somali Indians and the Seedies, and the dialects of the various other tribes or nations that lived on the eastern shores of that dark continent, Africa.

That was the land of Sambo's birth, and there he had spent the greater part of his life.

Seated by the blazing pine logs in Sambo's hut in the winter evenings, Stanley used to listen entranced to many a strange tale of adventure, the scene of which was laid in the African wilds, or on the bosom of the billowy ocean that laves its coralline shores.

Sambo's language was very simple, and his voice soft and sibilant, but all the more impressive on that account. There must have been a deal of poetry in the man's nature, for he seemed positively entranced as he dwelt upon the weird beauty of the scenery in and around his native land. Its opaline seas studded with fairy islands ; its deep, dark creeks and inlets, green-fringed with drooping mangroves ; its silent and solitary forests, where bright-winged birds flit songlessly from bough to bough, but where trumpet of elephant and roar of lion may still be heard by night ; its broad-bosomed rivers ; its mighty sand-banks, on which all the strength of the Indian Ocean breaks and thunders continuously ; its mountains and cataracts ; its glens and lakes,—of all these spoke Sambo. But when he talked of the terrible slave-trade, with its attendant horrors, then all the fire of his nature seemed to burn and blaze in his eyes. He was no longer the humble valet of Stanley's uncle. He seemed a chief, a prince, a hero, who, sword in hand, would fight and free his darling native land from the curse of a heartless invader.

"Oh !" young Stanley Grahame would say, "it is to this land of yours, dear Sambo, I fain would sail. It is there I would like to travel and roam. Dangers? Don't talk to me, Sambo, of dangers. Young as I am, a boy in years, I feel a man in strength, and I do not forget that I come of a brave Scottish clan, who for hundreds of years have wielded the sword in the cause of right. Sambo, I have made up my mind. If my uncle doesn't get me an appointment in some vessel sailing away to this dark continent of yours, I'll go back again to my native Highland glen and herd the sheep with old Ewen, or chase the wild deer in the forest of Cairntrie. There!"

VII.

A NIGHT ADVENTURE ON THE INLAND SEA

CHAPTER VII.

STANLEY GRAHAME was an apt pupil, and his dark-skinned tutor Sambo was justly proud of him.

"Der am jus' one ting," said the latter one day, laughing all over—and this is no empty figure of speech, for when Sambo laughed he did laugh. The spirit of mirth got a hold of him, as it were, wreathed all his round face with smiles, almost hid his eyes, but made up for doing so by exposing two rows of alabaster teeth, and ended by shaking him from head to heel. "Der am jus' one ting, Massa Stanley, yah! yah! You is perhaps jus' a leetle bit too big for a sailor."

Stanley was sensible enough of this fact, very disagreeably sensible at times, when the main-boom, for instance, came round with a rush and carried his cap overboard, and very nearly the head that was in it. Stanley's cap was not easily carried away either; it was one of those little blue Scotch ones, called in the army "forage caps," and in the Highlands "Glengarries;" but, though a gale and a half of wind could not budge it, it lowered its flag to the shifting boom, and was borne away into the lake to become the sport of the billows. For little accidents like these, however, Stanley was always quite prepared; he carried a spare Glengarry in his bosom, and when one was blown off he calmly mounted the other.

"Well, Sambo," replied Stanley, "I dare say I am fully tall for your *beau ideal* of a sailor, but then I'm only a youngster; I haven't filled out yet."

"Yah! yah! Yes, dear Massa Stanley, you is puffekly correct; you's nuffun more'n a piccaninny yet. By'me-bye you fill out proper, and den you be jus' such anoder big fellow as dis chile."

"Yes, Sambo, and I really wonder, with your immense height, you have managed to sail round the world without meeting more accidents than you have done."

"Yes, sah, to you," said Sambo, seriously, "and I hab often wonder so myself. Specs Providence had somefin to do wid de matter, ye know, 'cause I'se been wonderfully preserved. But when I'se on board de ships I always look out for my shins."

"Your head you mean, Sambo, don't you?"

"Yah! no, Massa Stanley, my head can look after his-self, he no take much hurt; but my shins, ah! young sah, dey are all de same's one maiden's heart—very tender and 'mpressionable. Yah! yes."

Sambo was squatting beside the tiller while he spoke, with his knees as high as his chin, and Stanley was stand-ing in the cabin with *his head* nearly on a level with the deck; for you must know that they were out on a cruise. The mulatto man was forward ready to take in sail whenever desirable, and Captain Mackinlay was lying on the sofa enjoying his after-dinner "caulk," as he called it.

They had left Beaumont Park the day before, and Canute Creek, near the south-easternmost end of this mighty inland sea, on the same forenoon, after spending a few pleasant and profitable hours fishing. Their intention at present was to sail far away north and west to the moun-tain lands where bear and wolf and bison were still to be found in forest or plain, and where there was accordingly reasonable expectation of good sport. It would be morn-ing or near it before they could reach their hunting-ground, but there was a full moon and a favouring breeze, and the yacht was strong and true.

Captain Mackinlay was an old sailor of the right school,

and he had himself superintended the building of this beautiful little vessel. Paint hid no faults in her; he had
examined every timber and every knee and bolt about
her, and knew the iron was good. So he could sleep
soundly enough, with never a dream to disturb him, for
had not his sailing-master himself got hold of the tiller,
and his eyes aloft ?

And a pretty display of canvas that was too. She had
a tall mainmast and a maintopmast as well, and right abaft
was a mizzenmast, not a sham of a thing with a sham of a
sail on it, like what you see on a fishing yawl, but a good
spar with a real topmast over it. Nor was the mizzen
a mere show, but good and strong—a "sonsy" mizzen sail.
Well, she had at present a foresail and jib set, and a fore-
jib and two gaff-topsails. In a word she was under every
inch of cloth she could display, and with the wind on the
starboard quarter she kept her course like a thing of life,
with never a wrinkle in rag that was on her, and the stars
and stripes at the peak coqueted with the breeze, as if it
were the happiest flag that ever floated over waters blue.

You may guess she looked a beauty, and her bows clove
through the water like the rays of the sunlight, softly,
without an effort, with hardly a sound. About two hours
after the sun was getting low on the horizon, the sky was
blue all over save in the west; on that horizon was a bank
of ugly clouds, changing to a sickly yellow on the margin,
as the sun approached, and seemed to make haste to hide
behind them.

The mulatto man was laying the tea-things in the cabin,
tea and buttered toast. That mulatto man was not gifted
with a great flow of language; terseness was his strong
point. Presently he nudged the sleeping captain.

"Fiddles, sah ?"

"Eh ? eh ?" cried the captain, only half awake. "Fiddles ? fiddles ? fiddles ? What are you fiddling about ?"

"Gwine to blow. Dirty night, I 'specs," said the mulatto.

As he spoke the *Saucy* gave one quick lurch to leeward, and cups and saucers, teapot and toast, went floating down the table, and emptied themselves, avalanche-fashion, on Captain Mackinlay's stomach and legs.

He jumped up and shook himself clear of the wreck.

"Fiddles, you ass!" he cried, angrily, "couldn't you see for yourself? Down with the sticks and get out more delf."

Then he ran on deck.

"Ah! Sambo, Sambo," he said; "what have you been doing? I'm drenched in boiling tea from top to toe."

A bit of a sea struck her fore foot as he spoke, and the thin edge of it cut the captain like a whip-thong across the mouth.

"That's it, is it?" said the old mariner. "And the wind going farther aft too. Well, Sambo, get in your jibs and down topsails."

There was no fear of her carrying her sticks away just yet, but she was not snug by any means. The sea got up momentarily, and she rolled in a way that was anything but pleasant.

Stanley was all alive now; all motion and action. He had been what poets call dreaming just before the captain came on deck. Dreaming of home; thinking, not without some degree of sadness, of his mother and sister and the little homely cottage near the great forest, and the wild, happy, free life he had led in dear old Scotland. This had led him to think of the parting scene, and his adventure at the *eirde* house on the moor.

"Dear me, how strange it would be," he had said, half aloud, "if ever I happened to meet daft Jean's son, and how pleasant a task to bring him home!"

"Oh! yah!" Sambo had cried, overhearing some of his words. "Am de poor piccaninny boy beginning to tink ob home? Yah! yah! 'Cause de wind begin to blow, and de ship begin to swing, eh? Yah! yah! yah!"

I am not sure that Stanley might not have offered some verbal reproof to stem the flood of Sambo's mirth, which he did not entirely relish, had not the captain's appearance on deck put a stop to further conversation.

"Down topsails!" But the rolling of the little vessel, although she behaved like a duck on the great seas that chased and seemed determined to swamp her, made anything like comfort down below an impossibility.

"Now, young sir," said the captain, "this doesn't half come up to my ideas of pleasure. I like tea and toast very well, and there is no one in the world can make either better than our good cook there."

The mulatto man grinned with delight.

"But," continued Captain Mackinlay, "I like peace to enjoy these blessings. So, ho! Away aloft with your long legs, and help Sambo to house the topmast."

Stanley only waited three seconds, just long enough to button his coat and pull his Scotch cap over his ears, then up he went.

The captain laughed when the work was finished.

"Had to hold on by your teeth, hadn't you?" he said.

. But the yacht now rolled far less.

The wind did not lull in the least, however, and the seas seemed to increase in size with the on-coming of night and darkness. There was a moon, but it barely gave light enough to show the huge dusky sheets of vapoury clouds that went hurrying across the sky, impelled by the force of the gale.

"When things are at the worst," said Mackinlay, "they usually mend. Now, in a couple of hours the storm will be just at its height; if we keep this course we give ourselves plenty of sea-room, and towards morning it will be all plain sailing again. We'll run into Freeman's Bay at the nor'-west end of the lake as gracefully and easily as a swan would; then, Stanley, you will see such scenery and have such sport as you never saw nor had before."

The worthy captain knew well what he was talking about. He was perfectly acquainted not only with the fierceness of the storms that so often swept over those inland oceans, but with their brevity as well, and he knew also that so long as he had plenty of sea-room he was safe. But that he was somewhat uneasy was evident from the frequency with which he went on deck and glanced from compass to sky, then around him at the bleak dark night and raging waters. This same uneasy feeling communicated itself to Stanley ; young though he was, he knew there was danger.

He fell asleep on the locker, and an uneasy dreamful slumber it was. It must have been long past midnight when he awoke. The lamp was burning dimly, and Captain Mackinlay was asleep. There was nothing to be heard but the roar of the breaking seas, and the whistling and shrieking of the wind in the rigging. He crept up and found faithful Sambo at the helm.

The yacht was flying along, and it was evidently all Sambo could do to manage her.

"May I speak to the man at the wheel ?" cried Stanley in his ears.

Sambo's eyes were aloft, and there was the glimmer of the binnacle light on his hardy sable face as he nodded assent.

"We're in danger of some kind, aren't we ?"

Sambo nodded again.

"That is all I want to know," said Stanley.

He lightly touched the back of the man's hand. It was cold as stone and wet ; he noticed also that the poor fellow's teeth chattered.

That was enough for kind-hearted Stanley. Sambo was only a black man, but—

Stanley went below, and opening the locker, produced the spirit-stove and kettle, which he carefully steadied among the fiddles on the table, then he lit the stove, and sat down to watch it.

Just ten minutes after he was on deck again with a great mug of steaming coffee.

It was only a very trifling act of kindness, but it was one that Sambo never forgot.

Stanley did not go to sleep again; he preferred reading by the cabin lamp, and so interested was he that he did not perceive from the yacht's motion that both sea and wind had gone down. He threw down the volume at last, and stretched himself with a feeling of relief; the danger, he thought, must be over, and morning would soon break.

Listen ! What is that strange noise—that rasping, scraping sound under foot ? Instinct seems to tell him the yacht is aground, and as she heels over and ships a sea there is a crashing of timber and a shout from Sambo; both masts have gone by the board and the helmsman is entangled in the wreck of the mizzen. Next moment Stanley finds himself, axe in hand, cutting away at the stays, in obedience to the orders of the captain.

There are times in the life of a sailor when the hardest work seems not only easy but positive enjoyment. This was one of them with Stanley, and every rope and stay was cleared, and Sambo erect, ere he stood up and looked around him. Once free from the wreckage the yacht not only assumed an even keel but floated again, and was drifted farther on the shore, where she once more took the ground to the leeward of a rock that broke the force of the wind and sea. And there was the ruddy glare of a camp fire in the forest above them, shining redly over the water. This fire had sprung up suddenly ahead of the vessel, and in keeping away to avoid one shore Sambo had run her on another. The yacht had made a far quicker run during the night than any one on board could have believed possible.

There were dusky figures around the fire hurrying to and fro, and it was soon apparent that the presence of the yacht was discovered, for close to the beach another and bigger fire was lighted, which soon eclipsed the other with its smoke and glare.

It was strange, however, that the figures that stood or moved by the second fire had all the appearance of harmless unarmed Indians.

"I feel sure the others," said Captain Mackinlay, "were men on the war-path. But daylight will soon enable us to get at the truth."

And day did break at last, hazy, cold, and grey; but for the present the mystery of the armed men remained a mystery, for the people on the beach could not have looked more peaceable than they did. By-and-bye some of them came off in their canoes, bringing fish, and inviting Captain Mackinlay and his party on shore.

"What do you think of it, Sambo?" asked the captain, with a quiet smile.

"I tink, massa," was the reply, "as you tink, though you not speak it. Dey are one bad tribe. If they get us on shore, den dey scupper us all plenty quick."

The captain determined not to land, and the whole day was spent in rigging a jurymast and staying it, in the hope that with a shift of wind the yacht might be got off.

Watches were kept as soon as night fell, Sambo and the mulatto remaining on duty till twelve o'clock, then Stanley and the captain taking their turn till morning. Stanley Grahame was stationed in the bow, and more than once in the uncertain light of the moon he thought he could perceive canoes laden with dusky warriors coming towards the yacht. Next day passed by without even the sight of an Indian, and this only made matters all the more suspicious.

"They will attack us to-night," said Captain Mackinlay. "I know their tricks and their manners well. Stanley, dear boy, I fear there won't be any hunting this trip."

In the afternoon a breeze blew off shore, but the yacht moved not, with all exertions that could be made. It was a question, too, if she would float even if they succeeded in getting her into deep water; for as she bumped a good deal against the ground bits of timber came floating to the surface, that told only too plainly what was going on underneath.

No one thought of sleeping this night. There were plenty of arms in the yacht, and everything was got ready in case the Indians returned.

With the change of wind the sky had cleared, and at nine o'clock up rose the moon and flooded all the glorious scenery with its light. So quiet looked the woods now, so placid and still the water, that it seemed hard to believe that a hostile foe was lurking not far off preparing for pillage and murder. On board the wrecked yacht never a light was shown, and on the shore there was no sign of life. Two, three, four hours went slowly past, and Stanley was beginning to think the night would pass in peace, when suddenly a dark object became visible on the water coming from the wooded point to the north, and silently but swiftly approaching them.

"Here they come," the captain cried. "Be ready, Stanley; be ready, men, to do as I tell you."

Then he hailed the advancing boat, an immensely large canoe, in which the stalwart forms of over a dozen painted warriors were now distinctly visible.

The reply was a well-directed volley, and a wild yell of defiance, and both volley and yell were reverberated from afar, and must have startled the denizens of those wild woods. The volley had only one effect, and that a good one—it put these brave yachtsmen on their mettle.

"Don't fire yet," cried the captain. Then a minute or two after, "Now then, now together," he shouted.

Perhaps the Indians had not expected so warm a reception, and had counted on an easy victory. But in no way daunted, on they came with redoubled shouts. There was no time to fire again from the rifles, but revolvers were at hand, and with these good execution was done. But the

fiercest part of the fight took place when, the canoe alongside, the savages were repelled with pike, cutlass, and
clubbed rifle.   Sambo fought like a lion, if it is not invidious
to say so where all did so well.

The struggle was virtually over in but little more time
than it takes to tell it, and the canoe was rapidly making
for the shore again.   But it can hardly be doubted that
they suffered severely.

"Just ten minutes to rest," said Mackinlay, "and then to
get our boat provisioned and lowered.   These fellows will
return in more canoes than one, and next time we may not
come off victoriously."

The work was gone about in a business-like fashion, but
as quietly as possible.

"Let us be thankful for the friendly wind, Stanley," said
the captain, as he took his place in the boat.   "Step the
mast and up with the sheet.   Did you arrange everything
nicely below, Sambo?"

"Oh! yes, sah," cried Sambo, "tar and tow, sah, and
petroleum; presently you see de smoke and de blaze ob
our poor leetle ship."

It needed a stroke or two of the oars to get the boat past
the point, but soon she felt the force of the breeze, and the
oars were no longer required.

Are they to be allowed to depart thus peacefully? Nay, for they are already perceived, and not one canoe but a dozen at least start in pursuit. They start in a line parallel to the shore, but soon one or two better manned outstrip the others, and seem to come up hand over hand.

The mulatto took the tiller, keeping the sail well filled, and the others commenced a running fire on the foremost of their pursuers, and the fire was well returned.

"Courage, Stanley," said the captain, "we are safe as yet; a stern chase is a long chase, and their arms will tire, but the wind won't, unless indeed they cripple our sail. But look, look: see how the flames begin to mount around our poor lost yacht, and the enemy are already wavering and slackening their fire."

It was true. Revenge is sweet to the American Indian; but the hope of plunder is a feeling that overcomes even revenge.

One last yell of anger and disappointment, one last hurried volley, and the chase was over; but at the same moment Stanley Grahame started and fell backwards in the boat, with a pale face turned skywards, and the kindly hands that hastened to help him were stained in warm blood.

VIII.

LIFE AT BEAUMONT PARK—PARTING.

CHAPTER VIII.

LIFE AT BEAUMONT PARK—PARTING.

A DARKNESS, almost akin to that of death, eclipsed for a time the young life of Stanley Grahame, from the moment he was shot down in the boat by that cruel Indian bullet. He felt no pain as he fell, indeed how could he? He heard not even the frantic lamentations of honest Sambo, nor the quiet, stern, but mournful tones of Captain Mackinlay's voice, as he gave directions for the staunching of the blood and temporary bandaging of that terrible wound. He knew nothing of the journey home to Beaumont Park, nothing of the lying in bed, nothing of the visit of the surgeon, who came from a far-off town to see him and pronounce upon the case.

No pain; not even when he opened his eyes, after weeks of burning fever for himself, and heartfelt anxiety for his friends around him, only a confused consciousness of weary racking dreams, of toilsome wanderings over lonely moorlands, by rocks and by waters, on mountain and in forest. He was only half aware that these were dreams; he was not sure that there was not a mingling of the real with the imaginary; but the moorlands had been very long, and the rocks oftentimes fearful precipices, over which he had fallen headlong into abysses of insensibility, and the waters had been deep and dark, while in the woods and forest he had contended and fought with creatures of strange shapes, that had tried to prevent him from going he knew not whither or doing he knew not what.

But where was he now? In bed, that was all he could tell.

He gently breathed his sister's name, " Ailie, Ailie." A soft footstep was heard, the curtain was drawn aside, and a slender girlish figure stood beside his pillow.

" Ailie ! "

It surely was Ailie. And yet those dark eyes and those raven tresses were not his sister's, though something in her looks was the same.

He essayed to talk, but she held up a warning finger and shook her head. Then she was gone, but back again

in a moment, holding something to his lips, which he knew he must swallow. Then his eyes, weary, hot, and half shut, rested on the face of his little nurse.

" Oh ! " he thought, " it *is* Ailie. Must be Ailie. How could I have been deceived ! "

Yes, to all intents and purposes, she was Ailie to him now, for he was fast asleep again. But no more racking, worrying dreams, no more toilsome wanderings. He was back once more in the great forest, high up again in leaf-land, and Ailie was seated on a bough by his side, the myriad leaves were gently sighing in the summer wind that fanned his brow, and the bees made drowsy music above, beneath, and around him.

Anon the scene was changed. He was seated in the strange *eirde* house on the moor, and near him "daft" Jean. She was telling him again the story of her long-lost son, and earnestly pleading with him to bring him back to her—to bring him back to life.

Bring him back to life? Why, the words were not daft Jean's at all, but those of a gentleman who sat in the room not far from his bed; a cheery-faced little gentleman with steel-grey hair and apparently steel-grey eyes, so brightly did they sparkle. He was nursing his hat and nursing his gold-headed cane, and talking earnestly to the demure little maiden whom Stanley had mistaken for Ailie, and who, by some means or other yet unexplained to him, had been constituted his nurse.

"No," he was saying, "all danger is now past; skin cool and fever gone. I needn't come again for a whole week, for, as I said before, it needs but my medicine, regularly given, Sambo's attention, and your gentle care to bring him back to life. You are my little lieutenant, don't you see? and I'm so sure that you'll obey orders, and carry out my instructions to the very letter, that I'm going to leave the case in your hands for that time. And then—but see, our patient is awake, and has been listening, perhaps, ever so long to all we've been saying."

Stanley smiled.

The doctor approached the bed and laid his fingers on his wrist. "Bless the boy!" he said; "he'll be all right soon. But it was a narrow shave he had of it—within half an inch of the heart. Yes, he'll be running about again in a couple of months. That smile tells me so. Heigho! If I could get all my patients to smile like that I'd soon be the richest man betwixt here and Boston. Good morning. You'll do. I guess I won't come again for a whole week."

Stanley's life for the next three or four days seemed to consist of a series of long, refreshing sleeps, his waking moments being but short, and occupied principally by taking nourishment and holding his tongue.

But though forbidden to talk, there was no provision made to prevent him from thinking or wondering, and he did a good deal of that. He wondered, among other things, where his gentle and attentive little nurse had dropped from, why she was dressed in black, and what that something in her looks and manner was which caused his thoughts always to revert to his sister Ailie.

" You are to be allowed to talk a little this morning," she said, on the fifth day after the doctor's last visit.

" I'm so pleased ! " he said.

" And to sit up a little in bed Only for twenty minutes,' she continued, consulting a dainty wee gold watch, no bigger than a florin ; " twenty minutes—doctor's orders."

Then the curtain was drawn back, and Sambo himself, who had been hidden from Stanley's view till now, came forward and raised him gently on his pillows.

Sambo was smiling from end to end of his mouth—or from ear to ear, as one might say. He sponged his patient's face and hands, then put away the things, and, returning to the bedside, relieved his feelings by getting rid of a big sigh. Then, "Oh, I *is* so glad !" said Sambo—"I is so puffukly happy, that byme-bye I shall go out into de woods, where nubbudy can hear me but de 'possums, and laugh !"

Stanley pressed his hand.

" I'm sure, good Sambo," he said, " I shall soon be all right again now, and then we will go down into the woods together and—and laugh."

" Oh ! yes, sah," said Sambo, "and do all kinds o' fine doin's when you is fit. We'll hunt de 'possum and catch de 'coon, and—But, la ! young sah," here Sambo's face got as long as a bootjack, " w'en de skunks of Injuns make de bobbery and shoot you down, I tink den you am murdered for sartain.

"I tink you plenty—too—much—quickly die. Den you lie on my knee, and you bleed and bleed 'spite ob all massa and I can do ; and all de while you look so white, all de same one bladder ob lard."

"Did I, though ?" said Stanley. "You describe things very graphically, Sambo."

"P'r'aps," replied Sambo, "I not speak so geographically as I wish, but den, sah, I speak de troof. W'en Sambo see you lie all same's one dead pigeon, den he want to die hisself. His heart come up out ob his place and stick in his throat, can't swallow 'im down again nohow."

All at once Sambo's face lost the boot-jack shape ; it broadened and rounded up again, and his eyes sparkled with delight.

" But I say, sah," he cried.

" Yes," said Stanley.

" What you tink ?" asked Sambo, all a-grin.

" I couldn't say."

"No, you nebber, nebber could guess. But, sure I got de gemlain safe and sound dat nearly murder you."

" What !" cried Stanley, " you caught the———"

" Yes—ess, sah," cried Sambo, laughing delightedly, "sure enuff I catchee he for true. I put he in one box for safe. 'Now, gemlam,' I say, 'out ob dat box you not can come until young Massa Stanley is better, and if poor young massa die, den out ob dat box you nebber come.' I go fetchee he, sah, plenty quick."

Stanley waited with a good deal of anxiety, expecting that Sambo would presently return, accompanied by an Indian prisoner of the warlike and nomad tribe of Apaches.

But Sambo returned alone, and in his hand a pill-box, from which he pulled out a much-indented rifle-bullet, and handed it to Stanley.

"You are a funny fellow, Sambo," said the boy, much amused. Then he took the bullet and examined it, with the same kind of interest that one would look at one's own tooth, extracted by some cruelly-kind dentist.

The same afternoon Stanley was permitted to sit up and talk a little more. The French window of the room where he lay opened on to a beautiful verandah, whence he could see away, over miles on miles of meadow-land and woods, to where the view was bounded by the far-off hills. It was the Indian summer, the trees were arrayed in the tints of autumn, and the fresh air felt to Stanley redolent of returning health and happiness.

Presently in through this window, accompanied by a beautiful setter, came Captain Mackinlay, booted and spurred, as he had leapt off his horse. With his bright, rosy, beaming face, his sturdy form and hair of grey, he looked the very genius of the lovely landscape on which Stanley had been gazing.

He did not say much, but sat down by the bedside, and took the boy's wasted hand in his.

"It makes me feel better only to look at you," said Stanley, smiling.

"Well, then, my boy," replied Mackinlay, "you'll get better every day, for I'll come in every day after my ride, and if I can't do anything else I'll sit and let you look at me."

"Everybody is so kind to me," said Stanley a week later on, "that really getting well is a pleasure. I don't think I would mind being shot again at the same price."

When he was able to be up and dressed Sambo was indeed delighted.

"I'se de happiest nigger," he told his patient, "on de whole plantation."

Then reclining on the sofa, which was wheeled near the open window that he might inhale the life-giving air, Stanley used to listen entranced to the poems and tales read to him by Ida, his child-nurse. He had never thought the wild lays of Scott, or the poems of Coleridge and Campbell, half so delightful before, much though he used to love and enjoy them, for now to his ear they seemed set to music.

It was weeks before Stanley knew anything more of the girl his medical attendant had placed such faith in than her name—Ida Ross. He knew, from the dress she wore, she was in grief of some kind. What that grief was he would not for the world have been rude enough to ask, but his uncle, in her absence, said one evening, in his blunt, straightforward manner,—

" You are wondering, my boy, who little Ida is, aren't you ? "

" I have been, sir," said Stanley.

" Poor little dear ! " the captain said ; " she has recently lost her mother, while her father, Captain Ross, an old and dear friend of mine, is at sea, so Ida has no one but myself at present to protect her."

Stanley could not help feeling even more tenderly towards her now. It seemed so good and kind of her to interest herself in his welfare while her heart was breaking with her own grief.

So the time wore on. The balmy Indian summer gave place to winter. Snow fell, making the great cotton-trees and the cypress-groves a sight to see. Stanley was not permitted to take outdoor exercise yet, so he still was Sambo's patient and Ida's.

He took her hand one day in his.

"Ida," he said, "you have been very, very good to me."

" Have I ? " she said, innocently ; " but not more so than I ought to have been. Oh ! no, not a bit more."

" Ida, I have written to Ailie and to my mother, and told them all about you and your goodness to me, and Ailie says you must be a sister to me, quite a sister, and mother says she loves you, and will pray that some day she may meet you and thank you.   Ida, will you be a sister to me, and may I call you so ?"

"Oh! yes," said Ida; "I will like it very much, Stanley."

" Ailie always calls me 'Stan,'" said the boy.

" Well, then, I will always call you Stan."

" Read to me, Sis."

" What shall I read, Stan ?"

"'The Rhyme of the Ancient Mariner.'"

" But is it not terrible ? "

" Yes ; but the last verses, as you read them, Ida, are like a prayer.   They make me feel better."

In a low, sweet voice, that lacked not solemnity, Ida read that weird poem, and at some stanzas, with a little shudder she crept closer to her " brother's " shoulder.

The surgeon who treated Stanley's wound had not done wrong in making this strange girl his nurse.   She was one of a type that you seldom or never meet out of America, who combine the wisdom of the woman with the innocence and tenderness of the child.

There was in the room where Ida, the captain, and Stanley used to spend the evening, a small harpsichord. Ida often seated herself by this, and played and sang the simple but affecting melodies so common during the last fearful civil war.   This was the sweetest music, to Stanley's thinking, he had ever heard, and he wondered how his uncle could go to sleep.

Spring comes all at once, almost, in the country where Captain Mackinlay had his home.   In one short week the fields are carpeted with green and studded with wild flowers, butterflies flit in the sunshine, birds sing gaily in the woodlands, and there is life and love and beauty everywhere.

From the time he regained consciousness up till now, when he regained strength, Stanley Grahame's life had been quite an idyllic one; too much so, perhaps, for a dreamy life of ease is not suited for manly youth. And to tell the truth, now that he could go out of doors, and ramble about in the woods, and row or fish in the river, the boy was somewhat ashamed of himself for having given way to the pleasure of such a dreamy existence as he had led all the autumn and winter through. He did not now ask Ida so often to read or sing to him. This was, perhaps, somewhat ungrateful. To do Stanley justice, he knew and felt it was, and, to make up for it in some measure, he used in the evenings to recount to her all his adventures in the woods or by the river, show her his fishing tackle, descanting on the merits of various flies, which he even taught her to make from the feathers of birds he procured.

Sometimes she used to accompany him in his rambles, but not very often. I fear he preferred Sambo.

"Oh, Sissie," he cried, as she came joyfully to meet him one evening in the hall, "what a day Sambo and I have had! Such sport! Such fun! You can't conceive how much we have enjoyed ourselves."

As he spoke she had her two hands on his shoulder, and was eagerly watching his animated face.

"How I wish," he continued, looking down at her, "you had been a boy! girls really are so little use, you know."

Tears rushed into the poor child's eyes, then her arms drooped nervelessly by her side, and next moment he was alone.

Stanley would have given all he possessed in the world, and a deal more if he had had it, to have been able to recall those words. Alas! it was too late. "A word spoken—" You know the proverb, reader.

"Stanley boy, Stanley," cried his uncle from the sitting-room; "come along in, lad, I've news for you that will make you jump for joy."

At any other time, perhaps, what his uncle told Stanley might have made him jump for joy; at present it had not half the pleasant effect it ought to have had.

"Sit down and listen. Now, you see I have been thinking about you for months and months, and planning how best I could serve you. Truth is, Stanley, I want to make a man of you, because the fact is there are the makings of a man about you. Well then, you want to be a sailor, and I've got you a ship. You see you are far too old to enter the fighting navy, and I'm not sorry, for in these days of floating rams—box-heaters I call them— seamanship is quite unknown, even in the Royal Navy of England. But the merchant service is the place for you. Well, lad, I could have got you apprenticed to one of the finest liners afloat, where you would have been treated like a young gentleman, and fed like a lady, and seldom required to soil your fine fingers. But would that make a man of you, think you? No, nor a sailor either. I want you to rough it a bit, just as I roughed it in my young days, and as every good man and true that now sails as master mariner has roughed it. Are you afraid to rough it, lad? Say so if you are, and I'll send you home again to your mammie."

"I'm not afraid of anything that's right," replied Stanley, boldly but respectfully.

"Well spoken, lad. I knew what you'd say, but I wanted to hear you say it. Now this is a letter from Skipper Allardyce, of the good barque *Trincomalee*. It was brought by a messenger not an hour ago. Allardyce is down at Forestville to-night; he is off again to-morrow for New York; we must see him at once and arrange matters, and we have just an hour to catch the down steamer. Are you ready? Can you do it?"

"Of course," said Stanley; but——"

"So sudden, isn't it, eh? Take the word of an old sailor, boy—every event in this world worth calling an event happens without warning. A man should be always in marching order, and always ready to do his duty, even if that duty be to die. Get out your knapsack. Heave round, there isn't a minute to spare. We'll dine in the boat."

"I'se got de habbersack," cried Sambo, "and ebberting you want, sah. Horse ready all same too, sah! We got to ride good ways down de ribber dis time to catch de boat. Suppose you no plenty quick, sah, 'ssure you for true you no catchee he."

"I won't be a moment, Sambo."

Stanley hurried away as he spoke.

No need to say he was looking for Ida to say good-bye, and to ask forgiveness for the cruel, ungrateful words he had inadvertently spoken.

But where was she? Not in any room below. He was hurrying across one of the corridors when he met her maid coming on tiptoe down the broad staircase.

"Hush!" she said, raising her finger. "Your boots make too much bobbery. Poor missie sleep. She been cry. She not well. Hush!"

"Stanley! Stanley!" cried his uncle.

Only a few hurried words, incoherently spoken to Ida's maid. Words that she hardly knew the meaning of—words she would scarcely remember—and Stanley was off.

How beautiful the woods looked in the sunset; how quiet and still they were!

> "And nought within the grove was heard or seen
>   But stock-doves plaining through its gloom profound,
> Or winglet of the fairy humming-bird,
>   Like atoms of the rainbow fluttering round."

Stanley had never seemed to love them half so much as he loved them now. But why this sadness on his heart? He would be back again to-morrow or the day after, and tell Ida how much he had suffered and sorrowed for what he had said. Then for a time at least the dear idyllic life would be resumed.

But then he *might* not. He might *never*——

"Now then, Stanley; jump, lad! Now we're off."

The great paddles dashed slowly round, and down the river dropped the steamer, and next morning found Stanley Grahame far away from Beaumont Park.

IX.

A SAILOR LAD ON HIS BEAM ENDS—HUNTER'S HOWE—FRIENDS IN NEED ARE FRIENDS IN-DEED.

CHAPTER IX.

IT was near the close of a summer's day about six years
after the events narrated in last chapter. It had not'
been a very bright day, nor a very beautiful one, and the
tourist passengers homeward-bound from Rothesay or the
western isles had good cause for grumbling, especially
those who had never before steamed up the broad and
romantic Clyde, for though glints of the green woods, the
bosky dells and bonnie glens, could be seen on either side,
the grand old hills remained sullenly encapped in mist.

Opposite Greenock the boat was stopped for a few
short seconds, barely allowing time for two or three steerage passengers, with their bundles and sticks, to scramble
over the bows into a wretched-looking shore boat or cobble.

Ten minutes afterwards these passengers were landed
on the quay, and immediately separated, each going his
own way on his own business, probably to meet no more
again in this world.

But one of them lingered for many minutes behind the
rest, a tall handsome young man or lad, for he might have
been any age between seventeen and five-and-twenty.
"Younger probably than he looks," any one would have
said who had glanced at him, "but how careworn he
seems."

Yes, there was anxiety in his large eyes, and his cheek-
bones were certainly higher than health required them.

He took from his trousers pocket a few pence and gazed half wistfully at them.

"I should have liked to have gone all the way to Glasgow in the boat," he said to himself, half aloud, "but —seven— nine—ninepence-halfpenny and a threepenny-bit; no, I couldn't have afforded it.   But what is a twenty-mile tramp to me, to long legs like mine, long legs and a good stick? Ninepence-halfpenny and a threepenny-bit.   Ha! ha! ha!

It's good fun.   At least it would be if I wasn't quite so hungry."

He sat down on a great log of timber, put one knee over the other, and whistled.   He was whistling a beautiful dreamy melody from Mozart, but I'm sure he didn't know what he was whistling.

"So hungry," he muttered.   "Ever since I had yellow fever I have hardly been able to eat enough to satisfy myself.   Well, I'll spend that threepenny-piece, anyhow. Bread and coffee, Grant's coffee house in Borlem's Close the steward said.   So here's for off."

He grasped his stick, started up, and marched away, swinging his bundle and singing as he went.

"You're a merry lad," said a great hulking shore porter that he nearly ran against. "And not much on your back either. A pair of duck pants and purser's shoes, a blue jersey, and a straw hat; sailor evidently; but maybe you carry your wealth in that bundle?"

"Yes," said the lad, "all I have in the world—my jacket. But, say, can you direct me to Grant's coffee-house?"

"Have you a plug o' baccy?" was the reply.

"Really no; I'm sorry I haven't," said the lad.

"Have ye the price of a pint?"

"Well—yes—if you really want it I can just manage that. I have nine·——"

"Keep your dibs," cried the porter, laughing. "You're an honest-faced lad, and an open-hearted. Here's my card. I'm called English Bill if ever you want assistance. Now come on, and I'll show you Grant's."

"Thank you. Good-bye," said the lad, when he had brought him to the house.

Grant's coffee-house was certainly not a palace. But it did not pretend to be; only it was clean and cheap. There was not a soul in it when the lad entered and seated himself in one of the little partitioned boxes that did duty for private rooms. The dividing partitions of these were canvas, papered on both sides. They looked solid, but were not even pin-proof. Yet each box had a door of its own, and, when once inside, looked far from uncomfortable. When bread, butter, and coffee were set before this tall, hungry sailor lad by the not over-tidy waiting-maid he considered himself in luck indeed.

"And all for one small threepenny-bit," he thought. "Why, hungry as I am, I'll hardly manage to get through it."

But he did though.

"And now I'll think," he said, pushing aside the tray, and dropping his weary head on his bundle. "Then I'll set out and tramp all night."

If thinking meant sleeping and perhaps dreaming, he certainly was not long in commencing operations, for hardly was his head down before he was off to the land of forgetfulness.

It might have been three hours before he stirred again. The girl had come in and taken the tray away.

"Poor laddie! he's tired," she thought. "I'll leave him in the dark, else master'll turn him oot."

He awoke with a kind of a start and a cold shuddering feeling, for which he could not account.

There were voices talking close beside him in hoarse whispers, just on the other side of that paper partition.

"Hush!" one said; "are ye sure no one can hear us?"

"I looked into a' the compartments," was the reply; "they're a' dark. There's not a single sinner in Grant's the nicht but the auld man himsel', and he's noddin' ower the fire. No, lads, as I was sayin', the job can be done easily and safely. He has oceans o' gold in a belt round his waist. Sally told me. She saw it the day. Ye ken what a tongue she has, and how she can wheedle roun' the sailors, and this chap, she says, is safter than any she ever came across."

"Go on," said voice No. 1, "but whisper, man, whisper. Wa's hae lugs."

Thus admonished voice No. 2 was lowered, and our sailor lad, now all alive and listening, had considerable difficulty in following the thread of the discourse. But he heard enough to make his blood curdle. He heard enough to let him understand that robbery and violence, if not even murder, were being planned by the three villains in the next compartment; that the victim would be some poor sailor man newly returned from abroad with his savings all in gold in a girdle round his waist; that this girl Sally, whoever she was, and he were now at a concert; that after the concert she was to walk three miles into the country on pretence of going home to her mother's cottage, and that the sailor was to give her escort. He did not hear the name of the cottage. Perhaps there was no cottage, but repeatedly he heard the name "Hunter's Howe" mentioned.

"Mind, Jock, there maun be no knifin' this time," said one voice.

"Unless, ye know——" said the other.

"But remember that affair at Paterson's——"

"Bah! man, come along out and have some whiskey. You'll maybe no be sae squeamish after that."

As soon as they were gone, "What shall I do ?" said our sailor lad to himself.

"Go and alarm the police? No, they would but laugh at me. I'm not over respectable-looking, and they might—oh! I have it. I'll go and see English Bill. He looks honest. Here's off again once more."

He had to ask his way several times ere he found Bill's garret. Haply Bill was in, and had his boots off.

"What, my sailor boy!" cried Bill. "Well, well, but what's in the wind, matey? You look as white as a sheet."

The lad hastily told him all he had heard, and Bill began to put on his boots before he had half finished.

"Did you see them ?" he said, quietly.

"I did," said the lad, "I opened a tiny hole in the partition with my knife, and I'd know them again easily."

"Come on," said Bill. He buttoned his coat as he spoke, previously pocketing a sturdy truncheon. "Very likely they've started before now. If not we'll go on first."

"But how shall we know ?" asked the lad.

"Easily," was the reply. "We'll just take a look into the whiskey howffs near Grant's. Folk that love the drink never go much beyond the nearest inn to get it."

The moon, a great round red one, was rising and struggling with the bank of fog that lay along the braes beyond the

town, when they found themselves in front of a brightly
lighted tavern.

"This is Paterson's," said Bill.   "There have been queer
doings here before now."

They entered.   Three evil-visaged fellows sat drinking
neat whiskey on the top of a barrel that did duty for both
seats and table.

The sailor lad touched Bill lightly on the arm.   That
was enough.   They had some refreshment, which the
youth paid for, and once more sallied forth.

"Now, then, we're sure they are not before us.   Let us
on to Hunter's Howe.   They look strong villains, but if the
poor beggar they mean to murder is anything like me, we'll
be good enough for them."

It was past ten ere they started ; the sky was now
bright and clear, and the moon shining brightly enough for
any purpose.   That is, it shone brightly in the open, but
when the trees began to close overhead, and finally, when
the road descended into Hunter's Howe, the heroes in this
night's adventure thought they could have done with a
little more light.

Hunter's Howe was an eeriesome enough place even by
day.   It was a place that bore a bad name too, for many
a highway robbery had been committed here in days gone
by, and if countryside talk were anything to attach importance to, murder itself had stalked red-handed among the
gloomy firs in this uncanny dingle.   Bill and his young
companion hid themselves behind some spruce firs, near to
the entrance to the Howe, nor had they very long to wait
ere down the road came the selfsame three scoundrels
they had left at Paterson's Inn.

"I feel sure," said one, "I saw some one in front of us."

"Nonsense, man," cried the tallest and roughest-looking
of the murderous trio.   "You're squeamish, man.   You're
an auld wife.   What for do you no' gang hame ?   Jock
and I can do the business our twa selves easy eneuch."

"Ay," said Jock, gruffly, "and we can share the gold between us as well."

Then they hurried on, and no doubt hid themselves in the wood lower down, for the sound of their heavy boots was soon inaudible, and all was now silent in the Howe, save the occasional cry of the brown owl, or the frightened and mournful scream of some night bird.

It was a long weary hour that followed, for time always does seem long when one is waiting.

Bill put his arm kindly across the sailor lad's shoulder. He was shaking with cold, for the air around was damp and chill.

"You're not afraid, are you?" whispered Bill.

"Not I," replied the lad, "only cold."

"Well, you're only a young 'un, you know. But take a pull at this flask. It is good whiskey."

"Thank you, no," said the other. "Dutch courage, Bill. I will not touch it now, nor ever, I trust. Young as I am I know the cost of that."

"Hush!" cried Bill; "listen."

Nearer and nearer it came. Only some manly voice trilling a song, a brave old sea-song, to a ringing old sea melody.

> "The busy crew the sails unbending,
> The ship in harbour safe arrived,
> Jack Oakum all his perils ending,
> Jack Oakum all his perils ending,
> Had made the port where Sally lived."

"Poor fellow!" whispered Bill. "He comes singing on to certain death if we can't manage to save him. And that girl on his arm. Look at her face."

It certainly seemed a pretty enough one in the moonlight.

"I know her well," said Bill, "and many a poor sailor does so to his cost.'"

The girl was glancing uneasily around her. as if she

expected every moment that the assassins would leap into the road and fall upon their victim. The latter was well dressed in a suit of blue pilot, and was probably mate of some merchant ship.

The pair had come along through the fields, and not by the highway, else it might have been easy to have met them and warned this innocent sailor not to enter the wood—a warning which, even had it been possible to give it, would in all probability have been disregarded, for sailors are proverbially headstrong and careless.

Even now Bill hesitated how to act. Bill would have made a good soldier, but a bad general. That hesitancy almost cost a life, for while he was still deliberating the girl shrieked and ran back towards the town, and at the same moment the sailor was felled to the earth by a blow from behind.

There was no more hesitating with Bill now.

"Hands off, you cowards!" he shouted.

Next moment the three assailants had turned fiercely round to meet the attacking party.

Three to two. Yes, but Bill and our sailor lad had right on their side, stout hearts and heavy cudgels, and the would-be robbers fell back before the suddenness of the first attack as if they had been but schoolboys.

"Knives, lads, knives!" shouted the biggest of the three. "Give them Greenock!"

"Ay!" cried the others; "hurrah for Greenock and Cardiff!"

Knives now flashed in the moonlight, and although one of the ruffians almost immediately after measured his length on the ground he was speedily up again, and it would doubtless have gone hard for our heroes had not the sound of rapidly approaching wheels at the same moment put an instant end to the combat.

"Heels, boys, heels!" cried the ringleader, and he and his fellows rushed headlong into the copse and were seen again no more.

Timely aid had come in the shape of an honest old farmer, who was jogging homewards in his dogcart from the market.

Matters were soon explained to him. The form of the prostrate sailor was lifted into the cart, and half-an-hour afterwards they found themselves at Bill's humble home. The farmer had done his duty, and so retired. Not so Bill. He considered he had done but half of his, and he determined to complete his work, so he hurried away for a surgeon.

The doctor's verdict was soon pronounced. The wound was so severe that removal to hospital would be fraught with danger. If he could be nursed where he was it would be infinitely better; he had lost so much blood already.

"I'll stay beside him for a few days, at all events," said the sailor lad. "He is a seafarer like myself, and——"

The poor lad stopped short. He remembered he had little more than sixpence in the world. He hung his head and blushed.

"I know what you're thinking about," said Bill, bluntly, "and you are welcome to bite and sup in my garrets as long as you like to stay."

The wounded man's eyes had been resting on the sailor lad during the conversation.

He now beckoned him towards him.

"Stay," he whispered, "don't leave me."

"Yes, stay, lad," said Bill. "My two rooms are not big; they are only garrets, but stay, lad, stay."

"I will, then," said the youthful sailor.

"Then it's all arranged," said the surgeon. "I'll be here to-morrow to dress him again. Good night."

For more than a week the wounded man hovered between death and life, and the sailor lad watched by him night and day. Had it been his own brother, hardly could he have been kinder to him than he was. In ten days he was able to sit up a little and talk, and one morning Bill went to a drawer and took therefrom a sailor's leathern girdle and placed it on the bed.

"You'd better count your money," said Bill, "and see if it be all right."

The man's dark eyes were opened wide with astonishment and delight.

"What!" he cried; "then I wasn't robbed! Neither robbed nor murdered! Oh! Heaven be praised, and you be thanked. Most of this gold was for my old father. Had I lost it, as I deserved to, back to sea I'd have had to go for years more without even looking upon his dear face. But a portion of this gold—all I can spare—shall be yours, my dear young friend, and yours, good Bill."

But the sailor lad put his hand on the man's arm.

"Not a coin of that money do I touch," he said with a calm smile. "I'm on my beam ends, I grant you, but I'm young, I'll right again. The storm has nearly blown over."

"Then how ever shall I repay you?" cried the man. "And yet," he added, musingly, "there is no knowing where sailors may meet, or what they may have it in their power to do one for another. There is no knowing. *But,* lad, one thing you will not refuse me—you must get yourself rigged out in decent togs. There! I won't offend your pride, I'll give you no money, but I'll lend you that much, ay, and force you to accept the loan.

"You see," he continued, "you want to get a ship. You say you've been third officer. Who knows but we may sail together? But in that rig no ship-master would look twice at you. Come now, add to the favours you have already done me by accepting the trifling loan. Loan, mind, loan, d'ye hear?—and when you get a ship you can repay me."

The sailor lad consented now, and went off at once, in obedience to his newly-found friend's wish, to get "rigged out," as he called it.

Two hours after he re-entered the garret, smartly dressed, and sat down somewhat shyly by the edge of the bed.

"And now," said the wounded man, "there is one thing I've suspected, but am now sure of. You may have been before the mast, but you're a gentleman. Now tell me your real name. It is *not* Tom Smith."

"It is Stanley Grahame," said the sailor lad.

Well then, Stanley, let us know more about each other. My story is short, though strange enough. But you—how came a young lad like you to be taken so flat aback? and, Stanley, what keeps you on your beam ends? You were to have sailed again before the mast, were you not?"

"I was indeed," replied Stanley. "How could I have done otherwise? But you shall hear and judge for yourself."

X.

A PORTION OF STANLEY'S STORY TOLD BY HIMSELF
—THE FATE OF THE "IVANHOE."

CHAPTER X.

"HULLO! here is the doctor," cried Cooke, for that was the name of the wounded sailor that Stanley Grahame had volunteered to nurse.

"I like that 'hullo,' Mr. Cooke," said the doctor laughing; "it is a hearty one."

He placed his fingers on his patient's wrist as he spoke Then he touched his cheek.

"There is a bit of a flush just there that I don't quite like. Oh, I know how it is: you sailor lads have been spinning yarns one to the other."

"No," said Cooke; "but we were going to."

"Then you won't," replied the doctor. "D'ye hear? Never a yarn for a week to come. Your nurse can read to you instead."

"Very well," said Cooke; "you are head man here, doctor."

"Should think I was," said the man of medicine.

"And what a lot you've done for me."

"But what a constitution you have," said his interrogator, modestly.

"Well, then," he continued, "you are able to get up a little now, and sit by that open window and breathe the fresh air that blows over Bill's box of mignonette. Bill, where are you?"

"Here I am, sir," said Bill, entering the little room.

"Look here, Bill, you'll catch the down boat to-morrow, and run right away to Rothesay, and take rooms close by the sea, and in a few days I'll start the whole three of you off down there. My patient will get well in a fortnight there, and as I have business in the island twice a week I can always pop in, don't you see ? "

"You'll be obeyed, sir," said Bill. "The change will do myself good too. I haven't been picking so well of late."

The surgeon looked at him from top to toe, and *vice versâ*, then nodded his head and laughed.

"You're in a galloping consumption, Bill," he said; "consumption of victuals; galloping consumption, because I do believe you could eat a horse."

His friends hardly knew honest Bill next day, when he came into the back attic to say good-bye before starting for Rothesay. A blue cloth coat and vest of white, any amount of shirt-front and gold-chain, and a long black hat on his head. What with the hat and his height he had no room to stand in the little attic, so for his own comfort he had to assume the shape of a Belgian canary.

A very happy little group were seated on the lawn of a pleasant cottage down in Rothesay about a week after this. The lawn was gay with flowers, the birds made melody in every bush, and the sea rippled up to the very gate. There was honest Bill, the shore porter, who had just placed coffee on the table; and Stanley, looking infinitely better now than when he landed at Greenock with ninepence-halfpenny and a threepenny-piece in his pocket; and there was the young surgeon, who had dropped in to see his patient ; and the patient himself in a rocking-chair. His bronzed face was somewhat paler than it had been some weeks ago, but with his rich brown beard, his finely-formed nose, and dark eyes, and his cap stuck carelessly on the back of his head, he looked every inch a sailor, and a very handsome one too.

Stanley was talking. Not much of a story-teller was the

lad, however. When he began first it looked as though he were talking to his boot. He had one leg over the other, and kept poking his boot with the point of his cane, as if he wanted to impress the story on its darkened understanding.

He spoke of his arrival in America and reception by his uncle, and told his hearers—or his boot—all about the fight with the Indians and the burning of the pretty little yacht. He was loud in his praises of Sambo, and, of course, he did not forget to mention Ida, his child-nurse, and all her kindness. Then he came to the parting, the going away from dear old Beaumont Park, where he had been so very, very

happy. It was exactly at this point of his story that Stanley ceased to appeal any more to his boot. He lifted his one knee off the other, and, bending forward, began to make circles and triangles with his cane on the gravel. He was silent for fully a minute, but nobody spoke. Only the doctor winked to Cooke, and Cooke winked to Bill, and Bill winked back to both of them.

"That was the worst of it," said Stanley at last, giving a vicious blow with his cane to an unoffending pebble. Then he started up and took a few brisk strides down the path, and came back as suddenly as he had gone, and reseated himself.

"Yes, that was the worst of it, and I have never forgotten it all these years, and what is more I never shall."

"But," said Mr. Cooke, mildly, "you haven't told us yet which *was* the worst of it."

"Oh! didn't I though?" said Stanley, opening his eyes as if in wonder. "I mean, you know, having spoken so cruelly to poor Ida, and having to go away without saying good-bye. I expected to get back in a day or two, but never could and never have been. It is too late now, she is gone, and I'll never, never see her again.

"I'm sure, though," he went on, "that uncle meant all for the best, but he never could have imagined I would have been treated as I have been. Nor could he have known the captain of the *Trincomalee*, in heart and soul, as to my sorrow I came to know him before I had sailed two days in his ship."

"He was a tartar, was he?" put in Mr. Cooke.

"A tartar?" repeated Stanley, "ay, and a tyrant."

"I know his stamp and his style," said Cooke; "there are many of them still in the merchant service, though, thank goodness, not so many as there used to be. But no doubt you learned a good many of your ideas of sea life from books, as most boys do, and came to think it is all beauty, dash, romance, and moonshine. Go on, I'm interrupting you."

"Some of my ideas of sea life I certainly did learn from stories. My little sister Ailie and I used to get away up together into a tree, in our dear old forest, and there I used to read to her for hours, but the ship I crossed the Atlantic in first—oh! she was a model ship and had a model master. I wish I had time to tell you all about her."

"I can guess, my dear boy; but continue. Were you bound apprentice?"

"Bound a slave, it seemed to me.* You see, Mr. Cooke,

---

* The author deems it only fair to himself to state that the description of Stanley's treatment on the *Trincomalee* is no flight of imagination, but hardly half the truth.—G. S.

my uncle had an idea that the only way to make a man of
a boy was to make him rough it."

"Ha! ha! ha!" laughed Cooke, "a gentleman of the
real old 'school, I'll be bound, but gallant and true, no
doubt."

"Ay, that he is," said Stanley, his eyes brimming with
enthusiasm; "but he told Captain Allardyce to keep me
up to the mark in duty, seamanship, and everything else."

Stanley paused for a moment, then resumed, smiling—

"I can't help laughing, now that this man's cruelty is all
past and gone, at his ideas of duty and seamanship."

"I think I know," said Mr. Cooke.

"Ah! but tell us," said the doctor. "I know nothing,
you see, not being nautical."

"Duty," said Stanley, "in the opinion of Captain Allardyce, of the *Trincomalee*, consisted in the most abject
obedience to his will and commands, whether connected
with the regular ship work or not, at any hour of the
day or night, whether your watch was below or on deck.
Seamanship, constant 'cracking on' as he called it, at all
risk to rigging of craft or life of crew, a determination to
look after No. 1—that was the gallant skipper himself—and
a stern resolve to turn the fault of every little accident that
happened on board upon those beneath him. But duty
like this would not have been so difficult to perform to one
like me, brought up as I have been in the woods and wilds
of the north, had it not been for the fact that we were at all
times when on deck subject to horrid language, threats, and
kicks and blows from both mate and master; and while
below we were——"

Stanley paused again, and looked at Mr. Cooke.

"Starved," said the latter.

"I did not like to speak the word," continued Stanley;
"but really we were put on short commons, and very
common were these commons too."

"But, pardon my interruption," said the doctor; "on

what plea could you possibly have been subjected to such treatment, and whom do you include in the word 'we'?"

"The captain never went far in search of a plea," replied Stanley. "Sometimes we were accused of neglect of duty, or not working quickly enough or tumbling up on deck fast enough. At other times we were simply denied dinner because we 'looked cheeky' and were 'growing too fast,' and wanted taking down a peg. By 'we' I don't mean the crew and I. They were big and strong, and could take their own part; besides, they had an ugly way of going aft with their complaints, that both mate and master had some very good reasons for dreading. No, '*we*' were poor Watts and I. Friends in everything we were, friends in sorrow and in the few joys we had. One of these was to get together in our watch below and talk of home. Many are the hours' sleep we had to want for so doing, but we didn't mind that, because he, like myself, had a mother and sister who loved him. And sadly they must have missed him too, though I never heard anything about it. I know I missed him."

"But," said the doctor, "was he lost, then?"

"Yes," replied Stanley—"fell from the yardarm into the sea while reefing topsails one squally night near Cape Horn. I don't wonder. The wind came down in fierce blasts and struck you on the shoulders, as you leant over, with the force of a battering-ram; then it was dark and bitterly cold.

"I was," continued Stanley, "in that ship for nearly four years, during which time I seem to have lived a life-time and been almost everywhere. I grew a man, too—the man you now see me."

The doctor smiled, and so did Cooke, and Bill laughed right out, which was very unmannerly of Bill.

"The mate, who remained in her all the time, found out that I was handy, and he rated me, gave me a kind of promotion, and used to make me keep his own watch for him in dirty weather, or whenever from other reasons he wanted to remain below. Now, bad officers make bad crews. I've learned that, young as you all think me, and even on dark nights our look-outs were improperly kept, and I'm not sure that the lights were always what they should have been. But one night our vessel seemed as safe as ever ship was. We were bound to Valparaiso with a mixed cargo, and if the wind held should have hoped to reach that port in four or five days. It was in the queer season when storms and squalls may be expected, but all day the sky had been quite overcast with big, dark, bunchy clouds, and now and then heavy showers, but nothing of a sea on to speak of, so you may be sure that as soon as the sun got well down there wasn't too much light. There were flashes of lightning just now and then, but they did more harm than good. Perhaps that was the reason that took me forward when I came up for the middle watch, for I could not trust my men. If I'd been aft it would have been better for the ship, and better for the mate and master.

"It must have been considerably past four bells, for I remember wondering why they had not been struck. The man at the wheel could see the cabin clock, and it was his duty to call out the time. The man was gone, the helm lashed; but a strange smell of burning was coming up out of the captain's cabin. I ran to the hatchway and opened it, and smoke came pouring up. But down in that cabin there was visible fire as well, and as it came licking up and sought exit I could tell by the fumes it was burning spirit.

"A few seconds afterwards the bell of the *Trincomalee* · rang as it perhaps never rang before, and certainly never will again.

"My first duty was to my captain now. I had not forgotten the teachings of my uncle at Beaumont Park."

"And did you save him?" cried Bill, making his big

fist fall with a ring on the table, for at this part of the story
the honest shore-porter's face was full of excitement.

"The men," said Stanley, modestly, "did work well, and
at last we got him out, and the mate too, but both dead.

"Spirits must have been part of her general cargo. We
did all we could at first by laying-to to confine the fire to
the after part of the vessel. But, in spite of all, it broke
through the closed hatches ; then all was over. Alas! the
despairing crew, with but few exceptions, found their way
to the maddening liquor, and many of them paid the penalty
with their lives. Then ensued a wild scramble for the
boats. I think I and a few others would have been left to
go down in the burning ship, had the rest had it all their
own way. They did not, however, for while they were in
the very act of leaving the *Trincomalee* we discovered
several strange boats close beside us. They were those
of an outward-bound ship that, seeing the fire from afar,
had borne down to our assistance.

"Gentlemen," continued Stanley, "with the burning of
the *Trincomalee* my apprenticeship ended. Three months
afterwards I found myself in Melbourne. Thence I sailed
to China, from China to Japan, Singapore, Ceylon, Calcutta,
Bombay, more than once to Bombay, and there I stayed for
a time and passed for a mate. How very proud I was you
may be sure when I found myself second master of a
handsome clipper barque leaving that beautiful roadstead,
with its forest of shipping, its romantic city, a rippling sea
all around us, the distant island of Elephanta like a land of
enchantment on our weather quarter, and——"

"Go on, my dear boy," cried the doctor, "you are getting
quite poetic."

Stanley blushed, but added bravely, in spite of his hot
face—"with hope in my heart."

Cooke glanced slily over at Bill again, and the doctor took
to watching the ants running hither and thither on the
gravel, but nobody moved a muscle, for all knew this was

the critical point in Stanley's story. Bill remarked many a day after this that he knew "the lad was coming to something."

"I had the hope," said Stanley, "of seeing my own country again, my mother, and Ailie; and America also, and—and Ida. This was natural, you know, because—because—oh, bother!—because, don't you see, I had left her in grief because the last words I had spoken to the child had been those of ingratitude.

"I could have gone home years before, I could have gone years ago to my second home, to Beaumont Park, but I had promised myself I would not until I really had roughed it, and seen the world, and until I could show Ida—well, I mean my uncle—my mate's certificate. And now we were off, and with a favouring breeze too, right away to the Cape, and thence to dear old England. During all the years I had been voyaging I had had many letters, but for more than two years before my uncle had never mentioned Ida's name, merely putting in large letters in the postscript the sailors' words, 'All's well.'

"Our passage to the Cape was a wonderful one, but I didn't think, for all that, we went quite fast enough. At last the bonnie hills above Capetown hove in sight, and at last I had landed and rushed away to the post-office, where letters I knew would be awaiting me.

"I'll read you a snatch of one. I have it here."

Stanley put his hand into his bosom, and pulled out an envelope, which might have been an old pensioner's certificate, so frayed and worn was it. Then he read,

"'I dare say, my dear nephew, you will not have forgotten the little girl that nursed you here when ill. Well, lad, we will never see her again, nor my dear friend Captain Ross either. He took her to sea with him about two years ago, and the ship must have foundered, for she has never more been heard of, and a good ship too was the *Ivanhoe*, though with many new-fangled——,'"

But Stanley was able to read no farther, for Cooke, who had been watching Stanley's face earnestly while he read, now sprang from his chair, and leaning over the table,—

"What!" he cried, excitedly, "Captain Ross!—the *Ivanhoe*! Where have you been, then, that you have not heard the news?"

Stanley was now quite as much excited as Cooke.

"News," he exclaimed, "is there indeed tidings of her at last?"

"Ah! yes, but sad tidings, boy; sit down; answer me, where have you been?"

Stanley spoke quickly now. "Shipwrecked," he said, "and after waiting for a ship six months at St. Helena, I worked my passage home in a small schooner, and arrived in Belfast penniless; thence to Rothesay, then to Greenock, where we met. Quick, tell me, what of the *Ivanhoe*?"

"I have recently arrived from Zanzibar," replied Cooke, "and as soon as I'm well, will go out again. About the last news I heard before leaving that port was of a ship of that name, and with that captain, having gone down in the Indian Ocean, and of one or two boats having at last reached the Somali coast, and having been set upon by the Indians and all their occupants brutally murdered."

Stanley hid his face in his hands.

"All! all? Oh! don't say all!" he cried.

"Alas! dear boy," said Cooke, kindly, "I kept back the worst part of the news. They were not *all* killed. Some few were taken away into the interior—to a slavery worse than death."

Stanley left his chair now and stood in front of Mr. Cooke. His face was very pale, but his voice was calm.

"Cooke," he said, "you go out again to Africa in a few months?"

"I do."

"*I shall go.*"

The two men simply grasped each other's hands.

CHAPTER XI.

BY THE CLYDE—THE SCENE CHANGES—H. M. S. "TONITRU" IN A GALE OFF THE COAST OF AFRICA—PROSPECTS OF A FIGHT.

CHAPTER XI.

MANY a time and oft in his future lifetime did Stanley Grahame look back with pleasure to those few weeks spent with Cooke and Bill in their cottage by the sea in that beautiful isle of the Clyde. It was in reality the last days of his boyhood. Henceforward he was to be Stanley Grahame, the man. He was not sorry, as far as his apprenticeship and indentures went, for the fate of the *Trincomalee*, although he sighed as he thought of the dreadful end of the captain and mate, and the burning of the brave old ship. But it had set him free. He was his own master, to go where he liked, to do as he liked. He was as good a sailor—ay, and he knew it too; pray why shouldn't he?—as most young men of his age. Between you and me, reader, perhaps he was a better. He was not a mere swabber, nor was his knowledge confined to the feet-and-finger work which goes by the name of reefing, splicing, and steering. He had had a good education to begin with. He had not been all these years at sea with his eyes shut, and, rough though his life had been, and even more than busy, he had found time to study winds and currents and skies, and make himself conversant with the navigation of a ship, and I verily believe that if his modesty had allowed him he could have gone straight away from before the mast and taken his mate's certificate in Bombay, instead of spending some time in earnest study, as he had done.

Yes, Stanley Grahame was a man—a very, very young one, it is true. He smiled a kind of apology to himself for his very youth as he stood by the Frith of Clyde the day after he told his story to his companions, skipping stones across-the water.

"A man shouldn't be doing this sort of thing," he thought "but it is good fun. Well, one other shy, and then I'm off to do a think, as poor old Ewen used to say."

A few minutes afterwards we find him seated all alone by the waterside on the top of a brown, weed-covered rock ; and, mark this, his face is turned seawards, not up towards the Clyde. All the blue frith is studded with sails. Boat and brig and barque and ship are there, with white sails glittering in the sunshine, and yonder is a lordly three-decked steamer, making her way citywards, with the white churned waters forming her wake, and a long rope of grey smoke trailing behind her. Beyond are hills, and above all, the sky, far bluer than the sea that reflects its radiance, and flecked here and there with white feathery clouds. But Stanley sees nothing of all this. His thoughts are not on the scenery around him. He is reviewing his short but eventful life, and laying plans for the future. Not building castles in the air, mind you, but considering calmly what he had best do in order to raise his dear mother and sister, and, with them, himself, to the position from which the revolving wheel of fortune had cast them. He does not particularly wish to see them rich, but he wants to see them comfortable and happy. Might he not succeed in making them so if he remained on shore ? Perhaps ; but shore life was far too tame for Stanley Grahame ; besides, what right has a young sailor to live on shore ? But had he not prospects from his uncle ? Yes, and he had also pride. If his uncle really did mean to do anything for him he should at all events first prove himself worthy of it. He will go to America before starting with Cooke, and tell his uncle what he has resolved to do, and already in imagination he hears the old captain's voice ringing in his ear as he presses his hand and says, "You do right, lad ; you do right. Go to sea again ; go and seek your fortune, and may God's blessing go with you."

Then his thoughts revert again to his mother and Ailie, how rejoiced they will be to see their sailor-boy!

> " How glad to meet, how wae to part,
>   The day he gaes awa ! "

At this point he must jump off that brown rock, and take to skipping stones ag in. Oh, Stanley! I'm afraid you're only a boy after all.

But see, the last stone drops from his hand on the sand, and a change comes o'er the spirit of his dream and his face. He is thinking now of Ida. Will he ever— But no ; she is dead. That is certain. Drowned! She sleeps in the calm depths of the Indian Ocean. She lies where pearls lie deep. He hopes and wishes she may be, for to think of Ida, his innocent little child-nurse—albeit, if alive, a child no longer—in the hands of savages! No, no—but he will learn her fate. Sooner or later he will find out where and how poor Ida died. He *is* a man now. He goes and sits on the rock again for a while. He has not another thought of skipping stones, and by-and-bye he gets down, and, turning his back to the sea, slowly retraces his steps to the invalid's cottage.

*   *   *   *   *   *

Neither officers nor crew of her Majesty's gallant cruiser *Tonitru* were in the habit of expressing any fears for the safety of their vessel, even on the stormiest night that ever blew. They knew what she was made of and what she could do, and really, making all allowance for a little pardonable pride on the part of the brave fellows who trod her decks, it must be confessed she was, if not quite all they thought her, at all events as strong and bonnie a craft as you could wish to sail in and well deserved the title of

Cock of the 'Bique. The word 'Bique, I may tell you, is a contraction for Mozambique, so now you know where we are, or at least you can guess the coast on which the *Tonitru* was wont to cruise. She had been down south at the Cape of Good Hope, and had only sailed three days before. She had been paying her respects to the flagship, the good old *Princess Royal.* She had entered Symon's Bay about a fortnight before, with much flaunting of signal flags, and a deal of firing of shotless guns, but she came away from there quietly enough. The band of the big ship had simply played "Good-bye, sweetheart, good-bye," as she steamed past them, the officers of the big ship had waved their caps, the men had cheered. One man with lungs more stentorian than his shipmates had sung out,

"Hurrah! for the Cock of the 'Bique."

Upon which a midshipmite, for you couldn't call him a midshipman, perched upon the topmost crosstrees of the brave little *Tonitru*, had elevated his voice and given vent to a shrill but defiant,

"Cock-a-doodle-doo!"

And for this liberty the commanding-officer had bellowed an order up to him to—

"Remain there until you're told to come down."

When the commander had gone on shore to ask for leave to sail,—

"You'll have dirty weather," said the admiral.

"Ay, that is so," was the reply.

"And all in your teeth," continued the admiral.

The commander only smiled.

"Ah! I see," laughed his senior. "You don't mind it. You're anxious to get another slap at those slavers. Very well, I'm agreeable."

The admiral was right about the dirty weather. And this was a dirty night. A wild and dark and stormy night. I verily believe that had a landsman even been at sea on this night he would have been—well, not afraid, for landsmen do not know enough to be afraid, but he would have been uneasy.   And well he might.

Let us in imagination, you and I, reader, take a ramble round the ship, as the easiest way of realising in some measure what life is on board a fighting cruiser on a night like this.

Let us follow the doctor. He *has* to go forward to attend to his duty; he has no assistant, for the *Tonitru* only mounts six guns, and carries but ninety men all told.   But I assure you the doctor would never think of leaving the ward-room unless he were forced.

We find him first in the steerage outside the ward-room. The former is simply—in this ship—an open space between decks, dividing the engine-room from the officers' mess-room ; on to it open the pantry and two cabins, and *in* its deck is the screw-hatch, through which it would not be agreeable to tumble.   And here is the broad ladder that, standing athwart ships, leads to the deck above.

The doctor stops a minute to converse with the engineer on duty.   It is positively pleasant to gaze down among the engine gear, the glittering steel and polished brass work, and the cheerful gleaming fires.

" It's blowing a sneezer, isn't it ? " says the engineer, wiping the perspiration from his brow, as he gazes upwards at the doctor, who is holding on to the sides of the door.

" I should think it is blowing a sneezer, as you call it," says the surgeon, " and, worse luck, I have to face it.   Why there isn't a passage right fore and aft between decks in a ship of this size I can't tell.   And why a marine should choose to fall sick on a night like this, and send for me, is a puzzle, that is all, simply a puzzle.   The service is going to the bad."

" Doctor ! doctor ! " says the engineer, shaking a grimy finger * up at him ; " don't be——"

---

* Engineer officers do not wear kid gloves on duty in a small ship like the Cock o' the Bique.

What advice the engineer was about to give the doctor may never be told, for just then the saucy *Tonitru* ships a sea which fills her decks, and takes the liberty of pouring down the ladder.

"Wet to the skin," says the surgeon, shaking himself as a duck does when it treads the water and waggles its wings. "Now I'm off. I can't be worse and I can't be wetter."

"Good-bye," says the other. "Don't be long : I've got a couple of yams in here roasting."

"Yams!" cried the doctor, his eyes sparkling. "Well, I know we have butter in our mess, badly found and all as we are. Here's off."

He buttons his coat up and makes for the ladder. The ladder seems to make for him at the same time, and he finds himself floundering on top of it with a badly-barked shin. No sooner on than he would have been off again had he not caught the rope railing ; then he seems to hang head down for about five seconds, and as the vessel rights he makes a step forward, meaning to walk, but it is a run, or rather a running scramble, and thus he gains the top, and carefully withdraws the hatch, and, watching his oppor-tunity, steps carefully over the board that has been shipped to keep out the seas, quickly recloses the hatch, and stands for a moment undecided, if, indeed, you can call it standing, for he is clutching wildly at top of the companion and swaying about like a drunken man. He gasps for breath, and wonders which is the lee side. He hardly knows at first, the wind is so far aft.

The sails which he can just dimly descry are bellowing full, emitting many a roar and many a thud as the wind threatens every moment to rend them into rattling ribbons.

The doctor goes down to the lee side at last, much in the same graceful way that a person who has never worn skates before glides over a piece of ice, but he brings up by the shrouds with only a bruised shoulder, and so far he is safe. This is the worst part of the journey.

"Hush!" cry the seething, foaming waves close to his ear. So low down is the bulwark that, incautiously putting his arm over, with another little lurch his arm is buried in the water up to the elbow.

"What a fool I was!" says the doctor to himself.

"Hush! hush—sh—sh!" cries the boiling sea, as if it had some mighty secret on its mind, and was just going to tell it.

"I believe," continues the doctor, talking aloud—why, his voice would not have been heard in the howling of that tempest had he roared—"I believe I should have been better on the weather side after all."

A sea cuts him in the neck; he waits for the second, then the third, then there is a lull, as he knew there would be. Then he makes the best of his way and scrambles forward till he reaches opposite the fore-hatch, then pauses to glance around him.

Oh! but, dear reader mine, I should fail if I were to attempt to convey to your mind any notion of the dreary blackness of the night or the terrible hissing and howling of the restless waves, mingled with the "howthering" of the wind. There isn't a star, the clouds seem close overhead, the staysails are in them, the masts rake them. The wet wind comes in gusts that make the surgeon gasp like a drowning man. He looks awfully across or on to the sea —a sea that is only indicated by the combing, curling waves that here and there glint white against the ever-shifting horizon. But he can imagine all that is not visible, imagine the pyramidal seas twisted with the wind, the terrible troughs between, and the dreary black depths that lie beneath the surface of the storm-tossed ocean.

He shudders, and is fain to cast his eyes forward to catch a glimmer of light from the fox'le. There is comfort in that, comfort even in the yellow light of the dead-eyes that shimmer up through the slippery deck.

The doctor reaches his journey's end at last by rolling

down the forehatch ladder all in a heap.   He isn't put
about a single bit.

"This is precisely the way I expected to arrive," he says,
laughing, to the carpenter, who helps him to rise.   Then
the doctor goes to the sick man's cot, and having done what
he could for him, thinks he won't go aft again without
visiting the engineer's berth.   There is a song going on
there, and he stands in the doorway holding back the curtain
and smiling until it is finished.   He even joins in the
chorus, and a rattling one it is—

"Then come along with me to Scotland, dear,
    We never mair shall roam."

And so on *ad libitum*.

"Ho! ho!" says the doctor, when the song is ended,
"and so you are here, Stanley Grahame.   We thought
you had fallen overboard, and I'd just come forward to visit
the ship's tailor to see about a bit of crape for our caps and
sword-hilts, and your little mite of a townie MacDermott
has been crying about you, or pretending to, for that is
more his form.   And I've had the boy Green searching the
ship for you."

"Your loblolly?   Ha! ha! ha!" laughs the second
engineer.

"Yes, Snade, my loblolly."

"Well," says Stanley, laughing, "we are just going to
have another song and then I'm with you."

"But I say, though," adds the surgeon, "there are yams
for supper."

"Yams! Yams!"

Both Stanley and Snade spring to their feet.   There was
no more thought about the song.

"Come along, both of you, you are right welcome to
our mess, Snade, so don't hang fire."

Round the little ward-room table of the *Tonilru*, about
an hour afterwards, a right merry crew of eight were

gathered, discussing with many a friendly joke and laugh a meal of yams and melted butter.

A yam is a kind of very large potato, and, my dear boy readers, if you have never eaten roast yam and butter, I sincerely hope you may live till you do.

Little MacDermott the midshipmite's face was all a-pucker with fun and mischief. I'm sure he had a deal more than his share, because he sat between the doctor and Stanley Grahame, and whenever Stanley looked the other way he helped himself to a fork-load off his plate and winked to the doctor, and whenever the doctor happened to turn round to speak to any one, little mite Mac helped himself off the doctor's plate and winked to Stanley. Then he would say,

"I say, men, though, ain't this yam scrumptious?"

It was no easy matter sitting at the table at all, I can tell you. These young officers had got themselves wedged in, in all sorts of intricate shapes; some had their knees against the table, one gentleman positively had a leg on it, but really it was not a night for them to stand on the order of their sitting.

"Doctor," said little Mac, "don't you think I'm fading fast?"

"I think the yam is," replied the doctor.

"But really now, dear doctor, don't you think I'd be better of some fruit and rest—medical comforts, you know?"

"Oh! bother," said the doctor. "Gentlemen," he continued, standing up and swaying about as if he had been set on wires, "I have observed for some time that you all look somewhat pale, fading away in fact. If I could get round the table, a thing which is quite impossible under the circumstances, I would feel all your pulses turn about, and I'm sure I would find that they called aloud for medical comforts."

"Hurrah!" from Mac.

"Mac," said the surgeon, " if you're not quiet I'll pull
your ears.

"Well, gentlemen, it happens that the fruit is positively
spoiling, and there isn't a sick man in the ship except
a marine, who is suffering from the effects of two days on
shore, and whose leave I have stopped for two months.
So I will prescribe for you a bunch of bananas, some

grapes, and a dish of mangoes.   Steward, call the boy
Green."

This boy Green, this loblolly boy of the doctor's, was
somewhat of a character in his way.   I'm not going to
describe him very minutely at present, he will develop as
the story goes on.   When he appeared in the doorway,
touching his hat with a half-deferential bob of his head,

" Sir to you," said the boy Green.

He was dressed as a second-class be   'f the truth were told he was in some matters a very second-class boy; he was round-faced, squarely built—not lubberly, mind.   The boy Green was fairly well-built and as hard as a ring bolt, in fact looked as though he knew how to take good care of himself; he was smart and active—when he pleased.

But his one crowning peculiarity was that when he looked at you he seemed to sneer. This got him into many a row.   He was constantly getting smacked on the ear by the cook and the steward, and used to retaliate with belaying-pins, broom-handles, or saucepan-lids.

He was constantly being ordered to get his hair cut by the officers; not that he wanted it—it was so short through frequent applications of the scissors as to resemble a barber's block.   The hair-cutting was a punishment.

Just a word or two about the boy Green.   He was a London Yankee boy, having come to London from New York as a stowaway, thence found his way to a receiving-ship, and afterwards to H.M.S. *Tonitru*, where he was speedily elevated to the proud dignity of loblolly boy because he was no use on deck.   But at the first muster by-open-list, a ceremony of great pomp on board a man-of-war, when every one from the commander downwards must file past and answer to his name, the admiral stopped the boy Green, and asked him what or whom he was sneering at.

" Ain't a-sneering at you, I guess," said the boy.

"What are this boy's antecedents?" asked the commander of the paymaster.

"Ha! ha!" sneered the boy Green.   "I never had a father nor mother, let alone an auntie."

" Quartermaster," said the commander, " let that boy have his hair cut."

And from that day to th's boy Green was continually having his hair cut.

Now this boy appeared in the doorway, and obeying his master's orders, retired again to fetch the fruit.

"Is this all that is left of that splendid bunch of bananas?" asked the doctor, when he came back.

"Guess," said the boy, "the rats has been a-goin' in for medical comforts; and why shouldn't they?"

"Silence, you young rascal!" roared the surgeon "Silence! I say. Go and get your hair cut."

The boy took off his hat and rubbed his block sympathisingly. Then he turned to go, but speedily turned round again.

"Which I were a-going to say summut," he said.

"Well, then, what is it? Here is a banana for you, but I hate a pilferer."

"So do I," said the boy, peeling and swallowing that banana at two mouthfuls. Then he added, slowly,

"Which I guess I did hear the officer of the watch report to the captain 'a light on the lee bow,' and that it must be the slave dhow we let slip yesterday."

"Hurrah!" cried everybody round the table.

"She means fighting," said the second master, "if she is put to."

"That she will," said another.

"Oh, dear, dear! whatever would my mother say?" cried little mite Mac, making pretence to cry. "Her darlingest boy too. Doctor, I'm going on the sick-list. Do put me on, there's a dear old doc."

The boy Green was in his glory at even the remote prospect of a fight with a dhow, and found his way forward, as soon as he had filled his pockets with cold potatoes and ham from the pantry, to tell the cook that he felt sure a ball would smash his (the cook's) leg, and of the joy and pleasure he would feel in "helping" the doctor to cut it off and dress the stump.

CHAPTER XII.

SUNRISE ON THE SEA—A SAIL ON THE WEATHER BOW—CLEARING FOR ACTION—THE FIGHT.

CHAPTER XII.

MORNING broke, and clouds and sky and wind and sea all combined gave promise of finer weather, not to say a glorious day. Stanley Grahame had been up betimes. His mind had become possessed of the idea, how formulated he could not tell, that, in some way or other, the sturdy two-masted dhow that they had lately given chase to, but lost with the fall of night, would have something to do with his future life, or, at all events, be in some way connected with his interests. For Stanley was imbued with a little of that strange superstition which is never wholly absent from the minds and characters of those whose early lives have been spent among the wild mountain scenery of romantic Scotland. And strange it is, but true, that these presentiments are sometimes—nay, often, followed by the very events which they forebode. Stanley was up and treading the deck long before the sun appeared. The storm was over to all intents and purposes. The wind still blew down in gusts, but there were long lulls between each blast that spoke volumes to the experienced sailor. The sea still fretted and chafed and foamed, but the waves that had been hills high were now but houses high, and the good ship took on board no more water.

Then up arose the sun, its coming heralded by long strips of amber and crimson clouds.

"Up leapt the sun out of the sea." Nay, reader, these

are no words of mine. I have spent years cruising in tropical waters, and I never yet saw the sun leap all at once up out of the sea in the morning, nor sink as suddenly at setting time. Books and stories written by fresh-water sailors tell you there is no twilight in the tropics, that darkness follows sunset quick as a hand clap. Believe them not; there always is a short twilight, both morning and evening.

The sun rose, and the gold and crimson clouds changed into silver, and the clouds in the west that had been grey before turned scarlet and yellow. The horizon was a shifting one still, and every moment a wave seemed to wash the great red sun quite out of existence, but soon it defied them, and as it mounted higher it was almost impossible to look along the pathway that his beams made 'twixt the *Tonitru* and the east, for the crimson glory dazzled the eyes and almost make the brain reel. The still breaking wave-tops were dyed in the light, and the rippled sides of each wave shone and glittered like "coals of living fire."

Who could look on such a scene as this, after a n'ght of storm and tempest, and not believe that the Supreme Being who ruled on high loved all things here below! From some such thoughts as these Stanley Grahame, standing by the main rigging, was roused by the cheerful voice of his captain.

"What, Mr. Grahame!" said the latter. "Well, if I had been you I would have stuck to my hammock for hours yet."

"Good morning, sir," replied Stanley, lifting his cap. "I don't usually get up so soon, but I was thinking about that light we saw last night."

"I know," said Captain Orbistone ; "and you are longing to stretch your legs, aren't you? And have a good look round? Oh, I know what you merchant sailors are. Well, well, away aloft you go. But if you do see anything, come quietly down and tell me. I think that fellow of mine in the foretop isn't quite awake yet."

"NOR DID HE STOP UNTIL HE HAD REACHED THE MAIN TRUCK."

Page 147.

"Thank you, sir," said Stanley, smiling.

And away he went spinning spider-like up the rigging, for a wonderful fellow was Stanley considering his great length.

The storm of the previous night had come on quite suddenly about dusk, so there had been no time to strike royal masts. And now, not content with going into the highest top, Stanley, when ratlines would take him no farther, simply edged a leg and an arm round cornerways, as it were, and next moment he was shinning up the bare pole, very much to Captain Orbistone's amusement, and the delight of the brave blue-jackets around the fox'le. Nor did he stop until he had reached the main truck. Then he had a good look round.

He was down on deck again in less than five minutes.

"An immensely large two-masted dhow," he reported, "on our weather bow."

"That is she," said the captain.

"Foretop there!" he roared.

"Ay, ay, sir!"

"See anything of a sail on the weather bow?"

A long pause.

"There is no such thing, sir."

"Where are your eyes?"

"Pardon me, sir," said Stanley, "but they would need to be good ones. She must be a good three miles off, and even from my position I could only raise her rigging."

The captain said nothing more; he paced the deck rapidly once or twice, then sent Midshipmite MacDermott for the engineer and the first-lieutenant.

Both officers appeared, looking somewhat sleepy, with frock coats buttoned suspiciously near the neck.

"We can't go a bit closer to the wind, you see," Stanley heard the lieutenant say, after some minutes' conversation carried on in a lower key. "She is to windward of us now, and if the breeze holds she'll keep there."

"Well, bother it all!" said the captain, laughing, "we'll get up steam."

"Ay, we can do that," said the lieutenant, also laughing.

It needed but small encouragement at any time to make young Pendragon laugh. With his round, beardless face, and his fair curly hair, he looked little more than a boy; and as, instead of the usual French peak to his cap, he had one of those—now nearly out of fashion—that lie close over the brow, the boyish appearance was still more pronounced.

"We can get up steam, sir," he said; "but we mustn't forget two things, sir."

"What are they, Mr. Pendragon?"

"The first is," said Pen, as he was always called in the mess, "that she hasn't seen us yet; those chaps don't keep much of an outlook from their stump-heads."

"No," said the captain. "The Arab dress isn't quite suitable for going aloft. As well send an old woman aloft as an Arab. Well?"

"Second is," continued the lieutenant, "that she can sail as quick as we can steam—in this sea, anyhow."

The captain bit his lip with vexation.

"You're right," he said. "That dhow is a bad one. She'll keep full if she sees us, and we know what dhows can do before the wind."

"Fly," said Pendragon, emphatically—"fly, dance, dive, anything that ship can do, and a deal more."

"Keep her close-hauled, then, Mr. Pendragon, for a little bit, and clear away our old sixty-four; perhaps she'll want a taste of that to bring her to her senses."

"Perhaps," replied Pendragon, "if we get near enough."

If the dhow had not seen them at the time this conversation took place, it was not long ere she did. She then altered her course, keeping nearer to the wind, and, somewhat to the surprise of the officers of the *Tonitru*, began speedily to increase her distance from the cruiser.

And so the morning sped away till six bells in the fore-

noon watch, then something very fortunate for the *Tonitru*
occurred—the wind shifted round a point or two against the
sun, and fell considerably in force.

The captain of the *Tonitru* rubbed his hands, and walked
more briskly than ever. Pen's face was wreathed with
smiles. Midshipmite Mac, his mother's " darlingest boy,"
went down below to write a letter home, the clerk prepared
to take shorthand notes, the doctor went to the dispensary
and pulled out some ominous-looking bundles of tow and
bandages, and a long flat mahogany box, not unlike a
duelling-case. The dispensary opened on to the steerage,
so the doctor put the tow and bandages at the corner of the
counter; then he opened the case and had a look at some
awfully sharp knives, which, with a smile of grim satisfac-
tion, he placed " handy," with a bottle of wine and a bucket
of water, where neither would tumble down with the ship's
motion. Then he sent the steward for Snade, who was off
duty, and told him that in the event of a fight he looked to
him for some help.

The boy Green was here, there, and everywhere, com-
forting the men by assuring them that he knew as much
about amputating limbs as the surgeon, and that he would
do all he could for them.

Meanwhile steam had been got up, and the men were
ordered dinner an hour sooner than usual; and by-and-by,
" Birr-rr-rr-rr " went the drum, and " birr-rr-rr " a
second time.

The men did not wait for the third rattle; in two minutes,
if not less, every man Jack fore and aft was at his post, and
there was silence on the decks of the *Tonitru.*

While the men stand to their guns awaiting orders, and
all is expectancy and eagerness for the coming fray, let me
go back a short way in my story, and tell you how Stanley
Grahame came to be on board this gallant cruiser, and in
what capacity he was serving. This I can do in a very few
sentences. So pray read them.

Stanley, then, had quite fulfilled all his intentions with regard to his visits to his mother and sister, and across the Atlantic to his uncle. I must leave you to imagine the kind of welcome he got from each.

He worked his passage out to New York accompanied by Cooke, whom he took along with him to Beaumont Park. He told his uncle whither he meant to go, namely, to the shores of Africa, and Sambo received with joy the same intelligence and begged hard to be allowed to accompany the young master, as he called Stanley. In this matter Captain Mackinlay was obdurate. Perhaps he did not, even for Stanley's sake, wish to part with so good and faithful a servant. But Sambo's last words to Stanley were these :

"When you go, I get round de ole gemlam nicely, I do. You see byme by. I follow you plenty quick."

Back to Glasgow, where Stanley Grahame did not forget to visit his good cousin, and thence by merchant vessel as second mate, Cooke being first, straight to Zanzibar.

Here he was permitted to leave his vessel, Cooke, with whom Stanley Grahame was exceedingly sorry to part, returning in her, his ship laden with sugar and spices.

What to do in this strange wild city, Stanley for a time did not know. He was wandering aimlessly one day in the suburbs, when he found two officers having an altercation with some half-dozen spear-armed savages. Somali Indians they were, but as neither party could understand a word the others said, the matter was likely to end where it stood, unless indeed they came to blows, which they seemed very likely to.

Stanley's knowledge of African dialects, taught him by his dusky friend Sambo, stood him in good stead here. He begged respectfully to be allowed to act as interpreter, and, his offices being accepted, he did this so effectually that the dispute was speedily settled.

One of these officers was Captain Orbistone of the

Tonitru, the other his surgeon, and the matter ended thus : Stanley Grahame was appointed, much to his joy, interpreter to the cruiser on whose decks we now find him. If the truth be told, the captain thought he had made a very good bargain ; he soon found out Stanley's worth and the sterling stuff of which he was made, and, although only a supernumerary, Stanley was at his own request drilled in gunnery, and in all the duties of a man-o'-war sailor officer, and being a gentleman, was admitted an honorary member of the ward-room mess.

Just one word more. Stanley Grahame had no charge of a watch, of course, nor any charge of a boat, but he was told off to Midshipmite Mac's, and he always went in this cheeky little mite's boat, and he soon got to find out that he and not the mite was in reality in charge. Besides all this —But stay, the firing has begun. Pendragon is stationed in the foretop to watch the result of each shot.

The first fell far too short, nor did they ricochet along the water as they might have done, to the damage of the dhow's hull, had the sea been smoother.

Up till now the man-o'-war had been gaining on the dhow, but that wily vessel changed her tactics, filled, and kept away, and though this manœuvre brought her for a time closer to the fire of the *Tonitru's* great bow gun, she soon profited by her daring and got out of reach entirely.

Then the *Tonitru* ceased firing, and the captain was fain to fall back upon the skill of the engineer.

"I must get within shooting distance of that dhow," he told that officer, whom he had sent for to the bridge.

" I'll do all I can, sir," said the engineer, "short of endangering our lives by bursting the boilers."

"That's a good fellow," said the captain, "go and do it. No fear of the boilers."

Little Mite Mac was in the steerage as the engineer passed down.

"I say, you know," said Mac, "we must get alongside

that dhow somehow. I'm full of fight. I'd like to face
any number. Now suppose you tie down the safety valve
and I come and sit on it—eh ?"

The engineer pinched his ear for him and went on.
Then the mite went away to tantalise the clerk.

"I wouldn't be you for the world," said the mite.
"Fancy standing beside the captain all the time of a deadly
battle and taking notes ! How your hand must shake and
how your teeth must chatter all the time; and then there
is no chance of running down below, you know, and if you
happen to——"

Brrrang!

"Another shot," cried the mite, "they're at it again.
I'm off. But when t'other fellow begins to fire then I'll
come below, and finish the letter to my own dear mum.
That'll be only dutiful, you know."

Brrrang !

Still another shot from the *Tonitru's* bow gun. And
now the doctor, who was standing on the companion ladder,
heard a distant echo, as it were.

"Shell," he thought; "we are firing shell."

The deck was not the doctor's place, but he could not
now resist the temptation to run up. No, that echo was
no far-off bursting shell, but the dhow had positively hove
to, cleared for action, and commenced to return the fire of
Her Majesty's cruiser *Tonitru !*

The captain seemed incapable for the moment of believing
his senses. He had run up the rigging to make sure. The
men were dancing for joy, and when a round shot fell close
to the ship, Pen, in the foretop, stretched both his arms out
towards it in the way a Frenchman does when welcoming
a friend.

A few minutes after this Captain Orbistone called his
principal officers together on the quarterdeck, and in a few
brief sentences explained to them his plan of attack.
There was no word of defence. He knew his fellows, and

before to-day he had heard their cutlasses and pikes clattering in anger against Arab swords.

"We'll fight her," he said, "in good old-fashioned style.'

"And glad of the chance," said Pen, rubbing his hands in glee.

"Well, then, Mr. Pendragon, there is no time for talk. We'll go alongside. Pepper her rigging as much as you ' please while we are doing so, but remember, not a shot in her hull. Get grappling gear ready—kedge anchors, anything."

"I understand you, sir," said the lieutenant, pausing just a moment, "that we are not to fire into her hull."

"You do, Mr. Pendragon," was the reply. "I have good reasons for believing that this is no common slave dhow. She is too far south for your northern Arab. She is well armed, and she has white men—Spaniards probably—on board. Their intention, doubtless, is to slip off to Cuba, if they can."

"They never will," answered the lieutenant. Then, in a voice of command,—

"Stand by port and starboard guns."

That dhow seemed to bear a charmed life for the next ten or fifteen minutes, during which time the cruiser was "going for her," as little Mac called it, at full speed. Not a shot save one struck her. That one tore through her bulwarks right aft, and considering the confusion it created must have done deadly execution. The dhow fired so well that the *Tonitru's* rigging was damaged, and more than one man borne bleeding below. The former now began to divine the intention of the cruiser, for she ceased firing, and our fellows on the *Tonitru* could see them busily engaged spreading along the top of the bulwarks those horrible nets, a kind of defence against boarders, that has cost us the life of many a gallant man in these seas. But the *Tonitru* was prepared for everything. All hatches were battened down that could be conveniently closed. Our brave men needed no back door for escape. They meant to win, or die at their posts.

I do not think that even Captain Orbistone had ever seen so large a dhow, certainly not one so crowded with armed men. Mostly fierce-looking Arabs they were—tall, spare, wild fellows, stripped half-naked, their long dark hair knotted up behind their heads, and brandishing spear and sword and gun.

There was on that dhow a fire burning amidships, and on it a cauldron of immense size. It was filled with boiling cocoa-nut oil, and it was intended to be used in repelling British boarders.

But Pen had seen it and reported the matter to the captain, and for a minute or two way was stopped on the *Tonitru.*

"Plant a shot *there*," said the captain, quietly, to his best gunner, whom he had taken on the bridge to speak to.

The man went away with a heart swelling with manly pride. "Heaven nerve my hand," he said to himself.

The gunner took aim, giving directions as he did so to the men with one arm. Bar the noise of the hand-spikes nothing was heard, for no one moved on deck, so intense was the excitement. Now the gunner is leaning forward lanyard in hand,—

> "There is silence deep as death,
> And the boldest holds his breath,
> For a time—"

Crash ! goes the armstrong. In the very centre of that dhow's deck lands the shot, and well it does its deadly work. The Arabs are hoist with their own petard. There is now no more chance of their deluging our brave fellows with boiling oil.

But see, smoke and flame begin to rise from the dhow's deck, while down on her, like bloodhound thirsting for his prey, rushes the *Tonitru.*

There is no time to lose. There is fire on the dhow, and those armed Arabs seem somehow to be dancing among it, and the thought that that fire may extend below among the poor manacled slaves nerves every arm, steels every heart, on board the cruiser, from the captain downwards.

She is alongside; she rasps, she bumps against the dhow; the dhow's bulwarks crash and break with the violence of the collision. Everything is done quickly but quietly by our fellows. The ships are lashed together, spears are thrust through the network at our men, and shots are fired; but spear-heads are smashed, shots are returned with terrible precision, and the network itself is hacked in pieces by our cutlasses. Then there is a ringing British cheer, and, defying all opposition, in one moment more we are on board.

"STORM THE POOP, UP LADS, UP!"

CHAPTER XIII.

STORMING THE POOP—VICTORY—THE 'TWEEN DECKS OF A SLAVE DHOW—CAPTAIN MACDERMOTT OF THE " SEYD PASHA."

CHAPTER XIII.

THE fight raged most fiercely around and on the poop
of the fighting dhow. Thither the officers and
probably the owners of the vessel had betaken themselves.
Terrible as it seems to the minds of those who think of it,
they had hoisted two guns up to this place, and, loading
them with shrapnel, had commenced firing indiscriminately
on those below, regardless how many of their own poor
fellows they slaughtered, so long as there fell by their side
the men of the *Tonitru*.

It was a dastardly deed, and one that well merited the
punishment that followed.

It hardly needed the word of command, the captain's
voice shouting high over the din of battle,

"Storm the poop. Up, lads, up!"

The poop was a very tall one, and the ladders leading
thereto had been drawn up.

Our brave fellows fought their way aft. Nothing could
stop their wild rush. Pendragon was there at their head;
he had outstripped even his commander in his eagerness to
gain the poop. Stanley Grahame was there too; he used
his cutlass with both hands, as Highlanders in olden
times used the claymore. He was as tall as the tallest
Arab there, and, fine swordsmen though they are, the
enemy's guards were borne down before the fury of his

charge, tneir swords bent or broken as if they had been mere straws.

Will it be believed that close by his side fought little Mite Mac, dirk in hand ?   I'm not sure that he did not stick very close indeed to his tall countryman's side.   He was hardly noticed in the fray, yet many a lunge he gave with that dirk of his nevertheless.   Nor did his tongue cease to wag the while, and, being a shrill treble, it was pretty well heard.

" Bravo, Stanley ! " he would cry ; or " Well done, old townie ; " or " I gave it to that one."

Once indeed he was heard to quote the words of Scotland's great wizard, Walter Scott, and to shout,

> " Charge, Chester, charge,
> On, Stanley, on ! "

The lack of ladders seemed little drawback to our blue jackets.   They scrambled up, they pitched each other up, defying Arab spears and swords, those in the rear doing terrible execution with the deadly Colt revolver.

Stanley's long legs befriended him ; he was up and had cleared a space before even Pendragon.   An Arab made a vicious lunge at him as he turned round to assist Mac up, for that midshipmite was positively crying with vexation. A bullet from Captain Orbistone's revolver foiled the Arab's intention ; he fell headlong from the poop.

Then more quickly than I can describe it the battle came first to a climax, and then to a close.   Every Arab on the poop that was not slain threw himself headlong into the sea and became food for the sharks—those slimy monsters that never fail to sniff blood from afar, whether it be that of innocent seals in Greenland seas, or the blood that trickles through the scupper-holes of a battle-deck in more temperate climes.

Every Arab preferred instant death to the dishonour of capture and a pirate's doom at the yard-arm ; only some cowardly white men remained on board, and these were speedily disarmed and made prisoners.

The fight began at twelve o'clock by the sun ; by half-past twelve—that is, in one brief half hour—the carnage was finished, the battle lost and won.

There was no cheering over the fallen foe.   Many of our men were wounded, some lay slain.   Not all of the wounded, however, cared to succumb, but stood pale and bleeding against bulwark or poop or mast.

The Arab dead were laid reverently side by side and covered with their own blood-red flag ; ours were carried on board and laid in state till near the eventide ; then slowly and solemnly the captain himself read the service, and one by one they were committed to the deep.   During prayers more than one brave fellow had occasion to cross his eyes with the sleeve of his blue jacket, for messmates were lying there still and quiet who never more would speak or laugh again.

"Ah ! Bill," said one honest tar, and his eyes did look red, "I can't get over poor Fred's death.   He were such a happy-go-lucky larky chap, and there he lies——"

He turned away quickly and said no more.

Some great navy captain said that the most solemn moment to him was the short silence that precedes a sea fight, when every man is standing to his gun or in his quarters, when lips move in prayer that may never pray again, and thoughts are, mayhap, turned to the far-off home in England by men who may visit them never, never more. But, the heat and fury of the fight being over, the washing and cleansing of the decks and the ship's stained sides, and the putting of everything as nearly shipshape as it was before, the attending to the wounds, often ghastly in the extreme, of the men who have fallen, and the impressive service over the dead—these are things which, if but once witnessed, are but little likely to be forgotten.

From confessions made by those white men prisoners, it

turned out that Captain Orbistone was right in his surmise about the dhow. She was no ordinary northern slaver. Nor was this her first cruise; for, slave-laden to the hatches, she had twice before run a living cargo from Zanzibar and Pemba to an out-of-the-way port on the eastern shore of Madagascar, where a large three-masted ship was ready to receive them. Not directly, however, mind you. No, that lordly ship had cleared from a respectable American port with all her papers signed and right; she was a legitimate trader. The cargoes of slaves run by this dhow had not as yet soiled her decks, not a slave iron would be found on her if searched, not an extra bag of rice; the slaves were housed on shore miles and miles from the place where this legitimate trader lay, and as soon as there were enough of them got together to make the voyage pay, then she would lup anchor, and, slipping round, ship them all in one night and set sail before sunrise.

The fire that had commenced on board the dhow was speedily extinguished; almost before the battle was over indeed our fellows were playing on it with the hose, the donkey engine having been rigged for the express purpose.

Next the dhow's hatches were thrown open as well as those of the *Tonitru*, and on the latter ship everything was got ready both on the upper deck and on the 'tween decks for the reception of a portion of the unhappy slaves that were cramped and crowded down in the hold of the dhow.

Mercy on us! my mind sickens even now as I think on the sight that presented itself, on first entering the hold of that dismal dhow. Four hundred and thirty human beings were there stowed, living, dead, and dying. Do not be afraid, reader, I will not attempt to describe in anything like detail the wretchedness and extreme misery of their situation. I could not if I tried. But when you crawled down the ladder first, fully a minute elapsed ere you could see about you, yet during that minute your ears were assailed with a chorus of low moaning, despairing moaning, as from human beings sick in pain and in grief. The sound, or some of the sounds, if set to music would begin on one note, run quaveringly up half a tone, then mournfully end on the commencing note. It put one in mind of passages in Dante's Inferno.

Well, but as soon as you began to see, and got your back to the light that streamed down the open hatch, you perceived a dense multitude of black bodies seated back towards you on the deck, their heads all thrown over their shoulders and gazing at you with eyes that rolled horribly white in the uncertain light. The expressions on some of the faces were those of terror and wonderment combined, or dull apathy in some, and hope apparently in others. There was a little lane along the centre railed off with strong bamboos, and walking along that lane, as soon as your eyes became used to the gloom, you could not help seeing that there were many slaves there whose sorrows had for ever ceased, and that the heads of the dead were pillowed on the bodies or the limbs of the living.

I am not writing for effect, else I would describe the appearance most of those creatures presented when taken or helped on deck. I could do so graphically because I should do so truthfully, but I will not harrow the reader's feelings. What has often hurt my own feelings to notice when slaves were being liberated from the hands of their captors, was the signs of recent blows and brutal treatment on the bodies of both sexes, the marks and weals that bamboo canes had left, swollen jaws and eyes and curly hair matted with blood. Yes, slavery as carried on *sub rosa* even while I pen these lines is a fearful thing. All honour to those nations, like the British and French, who do all they can to wipe so foul a blot from the history of the world.

A large proportion of the slaves were transferred on board the *Tonitru.* The rest were left on the upper deck

of the dhow until her hold was thoroughly cleaned, disin-
fected, and dried by the busy hands of our own Kroomen.

These Kroomen are natives of Sierra Leone, sturdy, tall,
black fellows, who take service in out-going coast-bound
man-of-war ships, and are left again at their own homes
when the commission is over. They are brave, hardy, and
intelligent, and make very good sailors. They must not be
confounded, however, with the Lascars of our Indian ships.
One good Krooman is worth a dozen Lascars. I have
small respect for these latter. They are called Lascars,
but the same letters would bear transposing thus, L a s c a r s
—R a s c a l s.

Apropos of these Lascars I'll tell you a little anecdote.
There is really not much in it, but it may serve in some
measure to banish any feeling of depression my short
description of the 'tween decks of that slaver may have
induced.

I was coming up the Red Sea one time in a P. and O.
boat. I was an invalid passenger from the east coast of
Africa, and I happened to be forward on deck when the
second officer ordered the Lascars up for duty. With
them came their own head man, or captain, a tall, moonraking, raw-boned native of India. To some angry remark
of the English officer this Lascar captain replied with a
blow of his fist. The Englishman, I should tell you, was
short and stout—round faced at all events—more like a
ploughboy than a sailor.

On board a man-of-war that Lascar captain would have
been shot or flogged, so you may judge of my surprise to
see the Britisher take off his jacket, pitch it over the
capstan, and go for his man, like an animated steam-
hammer. In less than five minutes he had given him a
thrashing that the fellow doubtless remembers to this day.
He ended by getting his head in chancery, then threw the
fellow from him into the lee scuppers; after that, as Scott
says of Roderick Dhu,

> "Unwounded from the dreadful close,
>   But breathless all,"

the Britisher resumed his jacket.

Everything being made as comfortable as possible for the slaves on both vessels, and the white men slavers being put in irons, Captain Orbistone determined next morning to make the best of his way to Zanzibar, where the slaves would be liberated and their captors tried for their lives, the indictment being " piracy on the high seas."

The dhow had been in tow all night, but now she was to have a prize crew put on board, and she would then sail as consort to the cruiser.

Stanley Grahame had hardly finished breakfast when the captain sent for him.

Stanley's cheeks tingled with delight as his commander complimented him on his conspicuous bravery in the fight with the slaver. He then informed him that he had not a competent officer to spare to take charge of their prize, that he would willingly have appointed him, Stanley, to the duty, but that the service would not admit of his doing so, and therefore he had made up his mind to give Midshipman MacDermott the command, with Stanley Grahame as sailing master and factotum.

"Are you agreeable to this?" said Captain Orbistone.

Stanley assured him he was delighted.

"There," said the captain, laughing and shaking hands with him, "off you bundle, and get your things ready. I'll see that everything you require for the voyage is put on board, and you'll have a first-rate prize crew. Only," added Captain Orbistone, "don't, if possible, lose sight of us. But *if* you do, make the best of your way to Zanzibar ; you know the way?"

"Very well, indeed," said Stanley.

"Oh ! by-the-bye, though," said the captain, "should we happen to lose sight of each other you may as well call in at Johanna on your way up. I won't promise to wait for you there, but I'll leave a message with the consul. So good-bye. *Bon voyage.*"

Midshipman Mac was summoned to the cabin next; and when he returned and re-entered the ward-room, it would have been difficult to say whether his face were more full of impudence or importance. He had his dirk by his side, his best white trousers on, and his very newest jacket.

Pendragon looked at him as he stopped for a moment in the doorway, and he could not help smiling. The doctor happened to come up behind him at the same time, and little Mac being in his way, he simply caught him by the ear and led him into the mess-room.

"Let go!" cried Mac; "let go, you ridiculous old Saw-bones! You've no idea whom you have got hold of."

"Midshipmite Mac, I guess," said the surgeon.

"Certainly not!" replied the mite, drawing himself up to his full height—about four foot nothing—and striking his hand against the hilt of his dirk. "You are mistaken, Dr. Slops; you grievously err, Sir Surgeon."

"Come along, Mite," said Pen, laughing, "and finish your feed. Here's a red herring with a roe in it. We all know your weakness for a red herring with a roe in it."

"How dare you presume, sir," said little Mac, with mock severity, "to call me 'Mite'; and how dare you to talk to *me* about so sublunary a matter as a red herring? Bah!"—here the Mite waved his hand and turned his head away—"a red herring with a roe in it!

"Behold before you, gentlemen!" he continued, strutting up and down the ward-room on tiptoe—"behold before you Captain MacDermott, of the British dhow *Seyd Pasha*! And now I shall condescend to be seated. Mr. Pendragon, I *will* unbend so far as to taste that—that herring with the roe in it. Mr. Grahame, I will trouble you, sir, to hand your captain another cup of coffee, as the exigencies of duty demanded my presence in our worthy commander's cabin ere I had quite finished my matutinal meal. And do not

forget, sir, that you are to be on board the *Seyd Pasha*—
my ship, sir—at seven bells on this same forenoon watch.
Thank you, Mr. Grahame. I have no doubt you will obey
your captain's orders, and that we shall get on very well
together. If we do, I may safely promise you that I shall
not forget to report your good conduct to the proper
quarter."

"It's a good thing I'm not going in the *Seyd Pasha* with
you, Captain Mite," said the doctor.

"For what reason, sir?" inquired Mac. "Don't be
afraid to speak, Dr. Jalap."

"I'd jalap you!" said the doctor—"and wallop you, too!
I wouldn't be two days in the *Seyd Pasha* before I tied my
captain, head down, over a gun, and gave him a breeching."

"Below there!" sung out the navigating sub-lieutenant,
lifting the hatchway and looking down. "Are you ready,
Stanley?"

"I'm all ready," said Stanley, pushing back his chair.

"Then just get that young shaver under way, will you?
there's a good fellow."

"Here, you Mite!" cried the doctor; "come along smart
O, and pack your traps."

The doctor seized Mite and led him out of the ward-
room precisely as he had led him in—by the ear. Captain
MacDermott of the *Seyd Pasha*, however, stuck long enough
in the doorway, although the doctor still held him by the
ear, to say,

"Gentlemen, the service is going to the *bad*."

"Move on," cried the doctor.

And away went the two of them, leaving their messmates
and even the steward to enjoy the luxury of a hearty
laugh.

When the dhow was fairly cast off from the *Tonitru* and
the great sails were hoisted up into the wind, and the
first watch set, then Stanley Grahame and his boy captain
entered the saloon together, little Mac holding on to one of

Stanley's arms with both his, and almost dancing with delight.

"You dear old Stanley," he said. "Isn't it jolly to be roving the seas all by ourselves like this!"

Poor little Mac! he had quite a boy's love for his tall and clever countryman.

"And I'm so glad, you know," he went on, "that the captain didn't send old Surgeon Slops. He is so rough, and punches one so, though he isn't half a bad fellow either. But oh, Stanley! did you ever? I never!"

Captain Mite's ejaculations of surprise and delight referred to the furnishing and fittings of the dhow's saloon. It was large, roomy, and well-lighted, and everywhere about them were curtains of crimson, magnificent mirrors, and the glitter of gold and silver and glass. Along the deck were ranged low silken covered lounges, with small tables, also very low, here and there. The centre of the room was empty, the floor covered with a thick soft carpet; one or two rocking-chairs, and one taller table at the farther end. of the room, completed the furniture. On this table were books in the Spanish language and a small guitar, and above it an ebony and gold cupboard, with a front of glass, in which sparkled in bottles of cut crystal the rich coloured sherbets which the wealthy Arabs use instead of wine.

"It is indeed a splendid saloon," said Stanley; "and to think that those wretches lived in ease and luxury here within hearing almost of the groans and cries of their unhappy victims in the terrible hold below."

But I don't think that at that moment our boy captain was thinking about "those wretches" or "their unhappy victims" either. He had helped himself to a large glass of sherbet, and thrown himself back in a rocking chair, in order the more thoroughly to enjoy it.

"I say, Stanley," said he, "don't drone and prose and preach there. This sherbet is dee-licious. Come and have some, and we won't talk about anything or even think about anything but what is pleasant and nice. And I do hope, Stan, that to-morrow morning the old *Tonitru* won't be anywhere in sight. That will be jolly, won't it?"

Stanley laughed, and sat down. Perhaps he enjoyed the novelty of the situation every bit as much as the mite did, though he did not say so much about it.

XIV.

*THE TORNADO—THE CAPTAIN SENT TO BED TO BE
OUT OF THE WAY—AN UNLOOKED-FOR VISITOR.*

CHAPTER XIV.

THE sun seemed red with anger as it glared, for the
last time before setting, across the grey-blue sea.
It descended from behind a bank of leaden clouds, its lower
limb being already washed apparently by the waves ere the
upper emerged.   It was but a bar of ruddy light, therefore,
that shed that blood-red gleam athwart the ocean, tipping
the crests of the billows from the west eastwards to the
dhow, at the bows of which both Stanley Grahame and
little Captain Mite were at present standing.   Neither of
them had ever cast their eyes on so fierce a light before.
After gazing sunwards for a short time they were fain to
turn backs and look aft; but, lo! yonder was the light
again, reflected from the little windows of the tall poop, as
red as the glare of a railway danger signal at the darkest
hour of midnight.

The wind had forged round, so that what little there was
of it was dead against the dhow.   She was tacking, and far
away on her lee bow, but stern on, her hull already sinking
behind the northern horizon, was the *Tonitru*.   The sea
had a strangely unsettled appearance.   Stanley did not like
the looks of it, nor did he think that sun or sky either
boded any good.

Neither the mite nor he had ever sailed in a dhow before,
so they were not quite used to the peculiar independent
swinging motion of that vessel.   She seemed as wild and

erratic as her former Arab owners, now throwing herself almost on her beam ends, and trying hard to show her keel to the weather; now plunging bodily forward, bows under, then rearing her head like a gigantic turtle, and endeavouring ineffectually to poop herself, and go down stern first.

"We're going to have a blow, I think," said Stanley.

"Shouldn't wonder," said the mite, evidently very unconcerned about the matter.

Stanley paced the deck for some time, taking quick, long strides, and pausing now and then to cast an eye aloft or seawards, for night was already beginning to settle down on the waves.

"Ready about!" he cried at last.

When the dhow was once again on the other tack he sent for Mr. Miller.

Mr. Miller was the sailmaker. Stanley knew he was not only an old sailor, but a very good one. If the whole truth must be told, he had chosen him as one of the crew of the prize dhow because he had noted his good qualities when on board the *Tonitru*, and he knew, moreover, that, like himself, he had been a merchant-service man.

They took two or three turns up and down the deck together ere Stanley spoke a word. Then,

"What do you think of the weather?" he asked, abruptly.

"If not impertinent, sir," said the old sailmaker, changing his quid to his other cheek, "what do you think of it yourself?"

Stanley smiled. "I've been in these seas before," he replied, "and, from signs that I can feel more than I can express, I believe we are to have a bit of a blow, and we had better shorten sail."

"A bit of a blow, sir!" said the sailmaker. "Ay, that we be, sir, and take the word of old Dick Miller, that, beggin' your pardon, sir, has sailed the seas before you was out o' the cradle, it's going to be an all-rounder too."

"You mean a tornado?"

"I never calls it that, sir, but that's what I docs mean. There ain't a great many words begins with 'tor,' and they're mostly a bad lot, but that 'un's the worst, so I calls it an all-rounder."

"Look, Mr. Miller, look!"

Stanley pointed eastwards. There was a bronze moon glimmering over the water.

"We won't have he long, sir," said Miller, "and if I was you, *young* sir—"

He put special emphasis on the "young"—

"I'd get those sails down out o' there afore the clouds settle down on us more'n a mile thick, and the wind begins to whistle through the riggin'."

"But what can I substitute? We have no other," said Stanley. "Mac," he cried, without waiting for an answer "call all hands. Look sharp."

This was the way Stanley spoke to **his** captain, and his captain answered,

"Ay, ay, sir," as if by instinct.

"If ye rigs a tablecloth," said Miller, quietly, "you'll find you've too much afore morning. But down below I've found two bonnie wee bits of storm-sails. Ah! mind you, sir, them demons o' Arabs knowed what they was about."

Few more words were wasted in talking. The moon was mounting higher and higher, the light in the east had gained mastery over that in the west, but a terrible bank of dark clouds was slowly rising from the sea, while very high in the air tiny flecks of cloudlets seemed positively scudding against the wind.

The dhow seemed to resent interference as a young colt being put into fresh harness does. She plunged, and kicked, and reared, and rolled, till at times Stanley thought the very sticks would come out of her. But once rigged out in her new sails away she flew before the wind like a startled wild deer.   Both Stanley and his little captain were thunderstruck, they never could have believed that so unshapely a craft could speed along as this dhow was now doing.

She was heading south and by east.

Going out of their course ?   Yes, this was not the way to Zanzibar, but if they were going out of their course they were also, they hoped, going out of the course of the coming tornado as well.   There was a wise head on the top of those old shoulders of Sailmaker Miller.

They determined to make the most of the breeze while it lasted ; by-and-by, after an ominous calm, perhaps, it would blow from every point of the compass.

An hour or two afterwards it was dark indeed.   There was a moon somewhere away behind the clouds, but the sky had fallen on the sea, so to speak ; there was the gloom of night all around them, and the horizon close abroad on every side.

"Thank God," said Stanley, "I have *you* here, Miller. I'm so glad I brought you."

"Thank God, young sir, we have sea-room.   I think it'll only be the tail-end of this business we'll get after all."

No doubt you have read in books of those terrible storms called tornadoes, that sweep across the Indian and China seas with such fearful violence.   Some of my country readers may have seen in the fields, or on the roads, minute whirlwinds that raise the dust, and even catch the birds off the ground.   These are in reality tornadoes on a small scale, and they are generated and guided by precisely the same law of storms.   It will be noticed that they have two motions, one on their own axis and the other a progressive one, in which the whole storm moves on bodily.   A tornado may be hundreds of miles in extent ; its forward motion is about forty-five miles an hour ; the actual force of the circular wind from eighty to ninety miles an hour.   If a tornado falls upon a ship, so that the centre of the storm shall pass over her, she has but a poor chance of survival, but sailors know in which way to steer in order to get away from this centre.

The object of Stanley and Mr. Miller was now to get as far as possible from the presumable track of the coming tornado, but in this they were only partially successful, for the storm was preceded by all but a dead calm. Presently it came.

No words of mine, no language of the best descriptive writer on the might or mystery of the ocean and the wonders of God seen in the great deep, could convey to your minds anything like a complete picture of that fearful storm. But it passed at last, the *Seyd Pasha* was safe, and all hands on board, thanks to good seamanship and an all-seeing Providence, were alive and well.

It must have been long past two bells in the middle watch when Stanley, after one glance around at that troubled, wind-vexed ocean, on the breaking, boiling waters of which the round moon was now smiling peacefully down, found his way for the first time since sunset to the saloon.

" We can leave the deck now," he had said to Miller. " I feel a little tired, and I dare say so do you."

" That I be, sir," was Miller's reply.

The two of them were clad from shoulders to knees in yellow oilskins, with sea boots beneath, and both wore sou'-westers merchant-sailor fashion.

They entered the cabin ; a great lamp swung from the roof, and its beams fell full upon the wet face of our hero Stanley. I wish you had seen him then. The rude seaman's suit did not detract from his youthful manly beauty, I can tell you. Escaping from underneath the sou'-wester, the short brown curls clustered over his white brow. His well-chiselled nose and upper lip, the curve of which was barely hidden by the small dark moustache, his shapely chin and hardy cheeks, combined to form a picture that was very pleasing to look upon. The words of the old Jacobite song might have arisen to your lips as you gazed on him,—

> "Sae noble a look, sae princely an air,
>   Sae gallant and bold, sae young and sae fair."

But having looked on that picture, your eyes would naturally have followed Stanley's, and fallen on one of quite a different stamp—poor little Captain Mite lying on one of the couches on deck,—

> "Sleeping sound and fast."

Stanley smiled to himself as he thought of the last words he had spoken to this wee captain of his in the early part of the evening. They were these :

"Look here, Mite, you're only in the way. Off with you to bed. If I find you haven't turned in in ten minutes I'll pull your ears well for you. There now!"

So after this mutinous speech the captain had retired, said his prayers, had a drop of sherbet and a biscuit, and gone off quietly to bed.

"Come in, Miller, and sit down and have something, old man. Yonder is a bottle; help yourself. There lies our bold captain fast asleep."

"Poor little man!" said Miller, helping himself to a "glass o' ship's," as he called it. "Poor little man! What a shame to send a mite like he to sea! Hardly fit to be out o' pinafores, is he?"

The kind-hearted sailmaker patted his sleeping captain on the cheek as he spoke, and carefully covered up a leg that had strayed from beneath the sheets.

Stanley laughed heartily. "It's a good thing," he said, "that the captain doesn't hear you. He'd pinafore you. Why, he was sixteen last birthday."

"Be he now?" said the sailmaker, looking through his "glass o' ship's" at the light. "Should have thought that lollipops would have been more in his way than navy biscuits and big guns, sir."

Long after Miller left the saloon Stanley sat in a rocking-chair by the little table. The coffee the steward had brought him had got cold and stood untasted. He was not sitting up to safeguard the vessel. The danger was past; the dhow was once more on a pretty even keel, though the sea was still turbulent. No; he was deep in thought. He was reviewing the whole of his past life, and trying as well as he could to fathom the depths of a probable future. But something had occurred on the previous evening, to which his thoughts now reverted. It was something very strange indeed. Just before the storm came on, as he was seeing to the battening down of the hatches, the voice of some one singing had fallen on his ear. It was the voice of one of the slaves, too. The melody was a very old and somewhat mournful one. The words were words that he had often heard sung by the negroes in their little hamlets on the estate of Beaumont Park:

> " We hunt no more, for the 'possum and the 'coon,
>> By the meadow, the sea, and the shore ;
> We dance no more by the glimmer of the moon,
>> By the bench near the old cottage door.
> The day goes by like a shadow o'er the heart,
>> With sorrow where all was delight ;
> For the time has come when the darkies have to part,
>> Then my old Kentucky home—Good night."

The storm had driven all recollection of this event out of Stanley's head till now, but he resolved that as soon as daylight should come he would set himself to unravel the mystery.

"For good or for ill," he had said to himself, as he set foot on the dhow's deck to take charge under his nominal captain, "for weal or for woe, this vessel is to have something to do with the story of my life."

"For good or for evil, for weal or for woe—" he was repeating the words to himself now.

"For good—or—for ev——" His head dropped on his

breast, his eyes closed in sleep. Tired nature had asserted herself. Four bells struck—he still slept as peacefully as a child in its mother's arms. The motion of the dhow had become less irregular, it had resolved itself into the old swing and dip and roll. He was rocked in the cradle of the deep.

Sailmaker Miller looked in once to make some report or ask some question, but stole away again on tiptoe.

Five bells rang out, and soon after the saloon door was once more opened and the curtain pulled cautiously aside, and, holding it back with his left hand, a tall, powerful, and nearly naked negro stood in the doorway, and glanced eagerly at sleeping Stanley's face.

With his high cheek-bones, his glittering bloodshot eyes, and stealthy movements, as he dropped the curtain and advanced into the middle of the room, he looked a very dreadful apparition indeed, all the more so in that his frame was somewhat emaciated by ill-treatment or disease, or more probably by both.

He advanced cautiously to within a few feet of the still slumbering Stanley, then laid one hand lightly on his shoulder.

The sleeper started to his feet, his right hand clutching a revolver that lay on the table, and the two stood confronting each other.

" Young Massa Stanley !" said the negro, joy and sorrow both blended in the tones of his voice.

"Sambo !" gasped our hero. " Is it possible ? Are you indeed Sambo ?"

" Oh ! Massa Stanley," replied the negro. " It is indeed all dat am left of dat poor wretch."

" But how came you here ?" cried Stanley. " And in the guise of a slave ! Speak, my poor friend, speak."

" It am a long story," said Sambo, " and I'se tired and kinder weak. I—I——"

He would have fallen had not Stanley caught him and

seated him in the rocking-chair, drawing another close beside it, and sitting down himself.

"Drink this coffee, Sambo—and here, just a little to eat.
Now cheer up and tell me all."

"Cheer up, young sah ?" replied Sambo, putting down
the cup and forcing a smile. "Yes, I cheer up. It is ober
now. I hab found you. But dey use me so bery bad, sah.
See !"

He pointed to his poor ankles and wrists, that still bore
the scars of the cruel slave irons.

"Dey hab almost make one baby of me, sah ! I feel now
I hab found you I want to cry. All de cruelty dey put on
me not make me feel like dis before. Now you'se found,
Massa Stanley, I'se all ober quite 'sterical. I is, sah, for
true."

There were tears in honest Sambo's eyes as he spoke.

"See, sah !" he continued, producing a letter he had
hidden in his cummerbund. "All de time dey keep me as
one slabe I stick to dis— ha ! ha !"

Stanley took the letter; it was from his uncle.

In his broken but pathetic English Sambo then proceeded
to relate all his adventures since Stanley had left Beaumont
Park. He had no sooner gone, it seemed, than Sambo,
his own way, began to importune his master, Captain Mackinlay, for leave to follow Stanley to Zanzibar. The old
captain was kind-hearted and soft, and soon gave in ; and
shortly after this an opportunity offered in the shape of a
ship sailing from Baltimore for the Antarctic oil fisheries.
She was to call first at the Cape, and for this part of her
voyage Sambo, at his master's recommendation, was engaged
as cook. But Cape Town is a long way from Zanzibar, and
for a time this faithful negro could find no chance of secur-
ing a passage to that strange city. Opportunity offered at
last. He was engaged as seaman on board the very dhow
they were then in, and set sail presumedly for Zanzibar.
But alas ! he soon found that Zanzibar was about the last

place in the thoughts of the captain and owners of the *Seyd Pasha*. They gave that city a very wide berth indeed, and finally cast anchor about a mile south of the bar of Lamoo, on or very near the line. Here a party of these honest Arab traders landed in the mangrove forest. They took Sambo with them, and, much to his terror and disgust, after two days and two nights marching inland, they came to a barracoon or slave encampment, presided over by some rascally Portuguese, and the journey was, after a few hours' rest, recommenced backwards through the woods to the shore.

Sambo determined to watch a chance and run away. He would, he thought, march directly south along the coast until opposite Zanzibar, and take his chance of obtaining a passage thereto. The town, he was well aware, lay on an island.

The opportunity he looked for came that very night, and while the Arabs slept he stole away from the camp and was soon hidden in the darkness of the forest. But at daybreak he was missed, and those bloodhounds of Arabs were speedily on his track, and strong and lithe in limb though Sambo was, he was overtaken ere night fell and brought back. He was now most cruelly treated. Servant nor sailor he was to be no more, but a slave; his clothes were torn off his back, he was tied to a tree and beaten with bamboo canes till he fainted from loss of blood; then his wrists were ironed and he had to fall in with the captured gang, and so he once more stepped on board the dhow that he had left as a free man.

Sambo did little more than mention the cruel treatment he and the other slaves received in the slave dhow, the scanty supply of water, the handfuls of half-boiled rice doled out to them day by day, their sufferings through sickness brought on for want of fresh air and cleanliness.

"Den," continued Sambo, " byme-by we hear big guns fire on deck, and de drefful noise of de battle, and plenty much smoke and fire fly down de hatch; den I tink it am all ober. But oh! joy ob joys, sah! I hear my young massa's voice shout higher dan all de din ob de awful fight; and I'se so happy after dat, I feel I must cry like one leetle chile."

Sambo paused for a moment, then his face became lighted up as it were with a broad smile, as he continued,—

"Oh! young Massa Stanley, I'se no occasion to grumble now; I'se reason to bress de Lord for all His goodness. Suppose He not make me slave, den p'r'aps I not meet you. It seem all so dark at first, no hope, no nuffin. Den you come in dat fighting ship, and I'se free. But suppose you no hab come, den I a slabe for two, t'ree, p'r'haps plenty long year. I not see you, and all dat time poor Missie Ida and Captain Ross dey pine and die away in de 'terior ob Africa. Oh! sah, sah!"

"Ida? Captain Ross?" exclaimed Stanley, kneeling on the deck beside his old friend, and clutching him by the arm. "Speak, Sambo, speak quickly, I tell you."

"Ess, young massa, ess, I speak plenty quick. I hab heard where Ida—where poor Ida——"

"Yes, yes, go on, Sambo; go on, good Sambo."

"Ida is——" The poor fellow pressed a hand to his brow; he only muttered the words, "Dark—dark."

His head fell and arms dropped, and he lapsed into insensibility.

XV.

LIFE IN THE DHOW—CAPTURE OF A SLAVER—BOY GREEN MAKES HAY WHILE THE SUN SHINES.

CHAPTER XV.

"MAC, MAC! Mite, I say!" cried Stanley. "Wake, man! wake, and help me!"

Young as our midshipmite was, he had been at sea long enough to acquire the habit of waking easily when spoken to. He was, therefore, on his feet in a moment.

"Stanley!" he exclaimed. "Why, Stanley, what *is* the matter? Who have you there?"

"It is Sambo," said Stanley, "about whom I have so often spoken to you. Quick! he has fainted! Help me to lower him gently on deck. So—how light the poor fellow is! How he must have suffered!"

They laid him on the carpet, his head on a level with his body; they rubbed his chest with spirits, and chafed his poor thin black hands. Had he been a brother they could not have been more kind and thoughtful. When at length he began to show signs of returning life, and muttered some incoherent words, Mite was dispatched by Stanley for the steward, and a bed was made up for Sambo in a corner of the saloon. Hot water was placed at his feet, and he was soon fast asleep. And thus he remained till far into the forenoon watch.

"I say, Stan, old man," cried Mite, "don't walk so terribly fast, and don't take such awful strides! Just think of the difference between the length of my legs and the longitude of yours!"

Stanley laughed and slackened his speed.

"I'm keeping pace with my thoughts, I suppose," he said. "But only think, you silly little Mite——"

"Captain MacDermott, if you please," interrupted Mite.

"Well, Captain MacDermott," continued Stanley, raising his hat with mock courtesy, "just think—a letter from uncle, and probably news, when Sambo wakes, of dear Ida and her father! Isn't it glorious and funny, eh, Mite?"

As he spoke the last words, with a sad want of respect for his captain's dignity, he dug his thumb into that officer's ribs.

"What *is* the service coming to?" said his captain, pompously. "Sir," he continued, "I've half a mind to order you down below under arrest. Your want of discipline distresses me in the extreme. Your conduct before the eyes of the crew, too, is highly mutinous and insubordinate."

But Stanley now had his captain by one ear. He led him thus, much to the amusement of the bluejackets, to the door of the saloon and pointed to the couch where Mite had slept.

"Captain MacDermott," said Stanley, "I've half a mind, sir, to order you back to bed again. Have a care, sir, lest I do so!"

"Mr. Grahame," said Mite, about five minutes after this —and as he spoke he flourished a long battered telescope in a most impressive manner—"Mr. Grahame, it is my desire, as captain of this ship, to muster by open list. Let all hands lay aft, and summon the slaves on deck."

"Ay, ay, sir!" said Stanley, touching his hat. "Shall I act as clerk as well, sir?"

"Most assuredly, sir," replied Mite, seating himself three steps up the ladder that led to the poop.

So Stanley Grahame got a chair and the log-book and

as his name was called each man marched past his boy-captain, called out his rating, and lifted his hat as he did so. The last to march past and call out his name and rating was " boy Green, sir, surgeon's assistant."

" Stop, stop ! " cried Stanley. " How is this ? 'Your name is not here."

" No, 'tain't likely," sneered boy Green, " seein' as 'ow I took French leave of the old *Tonitru* ! My name ain't there ; *but*," he added, emphatically, " I guess *the man's here.*"

" You young rascal ! " began Captain Mite.

" Who are *you* a bullyin' of ? " said boy Green. " You ain't no bigger than I be, come ! See, sir," he continued, addressing Stanley, as if Mite was quite beneath his notice, " you wants to know vy I stowed away. I'se tired makin' poultices, that's vy. Besides, sir, you must have a surgeon o' some kind aboard this old sea boot, and a loblolly's better nor nothing, sure-ly ! "

" Silence, sir ! " roared Stanley. " Go down below, sir, and have your hair cut."

With one contemptuous glance at his captain boy Green retired.

The poor slaves when brought up seemed to think their last hour had come, but Stanley spoke kindly to them in the Seedie language and reassured them.

There was one lanky youth among them whose light-brown skin and more regular features bespoke him a Somali Indian. He was simply dressed in a cotton kilt, or cummerbund, and his hair was an enormous all-round pile, as big as an ordinary church-hassock. While Stanley was looking at the lad, " He ! he ! " sneered a voice behind him. " Some more o' us vants their hair cut, I guess ! "

It was that boy Green again.

" I beg your pardon, sir," said the acting boatswain, coming up and touching his hat to Stanley, " there is———'

"Stop!" cried Captain Mite, "you must make your report to me"—as he spoke he tapped his breast with the butt-end of that old telescope of his—"to *me*, sir! The captain of a ship is not to be practically ignored as he sits on the steps of his own poop."

"I beg your pardon then, sir," said the boatswain, trying to suppress a smile, "but there's a three-masted ship just hove in sight."

"Where away?" asked Stanley.

"On the starboard quarter, sir," replied the man.

"Hurrah!" cried Mite, forgetting all his dignity in a moment, and pitching his telescope into the lee scuppers. "Hurrah! here's for off!"

He was up the main rigging, hand over hand, ere Stanley had time to think or breathe.

"Follow your leader!" cried Mite, laughing. "Come on, daddy-longlegs!"

"What a merry little captain we has got, sir!" said the boatswain.

"We have indeed!" said daddy-longlegs, smiling, as he went off to follow his leader.

He took his glass with him, though, and after he had had a long look at the stranger he handed the glass to Mite.

"Now then, Mite," said Stanley, "can you be serious for five minutes?"

"You dear old stoopid! of course I can."

"Well, then, look here. Listen. This is the situation. The *Tonitru* is either in Davy Jones's locker or she has weathered the tornado and is holding on her course to Zanzibar. We've been blown nearly two hundred miles out of our course, and we are also out of the course of all ordinary traders, and in my opinion yonder ship is the Madagascar slaver having a look round for the dhow."

"Hurrah!" cried Mite again, "that would be jolly!"

"Hush!" said Stanley, "don't be so ready with your

'hurrahs!' If that is the slaver I think we should try to capture her—or at least overhaul and search her."

"I'll fight her!" said Captain Mite, boldly.

"Tush!" cried Stanley, impatiently. "A lot of fighting you'd do, Mite! Can you swim?"

"A little," replied Mite.

"To be sure you can!" said Stanley; "I never knew a Scotch boy that couldn't. Well, Mite, if you don't keep quite serious I'll fling you out of the top; then when you're hauled on board again I'll pack you off to bed till your clothes are dry. That's how I'll serve you, Captain MacDermott! Now, Mite, you are in charge of this ship— after a fashion, you know."

"Thank you," said the captain of the *Seyd Pasha.*

"And whatever happens you are chiefly responsible. And I'm second in charge, nominally, but really your master, don't you see? Well, Mite, we'll put it in another way. You're head of the ship, and I'm neck, and it's the neck that moves the head. Well now, if that be really the big slaver, and if we capture her, what a glorious thing that would be for you, Mite! You would be sure of your promotion, and I would be none the worse!"

"Capital!" cried Mite. "I see what you're driving at, Stanley, old man. Well I—Mite MacDermott, as you call me, captain of the *Seyd Pasha*—give you liberty to do what you like with that ship for the common weal. There now!"

"That's right, Mite, my boy! Now go down and change your dress, we mustn't have uniform showing on deck; and just tell the fellows, will you, to rig out as like Arabs as possible? And hoist the Arab flag, Mite."

"Give me the keys of your sea-chest," said Mite.

"There you are. What are you up to?"

"You'll see by-and-by!" cried Mite, sliding down a stay.

Mite had now found occupation congenial to his taste. He went to his own chest first, and it was not long ere he rigged himself out as a full-blown Arab, turban and all, for he had a dress which he was wont to wear while doing charades on board the *Tonitru.* He next opened Stanley's chest, sending the steward meanwhile for the boatswain and Mr. Miller. Between the three of them, with the help of Stanley's shirts and night-dresses and pieces of cotton cloth of various colours to represent turbans, and a free use of burned cork, in less than twenty minutes every man-Jack was changed so that his own mother wouldn't have known him. Mite even rigged out Sambo, who was now awake, in Stanley's evening dress-suit, and gave him a white beard and moustache, and made him take his seat in the rocking-chair with a book in his hand.

All this time Stanley remained in the top, his spy-glass fixed on the strange ship. The dhow had been kept away, and was fast bearing down on her. Very much surprised he was, though, when he came below at last to find the ship apparently in possession of a gang of cut-throat-looking Arabs. He laughed heartily and entered the saloon. Here another surprise awaited him, for seated in the easiest chair, book in hand, was, to all appearance, an aged missionary.

"'Pon my word!" cried Stanley, "I never would have known you, Sambo! Now sit down, old man; I'm burning to hear what you began to tell me last night when you fainted, poor fellow. I've just five minutes to spare, Sambo."

"I'se better now," said Sambo. "You have seen all de niggers—all de slaves on board?"

"Yes."

"And you have seen one Bushman ooy, yeller skin, plenty much hair all ober him head?"

"Yes, Sambo: I took particular notice of the lad."

"He was chain to me," continued Sambo, "all dis cruel voyage. I speak much of him in the Somali tongue, and he tell me——"

"Quick, quick, Sambo! that Somali boy knows of the whereabouts of poor Ida and her father—is it not so Sambo?"

"Ess, sah; ess, young massa. He know. He come from far, far inland, from the land ob de lakes, de land ob de raging torrent, and mountains higher dan de clouds ob de sky, sah. He come from dere, and he have tell me dat in an island, in de middle of a great lake, a beautiful white queen is residing, sah; he hab seen her. She is young and lubly, and dere is also one gemlum—white man, who make medicine—and de chiefs come plenty often to see dem both. Dat, young massa, is poor Ida and her pa. Dey are slaves, all same, and boy say she often, often weep."

"Dear, honest Sambo," said Stanley, taking his hand, "you have indeed raised hope in my heart; but from all I have heard, and also from what Cooke has told me, I have good reason to believe that there may be many white people slaves to the tribes that live in the far interior of that dark continent, Africa. How can we tell that this white queen, as the Somali boy calls her, is indeed Ida?"

Sambo rose and went quickly to the bed in the corner that he had recently left, and returned immediately, holding something in his hand. "She give dis ting to the Somali boy when he start on his long journey wid ivory to de city ob Lamoo. See, sah, see!"

Stanley seized it eagerly. It was a small tablet of ivory, not bigger than a florin; and roughly carved, or scratched, on its one smooth side were the words, "Ida Ross."

Delighted beyond measure, Stanley sent at once for the Somali boy and questioned him in his own language. He found out from him far more then even Sambo had. Ida and her father were indeed in slavery, and there were more whites in the same bondage, and in a far worse plight, for in whatever way they had managed it, both Captain Ross and his daughter seemed to have gained some ascendency over the wild tribes among which they dwelt. Prisoners they were; slaves only in name.

"Sambo," said Stanley, after he had finished questioning the lad, "I want you to be my servant here, in the saloon, all the voyage."

"Ess, young massa; ess, ess, sah."

"Well, you'll take off these garments; I'll give you a suit that will better become you, and I'll find one for—what is the boy's name?"

"Mbooma!"

"Oh!" said Stanley, "we'll call him Brown for short. I'll find a suit from Captain MacDermott's chest for Brown, as he has made so free with my outfit. You'll make him tidy Sambo. I know, and cut his hair. Boy Green was right."

"The ship has hove-to, sir," said the boatswain, entering the saloon, "and is making signals."

"Well, follow her example," answered Stanley.

He paused but for a moment to pick up the Arab signal-book, then hurried up to the poop.

Mite was there, and several of the quasi-Arab crew.

"That's right, Mite," said Stanley. "Now that they see your Arabs up here they won't smell a rat. Send Mr. Miller here. Mr. Miller, I want your assistance; we haven't many hands, and we may have to fight. See every gun loaded quietly and ready to run out, and have cutlasses, pikes, and revolvers all handy."

"Ay, ay, sir!"

"Why, look, Mite, what her signal says: 'Heave-to, I'll send a boat on board.'"

"Couldn't be better!" cried Mite, exultingly. "She is playing into our hands!"

A boat was now lowered from the tall-sparred ship,

though at least five hundred yards away, for Stanley did not care to get any nearer just then. There was a good time coming.

All the men in the boat that was now rapidly approaching seemed to be Europeans, and, as far as could be judged by looks, they were a mixture of Spanish, Portuguese, and half-castes. The officer in the stern-sheets was armed to the teeth, and the oarsmen wore daggers and pistols.

"Pass the word quietly," said Stanley to Mite, "to disarm the officer as soon as he steps on deck, and then seize the boat."

These orders were obeyed to the letter, and hardly had the look of surprise vanished from the face of the slaver officer as he stepped on deck before he was a prisoner and minus sword and pistols.

Almost at the same moment our fellows, six of them, threw themselves into the boat. There was a short scuffle, then all was over—no, not quite, for the crew of the boat had to be taken on board.

"There beant no use talking to 'em," said the boatswain, handing down a piece of hard rope. "Try 'em with this 'ere. That's the style! Give it to 'em proper!"

Our fellows did give it to them proper. This was a truly English way of explaining matters that these piratical scoundrels did not quite like, but there is no mistake about one thing—they understood it thoroughly.

Whack, whack, whack! Oh! didn't they just scream! They came floundering in over the dhow's bulwarks like a flock of geese, and dropped on the deck all of a heap, shouting, "Asesinato! misericordia! misericordia!" amid shouts of hearty Saxon laughter.

The boy Green was dancing for joy, and Mite was in his glory; even Stanley could not refrain from smiling to see the grimacing those foreigners made as they rubbed their smarting thighs. And Sambo must needs address the biggest of the lot as follows : "How you like fum-fum wid de rope-end, eh? You big white chap am de slave now. Dis chile am free. Eh? Yah! yah!

Stanley now hastily read a letter that had been taken from the officer in charge of the boat, then laughingly handed it to Mite.

"It's Greek to me, Stan," said Mite. "What *do* all these hens'-toes mean?"

"Oh! I forgot," replied Stanley. "This is a letter to the commander of this dhow ordering him to disembark his slaves as soon as possible at the old place, and then to proceed north again for the last cargo. This is quite enough to condemn her. We will now capture her, or burn and sink her if need be.

"Hullo, Mr. Miller!" he shouted; "look, the ship has filled her fore yard! Run out that little Dahlgren and send a shot through her rigging to show she is wanted. Down with the Arab flag, Mite! Haul up our own bit of bunting!"

Our men gave one ringing cheer as the bonnie white ensign floated out in the breeze, and crack! went the Dahlgren gun. But the shot tore over the ship without doing aught of damage.

And now the chase began.

"Go on firing, Mr. Miller!" cried Stanley. "Do your best to cripple her, but don't fire at the hull, we want no bloodshed. Bo'swain, get up the slave-irons, we'll give those chaps a taste of their own trade. What a providential thing the finding of that letter was, Mite; mind you take care of it."

Receiving no answer, Stanley looked behind him. Mite had gone.

The fact is that a few minutes before this Captain Mite noticed, very much to his astonishment, a lanky yellow youth standing beside Sambo in the saloon doorway, dressed out in one of his best suits of mufti—a recent importation from England—and had hurried below with the laudable intention of punching his head.

But when Sambo—the new steward, as he styled himself—explained matters, he passed on into the saloon, laughing. He threw the letter he had received from Stanley down on the table, helped himself to a drop of sherbet, which he rather liked, and went out again.

Two hours afterwards the mainmast of the big ship was shot away, and she lowered the crimson-and-orange flag of Spain that she had been flying at her peak. Then there was bustle and stir on board that dhow. Mite was ordered to proceed with an armed boat to complete the capture of the three-master. Stanley did not tell him, however, to load the boat up with slave-irons. This was an idea of his own. Mite believed in making sure. He even found time to run up to where Stanley was standing on the highest part of the poop and beg him to keep the ship covered with the guns, for fear the hauling down of the flag might only be a ruse.

" These beggars are up to all kinds of tricks, you know, Stanley," said Mite.

" Look here, Mite ! " cried Stanley, impatiently, " if you're not out of here in two seconds I'll go myself ! "

Then off went Mite, and in less than ten minutes the British flag floated over the Spaniard's decks. But when Stanley went on board her, very much surprised he was indeed to find every one of her crew, from the captain downwards, in slave-irons.

Meanwhile somebody was making hay while the sun shone. It was the boy Green. " There's nobody a-looking," he said to himself, " so I'll go and have a buster in the cabin. 'Tain't every day I gets sich a chance. Guess I'll do it proper when I'se about it ! "

He went whistling away aft as he spoke. He picked up a belaying-pin and sent it skipping along the deck. It struck poor Sambo on the shins and doubled him up.

Boy Green doubled up too—with laughing. Then he seized the Somali boy and whirled him round and round as if he had been a teetotum.

"Got 'em all on, then," he said, "eh? 'Air fashionable crop and all! My heye! you does look a guy!"

A minute after he was seated in the cabin, with cold fowl, ham, and sweet potatoes before him, and bananas and grapes and pineapples and nuts.

Boy Green was by no means shy, especially when anything good to eat was placed before him, and the zeal with which he applied himself to the demolition of that cold fowl was worthy of a nobler cause. All the while he kept talking to himself as if there had been two of him. "Help yourself to another slice, Mr. Green." "Thank you, I think I will." "A tiny bit more fowl, Mr. Green?" "Well, since you're so pressing." "Another glass of sherbet, Mr. Green? one glass won't hurt you." "Thanks; I don't think three would."

When boy Green had stuffed as much inside as he could hold, he commenced stuffing outside. "I hate waste," he said, cramming the remains of the fowl into his bosom, with the last pineapple and all the bananas, the ham-bone, and a few potatoes. "And there is them nuts and raisins," he continued. "It's a shame to leave 'em. Here goes!"

He picked up a letter from the table, made a grocer's bag out of it, and emptied the plate therein. Then he finished the last drop of sherbet, and "I feels like a giant refreshed!" said the boy Green, and off he went, whistling as before.

"BOY GREEN WAS BY NO MEANS SHY WHEN ANYTHING GOOD TO EAT WAS PLACED BEFORE HIM."

Page 19.

XVI.

*TRIED FOR PIRACY—DEATH SENTENCE—
BOY GREEN AGAIN.*

CHAPTER XVI.

IN one of the most beautiful of the many bays that indent the eastern shores of Africa south of the line, and about two weeks after the events narrated in the preceding chapter, three vessels lay at anchor. One we know well, it is the high-pooped war-dhow *Seyd Pasha*, not long since a prize to Her Majesty's ship *Tonitru*, and still borne on the log of that saucy cruiser under the heading, "*Seyd Pasha*, five guns, piratical slave-dhow, Midshipman MacDermott commander, prize crew, Stanley Grahame interpreter and second officer in charge."

The other we also know. Two tall masts still pierce the blue of the summer sky; the other is gone, and only an unsightly ragged stump remains.

The third vessel we have never seen before. She has but newly come on our stage. Alas! she came but to bring sorrow to two of our chief heroes—a Spanish man-o'-war.

But why is she here? and why does the crimson-and-orange flag now float lazily over the tall-masted slaver? This is a question that is soon replied to. In the heat and bustle of action but little lookout was kept on board the *Seyd Pasha*, and it was not until all was over, and the wreck of the fallen mast cut away, the dead—of whom there were several—placed reverently side by side to await burial, and the injuries of the wounded attended to, that a large steamer was noticed not two miles distant, and rapidly nearing them

Stanley had been walking up and down the quarter-deck in company with Captain Mite and Mr. Miller. They were considering how best they could divide the crew between the dhow and the new prize in order to reach Johanna, one of the Comoro group of islands, and the residence of the British consul, speedily and in safety.

"Hallo!" Stanley had cried, as he spied the great black frigate, "nobody on the outlook? What have we here?"

"A Spaniard, sir, sure enough," was Mr. Miller's reply.

"So it is," replied Stanley, "but our two nations are friendly, and Spain is under treaty to put slavery down as well as we are."

"She won't take our prizes away, will she?" said Mite.

"That she can't," was the reply, "not from under that flag."

"Flags don't go for much at sea," said Mr. Miller, smiling. "You see, sir, any ship may hoist any bit o' bunting she pleases, just to suit her own conwenience as it were."

"True, true," replied Stanley; "but we have good proof that this is a slaver."

"Not on board her, though, sir. I've just been all round her decks, above and below, and ne'er a bit o' me can find a westige o' slave about her. She has more bags o' rice than she needs, and conwenience for distilling more water than ten times her crew could drink; but them proofs ain't proofs, sir—leastways they won't condemn a wessel, sir, unless there's something else."

"Ah! but that we have," said Stanley; "the letter, Mite, the letter?"

Mite had turned ghastly pale; he staggered and had to clutch at the bulwarks to save himself from falling.

"Speak, Mite; speak quick. You have it; you have the letter?"

"Call away the dingy, Stan," replied Mite. "I believe it is in the dhow's saloon.'

Both the dhow and the *America*, the name the large slaver went by, were still hove-to.

Mite was back again in less than ten minutes.

"Oh! Stanley, it's lost, the letter is lost," was all he could say.

"Lost! Then Heaven help us," cried Stanley; "we are lost too."

"Don't say that, sir," said Miller.

"But I do say it, and I feel it. Though I have not been long on this coast, Mr. Miller, I have studied all the ins and outs of this accursed slave-trade, and you know as well as I do that neither Spaniards nor Portuguese ever went heart and soul into its suppression."

"I knows it, sir, I knows it; I've been over ten years in African waters, and the truth has been forced upon me like. The Portuguese, you see, sir, make a power o' money out o' gold-dust and slaves, and they don't like trade interfered with by interloping Britishers, as they call us. They——"

"Yes, yes, my good Mr. Miller, we know all about it; say no more. The question is, what now is best to be done? Did I not know we are in the right, I would look upon this half-wrecked ship as a testimony of our treachery and cruelty, the villains we hold in irons as ill-treated traders, ourselves as pirates, and yonder grim stains on the deck and bulwarks as the blood of murdered men."

"They are lowering a boat, sir."

"Yes," said Stanley. "Miller, you must act as interpreter."

In the midst of his sorrow and annoyance Stanley could not help admiring the workman-like way the boat was handled. She was broader in the beam and lower as to gunwales, but otherwise she might have been taken for a British man-o'-war's whaler.

In two minutes more the lieutenant in command stood on the quarter-deck, bowing low with head uncovered to Stanley Grahame.

Stanley introduced him to Mite, Captain MacDermott, of the prize dhow *Seyd Pasha.*

The lieutenant drew himself up, and after one haughty glance at poor Mite, who never looked to less advantage, he addressed a few words in Spanish to Mr. Miller.

"It's just as I thought it would be," said that worthy sailor to Stanley. "This wasp-waisted son of a sea-cook, with cocked hat and swabs, wants to know why the captain and crew of a British prize should be wearing the dress of piratical Arabs."

Stanley bit his lip with vexation. Everything seemed to be working against him.

He was about to explain when the Spaniard raised his hand.

"Not to me, sir," he said. "You will pardon me, I am sure. I have but to do my duty. You are our prisoners, and must accompany me on board the *Don Carlos.*"

This being interpreted to Stanley, he turned to Mite.

"Don't you fret and worry, Mite," he said, "and remember that this officer is but doing his duty. It is only the fortune of war. It'll all come right enough in the end."

Then he turned to the lieutenant.

"We are ready," he said, bowing.

Let us now betake ourselves on board the *Don Carlos,* lying at anchor out in the bay there on this lovely summer's morning. Here is a half-caste Kaffir in a log canoe, with outriggers as large as ordinary sheep hurdles. The little boat does not capsize if you sit straight, with head erect, and nose in a line with the keel, and have your hair parted in the centre. The savage creeps on board after he has floated the wonderful boat; he has no clothing save a filthy rag around his loins, but he manages the paddle well.

How calm and bright and blue the sea is! The beach is a broad belt of snowy sand, on which the waves are breaking in a kind of dreamy monotone, as if the sea were singing the land to sleep; and all asleep in the sunshine it seems to be, for other than that of breaking waves there is not a sound to be heard ; there is silence on the woods, silence on the hills, the smoke is curling upwards from the village that goes straggling up the glen, but no other sign of life is visible ; and yonder on the picturesque fort, from the embrasures of which guns look menacingly seaward, one white-coated sentinel alone can be seen. But see, a sheet of flame appears for a moment on the frigate's quarter, and the sharp roar of a gun falls on the ear and goes echoing and re-echoing all along the shore, and the white smoke rolls slowly to leeward.

What means it? Only this, the court is assembled in that ship-of-war's saloon to try two men on a charge of piracy on the high seas.

Very imposing the officers that crowd around the table look in their uniforms of white and blue and gold. The captain of the ship is president, a red-faced, white-moustached, but not unkindly-looking gentleman. At his right sits the commandant of the fort, and near him the Portuguese consul, while officers, both naval and military, make up the number to twelve.

The prisoners are brought in—Stanley calm and bold, for he is confident he will receive a fair and impartial trial, and poor little Mite, very pale, but taking the cue from Stanley and trying hard to look just as bold and calm as he.

Mr. Miller is there, also a prisoner, but at liberty to interpret every word that is spoken.

After a few words of explanation to the officers of the court,

"Prisoners," said the president, "you stand arraigned before us on one of the gravest charges that can be brought against mortal men—namely, that of murder and piracy on the high seas. You have even been taken red-handed in these acts, and as commander of a ship sent ou expressly by my Government to suppress and punish such as you, your shift would have been a short one, your trial a mere matter of form, had you not, to shield yourselves from your doom, hoisted the flag of a nation with which we are at peace. You are Englishmen both, therefore it may be supposed have a perfect right to attempt to shelter yourselves under England's flag; but I have yet to learn that officers of a British man-of-war, as you call yourselves, ever opened fire on an unarmed and legitimate trader. Your having hoisted that flag, therefore, but adds to the heinousness of your crime, if guilty you be, and will not defer retribution a single day if the charges are proved. Myself and my colleagues are willing to lend polite ears to any remarks you make in justification of your conduct, or any explanation you can give of the fact that both yourselves and crew were and are dressed in a garb, which in all my time at sea, I never have seen man-of-war's men of your nation adopt."

A murmur and laugh of derision went round the table as the president sat down, and looks that boded no good were directed towards the prisoners.

In clear ringing tones Stanley told his story—the story of the capture of the slave dhow by the *Tonitru*, his being sent in charge with Mite as their captain, his meeting the slave-ship, their dressing up as Arabs to make sure of the prize, of the arrival of the boat from the *America*, and the delivery of the letter, etc. ; in fact, he told them all that the reader already knows.

He was listened to most patiently, and at the conclusion of his speech, which he delivered with all the earnestness and eloquence of a man who knows he is verbally fighting for dear life, an officer arose, and bowing with a pleasant smile to the prisoners,

"I am here," he said, "as your special pleader. Your defence is good, and well worthy of the great nation to which you belong. That letter will save our case. You doubtless can produce it ?"

As soon as Miller had made this speech plain to Stanley,

"Alas!" he replied, "during the excitement and bustle of the action that letter has been mislaid."

His pleader's face fell.

"This is indeed sad," he said; "but the uniform of your men, and of the young officer beside you, where is that?"

"Oh! these," cried Stanley, brightening up, "can be easily got. They are on board the dhow."

"It is false," said another Spaniard. "It is false, sir. I myself had command of the party who searched the dhow, and who struck the irons from my captured countrymen, and nothing in the shape of uniform was found in the dhow—nothing British save the flag we hauled from the peak."

"The scoundrels!" said Miller, "they've been and gone and shied all our togs to the sharks. That chap that's just finished yarning has done it. He with the blacking-brush moustache and the mouldy chops. I say, Mr. Grahame, wouldn't I give ten years o' my life just to have five minutes of that swab, five minutes all to ourselves, fair wind and no favour. Oh!"

Then Mr. Miller seemed to lose control of himself; he threw himself into an attitude of a truly British character, but by no means complimentary to the august assembly he stood in front of. He drew himself back most artistically, his guards well up, then he landed one with his left straight from the shoulder at an imaginary opponent.

"Ah!" roared the president, stretching out his arm towards Miller, and with a face almost purple with rage, "Que—Que—Que significa eso?"

"Yo no se, señor," said the lieutenant.

"Yo pido pardon e usted, señor," said Mr. Miller, humbly. "I was but pointing out to my friends the manner in which some of the slaves of the *Seyd Pasha* must have pitched our uniform overboard. None of your brave and

honourable countrymen would have thought of so dis-
honourable an action."

The prisoners' solicitor once more addressed them. He
seemed to wash his hands with invisible soap, and there
was a cloud on his brow, although a sadly sinister smile
on his by no means beautiful countenance. Both Stanley
and Mite knew the meaning of this even before Mr. Miller
translated his language. "He threw up the case. He
was sorry, but he could do no more ; the ladder that ought
to have led to success was kicked from under them. It
only remained for him to wash his hands of the business
and throw up the sponge. In a speech that he had made
in their behalf, so he said, before they were summoned
to this tribunal, he had fought his ground inch by inch
(*palmo a palmo*), but in vain. He must now advise them
to submit to whatever was before them (*bajar la cabeza*)."

Ba ar la cabeza ! (Bow the head !) What a sad significance rested in those words, *Bajar la cabeza !* Criminals
on some parts of the Dark Continent stand erect for execution, by the sea beach or on the lovely river's bank, but
they bow the head to the sword's blow.

The court retired for half an hour, one of the longest,
saddest half-hours ever young Stanley had spent. But
hark ! They come at last. Our heroes could hear them
laughing and joking long before they reached the door of
the saloon. If the truth must be told, they had spent the
time discussing a light luncheon of fruit and wine and
coffee. They had never even mentioned the names of the
accused, till they had finished their repast, and then the
president had merely said, shortly,

"I suppose, señors, we are all agreed ?"

"All."

"And the sentence on these two young men ?"

"*Muerte*" (Death).

They were very grave when reseated around the table,
and every eye in the room was turned towards the presi-

dent. He stood there silently for a moment or two leaning forward with both hands on the table. His task was not a pleasant one, and he seemed deeply commiserating the position of the prisoners in front of him, that the words he was about to speak would consign to so early a grave. Who knows what thoughts might not have been passing through his mind during those few brief moments that he spoke not? He perhaps had sons of his own. He might —But hush! his voice now breaks the solemn stillness.

"Prisoners," he begins, "you have been tried and convicted——"

"Hold on, old stick-in-the-mud," cried a voice from under the table, "there is somebody else got summat to say as well as you, I guess."

Out popped the boy Green, to the astonishment of everybody present.

"*Quien esta ahi,*" cried the president. "*Quien esta ese muchacho? Que, que——*"

"*Que, que,*" sneered the boy Green, "as many k's as you please, but listen you'll have to. I've been afore bigger beaks than you, and a——"

"Away with him," cried the president.

"I've been lyin' in there all the time," continued boy Green, "and my conscience has been a-tumbling over on me. Hands off, I say! Hands off! I's not a-goin' to stand by and see them young officers murdered. Let go, will you. Not if I can help it. Let go, I say. Take that, then! There's one for your nob, and t'other for your shins."

Poor boy Green! I greatly fear his strange intrusion did not mend matters, good though his intentions undoubtedly were. Kicking and hitting and sprawling, he was borne off, and thrust below in irons.

*   *   *   *   *   *

While lying in their cell at night, with hands and feet in chains, worn out in body and mind, and just sinking into an uneasy dreamful slumber, from which the monotonous sound of the sentry's footsteps was not entirely banished, a voice raised in song suddenly fell on the ears of Stanley and Mite, and made them start and listen.

It was Sambo's, most unmistakably:

> " Weep no more, dear massa,
>   Oh ! weep no more to-day,
>   We will sing one song for de ole Kentucky home,
>   For de ole Kentucky home, far away."

Then there were heard the tread of hurrying feet and the sound of blows, and thereafter all was silent as before.

Two hours might have passed—the sentry had been relieved, so it must have been well on in the middle watch, when a splash was heard in the water alongside, succeeded almost immediately by the sharp ring of a rifle, and a wild shout of,

" *Escapado !   Ha escapado !* "

IN THE DUNGEON—SAMBO TO THE FORE—THAT UBIQUITOUS BOY GREEN NOT FAR BEHIND.

CHAPTER XVII.

"STANLEY! Stan!"

"Yes, Mite, yes."

"Oh! dear Stan, I am so glad to hear your voice again. I've had such a strange happy dream, and then to waken here in this dungeon, all in the dark! It is too, too terrible. And I felt around for you, Stan, and when my hand didn't touch you I thought they had taken you away and—killed you, Stan."

"You are nervous, Mite; but I do not wonder."

"It is being in the dark, Stanley; but don't fear for me, I'll keep up my heart like a man when it comes to the —end, Stan." His voice shook as he spoke.

"Creep closer this way, Mite. Now make a pillow of my knee. That's right. I think it will soon be day, little brother."

"Oh! Stan, brother Stan, do not talk in a kind voice to me, or else I'll break down, I'll——"

Poor little Mite! he did break down, and, with his head pillowed on Stanley's knee, sobbed as if his very heart would burst.

"It does seem so very cowardly of me to cry, being a Scotchman too; but *they* won't see my tears, Stan—no, *hey* won't see them."

An hour later it was day, but the bright sunshine that streamed through the tall narrow opening in the wall of their dungeon, brought neither hope nor joy to the hearts of the prisoners. The place in which they were confined was beneath the fort and partly underground, its walls were the bare stones, furniture it had none of any kind, its very floor was a portion of the sea-beach, and they sat or lay or walked on sand and shingle. There was but small room for walking, and had there been ever so much, the chains that bound their legs, and those cruel manacles, would have precluded the possibility of taking exercise So close to the sea were they, that they could hear the waves breaking on the shore, and had there been a sudden high tide the waters might have rushed in and drowned them in their cell.

Mite still retained his position by Stanley's knee, but he was looking up into his face.

"You feel better now, don't you, Mite?"

"Much, now that I can see you. Do my eyes look swollen? That padre will be here before long, and I would not like that even he should think I was afraid."

"The padre," replied Stanley, "is a kindly-hearted old man, and a servant of God, Mite, although his religion does differ in some respects from ours."

There was a long silence now, both were thinking and praying. The gecko lizards glided stealthily over the rough walls, intent on their prey; the tap-tapping one made when hammering a captured moth to death was distinctly audible. A great round-eyed bird, with wings and body of blue and crimson, alighted for a moment on the window-ledge, and gazed inquiringly at the prisoners, then took to flight again with a frightened cry.

How sweet to Stanley seemed the morning sunshine! What a glorious thing freedom would be he thought. Freedom and sunshine, in which even a bird could revel, but which were denied to him and his companion.

Death hath its terrors even to the aged; but to die so young, and to die innocent—to meet a felon's doom, to fill a felon's grave—the thought of it is too awful to dwell upon.

"Stan," said Mite at last.

"Yes, Mite."

"Do you think it will be to-day?"

"Dear Mite," replied Stanley, "I cannot even guess. You see the padre knows nothing, or he will tell us nothing."

"Oh! Stan, I do not fear death now, at least not an ordinary death. Not if they shoot us, Stan; but I have read of the terrible garotte, and how they place you in a chair and——"

"Oh! Mite, Mite, poor boy, do be calm. My heart bleeds for you. I seem to have lived a long, long time in the world, but you are so young. And yet you know it will soon be all over. It was so kind of the padre yesterday to bring us paper and pens and let us write to —to those we will never, never see again. But listen."

A key was inserted in the lock, and two men armed to the teeth brought in their meagre breakfast of boiled rice and water, and placed it beside them.

By-and-by the padre came in, a white-haired, kindly-faced old priest.

He sat down by the prisoners and took Mite's hand in his. He talked to them long and earnestly in their own language, not of things earthly, but of things beyond the veil. There was something in this priest's manner to-day more impressive even than usual. Stanley noticed this, but he kept his thoughts to himself. But ere long Mite noticed it too, and, more impulsive far than his companion in sorrow, he clutched the priest's thin white hand, and it would have melted a heart of stone to have seen how eagerly he gazed up into his face, as he piteously exclaimed,

"Oh! father, *is* it to be to-day?"

"Alas! my son," said the padre, solemnly, "it is to be to-day."

And the old man bowed his head and wept.

The last morning had come, then : the execution was fixed for the afternoon. And yet how slowly the forenoon seemed to wear away.

It must have been past two o'clock—they could tell that from the shadow of the strong iron bar that guarded the window of their cell—when music fell upon their ears— the music of a brass band ; a slow, solemn march was being played ; it increased in tone, seeming to come nearer and nearer, and finally died away in the distance. Mite crept closer to Stanley's side ; they both knew what it meant, but neither spoke.

A few minutes afterwards the dungeon door was thrown open.

Always before this, whenever the guard or any one came to visit the prisoners in their cell, the door was opened cautiously, and only sufficiently wide to admit the visitor with difficulty. But now it was dashed open wide against the wall. There was a terrible significance in even this.

The passage beyond, usually as dark as night itself, was now lighted up by the glimmer of lamps, revealing armed men in white uniforms. There were quick, short orders being given, and the rattle of swords and musketry. I think poor Mite would have fainted at this moment had not the aged padre pressed close to his side. Once out of the fort, although the bright sunshine dazzled him for a moment, the fresh breeze revived him, and he was able to march by Stanley's side as steadily as he did. Only he clutched his brother's hand—to do even this was a comfort to the boy.

No need for either to speak. No need for them to breathe the word farewell. They were together now hand in hand, and so they felt they would be—till the end.

*   *   *   *   *

We must leave this sad scene now for a short time, and fall back in our narrative to the morning after the trial, and very early on that morning, to the time when Stanley and Mite heard the splash in the water alongside, followed by the rifles' ring and the wild shout on board of,

"*Escapado—Ha escapado!*"

Sambo, for it was no other, had acted his part well. He had seen the "young massa" and Mite taken to the cells after the trial, and well he knew what the sentence had been. From that very moment he determined to escape, and to endeavour to do all in his power to effect their rescue. The song he had raised in the stillness of night was part of his plan. The writer of these lines knows from experience that Spaniards are not slow to draw and use the cutlass against unarmed men. Sambo knew so too. He had not reckoned without his host either. That was a cruel blow the sentry aimed at his unprotected head. What matter though he killed him, so reasoned the marine, he was only a nigger, and a pirate to boot! But Sambo held his hands up, and the blow fell crashing between them, severing the manacles; then Sambo fell backwards with a groan, and laughing to himself the sentry resumed his watch. Sambo laughed to himself also. In ten minutes more both his hands and feet were free, then he glided snake-like to the foot of the ladder, taking advantage of every shadow. His friend the sentry, who had so kindly attempted to split his skull, stood right at the foot of the ladder, gazing up towards the sky. Sambo was not revengeful, but this fellow was in his way, so he dealt him a blow with his clenched fist that felled him to the deck.

Although splendid swordsmen as a rule, Spaniards do not excel with the rifle, and though the night was clear and starry Sambo was perfectly safe. The shore was not very far off, and he soon reached it, and was well hidden in the bush before the boat was lowered to give him chase.

Once fairly in the woods, Sambo sat down to think. His young massa must be saved at all risks. But how?

Nothing could be done in the village, where all were
against him. Ha! he had it. Happy thought! To go
straight away north through the woods until opposite the
Comoro Islands; here, at Johanna, some British ship was
sure to be, perhaps the *Tonitru* herself. To make up his
mind was with Sambo to act. There was not a moment
to lose. Perhaps at daylight the woods would be scoured
to find him. He started to his feet, took off his cummerbund and wrung the water from it, and replaced it round
his loins, then with just one quick glance starwards, with
just one prayer on his lips to the Great Father, who is no
respecter of persons, and can show mercy to the black
man as well as the white, he started off and away through
the forest with almost the fleetness of a hunted deer, and
before morning broke, and the great sun rose red over
the purple sea, he stood on a distant hill-top, from which,
to his joy, he could see the tips of the far-off mountains
of those romantic islands in which his present hopes were
centred. Sambo's breakfast consisted of a root that he
dug from the ground, and a draught of cocoa-nut milk.
He rested for an hour, for well he knew he must conserve
all his strength for his dear young massa's sake. Then he
resumed his journey. He had a broad river to swim.
The water was brackish, for it was at no great distance
from the sea-bar; and here were monster sharks in dozens
—he could see their fins over the water and hear them
plash and gambol, for—woe is me!—even sharks play
at times, and they never seem more inclined to do so
then when there is a chance of a feed on human flesh.
Sambo feared them not—he was black,* they would not
touch him. He avoided the mangrove swamps; he had

---

* The belief that sharks will not attack a black man is a very
common one on the coast. I have my doubts of the truth of this; but
I have seen a Krooman dive into a river infested by these monsters
after an officer's cap, and come back sound in wind and limb, and
smiling.

an idea that crocodiles were not so fastidious in their tastes as sharks, so he kept to the woods and the open. In two days' time Sambo had reached a part of the coast almost opposite the Isle of Johanna. But how to get there, that was the puzzle. He walked onwards by the sea-beach, but coming presently to another mangrove forest, he made a *détour* and finally found himself at the top of a creek. It was almost entirely surrounded by forest, so he kept well away from the water's edge, and concealed himself in the banana groves. By-and-by he heard voices, and then there passed his hiding place a procession that he knew only too well the meaning of— Arab-driven slaves fastened by the necks by chains and bamboo collars, male and female, young and middle-aged. Newly come from the interior, evidently, for their feet and legs were cut and torn, and their sad dejected faces told a tale of woe which Sambo could read at a single glance. How he longed to set them free, to spring at the throats of those brutal Arabs, strangle them where they stood, and cast their bodies into the creeks to feed the sharks!

He dared not move. Nor did he move all that day; but when the kindly stars shone out again he crept from his place of concealment and made his way cautiously along the creek. It was not simply one long arm of the sea, this creek, but rather a series of branching gulfs, and some were almost hidden by the trees that grew by the banks, so narrow were they. In one of these Sambo noticed lights, and soon perceived that he was close alongside a small rakish-looking brig that had her topmasts struck—the better to effect her concealment. There was a boat floating astern of her, attached by a painter.

Now, in what followed I do not mean for a moment to defend Sambo's morality. I only describe what actually occurred, and the reader is quite at liberty to condemn the poor faithful fellow if he chooses.

Sambo, then, lowered himself gently into the water, then he got on board the boat. "Fust-rate!" he said to himself, "nuffin could be nicer nor dis is; oars and sails and mast all complete. Yes, I borrow dis boat for a little time. Must have somfin' to eat, though."

So saying, Master Sambo went ashore again, and pre sently came back laden with a dozen green cocoa-nuts and an immense bunch of bananas. These he carefully placed in the boat; then, cutting the painter with a knife that he found in the boat, he seized the overhanging branches one by one, and so quietly glided away seawards. There was a slight breeze, and as soon as he was fairly clear of the trees he stepped his little mast, shipped his rudder, and hoisted the sail.

Now Sambo was a good sailor—this the reader already knows; but to attempt to cross from the mainland to the distant islands of Comoro in an open boat, even under the most favourable circumstances, was a task at which even the boldest mariner that ever sailed the sea might be pardoned for hanging fire. But Sambo never dreamed of anything else save success; and so, when far away from land, he even prayed that the breeze might increase, and he damped his sail with water from the sea that it might draw the better. Although from the hill-top on the mainland he had been able to see the far-off island mountains, here at sea they were not visible; there was therefore nothing to guide him save the sun by day and the stars that shone at night. But land came in sight at last, though farther to the north than he had expected ; he had not counted on the currents. Yet, nothing daunted, he altered his course somewhat, and made use of the oar as well. Had he been content with his sail, misfortune might not have befallen him. It was easy enough to pull an oar at one side and take charge of the tiller with his naked foot, but seated thus he could not easily look ahead of him, and so did not perceive, until too late, the approach of one of those white squalls that **are** the terror of seamen in the Indian Ocean. The sail flapped listlessly for a moment, then, before he had time to take it in, the squall was on him in all its force, the canvas was rent in ribbons, and the boat capsized.

For two whole hours, until the storm passed away and sky and sea were once more serene, Sambo clung to the keel of his boat. Then, after great exertions and many failures, he managed to right her again, and clambering on board, he succeeded in baling her out. But, alas! his oars were gone, as well as the mast and sail, and even the cocoa-nuts and bananas, on which his very life depended, had been washed away.

He was helpless now, and hopeless. All day and all next night he drifted about he knew not whither; but when daylight came at last, there was no land in sight anywhere, only water—only the quiet blue, heaving bosom of the great ocean. He never thought of food, but the thirst was terrible to endure. His mouth was parched, his lips and tongue swollen, his eyes seemed balls of fire, and at length he sank down exhausted in the bottom of the boat, and darkness seemed to overwhelm him. Was it the darkness of death? No, for he began to dream; he was back again at the old plantation, his " young massa " was with him; they had been out in the forest all day shooting, and, tired and somewhat weary, they must bend down over a clear purling brooklet, and drink. How cool, how refreshing was that draught!

"I hope you feel better now," said his "young massa."

Sambo opened his eyes. It was not Stanley that had been talking to him, then. No; a kind-hearted British sailor was bending over him, and he was lying on the white deck of an English man-of-war."

"Drink a little more," said the sailor.

Sambo did so, and sat up, looking wildly and amazedly around him.

The sailor replied to Sambo's look by telling him they had found him in his boat only an hour since—that he was now on board the *Tonitru*, bound for Zanzibar.

"Zanzibar," cried Sambo, springing to his feet. Weak though he was, his strength for a moment returned. "Zanzibar! No, no, not dere, sah, not dere!"

Then, talking so quickly as to be hardly intelligible, he told the officers, who had now gathered round him, everything that had occurred since the dhow and the *Tonitru* had parted company.

Stanley and Mite in danger of death! And such a death!

The officer of the watch did not stop to hear the conclusion of Sambo's tale.

He hurried to the bridge. "Ready about!" he cried. "Stand by tacks and sheets!"

Then the order was given to get up steam with all speed.

Within the next few hours Sambo was made to repeat his tale a dozen times over at least, both in the captain's cabin and in every mess on board. For the time being he was the hero of the *Tonitru*.

The end of all this was that next afternoon, at the very moment when Stanley and Mite were marching, hand-in-hand, to a doom that it seemed no power on earth could intervene to avert, the saucy old *Tonitru* steamed round the point and commenced firing the usual salute to the Portuguese flag.

A boat was lowered with all haste, and the captain himself set out for the shore, even before the guns had well commenced firing. But would this hinder the execution? Not for a moment!

From the poop, in the position the *Tonitru* now occupied, the Spanish firing party were distinctly visible, and it was evident from their movements they had just got the order to load.

Pen was now in charge. He hurriedly beckoned the gunner, and pointed shorewards to the soldiers.

"There!" he cried; "quick, if ever you were quick in your life. Throw a shell in there. Quick and steady."

The gunner required no second bidding. The firing party on shore had just received orders to present. Their pieces were levelled, when "hursh!" came that shell. Was it an earthquake, or had the world suddenly come to an end? The dreadful missile burst with a roar louder than a thunderclap, right in front of them, and buried itself partially in the ground, where it made a hole that would have held a house, while the stones and *débris* it threw up literally buried the soldiers alive.

No one was killed, many were hurt, and before the commotion ceased the captain of the *Tonitru* was on the ground. Even he was astonished at the turn matters had taken—astonished, but certainly not sorry, albeit he afterwards confessed—confidentially to his officers—that he had never before seen a foreign flag saluted in such a slapdash fashion.

But look, some one else suddenly appears on the scene. It is that ubiquitous boy Green, and he now stands in front of his captain. A pitiable appearance he presents, for he has just escaped from the prison in which he had been confined, his clothes torn, his hair disordered, and wrists and ankles bleeding.

"Guess I'm in time," he sneered, " to turn the tables on that there. old beak."

This was the way he alluded to the captain of the *Don Carlos.*

"Here's the letter, sir. I took it. I rolled some nuts and things in it, and it's been a-tumbling over upon my conscience ever since, sir.

"They put me in gaol. But it ain't a furrin gaol as'll hold boy Green, I guess, when he's innocent. There's the letter, sir, and I hopes, sir, as how you'll 'ang the lot of 'em, 'specially the old beak."

After this strange address the boy Green rushed off to get rid of his extra steam by dancing round the rescued Stanley and Mite.

XVIII.

PREPARATIONS FOR THE MARCH INTO THE INTERIOR—BIVOUAC IN ZANZIBAR WOODS.

CHAPTER XVIII.

PREPARATIONS FOR THE MARCH INTO THE INTERIOR—BIVOUAC
IN ZANZIBAR WOODS.

IT was just two years and a day after the events
recorded in last chapter, and the *Tonitru* lay at
anchor in the roadstead off Zanzibar. There were many
more ships besides her lying there on that bright, still,
lovely afternoon. The Sultan's flagship, an immense old
tub of a concern, that a single shot from a British gunboat
would suffice to sink, and several other craft belonging to
that potentate, a graceful, airy-looking French frigate, a
sugar-ship or two, the Seychelles mail boat, and a whole
fleet of dhows of all descriptions and every size.

The day had been a hot one, but the sun was now
declining in the west, and a gentle breeze had set in
landwards, enough to cool the heated air and raise a
ripple on the water; and standing on the *Tonitru's* deck
one could hear the waves breaking musically on the sandy
beach that formed the city's foreshore. There was not a
cloud in all the blue sky; the long line of flat-roofed,
imposing-looking buildings stood out sharp and clear
against it, their whiteness relieved by here a waving flag,
and there a clump of feathery palm-trees. By-and-bye
those flags would be furled, for the sun would set; then,
though not a sound came from seawards, the city itself
would awake from its siesta—awake to the beating of
tom-toms, the sound of wild music, and strange wild
revelry, the shriek of Arab sentinels, and later on in the

night, perhaps, to cries that it has often made my blood curdle to listen to, but which neither I nor any one else could ever explain.

But here we are on board the *Tonitru*, and here is Mite walking the quarter-deck with the doctor and Pendragon. Not much difference is there in Mite since we last met him—a little ruddier and a trifle rounder, but not an inch bigger, he is still the *Tonitru's* midship*mite*, although he has been expecting to be promoted to the rank of full-blown sub-lieutenant for the last six months.

There is no difference in the doctor and no difference in Pen either; and here comes boy Green—well, I think he has grown fully an inch, but he certainly has not out-grown his independence nor his impudence either. But he has come to be a sort of a favourite on board; the surgeon forgives him now when he burns the poultices, smashes the bottles, or puts sugar instead of salt in the patients' beef-tea. He does not get quite so many rope's-endings, and he does not have his hair cut more than once a week, perhaps. But this is what the boy Green said to the doctor one day.

"Humph!" he grinned, "I guess you may all be proud o' me and thankful to me too; if I 'adn't found that letter it ain't likely you could 'ave condemned that Spanish slave-ship; there was nothin' else agin her as I knows on, and Mr. Grahame and the little officer might 'ave got hung arter all—humph!"

"You abandoned little rascal," the doctor had replied, 'you forget that you stole that letter in the first place!"

"Stole!" cried that irrepressible boy—"what do you mean by 'stole'? I only took the letter to put them 'ere nuts and things in. Where else was I going to put 'em, eh? I ax ye that. No London beak would convict upon such evidence. No, sirree."

Now, there is one thing you would have noticed had you been on board the *Tonitru* that afternoon—namely, that there was something unusual up. You would have guessed that much from the more than usually animated manner Mite talked and walked. Besides, Mite was in *mufti.* He carried a double-barrel central-fire gun over his shoulder, and there was a mysterious-looking bag slung across his chest; even his coat had "a knowing look about it," as an American would say, and his nether garments were of the cut and fashion adopted by bicyclists.

"The whaler is all ready, sir," said the coxswain, coming up and touching his hat to Mite.

"Thank you," was the reply, when just at that moment Stanley himself came aft and joined the group. How handsome he looked! He has filled out since we last saw him; he is more hardy in appearance, and his skin is tanned to a healthy red. He is inches bigger than even Pen, and Mite has to look a long way up to his big brother Stan, as he calls him.

"You're all ready, I see, Mite," he says, quietly.

"Been up here for hours," says Mite.

"Good-bye," cry the doctor and Pen, leaning over the bulwarks after their two friends are seated in the boat.

"Good-bye. Take care of yourself, Stan, and mind the mosquitoes don't devour poor little Mite."

Ten minutes after Stanley and his friend Mite stood alone on the beach, and the boat was pulling back towards the ship. They were alone to all intents and purposes, for no white man was near them, only a group of warm-looking, not over-dressed negro boys, soliciting pice.

"Yonder is the Glasgow ship," said Stanley, pointing to a smart-looking craft that lay in the bay, "but I see no signs of any stir on board, so very likely Cooke and the others have landed and gone on before."

"All the better," said Mite. "We can talk to our two selves. Come on. Isn't it glorious to be free of the service for a time, brother Stan?"

"Well," replied Stanley, "I don't know. Life on board

ship is, I must confess, a little irksome, but you and I have had it pretty much our own way, haven't we ?"

" That we have, Stan, and I think it so good of Captain Orbistone to give me six months' leave."

" You have the doctor to thank for part of that good luck, Mite."

" Yes," said Mite, " he did a deal, I know. Dear old Sawbones ! I'm sure he'll miss me."

"I should think he would," said Stanley, laughing. " He'll miss the horrid row you always made. He'll have a little peace in his life now, poor fellow. Hullo ! here we are at old Portuguese Joe's. Good afternoon, Joe. Seen anything of our friends ?"

" They come here, sir, one long time ago," replied the tall, dark keeper of a semi-civilised eating-house, with a friendly nod. " They have coffee, wait more'n an hour, then they go on to de bush. They say you know de road, and dat you sure to follow."

" That we will, Joe," said Stanley, " as soon as we have tasted a cup of your excellent coffee. There is nobody in the wide world can make it half so well, Joe."

Joe smiled, showing a set of teeth of alabaster whiteness. Then he hurried away, but, returning presently, he placed before them tiny cups of black Arab coffee, the very aroma of which was most fragrant and refreshing.

Having done justice to this delicate repast, the two friends hurried on again.

Out and away along the strange, narrow, windowless streets, and by many a winding short cut known only to those who have resided for many a month in this strange city, till they found themselves in an avenue of shops. Not such shops as you are likely to find anywhere out of Zanzibar, although some in the old part of Bombay are not unlike them. These emporiums have neither window nor door. The fact is, each shop is a shed. It is all one big window, or all one big doorway, as you like to call it. for

"THEY WERE ALONE WITH NATURE IN THE BEAUTIFUL WOODS."

Page 251.

there is nothing in front, and on the floor squats the Hindoo, Parsee, Arab, or Banian merchant, quietly smoking his hubble-bubble. There is nothing very inviting in these stalls to a European eye, unless, indeed, you are on the hunt for curiosities, nor is there anything very edible, with the exception of the fruit. That, however, would make your mouth water whether you were hungry or not. The long street was as crowded as a Welsh fair, so that Stanley and Mite could with difficulty push their way through. And what a motley throng it was! Natives from every land of the East seemed to be here. The blacks dressed only in the cummerbund, and probably a little skull-cap of straw; the Hindoos in robes of white and gilded turbans; the Parsees in more respectable black, with head-dresses bearing a wonderful resemblance to the top of a tin whistle; stately Arab soldiers, with handsome bold faces, and hair trailing in ringlets adown their backs, with cloaks of camels'-hair depending beneath their knees, and spear and sword and pistols, with jewels apparently stuck in every place where there was the slightest chance of their stopping.

Onwards past the fish market, where the odours did not entice them to linger, past the market devoted to beef for meat-eating Englishmen and other Europeans. There the bluebottle flies seemed to have it very much their own way, and our heroes were fain to hurry past the place for more reasons than one.

In one short half-hour after this they were alone with nature, alone in the beautiful woods. How different was everything here from the scenes they had just passed through in the city, where man in his savagery held sway. Everything around them looked as pure and fresh and lovely as if it had but newly left the hands of the great Maker. Rain had recently fallen to bless and fertilise the ground; the tall cocoa-palms that held their feathery heads far, far aloft, as if scorning the earth from which they

sprang, glittered green in the evening sunlight. Mango-
trees, bigger and wider than the mightiest chestnuts of our
own parks, drooped their branches fruit-laden towards the
ground ; and here was the bread-fruit tree, the orange, the
citron, and the fragrant lime-trees covered with fruit, and
trees begemmed with flowers, and everywhere the air was
perfumed with the sweet breath of the orange-blossom.

Soon the sun would set. Already the splendidly plumaged
birds were seeking with peevish cries the shelter of
the loftiest branches, so our heroes stopped not to admire,
but hurried onwards through the woods. The path was a
small one and very winding, and were they to miss it but
once it would be difficult, 'if not impossible, to find it again.

"We cannot be far off now," said Stanley, at last.

"No, I don't think we are," Mite replied ; "suppose I
fire my piece, then we can shout, you know."

"All right, Mite, fire away. I know you are anxious to
hear the sound of that new gun of yours. Stop—what are
you going to do ? "

"I was going to hit that bird, Stan."

"Oh ! Mite, it would be cowardly."

Mite said no more, but fired both barrels in the air.

Then they shouted and listened. And presently they
were answered, for borne along on the faint evening breeze
came a long, shrill, and quavering yell.

"That's the Arab," said Stanley. "No British lungs
could emit a shriek like that."

They left the path now, and made straight in the
direction from which the sound had come, sometimes
stopping for a moment to halloo, then going on again as
soon as they were answered. In about ten minutes more
they were in the company of their friends, who had come
out to meet them.

Then ensued such a shaking of hands as surely never
was witnessed before in such a place.

But "Sta .l y ! " was the cry. Stanley was the attraction

Mite afterwards told his friend that he had positively felt nowhere in particular just then, so he was content to stand aside. He leant upon his gun and waited.

But he was not forgotten long.

"Gentlemen," said Stanley, " let me introduce you to my friend, brother, countryman, Midshipman MacDermott, o¹ her Majesty's cruiser *Tonitru*, usually called Mite for short. Mite, step forward here. Mite, behold my cousin, Tom Reynolds, a' the way fra Glaiska, my good friend English Bill, another importation from the city of merchant princes, and Cooke, whom you've seen before."

Then there was more handshaking, and a good deal of laughing, and together they all started off again through the woods. They had not gone far, however, when they came to a wide clearing, in the centre of which stood two tents, a big and a small, and not far off several others still smaller.

A tall, handsomely-dressed Arab, armed to the teeth, and glittering with gold and jewellery, stepped forward, and pressing both palms to his brow, bowed gracefully before Stanley and Mite.

They returned the salute.

"Dinner is all ready," said Soolieman, for that was this Arab warrior's name—" all ready, Sahib."

"Then, my good Soolieman," said Stanley, " lead the way, for the plain truth is I'm so hungry I think I could eat a horse."

"Well," said Mite, " I myself could manage a good-sized Shetland pony."

"Well done," cried Tom Reynolds—"well done, Mr. MacDermott! Ye're just as clever as my cousin Stanley, if no' a deal cleverer."

Mite stopped short.

"Look here," said Mite.

"Everybody *is* looking there," said Stanley. " What have you got to say that you stop the procession, and everybody dying of hunger?"

"Your cousin called me ' Mr. MacDermott,' " said Mite, pretending to be dreadfully serious; "now I'm not going to stand it, Stan. What I say is this—we ought to begin as we mean to go on. I may as well be ' Mite' at once; it'll come to it, you know."

"That's right," said Big Bill—"that's fair and manly. We're all in one boat."

"Well, then," Stanley said, "let everybody call out his own name. I'm Stan."

"Bill."

"Tom."

"Alf."

"Mite."

"Sool."

"Sambo."

"Brown."

"Ha! ha!" laughed Sambo. "I is de only chile among you dat has two syllabubs to his name. Yah! yah!"

The boy Brown—the Somali Indian or Bosjesman whom we first met on board the slave dhow *Seyd Pasha*—was dressed in white from top to toe; on his feet he wore sandals, and round his brow a turban. This was to distinguish him in some degree from the other so-called "boys" of this memorable expedition, for Brown was, indeed, an important factor. He was to guide them far inland to the country where poor Ida and her father were kept prisoners.

Once inside the tent, both Stanley and Mite opened their eyes in wonder and delight, for neither of them could have believed that it was possible to arrange such a feast in the wilderness.

The tent was conveniently large, but had it been twice the size the lamps that depended from the top would have furnished ample light. It was lined all round with crimson silk. The floor was spread with a carpet; in the centre rose a table about fifteen inches high, and around it cushions were placed as seats. The cloth was white as the driven snow; glasses and silver sparkled thereon like jewels rich and rare; in the centre rose an *épergne* filled with the most lovely flowers that eye ever dwelt on, and ferns that seemed to have been culled in elfin-land, so graceful and beautiful were they.

Sool stood for a moment with a pleased smile on his face, evidently enjoying the bewilderment and admiration displayed on the faces of the new arrivals. Then,

"Pray be seated, gentlemen," said Sool.

"What a capital caterer your are, Sool," Stanley remarked more than once that evening, and no wonder, for he had expected no such fare as this. It was not a dinner, it was a banquet fit for a prince of Ind. Stanley had never dreamed of such luxury, never read of anything to resemble his surroundings out of the Arabian Nights Entertainments.

"Sool," he said at last, " do you mean to keep this sort of thing up ? "

"I do fear me much we cannot do that, sahib. It is the custom with us Arabs to live well while we can, but not to grumble too much when Kismet changes our bed and diet. Allah is great. We are thankful."

After dinner an adjournment was made to the woods to sit and talk until Sool should prepare the tent for the night.

"Now you know, Stan," said Tom Reynolds, "I want to hear some o' your history from your ain mouth. I've got a' your letters by heart, man. Tell us, then, what you've been doin' for the last twa lang years."

"Well," replied Stanley, " I will gladly enough do that, but though it is very pleasant out here in the starlight, and very cool and nice, still I like to see people's faces when I speak to them. Suppose we wait a little till Sool summons us to coffee."

"Ay, you're right there," said Tom ; " we'd better bide a wee."

They had not long to wait. Sool's white-draped figure

soon advanced from the entrance of the tent to tell them their couches were prepared.

And, indeed, during the short time they had remained "out of doors," as Tom called it—for Tom was but little used to camp life—Sool had transformed the tent in which they had dined so sumptuously and well into a splendid sleeping saloon. In a semi-circle round one end of it were hung hammocks of netted grass for Stanley and his friends, each hammock occupying a little cabin of its own, so far as a cabin could be composed of curtains. These last were composed of crimson silk lined with blue, and gracefully looped up so that the interior of each little bedroom was visible, the cool white sheets in the hammock seeming to invite to repose.

No wonder that Tom Reynolds opened his eyes in astonishment when he saw the preparations that had been made for their comfort.

"Pshaw!" he cried; "this is grand, this is wonderful. It beats the best hotel in the whole great city o' Glaiska. I couldna have believed that such bountiful livin' or such splendid couches could have been prepared in the wilderness. Man, Stanley, that lang nigger Sool must be a vera clever kind o' a chiel."

Stanley and Mite laughed, and so did Cooke.

"You'd better not let him hear you calling him a nigger," said Stanley; "perhaps he wouldn't like it. Sool is a gentleman Arab."

"And I beg the gentleman Arab's pardon wi' a' my heart and a big lump o' my liver," exclaimed Tom. "I wadna offend the poor chiel for anything. He has a soul as well as you or me, Stan, though I fear it is a sadly benighted one."

"You were asking me about what I have been doing for the last two years. They have been weary years to me; Mite here knows this." It was Stanley who was speaking now. "And there is some one else knows it too; Sambo come in, Sambo. Don't be shy."

"This good fellow, Tom—and I'm speaking to you too, Bill—saved my life and Mite's to begin with."

"Dat is nuffin, massa," said Sambo, "nuffin at all. You save poor Sambo's life once, young sah, far away in dear ole Virginny. Sambo not forget dat."

"Our very first thought when we were free was how best we could succour and deliver our friends in captivity. To set up an expedition at once was, alas! beyond my power and means. We had no money. All representations of the matter to the British Resident in Zanzibar failed. Even the proof that both Captain Ross and his daughter were captives was not enough to get the assistance I required. . It was not deemed satisfactory, and, even had it been, neither poor Ida nor her father was an English subject. That would have made no difference could I have gained a hearing from my countrymen in England, but official red-tapeism prevented that. Then I wrote to uncle, and six months afterwards he received my letter. How it had not been delivered sooner I cannot tell. I know now that money was sent out by him, but till lately it had not reached me, and except for the kindness of you, Cooke, I should not have it now.

"But, Tom," continued Stanley, "Sambo and I determined to penetrate all by ourselves and one or two followers into the interior of Africa. The boy Brown was our guide. Of our dangers and our sufferings I will say nothing. I am glad, however, we undertook the journey, perilous and terrible in many respects though it was. We succeeded in communicating with the captives, we have given them hope, and now with Heaven's blessing we will set them free."

"And," said Tom, "the savages really kept you prisoner in that terrible country, so well named the Dark Continent, for a whole year? Eh! man, but that must have been dreadful!"

"Yes, it was certainly not agreeable," answered Stanley; "but there is good in everything, for during that time I managed, by means of our Somali guide-boy, to write and receive letters from our friends, and but for this I never would have known that the runaway son of that strange wild woman whom I met on the moor when a little boy just leaving home was also a prisoner along with Captain Ross and Ida."

"Ay, ay!" exclaimed Tom, eagerly, "that was strange—wonderful! but, don't you see, my boy Stanley, how Providence turns things round for good ? For as soon as I went to see poor daft Jean—oh! you should have seen her, Stanley!—'My lost laddie found!' she cried; 'tell me—tell me again! This is a joyful day for poor daft Jean. My lang lost laddie, that I've mourned for through a' these dreary years!' Then, Stanley, the poor creature fairly broke down and wept like a bairn. It nearly made me cry just to see her. Well, cousin, I wrote and told you about the gold Jean had found in the *cirde* house. How long it had been there no one can tell. It was treasure-trove, but after the Queen had her share there was enough and to spare, not only to pay for this expedition, but to keep daft Jean—but, oh! she is daft no langer, Stan—and her son, if ever we see him, comfortable, as long as it pleases Heaven to spare them."

"But what I cannot get over," said Stanley, laughing, "is your coming out, and honest Bill here, though I could understand his venturing abroad. It isn't the first time. But, Tom Reynolds, a stay-at-home like you!—a quiet citizen of Glasgow! Why, it puts me in mind of——"

"Of what, cousin ?" asked Tom.

"Why," replied Stanley, "of the Glasgow bailie venturing to trust himself among the wild Rob Roy Highlanders."

XIX.

EN ROUTE FOR THE WILDERNESS—"BUMPING" OVER THE BAR—LAMOO.

CHAPTER XIX.

LONG before the first glimmer of light appeared in the
eastern horizon, while the stars still shone as
brightly as they had done at midnight, ere ever there was a
twitter of birds among the branches or rustle of monitor
among the dead leaves, Stanley had stolen silently from his
couch and quietly left the tent. At so early an hour no
one, he thought, would likely be astir. No one was awake
in the tent, as the silence, broken only by the measured
sound of the breathing, soon convinced him. Just within
the tent, and not far from the doorway, each on his mat of
grass-cloth, lay Sambo and Brown, while outside pacing
backwards and forwards were the two armed Arab sentries.
Little need for these in the peaceful woods of Zanzibar.
By-and-bye there would be, however, and as he passed them
and returned their salute, Stanley mentally thanked Sool
for being so careful, even before the expedition had actually
commenced.

Where, he wondered, did Sool sleep ? His little tent was
empty, and he was nowhere visible ; indeed, with the
exception of the sentinels, the whole camp seemed wrapped
in slumber. Fires of wood here and there in the clearing
still gave a fitful kind of light, as their dying embers flickered
and glared in the changeful breeze. Many a dusky form lay
near these smouldering fires, for warmth it could not be,
but the smoke and sparks, that ever and anon formed a

kind of cascade over their bodies, must have kept mosquitoes and insects of every kind well at bay.

Stanley moved onwards into the forest, taking the little path that led citywards. When far enough away from camp to feel entirely alone, he seated himself on a fallen tree, and gave himself up to meditation and thought. He seemed to take a review of his whole past life from his earliest boyhood up till now. How filled with strange and stirring events it had been; how very old he felt as he thought of them all, though even now he was barely twenty-three! Young in years it is true, but old in strange experiences. What a long, long time it seemed since he used to sit with his little sister away up in leafland, in the summer days in the forest of Cairntrie. "Dear sister," he said to himself, "she is quite a little woman now, though always a child to me. And my poor, pale-faced, gentle, loving mother—ah! how precious those tears she shed when she bade me good-bye last! How she would have wished me then to stay at home, but how well she knew that it was for my good to go! Her prayers have saved me from death —and such a death! How anxious my dear old uncle will be to hear of my success! 'Bring back with you,' he says, 'my good old friend Ross and his daughter, and all I have is yours even before I'm laid under the daisies.'"

When Stanley Grahame's thoughts reverted to Ida his heart gave a great jump with delight, it seemed to thud against his ribs with very joy.

"Yes," he cried, half aloud, "I will save you, Ida; I'll bring you out from the terrible slavery you are undergoing, in the darkest corner of that dark land. With Heaven's good help, I will, or perish in the trying. Poor Ida! the thoughts of my base ingratitude to my little child-nurse, and the cruel words I spoke to you that last sad day at Beaumont Park, have haunted me ever since, and will continue to haunt me until I hear from your own lips that you have forgiven me. Ha! there is the light of the coming

"HE KNELT DOWN BESIDE THE FALLEN TREE."

morning over the mainland. It will soon be day. I'm all alone here—I'll—pray."

He knelt him down beside the fallen tree, and hiding his face in his hands, humbly thanked the Father for all His goodness to him in his past life, earnestly sought His help and blessing on the work he had undertaken, and ended his own supplications with that beautiful prayer that was dictated by Him who spoke as never man spake. He did not merely repeat that prayer—he prayed it every word and every sentence of it, bowing low but hopefully at those grand words which many a Christian finds so hard to utter, " Thy—will—be—done."

When he got up from his knees, Stanley felt every inch a man ; he was ready now for whatever might happen, for whatever might be before him, and he even glanced impatiently eastwards as if longing for the sun to rise. It was dark still, however, but there was light enough to perceive a tall figure draped in white coming gliding towards him, not from the direction of the camp, but from the deepest part of the forest.

" Who goes there ?" cried Stanley.

" Sool," was the reply.

Next moment they stood hand in hand.

Hand in hand under the stars, hand in hand and face to face, stood these two brave men. Sool had a bit of carpet over his right arm, and Stanley knew that he had been down into the quiet still woods to pray. They both worshipped at the same throne, both adored the same great Father ; both had been praying to Him, though in different languages and words.

" Soolieman," said Stanley, " something tells me we are going to be successful."

" Stanley Grahame, Allah is good and great. Allah tells you."

They pressed each other's hands just for one brief

second; in that stern clasp heart spoke to heart.   Words were useless.

"Sit down now," said Stanley.   "We have still a few minutes to talk before sunrise, and we are alone.   I need hardly ask you now if everything is ready."

"Everything is here," said Sool; "nothing has been forgotten.   That, sahib, was my reason for camping here one night before we start for the mainland—to see that we were all ready, quite prepared."

"And the boys, Sool ? "

"Brave, good.   I have brought them all from Lamoo. The vile fire-water of Zanzibar has never warmed their lips.   They are true, I have tried them.   They know chief Soolieman."

He smiled sternly as he spoke.

"And the boats and ammunition, and merchandise or presents ? "

"All ready, sahib, as by-and-bye you will see.   Boats have been put together, and are now packed.   Not a bolt or rivet is wanting, not a rope, not an oar that we have not got a duplicate of.   Every spear is ready, every gun, and the merchandise and presents ready for carriage."

"Thanks, good Sool.   Then after breakfast if the dhow is ready we will start."

"The dhow is all ready at anchor.   We can embark in one hour.   Now, sahib, of your own people what shall I say ? what shall I ask ? "

"Whatever you like, Sool; I shall not be offended."

"I have been with you, Sahib Stanley, in the desert and wilderness ; Sahib Mite is a British officer ; Sahib Cooke is a sailor ; that is enough.   Bill, as you name him, is strong and brave-looking ; he will do.   But is Tom a warrior, a soldier of your nation ? "

Stanley laughed.

"There isn't much of the warrior about poor Tom my

cousin," he said, "though he has some of the blood of the fighting clan Mackinlays in his veins. Suppose, my dear chief, we make him superintendent of the stores, as you seem doubtful about his abilities as a traveller, warrior, and sportsman."

"Good," said Sool, "now I am pleased. Now I go to prepare breakfast. Look, the sun comes."

It was true. The glorious sun had already risen, and his red disc gleamed through the branches of the cocoa-palms as if his beams had set them all on fire.

About five minutes after this Tom Reynolds rushed scared and breathless out of the tent into the clearing with his night-dress fluttering about him, for Stanley had commenced to play a solo on the gong. Low at first, with muttered growls and moans, he finally made it roar and bang, till there wasn't a bird in the woods within half a mile that didn't fly shrieking away at the terrible sound.

"Man! how ye scared me!" cried poor Tom. "I thought a' the wild lions and the untamable hyænas in the forest 'o Zanzibar had attacked the tent, and were tearing everybody limb frae limb."

"Bravo, Tom!" said Stanley, "but there isn't a single lion nor a hyæna either within a hundred miles of you. Now, off you go, lad. I'm glad I've waked you, anyhow; but the dress you're now showing off in is hardly sufficient even for this climate, Tom."

"Ma conscience!" exclaimed Tom, "till this vera minute I hadn't a notion I was standing here half naked."

And away he flew, and in a short time after out came Cooke and Mite and Big Bill, dressed, and ready for breakfast, and, as Stanley assured them, looking as fresh as April daisies.

Immediately after breakfast a grand review of stores was held, and the whole equipment thoroughly overhauled and carefully examined. Stanley then assembled his "boys." Nearly a hundred of them all told there were, counting carriers and spearmen. He also did what was a most unusual thing for Stanley—he made a speech. He spoke in the Somali language, which was Greek, and worse than Greek, to his own countrymen. He was glad to see, he said, that every one of them looked so brave and willing to work. Each one most have the success of the expedition at heart. Once landed on the mainland, there must be no going back until they had accomplished the end they had in view. It was unlikely that they would all return. The dangers they had to encounter were many and varied, but they were the same to all—to the white as well as to the dark-skinned among them. And who feared death? His white companions did not, and he could see by their countenances that they (the Somalis) despised all danger. He noticed that the boys were divided into two sections, carriers and spearmen, but this must be more a distinction than a difference. They must hang together, and each man help his neighbour. Those that returned to Zanzibar would have riches enough to buy clothes and canoes, and live in happiness all their lives to come.

Not much of a speech this, but it was delivered with a manly straightforwardness that appealed to the very hearts of those savages. Some grasped and shook their spears, others clutched and shouldered their burdens, and one and all evinced a wish to be off without further delay.

So the march beachwards was begun.

Three hours afterwards the dhow that contained the expedition was heading away northwards, the green islands around Zanzibar disappearing on the southern horizon, and the mainland showing as a mere hazy cloudland miles away on their weather quarter.

The captain of the dhow was a tall, wiry Arab, about as different from an Englishman's *beau-ideal* of a sailor as any one could well be, but he knew these seas well, and every shoal and landmark; and he knew, too, how to take the advantage of every breath of wind that blew. Sometimes he crept so close in shore that the leaves could be counted on the mangrove-trees that fringed the beach, and at other times he lay well off. Such navigation quite astonished even Cooke, but nevertheless just three days after leaving Zanzibar they found themselves outside the bar of Lamoo river, and, with sails well filled, steering straight to what seemed to the white men on board almost certain destruction. There were long lines of dark, threatening breakers, so high that, as the dhow neared them, they quite hid the shores at each side of the river from the view of those on deck. How silently and insidiously those breakers crept up out of their ocean bed, like long, slimy monsters of the deep; how they gathered strength and size as they rolled swiftly onwards towards the bar; how terrible they seemed in their might as their perpendicular sides were raised on high, their sharp crests curling in anger for a moment ere the whole body of each awful wave broke into foam, and went rushing onwards with a noise like muttered thunder! On that bar was a gateway of deep water, narrow enough in all conscience; but the captain of the dhow must steer for it, and go in on the top of the highest wave or be dashed in pieces. Well he knows his duty. Look! the sturdy vessel is among the breakers, destruction seems inevitable. She is shot along with the speed of an arrow, but the wave that carries her so far recedes, and she strikes the bottom. Not a man on deck that is not thrown off his feet. Again and again she strikes, and it seems certain she will go to pieces, when suddenly a bigger wave than all the others catches her under the stern, and hurries her along with a speed that makes every one sick and dizzy. The water breaks on board. For a few moments the dhow is tossed like a cork in the midst of a mass of seething foam. She reels from side to side, as if trying to shake herself clear of the blinding surf, the sails fill again, and next moment she is borne into the still and placid waters beyond.

I think I am right in saying that Tom Reynolds kept his

eyes fast closed all the time the vessel was being forced over the bar; but now when he ventured to look back on that chaos of foam and those fearful walls of moving water, his teeth positively chattered, and his eyes were opened wider probably than ever they had been before in his life.

"Ma conscience!" said Tom, "the Fall o' Foyers * is nothing to that."

They were now in the centre of a broad, quiet river, with high banks, tree-clad, on every side. From the number of boats and canoes they met it was evident they were not far from a town or city of some importance.

In less than two hours the vessel was lying at anchor close to the city of Lamoo. Very much smaller in size than Zanzibar, with quainter and more romantic streets, and a population quite as mixed and quite as destitute of anything that a European would look upon as civilisation, Lamoo is but little known to travellers, but nevertheless it well repays a visit, and the sporting artist would, in the city itself and the country around, be able to make many a good bag and many a good picture. The palace of the sultan is by far and away the most imposing edifice in Lamoo. The sultan himself is by far and away the most imposing looking individual in Lamoo. Stanley thought so when that potentate did him the honour of visiting his encampment some four-and-twenty hours after his landing. Perhaps the splendour of the dress of this Arab sultan, and his large retinue of friends and soldier-guards, had a good deal to do with the imposing character of the visit.

The sultan deigned to squat in the great tent, deigned to soil his lips with a mango, and even to sip a little sherbet, smiling all the while upon Stanley and Mite in a manner that was meant to be quite impressive. Yes, the Sultan of Lamoo seemed pleased—without doubt he did; but if he had heard and understood a remark made behind his back by

* A celebrated Scottish cataract.

innocent Tom Reynolds, I question if he would have smiled quite so much..

"Man!" said Tom to his cousin, "what a grand-lookin' auld nigger! I couldna have believed there were such finely-dressed savages in a' the world!"

It was no part of Stanley's plan to stay for one hour longer than was necessary near this city of Lamoo. Indeed, had not Soolieman advised him otherwise, he would have commenced the march into the interior the very moment after landing.

"This would not do, sahib," said Sool, "the Lamoo boys would follow—one, two, perhaps three hundred of them. They would steal, then fight with our own boys."

So at midnight the camp was broken up, and the expedition commenced in reality. Sool led the van through the forest-path, striking away northwards and westwards until they reached a wide, elevated, arid plain, where not a shrub and scarcely a green thing grew. Across this, guided only by the stars, they took their way in silence. They had left the camp-fires burning so that their departure would not be discovered until daybreak, and they hoped to leave so little trail behind them, that it would be difficult if not impossible for any one to follow them.

This sudden departure from their camp made matters very awkward for one individual. We must return on board the dhow to find out who this was.

The captain of the vessel had business in Zanzibar that demanded his return to that city as soon as possible, so he determined to take advantage of the evening breeze that in these latitudes generally blows off the shore, and to slip away to sea soon after sunset. But long before this he began to get up anchor and go down stream. It was pretty dark down in the dhow's hold; it wouldn't have been a nice place in which to live for any length of time under any conditions, but to be cramped up for two days and two nights in an empty flour-cask, in the blackest nook of that hold, could not have been otherwise than irksome. The conclusion that boy Green arrived at just as the captain of the vessel was getting up anchor was that the sooner he got out of that barrel the better.

"I've done a lot o' stowawayin' in my time," he said to himself, as he crawled out of his hiding-place, "but that 'ere barrel 's been about the crampiest corner ever I got into. It's been plaguey hot, and precious dusty too, and the ship a colly-wobbling like mad! The cockroaches more'n lively, and nothing to eat all the while but this old ham-bone. It ain't half picked either. Hullo! why the ship's moving! I've no time to lose. If that 'ere nigger skipper in the long nightgown dares to——"

He ran on deck without finishing the sentence, with his ham-bone in his hand.

No wonder the captain started and looked frightened, when he saw emerging from the companion what looked like the ghost of a defunct British sailor, for boy Green was white with flour from his cap to his boots!

"Hullo!" roared boy Green, "stop the ship—stop her; ye cawn't go yet, I tell yer. The expedition ain't all on shore; the best 'arf of it is here. Stop her at once!"

When boy Green grasped the captain by the arm, the Arab knew it was no phantom, but a young wretch of a man-o'-war sailor, with an excessively horny fist, so he recovered his presence of mind and half drew his sword.

"How dare you touch me," cried the captain, "with your infidel fingers, you pig-eating unbeliever you?"

"Easy now, my friend," continued the boy Green; "easy, I tell yer. Who are ye calling names, I ax yer? There's a picking on this bone yet, or I'd make you better acquainted with the thick end of it. Now look 'ere, old Kafoozlum! *Do* you know who you're a-talkin' to? I puts the question to ye calmly and quietly, out o' pity for yer ignorance. Now *do* you know who I am, come?"

"Begone, sahib!" cried the Arab, losing all patience—

"begone, I tell you, out of my dhow. I know not nor care not who you are. I say begone, before I plunge my sword into your breast!"

Then that saucy boy Green put his ham-bone under his arm, in order that he might place both his hands un-trammelled into his breeches pockets, then he struck an attitude right in front of the Arab, with his legs very far apart, and with his eyes fixed on the captain's face, and positively whistled three or four bars of a bright air right at him, as it were, before he spoke. "I whistles," said the boy Green, "to show my hindicpendence, to prove to you that I ain't scared. Now answer me this, old Kafoozlum. Do ye 'appen to know what the penalty is for threatening a British officer? Course ye do; and ye daren't draw that cheese-knife o' yours for the world. Secondly, do ye know that I'm an English subject? Thirdly, did ye ever hear of a paper called the *Times?* No? Shows where you've been brought up! Now, then, 'pologise quick! then call away a boat and send me ashore. I don't mind dinin' with yer first, though. Eh, Kafoozles? Ha, ha!"

If the boy Green had not dug his thumb into the Arab's ribs by way of emphasising his words, matters might have ended differently. As it was, the fire seemed to flash from that captain's eye as the sword flew from its scabbard.

"Darest thou?" he shrieked.

I do not know where that boy Green's head would have been next moment but for that handy ham-bone—it came into collision with the Arab's skull with resounding force and rolled him into the lee scuppers.

Twenty spears were clutched in a moment; twenty men, spear-armed, rushed pell-mell at the boy Green. The boy Green hurled the ham-bone at the head of the foremost, and, springing aft, he cut the painter of the boat that was drifting astern and jumped into the sea.

The confusion on board was too great to allow the dhow's crew to do anything speedily and well, and boy Green had landed and kicked the boat adrift before the dhow could be stopped or rounded to.

Now if that boy Green had acted wisely he would have gone off at once and reported himself in camp by way of making the best of a bad job. But no ; he meant to enjoy himself for a little bit ; so, as soon as he got his clothes dry by tumbling on the sand and lying in the sun, he turned his face towards the town, hands in pockets, whistling as usual, and looking altogether as unconcerned as though he were merely taking a walk along Oxford Street instead of among a race of semi-savages, where no white man's life is worth an hour's purchase after sunset. The sun was not yet set, though, and would not be for an hour, and that hour boy Green seemed bent on making the best of.

"Now," said boy Green to himself, "the werry first thing to be done is to try to get summut for the inner man. I'se precious hungry, I is. What a pity I parted company wi' that 'am-bone ! There was a good pickin' on it, too. And it was quite thrown away on those niggers. Yes, I'se hungry, I grant ye; but then I'se free ! What a fine thing it is to be free ! Nobody to scold ye, nobody to say, ' Silence when ye speak to an officer !' nobody to tell ye to go and get yer 'air cut. Yes, freedom is a fine thing ! 'Ullo ! 'ere comes 'arf a dozen little nigger boys and girls. I'll get behind a tree. Won't I scare 'em just ?"

*BOY GREEN BEARDS THE LION IN HIS DEN,
AND ENDS BY MAKING A DISCOVERY.*

CHAPTER XX.

"WHY, there is seven on them," said boy Green, lying close behind the bush. "Won't I scare 'em just? Guess they never saw a white man afore.

"Yah! young niggers," he screamed, rushing and extending both arms skywards. "Yah! yah! does yer mother know you're out? Go and get your hair cut. Yah! yah!"

Seven little niggers shrieking at the top of their seven little voices, boy Green shrieking louder than the lot of them. Seven little niggers flying along the dusty road, boy Green in chase of the seven of them. Fine fun for boy Green, but those seven poor little nigger children had their seven little hearts in their seven little mouths, as they fled along in front of their terrible white pursuer. Those little niggers seemed all legs and arms, eyes and mouths, with no bodies at all to speak of. They took to the woods, so did boy Green, and the seven little niggers never stopped running until safe in their little village of bamboo huts beneath the shade of the plantains. There parrots and monkeys joined the chorus, and cocks and hens lent their cacklings to increase the terrible hullabaloo. But tall black savages rushed forth from the tents armed with long spears, and shields made from the hides of buffalo humps, and prepared to give boy Green a warmer reception than ever he had had in his life before, or than ever he was likely to have again, for there was a glitter in those men's eyes that meant mischief.

It suddenly occurred to boy Green that he had carried his joke just a little too far. Only he was not quite such a fool as to run away, although at that moment he would have given the teeth out of his head to be back once more in the flour-barrel on board the dhow, with no more terrible companions than cockroaches, and picking away at that old ham-bone. If he ran he knew those spears would fly after him thick and fast, and then—! Why, then boy Green would drop out of this story, they would bury him in the sand, and grow curry over him. Boy Green forced a laugh. Boy Green knew what he was about; he laughed and laughed and roared and laughed. He knew those savages wouldn't kill him so long as he laughed, and at long last every one of them was obliged to laugh too, and the little ones all came back, and they laughed, and such a chorus of laughing was probably never before heard in the suburbs of Lamoo. Finally all the little nigger boys and girls, and all those spear-armed men, joined hands and danced and yelled around the boy Green.*

Well, boy Green had gained a point : he had saved his life, but he knew he must also effect his escape. He did it very adroitly. He took out a handful of copper pice, and showed them and shook them, still laughing as if it were the best joke in the world. Then he pointed at the fowls, then away seawards to an imaginary ship, then he shook the pice again, and grinned from ear to ear, for boy Green's mouth was not a small one. Alas for those unhappy hens! round and round the huts they fled before their pursuers, and boy Green was fain now to laugh in earnest. In less than five minutes fifteen hens lay dead at boy Green's feet. Then boy Green counted out fifteen pice (halfpennies) and handed them over.

"Ye can keep the change," said boy Green. "I ain't a hard one to drive a bargain.

* Ridiculous though this scene may appear to my readers, everything actually occurred as described. The boy Green is himself a sketch from the life.

"And now," said the urchin to himself, "there's nuffin beats cheek. I must do summut to make these niggers respect me."

So he went whistling around till he found a piece of bamboo rope. With this he deftly tied the dead fowls all in a bunch. Then he singled out the biggest savage in the crowd, an immense ogre-looking, pock-pitted, one-eyed fellow, and pitching the rope over his neck, coolly deprived him, gently but firmly, of his spear and shield.

"Ye don't want this toothpick," he said, "nor this old pot-lid either. Carry these fowls, and I'll give ye another coin. Another sixpence!" shouted boy Green in the fellow's ear, as if shouting would make him understand. But lo! that savage was cowed by this impudent boy, and looked as like an overgrown baby as it is possible for a savage to look. So, boy Green leading the way singing, the fellow with the string of fowls following, and the other natives bringing up the rear, they left the forest and got back to the road.

As boy Green neared the town, or city, the crowd about him got larger, and by the time he found himself in the streets it probably numbered many hundreds. But boy Green was now in what he considered fine form, and although the beings that surrounded him were about as motley and dangerous-looking as savages well could be, he was nothing daunted. If his feelings were to be analysed, perhaps, down at the very bottom of his heart, a little doubt might have been found lurking, that he was not quite safe from the danger of having his ears cut off and handed round, or his nose slit open; but he knew, at all events, that there was no good showing fear. And when he caught another gigantic Indian and mounted on his shoulders and waved his cap, and once more intimated that there was not the remotest chance of Britons ever becoming slaves, he completely subdued and captivated his hearers. To be sure, they did not understand a word he said, but that was nothing ; they yelled and shouted and waved their spears just the same, and boy Green began to think that he was a very big gun indeed. About the same time he became sensible of something else—namely, that he was getting exceedingly hungry.

"I could eat most anything," he said to himself; "but there don't seem to be nuffin to eat, which is ill-convenient. There don't seem to be no Spiers and Pond about nowheres, nor no eatin'-houses o' no sorts. I guess these white-eyed niggers eat each other when they feels a bit peckish. I feels now as how I could eat one 'o them fowls raw. Hullo, though ! where are the fowls ? The big fellow's bolted, I do declare ! And there isn't a perlice officer to be had, and ne'er a beak to take the prisoner afore if there was. Well, never mind, I didn't want the fowls. They saved my life, though. Paid fifteen pice for 'em—sevenpence-halfpenny ! Fool I was, to be sure, when fippence would have done ! 'Ullo ! what's that ? I never felt such a delicious smell in my life before !" .

The boy Green stopped the nigger he rode on and began to roll his head—his own head, not the nigger's—round and round in the air, the better to inhale the delicious perfume. " Wherever is it coming from, I wonder ? From that balcony, eh ? "—sniff, sniff, sniff—" yes, I'm sure it is "—sniff, sniff—" and it's curry, too ! Oh, I'm so fond of curry !"

As he spoke he unceremoniously wheeled his " niggerhorse," as he called the savage he rode, round by the ear till he faced the house. Then he stood right up on his shoulder till he could see in over the balcony, whence the smell of the curry emanated. There he beheld a beautiful room, furnished Arab fashion, apparently all curtains and crystal, rich mattings on the floor, rich lounges around it, and a punkah depending from the roof, kept in motion by invisible hands, to cool the apartment. But what riveted boy Green's attention most was the low table in the centre, on which, amid coloured glasses and vases and flowers, stood a banquet so inviting, so delicious to eye and nose, that this cheeky boy at once concluded he must have got into very good quarters indeed.

"Ho, ho!" he said; "all ready, is it? Guests hain't arrived yet. Well, here comes number one. As for you, old nigger-horse, I don't want yer services any longer, so go!"

Boy Green had got clear hold of the balcony now, and just as he did so he lifted one leg and administered to his horse a kick that sent him sprawling on his back.

"Good-bye, ye beauties!" he said, addressing the yelling but laughing mob from his coign of vantage. "I adwises ye all to go quietly 'ome for fear of the sun spilin' yer complexions! Good-bye; 'member me to the old people. I'se going to dine in here. Bye-bye!" and, kissing his hand to the spear-armed savages, boy Green gracefully retired to what he called "the privacy of his 'partment."

"Scrumptious!" he exclaimed, eyeing the table over. "First course fish; second, curried rats or summut and rice; third course, curried something else and more rice. Fixings: yams and sweet potatoes, all 'ot. Dessert: pine-apples and guavas. Vy, I do declare they must have been hexpecting of me. Hullo! who have we here?"

As he spoke he pulled out of a corner an exceedingly small and excessively black little naked nigger boy. He held this frightened, round-eyed urchin aloft—he did not weigh apparently more than an ordinary-sized Patagonian rabbit.

"Ho, ho!" said the boy Green, replacing him again in his corner. "Yer a keepin' of the punkah moving, are ye? Well, do yer duty and ye won't be touched. I likes a good little boy, but I eats bad 'uns!"

After making a face or two that would have made the unhappy little nigger boy get inside his boots with fright if he had had any boots on, our young sailor settled himself down at the table and applied himself vigorously to the operation of making a hearty meal.

" That fish," he said to himself, but speaking aloud, " is truly excellent. The dash of garlic in the melted butter is perfection saucified. Another slice, Mr. Green ? Thanks, I think I will. Try that sherbet, Mr. Green; it is iced, and I'm sure you are rather tired after your long ride. Well, I do feel a little tired, just a leetle. Yes, the flavour of this sherbet surpasses anything ever I tasted before; forgive me if I seem to make too free with it. Make yourself quite at home, Mr. Green. Help yourself to a little more curry. Thanks, I guess I will, but I mustn't forget to leave a place for some 'o those guavas, and maybe about a half o' one o' them pineapples. Good health, Mr. Green. Glad to make your acquaintance. Same to you, and many o' them."

" Well, I do declare," said a rough voice close behind him and in good plain English. " I've seen cheek and impudence before in many ways in my time, but this beats everything."

Before boy Green had time to reply he was seized by the back of the neck with a fist that gripped him like an iron vice, and held fast.

" What do you think of yourself, eh ? " said the voice.

" I'll tell you what I think o' you in a minute, old cockalorum, if ye don't quit a hold o' my neck. What do you mean, eh ? D'ye know that excitement spiles digestion, and I ain't half done dinner yet ? There now, ye don't know who ye have the honour o' hentertainin', else you'd be down on yer knees and beggin' for your life in a minute."

" Ha ! ha ! ha ! " roared the voice, letting go his hold and permitting boy Green to look round.

There stood a tall, brown-bearded, red-faced Arab, in gilded turban, cloak of camel's hair, with jewelled sword-belt, scabbard, and pistols.

" There's nothing like cheek, when it's well carried out," said this burly Arab.

" Them's my sentiments to a T," cried boy Green

"Shake hands, old chap. Now I don't mind ye sittin' down free-and-easy like and having a bit o' dinner with me. You'll find that curry really excellent. I'm afraid the fish is cold, though."

"How did you get in here?" said the Arab.

"By the window," said boy Green, with his mouth full; "how did yerself?"

"D'ye know," said the Arab, "I've half a mind even now to cut your head off?"

"Better that," replied boy Green, "than if you had a whole mind to cut the half o' my head off. But sit down, don't stand on ceremony. 'Ow is the old lady, eh?"

Very simple words these last, and impudent enough the inquiry. Boy Green did not mind that a bit. But he was very much surprised indeed to witness the effect they had upon the stalwart form that stood before him.

"Boy," he gasped, "is it possible you know me?"

"Never clapped eyes on yer in my life afore," was boy Green's reply, "but ye don't seem 'arf a bad sort."

"Then, why that allusion to—to my mother?"

"Just to be friendly like. Dessay she's a wery deservin old creachure as far as mothers go. Sit down. Ye're a fidgetin' o' me. I likes peas with my meals, as the pigeon said. Ye looks to me like a Forty-second Highlander that had swapped togs with a scare-the-crow. Sit down; curry's cold."

"What's your name?" said the tall stranger.

"Boy Green. What's yourn?"

"Archibald Weir!"

"Whew—ew—ew!" whistled boy Green, starting up from the table and looking at the figure before him. "Whew! Vy, sir, you're one of the customers as the hexpedition was got up to go to the relief o'. You're a slave, you are—or ye ought to be—somewheres in the 'terior of Afriker. Ye ought to be there now, I tell ye, and it ain't fair to the hexpiedition that ye ain't. Ye sees before ye, sir, the medical officer in charge o' that hexpiedition. Dr. Green, sir, at your service."

"You're a bright youth," replied Weir, "a bright youth indeed."

Then he threw himself on a lounge, and for a time seemed lost in thought.

This was a shining hour for boy Green, and he duly improved it by renewing his attack on the viands before him.

"When did this expedition start?" asked Weir.

"This morning."

"Ha! and from here?"

"Yes."

'I've been hunting, and so missed seeing them."

'Have you now?" said that cheeky boy. "Hope ye shot summut for breakfast to-morrow. But I say, suppose ye order lights. Carn't ye see it's gettin' dark? I can hardly find the way to my mouth. I'll sleep here to-night if ye can make me pretty comfortable, and join the hexpiedition to-morrow—arter breakfast, in course. Probably I shall pay a visit to the sultan before I start. D'ye think he'd be glad to see me?"

"I think," said Weir, "it is very probable you'll come back with your head under your arm."

"Well then, I'll think it over first," said boy Green.

"You'd better," said Weir, smiling grimly. "Make your self at home here to-night, anyhow."

"Boy," said Weir, after a pause. "have you a mother?"

"Not much," said boy Green.

"Ah, lad!" continued Weir, speaking more to himself, as it were, than to his uninvited guest, "I had; and my prayers for many and many a long year have been that I may return once more to my own country and get her blessing ere she closes her dear eyes in death. How she loved me, lad! But how ill I requited her for all the love she bore me. I scorned her, I fled, I fear I broke her heart.

I heard since then only once about her. They told me she had gone mad, that she lived all by herself on a wild moor in Scotland, that her little house was haunted, and she herself known but to be feared in all the country round. But she taught me when a boy to pray ; and in my manhood, in my bondage, a slave to savages in this dark continent, with tears in my eyes and wildest grief in my heart, I turned to Him at last and He has set me free."

"Well," said boy Green, "I'm glad to see ye. And if it's any comfort for ye to know, your mother is still alive : I know that for certain."

"Comfort ? " cried Weir, seizing boy Green by the hand. "God's blessing on you, my lad; you have made me the happiest man in the world."

It occurred to the boy Green next morning to go alone to the encampment of the expedition ; he wanted to make his peace, and if he went with good news he rightly judged this would not be difficult to do.

He found the fires still smouldering, and a hungry crowd of Somali savages around them, picking up whatever they could find, but his people were gone. So boy Green made the best of his way back to the house where he had found poor daft Jean's son.

"It's a kind o' wexing," he said to himself, "but it's one o' those things as can't be helped."

As he mused thus he was passing the palace of the sultan, and a thought struck this bold boy Green, which he proceeded forthwith to put into action. He marched straight up the steps and confronted the officer on duty.

"Good morning," said boy Green. "You don't know me. But don't apologise. I've come to see your master, the sultan, on most important business; I ain't got my card-case, but that don't signify. Give the sultan that."

He presented the officer with an old envelope as he spoke.

"See sultan ? You ? " said the gaily-dressed official, whose English was of the meagrest.

"Certainly," said boy Green. "An' you look bright about it too, and maybe I'll say a word in your favour."

"Sultan sleep," said the officer, "no can see you."

"What!" cried boy Green, drawing himself up. "Not see me. Sir, I'm Dr. Green, of her British Majesty's service. If you don't go at once and deliver my message, the Queen might send a ship and blow this old barn about your ears. Now then, will you go?"

There is no saying how matters would have ended, had the sultan and his retinue at that moment not happened to have come forth. Seeing a sailor in English uniform he at once ordered him to be brought before him, and proceeded to question him.

Not a bit abashed, boy Green told his highness that he desired private audience of him. Behold that cheeky youngster then, fifteen minutes after this date, squatted on a scarlet cushion in the presence of royalty, and eating mangoes with the air of a prince. The sultan and two of his intimate friends were listening amusedly by means of the interpreter to the boy's discourse, and he certainly did not neglect to enlarge on the subject of the greatness of the British Empire, or rather of that happy combination the British Empire *plus* boy Green, and from all he said—if the sultan believed him—he must have concluded that the British Empire was nothing at all without boy Green, and that it would speedily go to wreck and ruin if boy Green ceased to exist.

After about an hour of this pleasant confab,

"Well, sir," said the sultan, "there is one remark I must make."

"Out vith it, sultan," said boy Green, "you're an older man than me, but never be shy."

"I was going to say," said the sultan, smiling, "that you blow your own trumpet very well."

"'Cause vy?" replied boy Green, when the sultan's

words were interpreted to him—"'cause vy? Who vould blow the boy Green's trumpet if he didn't blow it his little self? It strikes me, sir, that that is the correct way of lookin' at the matter."

"Well, you have amused us so much," said the sultan, "that we really cannot refuse you the escort you ask for. Twenty of our very best soldiers shall therefore conduct you to your people."

Boy Green jumped up. "I ain't usually impulsive," he said, "and you'll 'skuse me for shaking 'ands with you. But, Mr. Sultan, you are a brick, sir, and nuffin else; and you're about to confer a favour not on boy Green only, not on the Queen of England only, but, sir, on the whole boundless British Empire! And I takes leave o' ye, sultan, with the tenderest feelings o' gratitude in my buzzom, and I'm sure ye won't mind me takin' a few of these 'ere mangoes in my pocket, will yer?"

*   *   *   *   *   *

It is time for us now to follow the footsteps of Stanley Grahame and his party.

Soolieman was a good traveller. He determined not to be followed, and he hardly left trail enough behind him for an Apache Indian to puzzle out. For two or three days he led the expedition over an arid desert, where hardly a green thing grew—where, saving the tents, there was no shelter from the burning midday sun. They then struck the river; the boats were put together, and they embarked. If the desert told no tale, the river would be doubly silent as to their route, and unless some wandering savage met them and bore the news to boy Green, Archie Weir, and the soldiers the sultan had lent them, there was a likelihood of their never being followed up at all.

Three days on the river, then they landed again and marched more directly into the interior. And so for days and days they journeyed on, and ever as they went the scenery grew wilder and more romantic, and the dangers they had to encounter greater and greater ; for now by night sentries had to redouble their vigilance, for howl of hyæna, bark of jackal, and the deep and terrible bass of the lion's roar resounded from forest or jungle and mingled fearfully with the dreams of the sleepers in the tent.

XXI.

*CAMP LIFE—A NIGHT ADVENTURE—THE DISMAL
SWAMP—ATTACKED BY CROCODILES.*

CHAPTER XXI.

"THE weather keeps up, doesn't it?" said Tom Reynolds one day as they were all sitting down to dinner in the splendid marquee.

"You dear, droll old Cousin Tom!" said Stanley, laughing. "Why, of course it does, and I shouldn't wonder if it would be another hot day to-morrow."

"Why," cried Mite, who was in fine form, "Tom thinks he ought to have it showery one day and misty the next—the same as it is in Glaiska!"

"Ah!" said Cooke, joining the laugh at Tom's expense, "in Glaiska the weather is sold retail in small packets, duly assorted—just enough to last for a day. But here in the tropics we've got to have it wholesale, and enough of the sort to last for months."

"Weather doesn't keep well in hot climates, eh?"

That was Bill's little joke.

"But you like the climate, don't you, cousin?" said Stanley.

"Man, I do!" replied honest Tom—"apart from the midges."

"You mean mosquitoes, Tom, don't you?"

"Well, maybe I do. But they do bite uncommonly hard," replied Tom.

"What a lot you'll have to tell when you gang back!" said Mite.

"May we a' gang back," laughed Tom. "They say Scotchmen never gang back."

"*Avertit omen !*" said Stanley, solemnly; "we are in a strange country, surrounded by danger of every kind. We must trust in Providence and do our duty."

"That's it, boys!" said Cooke; "trust in Providence and do our duty."

"Amen!" said Big Bill.

There was a moment's lull in the conversation, broken only by the roar of a cataract in the river, near by which they were encamped. It was a branch of the great Congo—that mighty stream near the banks of which, ere many years elapse, will arise the nucleus of a new nation that will go on spreading in all directions, till it rivals in wealth and wisdom the great American Republic itself.

They had crossed this river high above the falls, where the water spread itself out over miles and miles of a pebbly bed, and was everywhere as clear and translucent as crystal itself. But pleasant though it would have been to have journeyed along by its banks, it would have taken them out of their course and very much too far north.

"To-morrow night——" said Stanley.

"Yes," responded Mite; "go on, Stan. What about to-morrow night?"

They had left the dinner-table and left the tent, and as they spoke they stood together in a group, Stanley and Mite side by side—a position that the latter was very fond of, especially in the dark, as they now were.

"Stop!" cried Stanley. "Listen!"

Mite could just see that his friend held one hand aloft against the starlit sky, as if commanding attention.

Deeper far than the roar of the cataract, more appalling than the loudest thunder, it was a voice that seemed to shake the very forest trees.

Mite clung to brother Stan's arm. "Let us get nearer to the camp-fire," he half whispered.

Bill and Cooke and Tom were there already, and Stanley prepared to follow.

"There is no danger now," said Stanley.

"No danger," repeated Mite, "and that terrible lion so close to us !"

"No, Mite, there is no danger *now*." He emphasised the word "now." "In a thunderstorm as soon as you hear the peal the danger is over for a moment; it is the silent flash that brings the bolt. That lion growled with disappointed rage; he had been watching us probably for five minutes, and had not made up his mind to spring; then he became alarmed."

"Oh, dear !" said Mite; "I hope he wasn't thinking of springing on me, Stan, or you, you know."

"It was the very uncertainty," replied Stan, "in the brute's mind as to which of us would suit him best, that caused him to hesitate, I have little doubt of that, and that is what saved us. He wouldn't look twice at you, Mite, you may be sure. Why, you wouldn't be a bite to him !"

"Unless," said Bill, "the lion wanted a light supper."

"Don't you laugh, Bill," Stanley said, "lions don't care for light suppers. It was you he was thinking most about."

"Yes," cried Cooke; "but he wasn't sure if he could carry him off."

"No, that was it," continued Stanley; "and so as you, Cooke, looked so tough, and I'm all bones, I believe that lion would finally have made up his mind to sup upon Tom."

"Don't !" exclaimed Tom; "you make my blood creep ! Hark ! there he is again !"

"There is more than one lion there, gentlemen," said Sool, who had suddenly appeared on the scene.

"How very cold it has got all of a sudden !" said poor Tom, whose teeth were chattering.

He crept closer to the fire as he spoke, kicked the logs, and made them blaze.

"Much more wood will be needed to-night," said Sool. "Who will come with me to the forest ?"

Mite jumped up. "I'll go for one," he said, boldly clutching his rifle. "Tom," he continued, "you come too, and just keep behind me if you're afraid, you know."

Sool retired for a few moments, then he returned with torches, which he proceeded to light, afterwards handing one to each.

"These," he said, quietly, "will be of more use than rifles. Come !"

Then, axes in hand, ten of the boys went with the party. They struck directly into the forest, and a strange and weird-like appearance it had, that wood lit up thus by torchlight. There was no undergrowth, only the tall stems of the trees standing up around them like pillars in some mighty cavern ; but beyond the circle where the torchlight gleamed all was shrouded in darkness. No undergrowth. but presently they came to a spot where a great tree had fallen ; then the work commenced. The boys plied their axes, and, with great burdens of wood on their backs, they soon made their way back again to camp, around which fires were lit to protect it, for once more the deep bass of the lion's voice and the shrill, unearthly laughter of hyænas awoke the echoes of those ancient woods.

Even in the marquee it was considered safest to have loaded rifles close at hand.

"Stanley," said Mite, "when we went out that time, after dinner, you began a sentence and never finished it— something about to-morrow night."

"Oh, yes," replied Stanley ; "merely this. To-morrow night we'll have no bed but the green boughs, no roof above us except the sky, for it will not be safe to sleep even under trees. We can't take tents, nor anything that belongs to civilised life, with us for even another mile."

What Stanley said was strictly true, the rest of their journey inland must be made with free hands, untrammelled save by the arms they carried for their protection from dangers as yet unknown.

The part of the country they were now in was to all appearance uninhabited—by human beings, at any rate. Some little way up stream, and right in the centre of the river, was a small rocky island. The boat was put together on the bank opposite, and all tents and stores, and even ammunition that was considered extra, conveyed thither and hidden in a little rocky cavern, care being taken to barricade the entrance well against the inquisitiveness of wild beasts.

They now bent their footsteps farther northwards, intending to strike the country of the Makalala from the equatorial side, and thus avoid crossing the lands where dwelt those savages who had kept our hero and his little party so long prisoners, in their first attempt to reach Captain Ross and his daughter. They would thus, however, have to traverse regions quite unknown to them, and known even to Mbooma, or Brown, only by hearsay.

But Cooke and Stanley had compasses and quadrant, and right well they knew how to use them. All through this long and wearying journey they had kept a log and marked a chart just as if they had been at sea.

Sool had his little army well under command, and on the march every precaution was taken to avoid surprise either from wild beasts or still wilder men. All the natives they had hitherto met were, however, peaceably inclined. Many were the villages they had passed through that still bore the traces of dreadful raids having been made on them for the purpose of carrying the inhabitants off into slavery. The woods and bush around some of these were scorched and blackened with fire, on the lower trees hardly a branch had been left, and the lofty cocoa-palms, many of which had escaped owing to their great height, waved green above a wilderness of black. The little towns themselves had been laid waste by fire and sword, and only old men and women

and tender children had been left alive. They fled at sight
of the expedition—fled and hid themselves in holes in the
hill-sides, looking, as they peeped occasionally over or around
the boulders, more like poor hunted coneys or stricken
deer than anything human.

Tom used to go among them with the boy Brown as
interpreter, and he never failed to win their confidence and
bring them back with him to their deserted villages.

"Oh, Stanley," he used to say, "my heart bleeds for the
poor things! If we had but time, would it no' be a grand
thing to stop among them and tell them the Gospel story?"

But Stanley's answer was ever, "On, on; our first duty,
dear Tom, lies beyond those hills. Another time, perhaps
—another time."

"Ay," Tom would reply, "another time; it will and shall
be another time!" for honest.Tom Reynolds had formed a
great resolve.

But now they traversed a large belt of uninhabited
country—a land given up entirely to the beasts of the
field. Here was a region in which a sportsman might
indeed have revelled, and a naturalist felt in a kind of
earthly paradise!

The fact that the boys were laden with the pieces of the
boat, which had often to be put together to enable them to
ferry across some broad river or lake, retarded their journey
considerably. They still bore provisions along with them,
but on their guns they depended to a great extent now for
what they had to eat, so that, upon the whole, from ten to
fifteen miles made up the extent of a day's march. But it
must be remembered that there were no roads properly so-
called of any kind, the track of the denizens of wilds and
forests being excepted.

Sometimes their path led through deep, dark woods bare
of underwood, the home of thousands of wonderful monkeys
and baboons—the home, too, of immense flocks of parrots
and other birds. Especially did these latter congregate

near the banks of the streams, flying up into the air in screaming clouds at the approach of our travellers, the variety and splendour of their plumage and their gay colours as they wheeled and tumbled in the air forming a sight that, once seen, could never be forgotten. There were some parts of the forests where the branches were laden till they bent and broke with the weight of the nests of these birds. Different species lived in different colonies, and it was remarkable how careful each colony was not to disturb or invade in any way the birds that belonged to another.

With these woods, wide and fertile grassy glens or straths alternated, and next perhaps would come a perfect wilderness of mountain and forest-land combined. No lack of game here. There were deer and antelopes of a dozen different species among the hills, and the streams teemed with fish, and little lack of fruit either. There were fields of pineapple-bushes, the delicious perfume of which was wafted on the air for miles. There were groves of plantains, bananas, and oranges, and trees laden with guavas, mangoes, and a thousand other fruits that they could not even name, nor, for the matter of that, could they tell whether or not they were poisonous. But many of these that had quite a sickly flavour to our heroes were eaten with avidity by their carriers, and even by Sool and Sambo.

Water they seldom drank, the cocoanut-milk, as it is called, supplying its place. This is the fluid that is contained within the shell of the young cocoanut before the nut itself has more than just commenced to form, and very delicious and cool it is, one young cocoanut containing about a quart of it. Many of the mountains were tree-clad to the very summits, while others were all ablaze with the most gorgeous heaths and geraniums.

For more than a week they journeyed through this new and lovely land, without seeing a single sign of human being or human habitation.

Had our travellers been inclined for sport they might now have indulged in it to their hearts' content, for herds of immense hippopotami swarmed in the deeper pools of the river, rhinoceroses swarmed in the jungles, browsing on the roots and twigs, while elephants roamed in forest and plain, but, unless killed in self-defence, not one of these animals fell to their guns.

One evening Mite, in company with Bill, was returning to the camp, the former chatting away just as lively as he always did, Bill staggering along under the weight of a couple of antelopes, large enough to form food for all hands for a day at least, when, trotting along with its calf in front, came a huge black rhinoceros. It scorned to leave the beaten path, but came on with a rush, head well down, straight at little Mite. He fired and laid the poor calf dead, and next moment would have been hurled higher into the air than ever he had been in his life, without something to hold on by, had not a bullet from the rifle—the pet bone-crusher—of Stanley Grahame laid the animal dead at Mite's feet.

Mite was very much frightened, and just a little sur-prised, but he pulled himself together sufficiently to doff his cap and say smiling, "Thank you, brother, for saving my worthless life. But mind," he added, "I never meant to kill the calf, only to shoot the old cow."

"You might just as well have stepped aside and let tne old cow pass," replied Stanley. "However, it can't be helped. The boys will have veal to-night."

The boys certainly did have veal, and beef too, and after them, as soon as darkness fell, came the lions and tigers to the feast. Such a terrible roaring, fighting, and growling our travellers never yet had heard ; it seemed as if all the wild beasts of the forest had assembled to eat the flesh and gnaw the bones of that gigantic rhinoceros. Silence came at last, however, broken only by an occasional low yawning roar, as if some great beast out there in the jungle slept but badly, and woke up now and then from a terrible dream, the result of too much rhinoceros for supper.

The travellers lay around the largest fire, rolled in their blankets, for even in the torrid regions of Africa deadly night-dews fall. They slept feet towards the fire, and with their loaded rifles within easy reach, while not far off lay the boys asleep. Sentinels, whose duty it was to see to the fires and give alarm in case of danger, paraded silently hither and thither, and Sool himself never failed to keep the first watch.

It must have been well on towards morning; the fires had got low; I fear the sentries had fallen asleep. But out from the jungle a monster lion had crept. Right silently he approached the sleeping camp; never did cat stalk mouse or bear creep up to seal with greater caution. Nearer and nearer, stopping every moment to listen, all a-quiver from head to tail with excitement, but making no more noise than yonder snake that glides around the foot of the cactus-bush. Nearer and nearer, then raises himself gradually for a spring, but crouches again as some one moves or moans in his sleep. The lion is in luck, the whole camp is wrapt in slumber. The whole camp is at his mercy! He glares from form to form, from face to face, and lashes his tail from side to side. The fire flares up for a moment and falls on the sleeping face of Mite; the boy is unconsciously rubbing his cheek where a mosquito has bit. The motion seems to invite the monster to spring, as anything moving tempts a cat, and he " down-charges " once again.

But just then one of the sleeping sentinels raises his arms and yawns. In one moment the lion has changed his mind and springs upon the sentry instead of Mite, and bears the poor fellow, shrieking, away into the darkness of the night. The camp is all aroused in an instant. There is no more sleep this night for any one. As for the poor sentinel, no power on earth could save him. Fainter and fainter grew his yells, then abruptly ceased, then—every one shuddered to think of the dreadful deed that was being enacted in that dark and dismal jungle.

*   *   *   *   *   *

"We have already exceeded our orders," said the chief of what we must now dignify by the title of Boy Green's Expedition. "We have exceeded our sultan's orders, young sahib. We have followed up your friends' trail for five days now and there are no signs of them. We must return."

"Exceeded yer orders, eh?" laughed boy Green—"exceeded yer orders, hey? Why, that's nuffin! I often exceeds my orders. Won't go any furder? Nonsense! I tells yer this : if you goes back now you leaves my friend Mr. Weir and myself—Dr. Green, of her Majesty's ship *Tonitru*—to our fate. We goes on. Our blood will be on your head, and what if England should demand a just retrybooshin? Think o' that, I say," continued boy Green ; "suppose you were to be paid for going on, and on, and on till we finds the other part o' this memorable expedition, delivers our friends from the jaws o' death, burns old King Kafoozlum's kraal, covers ourselves with honour and glory, and all that sort o' thing, eh?"

"Who is to pay us?" asked the chief, somewhat mollified.

"I'll see that you are well rewarded," said Weir, laughing. "Come, make up your minds to go on with us. We cannot find the trail of our friends, perhaps, but I know the way to the country of the Makalala. I have good reason to."

So a bargain was struck, and that is how there came to be two distinct expeditions marching into the interior of the Dark Continent to the relief of the unhappy captives.

For the present, however, it is with the expedition commanded by Stanley Grahame we have most to do.

Hitherto it had been all "pretty plain sailing," as Mite

called it, with them. The first part of their journey was nothing less than one long picnic, with just a spice of danger about it, and one or two trifling adventures—such as Mite's with the rhinoceros; a fight between Bill and a boa-constrictor, in which Bill came off victorious because there was not a tree handy for the boa to take a turn of his tail round ; an exciting race between Tom and an alligator, Tom winning by a length, with merely the loss of the heel of his boot ; and so on, and so forth. When the tents had to be stowed away the picnic came to a conclusion, and since then they had had to rough it. They were surrounded by dangers of every kind, and now at last those dangers began to thicken. There was trouble and sorrow ahead. But they bravely faced all. One day from a hill-top they saw spreading out before them what seemed to be a boundless prairie-land. It lay right in their way, however, and so they prepared to march across it.

They had not gone far before they found it was damp as well as level and flat—a vast morass, a dismal slimy swamp.

For a whole day they toiled on over it, often up to nearly their waists in water, and as the sun went down behind the level horizon they found themselves apparently as far from any place where it would be possible to bivouac as ever. But the night was clear and starry, and before long the moon rose, making everything around them as bright almost as midday in some less sunny lands.

They had reached a part of the swamp where stunted bushes grew here and there, the bottom feeling somewhat more solid than in other places, as if the water had simply overflowed on dry land. Sool was in front, stalking silent and ghostlike in the uncertain light. Suddenly there was a hoarse and horrid sound in the water on ahead. The noise seemed to be re-echoed from every side, and was accompanied by a sound as of rushing water.

"Allah ! il allah !" cried Sool. "Come hastily back ! Quick, gentlemen, quick ! the crocodiles ! the crocodiles !"

"Quick!" repeated Stanley.   "Yes, Sool.   But what can we do? Look yonder!"

It was indeed a fearful sight, and with a low frightened moan like that which escapes from a crowd when danger is terribly imminent, when a house is falling or a ship reels before she sinks, the members of the expedition one and all crowded together as if paralysed with dread, for as far as they could see in the moonlight the water seemed alive with monstrous crocodiles coming swiftly on towards them, and evidently bent upon their destruction!

XXII.

FIGHTING THE CROCODILES—THE HOME OF THE GORILLAS—"THE KING WITH THE CLICK"—NEARING THE LAND OF THE MAKALALA.

CHAPTER XXII.

FEW travellers have ever had so fearful an experience,
or stood face to face with so hideous a danger, as an
attack by crocodiles in an open swamp by night. It was
strange that these monsters should have been in such
numbers in the place, and stranger that they should have
proved themselves possessed of so much courage and
daring. The crocodile is not naturally so savage as some
have supposed, and as a rule depends more upon his
cunning and wariness than on his pluck. But here the
brutes were in their element, and the fact that it was night
no doubt tended to increase their daring.

Chief Soolieman now showed himself a good general,
and the occasion was one to try the mettle of the very best
of men.

"Quick," he cried to the carriers, "throw down the
burdens. We must make a rampart of these."

A well-directed volley tended for a time to check the
advance of the scaly foe, but only for a time; then the
boldest and biggest came speedily to the front, and the fight
began in terrible earnest. They raised themselves on the
hastily thrown up barricade, and with teeth and arms tried
to tear the men from behind it. They even raised themselves one on top of the other, and rolled on top of each

other in their fury. In so doing they exposed the more vulnerable parts of their bodies to bullet or spear, and the slaughter was therefore great.

Not the least appalling thing about this terrible fight was the noise these monsters made, the roaring and champing and splashing; and this, combined with the shouting of the men, the rattle of spears and axes, the sound of the rifles, and the awful appearance of the angry brutes, made a scene I should try but in vain to describe, and which the weird pencil of a Doré only could do justice to.

But even crocodiles have sense enough to know when they are beaten, and presently, as if by one accord, they drew off to what seemed deeper water in the rear, where they disappeared, and silence once more prevailed over all the dismal swamp. But there was the dead left on the field where they had fought, and the moon shining down on torn and trampled bushes, and on water stained with blood.

Had they retreated entirely? Or only to recruit their strength for a renewal of the struggle? These were ques tions it was impossible to answer. And so our heroes had to stand to their arms and wait.

As it was, the crocodiles had done damage enough to their human foes in all conscience, and more than one poor fellow had been hauled by them over the barricade to meet a fate it is too awful to think about.

Big Bill had had a narrow escape; he had been seized and pulled half way over the rampart; but, axe in hand, strong-armed Sool was by his side in a moment, and saved him, though Bill's arm was badly torn and bled profusely.

Little Mite looked as pale as a ghost in the moon-light.

"I hope, Stan," he said, "those beggars won't come back. I've had enough of crocodile fighting to last me for a lifetime.

"Ma conscience!" said poor Tom Reynolds in his broadest Scotch—for there were times when English was frightened out of him, and this was one of them—"Ma conscience ! Mite, my laddie, dinna speak aboot their comin' back. My heart was in my mooth a' the time o' the row. Sich a colly-shangy I never want to see in this world again. But, Stanley, man, d'ye no think it would be better to make oor feet our frien's, and leg back o'er the moor at ance ?"

"I think we are safer here," was Stanley's reply; "if they saw us moving off I think it is very likely they would change their minds and show up again."

"Dinna speak aboot it," said Tom, "dinna, dinna, dinna! I never believed that a man's hair could raise his hat till this awfu' nicht. Just look at that dead monster yonder—look at the fearsome limbs o' him and the terrible head and claws. I'll see him in my dreams, that is if ever one o' us comes alive oot o' this moor."

Thus our heroes waited, and hours and hours went by, so slowly. They made as little noise as possible, and even talked in semi-whispers.

A low wind blew over the marsh, and went moaning through the bushes, and more than once as they stirred the men clutched their arms, and stood silent but firm, to meet the danger they thought nothing could avert.

But the night wore away, and the moon sank lower and lower in the west, and never, I ween, did travellers welcome with greater signs of joy the first streaks of early dawn.

Then the glorious sun arose, and with one accord they fell on their knees, just where they stood, and thanked the Deliverer, who alone had brought them through this night of fearful peril.

"Is it onwards now?" said Sool, smiling.

"No, thank you," answered Stanley, "a very little crocodile fighting goes a long way. These brutes will not attack us in broad daylight. Let us hark back ; we cannot cross the swamp, we must therefore go round it."

I do not think there were two happier men in that party than Mite and Tom when they once more found themselves on high and dry land.

"I could eat something now," said Stanley.

"And I also could pick a bit," said Cooke.

"But isn't it better to eat than be eaten ? " said Mite.

"Yes," said Stanley, solemnly; "think of the fate of our poor black carriers."

It took a whole week of wandering to get round that swamp, there seemed to be no end to it, but at last they stood on the wooded hills beyond.

But dangers seldom come singly, they proceed in series. They had many an attack from wild beasts. These animals, especially the lions, appeared to have no fear of mankind, and it was often difficult to find a spot open enough for the nightly bivouac. Watches were kept as a matter of course, and fires burned, so the lions had to be content to remain at a distance.

"I do believe, you know," Mite said one morning, " those brutes walk around us all night."

"Yes," laughed Stanley, "just licking their lips and looking on."

"It's awful music they make, though," said Tom, " awful music to go to sleep with in your ears."

Big Bill's wounded arm was weeks ere it healed, then Cooke fell sick of fever, and there were thus two of the party on the invalid list.

This was awkward, so Stanley determined to call a halt for a week. There was plenty of sport, plenty of deer and antelopes in the woods, to say nothing of monster lions and lordly tigers, while herds of elephants went crashing past them at times, and rhinoceroses scoured the valleys.

The country was not only wildly romantic, but the heaths, geraniums, and other flowers were very pretty. There were tall trees adorned with flowers at which Mite marvelled. There were birds of every shade of plumage and birds of every size, in such numbers that they positively darkened the air like clouds as they flew.

It would be difficult indeed to tell my readers one half of what these woods contained, but there was a race of creatures that Mite found the first signs of, that did not add either to the beauty or safety of the woods. These were gorillas. They lived in the deepest, darkest recesses of the forest, and very terrible they were in shape and appearance.

One encounter, and only one, with a monster gorilla is worthy of record. Sool on this occasion was the hero ; nor had the battle been one of his seeking, but forced upon him. Indeed, as commander of the expedition, Stanley had given strict injunctions that no one was ever to take life for the mere sake of killing. In self-defence, or for the sake of providing food for the party, was a different matter.

Sool met his antagonist while out with Mite and Tom in a tiny boat, all being bent on a foraging excursion. The creek into which they ventured was the back reach of a great river. It went winding away westwards, between two lofty wooded mountains, and was nowhere of any very great breadth, but the mighty trees grew close down to the water's edge, and, as there was not the slightest portion of underwood nor even creepers, and no branches grew on the two lower thirds of the tree trunks, viewed from the water the forest in many places had the appearance of a vast and dimly-lighted cavern, where great pillars supported a series of vaulted roofs. This was the home of the gorillas, and it was a place few would care to visit.

Our friends were fishing, and, considering the black depth of water, getting very good sport indeed. Tom was rowing, when snap went one of the small oars.

"This *is* provoking," said Tom.

"Yes, and five miles from camp," said Mite.

"Won't it mend ? " he added.

"There is nothing to mend it with," replied Tom; "and that just teaches us a lesson, never to discard tools or gear from a boat, by way of lightening her, when going from home."

"Now if we had but taken friend Sool's advice ——

"There is one way, gentlemen," said Sool.

"What is that?"

"To land and cut a branch."

"Seems the only alternative," said Mite.

"But a terribly risky one," added Tom.

"I'll take the risk," said Sool, smiling.

The boat was accordingly urged towards the bank.

"Don't you leave the boat!" cried Sool, springing on shore.

"And don't you go far away." This last from Mite, one of the prevailing traits of whose character was caution.

I have already said there was no underwood, and Sool knew enough to prevent his venturing on a voyage of discovery up through the partial darkness of those deep woods.

As he had to climb, a near tree would do as well as any other. He soon made his choice, divested himself of both turban and jacket, girded his loins up and slung his hatchet, and up he went as easily as if it had been a stair he was climbing.

"Look!" cried Tom, "look at that. Why auld Sool is like a cat amang the limbs."

"Limbs of what?" asked mischievous Mite.

"His ain limbs," was the reply; "he hasn't gotten the length o' the limbs o' the tree yet. But he'll no be lang. Ma conscience: when I was a laddie I could get my nose above any hoody craw's nest in the country-side. Look, he is out o' sight now amang the branches. May Providence send him safely down again. It is a fearfu'——"

Tom got no further. He was interrupted by a scream or rather yell from the tree-top, that chilled the marrow in

their bones. Fierce, wild, "eldritch," unearthly, and de-
moniacal in the intensity of its rage and hate. This was
followed by a crashing of branches, then all was still. The
silence appeared to those below to last an hour, but it was
broken at last by the rushing descent of what looked like a
human form of immense proportions. It reached the earth
with a dull thud, and lay extended on the ground in all its
ghastliness—a gigantic gorilla. A branch came down
nearly immediately afterwards, and then Sool himself. No,
not quite so fast, but he needed all the speed he could
muster, for presently the whole wood resounded with yells,
and Sool had hardly time to get into the boat, push it off
shore, dragging the branch after him, ere as many dusky
forms were seen as to fully convince them that these dark
woods were indeed the home of the gorilla.

Monkeys in millions of all kinds inhabit the woods and
hills of Africa, but the non-dangerous classes of them frequent the sunnier or opener forests. A merry life they
seem to lead too ; they are ever on the chatter, and ever
playing little harmless jokes on each other. Indeed so fond
of fun are they, or so full of it, that it is part of their very
lives to prattle and play. But the gorilla is different in
every way. He is more solitary and retiring, and dwells
remote in regions sometimes all but inaccessible to any but
the boldest of travellers, and he never courts but shuns the
presence of man.

For all this, I am loth to believe there is not some good
in the heart of even a gorilla. Having hauled the boat well
beyond the region of danger, our heroes rested to look
shorewards. A group of gorillas had surrounded the dead
one, but most of them withdrew after a little, giving place
to one that had thrown itself on the breast of the dead giant
with gestures of grief that were almost human.

Even Sool was touched at the sight.

Tom was simply silent.

"I never would have slain it," said Sool, "but had I rot

struck in self-defence it would have hurled me from the tree."

*   *   *   *   *

For a whole month after the above adventure Stanley Grahame's expedition went steadily but slowly inland. He was well provided with money and ammunition, and had a good little army behind him, so he determined to brook no resistance from man or beast. The former he soon found more troublesome, deceitful, and dangerous to life and limb than the latter. Well, he kept a watchful eye over everything that happened in or near his path of advancement. Cooke was soon able to travel, and Bill cared little for pain, but hardly had the march been resumed ere the party fell in with kraals. Some of the tribes he came among were small. These Stanley could afford to despise. He rewarded honesty with a string or two of beads, he scorned cajolery, and when he met with a display of force he showed a bold front. He would not be turned aside. This soon led to skirmishes. But these had more the effect of detaining him than anything else. None of these savages had ever seen or heard firearms. Sometimes when they pressed threateningly upon Stanley's brave little party, the order was given to fire a volley with blank cartridges. This at first had the desired effect. It sent the tribes back very speedily indeed. But it came to pass that when they found none of their tribe hurt, they took heart, and matters looked a deal more serious. A ball cartridge or two mended matters entirely, and the tribe kept at a respectful distance.

When they had followed for some time they dropped back and away altogether, because they respected boundaries, and no chief was foolish enough to invade the territory of another, or, as Tom phrased it, to put foot on another man's land.

They came at last to one tribe, and a very large one it was, who were ten times more friendly than any of the others   As soon as these people found out that the expe ditioñ had not come to despoil them, they welcomed it with open arms. The king, a very reverend looking old patriarch, averred, with much gesticulation, that if Stanley cared to stay and make this country his home, all that he —the king—possessed should be at his service.

A strange country this indeed, an oasis of civilization in a desert of savagery. They cultivated land, grew rice and curry, they had pigs and goats, and they wore a cloth of grass, which they manufactured themselves. They seldom went on the war-path, and never except on strict defence. The name of the king was N'tooba, and our people called the place N'tooba Land. (The apostrophe after the N represents a kind of sound like a " click " made with the tongue. Country people at home make a similar or nearly similar noise when urging a horse to advance.)

The king prevailed upon them to stay with him for three whole days. Stanley was the less disinclined to accede to this request because it would give his boys a rest, and he had a notion they would all need their strength ere long. But they received much information about the lay of the land and the strength of the Makalala warriors.

There was, they were told, wooded land to the south, with many wild beasts in it, then a great lake, with an island, then the country of the Makalala. But eastward was a land they must of all things avoid. It was peopled by millions of fearful and spiteful dwarfs, who lived on tree-tops or in holes in the earth, and were the terror of all the tribes for hundreds of miles on every side.

Stanley was unable to learn then whether these creatures were really human beings or wild beasts.

When the day for departure arrived, old N'tooba—"the king with the click," as Mite called him—was in great grief. He entreated Stanley with tears in his eyes to change his mind. Of one thing, he said, he felt certain, and that was that neither he—Stanley—nor any of his people would ever come alive out of the country of the dreaded Makalala.

Stanley had made up his mind to try, at all events, and so he told the old man, but he promised to keep clear of the country of the dwarfs.

Then, bidding the " king with the click " an affectionate farewell, they journeyed on, and were soon after swallowed up in the darkness of a great forest.

XXIII.

*THE LAKE OF THE WIZARD WATERS—IDA'S ISLE—
FATHER AND DAUGHTER—SIGNS OF THE COMING
STRUGGLE.*

CHAPTER XXIII.

IN the centre, in the very heart, one might say, of the Dark Continent is a lake, that the warlike tribes and peoples who dwell in these regions call Unga Noona, or the lake of the wizard waters. It lies a few degrees south of the equator, and about midway, if my memory serves me aright, betwixt the western and eastern shores of Africa. Hardly an atlas you are likely to possess will be able to show you its exact bearings, for in most maps the region hereabouts is marked "desert," or more truthfully "unexplored." It is, nevertheless, one of the most wildly fertile and beautiful districts in the whole of equatorial Africa.

Our story commenced with a brief description of the great forest of Cairntrie, near which our chief hero, Stanley Grahame, spent the first years of his boyhood. Lovely indeed is this forest, with its wealth of waving woodlands, its mountains snow-capped till far into the summer, its mighty pine-trees, its lonely glades and glens, and fairy-haunted dells. Lovely, indeed, but nothing to compare to the grandeur and romance of the scenery around Unga Noona.

The very memory of my own mountains has seemed dwarfed as I gazed upon the hills that here, in pile above pile, and tier above tier, yet mostly tree-clad to the summits, pierce the blue of the sky in this land of eternal summer. The waterfalls of Scotland would sink into the merest insignificance in view of the mighty cataracts that dash and foam, and fall and bound from rock to rock in the river-beds here. Scotia's rivers would seem but burns beside the majesty of the great sheets of water that in these regions move onwards to seek the far-off seas.

Unga Noona! It is a strange name; nor is the lake in itself a large one, albeit the river that feeds it falls sheer down into the waters beneath from a precipice many hundreds of feet high, causing the water to bubble and boil for miles around, and shaking the woods that wave luxuriantly on its shores. In length barely fifty miles, and in width nowhere exceeding ten. Yet the savage races who live near it look upon it with a kind of superstitious reverence and dread. So clear is the water of Unga Noona, that fathoms beneath its surface, when the sun shines, can be seen the gliding, gambolling fish, and eels that wriggle and glide hither and thither, or hide themselves in the silvery sand.

Unga Noona! The lake of the wizard waters! It bears a charmed reputation, and I have been told that these waters will cure all the ills of man or of beast, that the hunted koodoo or fleet inkonka has but to dip its parched lips in the lake to restore itself to life and energy, and that wild beasts, the lion, the tiger, the black rhinoceros and hyæna, come from afar through jungle and forest to drink the limpid waters, and bear for ever after a life that may defy spear or arrow of native sportsman. Strange noises they say are often heard after nightfall coming from the bosom of this lake, and chiefs that have died of wounds or fallen in battle are said to glide bird-like over its surface in the starlight, uttering cries that make the blood of the listener turn cold and his flesh creep. I believe nothing of all this; yet true enough it is that there are times when the bosom of limpid Unga Noona is seen to be ruffled as if a spirit troubled its waters, or as if a breeze were blowing over it, the while there is not so much as a breath of air to rustle the leaves of the feathery palms, or toy with the foliage of the silver acacia.

Some fifteen miles from the south-eastern end of Unga Noona, and about five from either shore, there is a lofty wooded mountain island. I cannot better describe it, for the whole isle is but a hill cut off at the top, and tree-covered on every side. In the distant ages of the past, there is little doubt, this was a burning mountain, for the top even now is hollow, a crater in fact, but, as we shall presently see, fertile in flower and foliage of every kind indigenous to the district. In the centre of the hollow top is a bubbling spring of purest water. May not, deep down beneath this beautiful island, fires still smoulder, and may this not account, in a great measure, for the troubled appearance of the lake at times, and for the strange sounds and noises that seem to emanate from its bosom ?

Let us land on this mysterious island.

It is a lovely morning. Gazing shorewards from our skiff, that bounds swiftly over the waters, we can hardly imagine that the woods on either side of this lake, that seem to sleep so peacefully in the sunshine, could harbour aught of danger or evil, or that yonder village half way up the mountain's side, and from which the smoke of many a hut or wigwam is now ascending like incense in the morning air, was the residence of a king who sacrifices to his lust for blood hundreds of innocent victims annually, who counts skulls as hunters do tails of beasts killed in the chase, and builds stacks of them before the blood-reeking threshold of his miserable kraal. But so it is, for in that village dwells Lambabeela, who dominates with a rod of iron all the country round, and all the tribes that dwell therein. He is king of the terrible Makalala—sometimes called Makula-men, whose motto is "war," constant war with every race they come in contact with, and who, horrible to say, capture victims but to kill them, and rear slaves only to minister to human sacrifices.

But here on this lonely island we are safe for the time. Lambabeela himself seldom visits it, his warriors still more seldom; and here is neither deadly snake nor treacherous wild beast, and, as we enter a little leafy harbour and draw our boat up on the green bank, we cannot help feeling alone. There are bright-winged butterflies floating in the sunshine that shimmers down through the trees, emerald lizards scarlet-striped creeping lazily on the branches, and birds gorgeously arrayed in black and gold, that hop nearer and nearer, and gaze on us curiously with bright inquiring beads of eyes, then, twittering peevishly, fly off again; but nothing to indicate by sight or sound that we are anywhere in the vicinity of human beings. But push aside the branches here, and lo! a little pathway ascending zigzag up the mountain's side. And we follow it, up and up and up, through bush and brake, through wild flowers and ferns. So steep is the path that our hands are fain to clutch at every aiding branch, or bush or stone. It seems like climbing a hill in a fairy tale. Up, and up, and up; where will it lead us to at last? But when we pause occasionally to take breath and look behind us, from between the branches and the tree-stems we catch glimpses of scenery so wildly charming, so picturesquely lovely, that were I poet and painter both in one, I would fail, if I tried, to give my readers any just notion of it.

But here we are at the top at last, and a cool breeze fans our faces. We have reached the edge of the crater of, or depression in, this extinct volcano, and looking downwards we find the surface of it is acres in extent, and only some twelve feet below the top of the hill, which in some parts forms a continued unbroken wall of rock, almost hidden by the foliage and flowers of luxuriant creepers. In other parts this wall is not continuous, but broken up into needle-like rocks, from between which we can see all the lovely landscape beneath us, lake and woods, hills and dales, and mountain peaks.

What strikes us as strangest of all, however, is that the whole surface of the crater has been transformed by human hands into a bewitching landscape garden. Here are walks and lawns and terraces, trees laden with ripe fruit, and flowers of every shape and colour. Yonder, too, in the centre is a rustic cottage, with walls bedecked with climbing plants, and flowers trailing in festoons around porch and verandah. Truly the little zigzag path seems to have led us into a kind of fairyland.

A fountain, too, is playing on a lawn in front of the cottage, pigeons strut cooing over its roof, and tame deer and antelope, the tiny teemba and the fairy-like ingo-loo-loo play and gambol on the walks or climb the rocks with perilous speed, and stand fearlessly forth against the blue of the sky on the very summit of the crags that bound the crater.

And this is all I have to tell you about the mountain isle of Unga Noona.

But surely this aërial garden has both a history and a presiding genius.

Alas! it has both. With all its beauty the place is but a prison. See yonder, coming slowly down the centre path, a white-haired man, partly clad in skins, and a beautiful girl, with dark eyes and sadly pensive face, and hair that floats over her shoulders in wavy but careless luxuriance. She is clad in gown of white; her hand leans lightly on the old man's arm, seeming neither to seek nor to afford support, for though somewhat bowed with care, he is still sturdy and strong, and his face has all the hardiness and colour that is never wholly absent from the countenances of those who have been used to a life of . exposure; and though slight in form and wearied by years of grief, there is a glance in the girl's dark eyes which tells of a high-born courage and firmness of purpose that it would be hard indeed utterly to subdue.

He is Captain Ross, and *she* his daughter Ida, the quondam child-nurse of the wounded Stanley Grahame. We already know a little of their story, but who shall tell the extent of their sufferings in all these dreary years of imprisonment and bondage ? Wrecked on the treacherous and inhospitable shores of Somali-land, captured and bound, the child Ida and her father, with many others, were dragged inland a long and terrible journey, and sold as slaves to this black tyrant Lambabeela. Some of their companions were speedily put out of their misery, others suffered from tortures previously to bitter death, and the rest fell victims one by one to disease or violence. More than one of the latter had been killed while trying to escape from the country of the wild Makalala. Death itself would have been preferable to a life of slavery, so thought Captain Ross, had he not had his child with him. For her sake he schemed and plotted to make life endurable, and he had not been many months in the country ere he was elevated to the rank of what might be called Lord High Medicine Man. This served his purpose well. He had some knowledge of simple herbs, and with these he managed to raise many of Lambabeela's officers and houschold from dangerous sicknesses. But it was not the medicine he gave them, so he told them, that worked such wonders, the inspiration came from Ida. If harm came to her it would soon be all over. In this he spoke truly, for he would not long have survived his daughter's death. In time Ross and his daughter were deemed far too precious to reside in the village or chief town of the king's territory, and so they were taken to the mountain isle in which we now find them. One or two servants were allowed them. Archie Weir—who had been years in slavery before them—was among the number.

By his assistance, and an industry born of despair—for they hardly hoped ever again to be free—they turned the mountain-top into the garden we find it. Had this spot been in a civilised land, with all its floral beauty and all its wealth of lovely foliage, it would indeed have appeared a kind of earthly paradise.

" And how has my little girl slept ? " said Captain Ross, passing one arm fondly round his daughter.

" Oh ! dear papa," said Ida, " I had such a dream."

" What ! more dreams ? " her father said, smiling ; "very well, let's sit down here, and you shall tell me all about it. How pleasant the breeze is, but how warm the morning sun ! "

" Not there, father ; see, Tom wants to get up there."

Tom was a pet lizard, a great grey monster nearly as large as a small alligator, and ten times more ugly. Ida smoothed him tenderly, nevertheless, and Tom seemed to like it. Then father and daughter turned away down another pathway, where an immense tiger came bounding towards them—nay, not to kill and eat them, but to be fondled and to be made much of, then go off on the bound again, making terrible pretence to catch and slay an ingo-loo-loo.

But Ida was after him, nearly as quick in all her movements as he was.

A pretty picture it made—the creeper-clad rock with the tiny frightened deer, against which the great tiger was making pretence to spring ; the young girl, both arms round his neck, her cheek on his broad brow, laughingly holding him back.

She went next and pulled a twig from a bush, and . denuding it of its leaves,

" I shall punish you most severely, Sir Stanley," she said, with the air of a queen of tragedy.

The tiger threw himself on the ground, and crept close to her feet.

" There," she cried, " I forgive you, but you really must go to cage for an hour, for you are positively frightening every bit of appetite from my poor teembas. There now, there. Follow."

Her father looked after her fondly, yet fearfully. The tiger was not the ordinary leopard or tiger-cat so called of Africa, but a real Bengalese. It had been brought as a gift, when only a cub, to Lambabeela, and given by him to Ida. Yet her father often trembled when he saw the freedom his daughter made with the monster.

Ida ran off with Sir Stanley, leaving her father alone. She would be back, she cried, in less than a minute; but if there was one strange pet to demand her attention, there were fifty at least—monkeys and mongooses, goats and deer, birds of every shape and feather, to say nothing of a variety of wonderful creeping creatures, that—not so demonstrative in their affections as pets of fur or feather—eyed her kindly from cool corners, under bushes or behind rocks and stones, and would have broken their hearts if she had not said a word to each. So it was fully half an hour ere she was free to rejoin her father. She found him seated in one of the rocky embrasures of this strange natural fortification, spy-glass in hand, anxiously scanning the mainland.

A wonderful glass this, so thought the king and the chiefs of the Makalala race. Most of them had had one peep through it. None of them would venture on another. It was part of the wreckage of the good ship. It was sold into slavery with Captain Ross. With it he was supposed to see into futurity. When he and Ida were permitted to visit the mainland, he always carried his glass drawn out to its fullest extent, and sometimes—in order to impress the mob of spear-armed savages that never failed to surround them—closed it with a snap that sent a shudder through the hearts of the sable crowd. If at any time Captain Ross was, on these great occasions, inconveniently crowded by the natives, he had but to clap one eye to his spy-glass and point it towards them, they fell back helter-shelter, shrieking and yelling, tumbling heels over head, as if the glass had been a veritable *mitrailleuse* and he the best gunner that ever pulled a lanyard or drew a trigger. It was a handy glass.

"I knew I'd find you here, dear father," said Ida. "You have been thinking again, I know. Oh! father, and you promised not to."

"And you have been dreaming, Ida. There, we are quits. Come and sit beside me, and tell me your dream."

"On one condition, father—that you tell me your thoughts. There is an anxious look in your face that hardly accords with the hope in my heart."

"The hope raised by a dream, Ida?" replied the father, smiling.

"Not altogether," said Ida: "you and mamma taught me to pray. I have prayed, oh! so earnestly, that I feel He will hear us at last, and take us away from here—away from the vicinity of these terrible savages. I dreamt such a happy dream. It was about our old home, and about dear old Beaumont Park. We were there, you and I and Stanley, of whom you have heard me talk so much. He looked so brave and tall, and *all* a hero."

The girl paused for a moment and gazed away at the distant landscape; then she sighed, and seating herself beside her father she nestled close to his shoulder, as she continued,—

"Yes, I have hope. Such hope too as I never had before."

"I fear poor Archie would never reach the coast," said Captain Ross.

"Oh! but Mbooma, father, you forget our poor boy. There is nothing Mbooma would not do for us."

"Our own people here in this place, Ida—can we quite trust them?"

Ida ran rapidly over the names of eight men who lived in the island garden with them. English names every one of them, though they were black men, savages. Nay, not now, for Ida had not left them in their darkness all these years. She had taught them to pray, and though books were things unknown in these regions, Captain Ross and Ida every morning and evening gathered them together and told them tales, and one tale that they all delighted most to listen to was the Gospel tale—the story of the cross. There were in addition to these men, or boys as Captain Ross called them, three female servants, one a grey-haired negress who took quite an interest in her "dear chile Idee," as she called our heroine.

"Trust them, father! Yes, they would die for us. But why do you ask that question *now?* Speak, father, speak! You frighten me."

"You are so young, Ida—a child. I fear to alarm you, and yet——"

"Fear nothing for me, father, I am quite old. Oh! think of what we have come through and suffered together. Could anything be more terrible ? Not death, father—no, not even death."

He drew her close towards him.

"Ida," he said, "last night when you slept I was up on our watch-tower yonder. It is five miles to Lambabecla's camp, but sound travels far. There was much commotion, much wild shouting, and tom-toms were beaten all the night. The tribe is at war and preparing to resist invasion. Who dares to carry war into the land of the Makalalas ? Who would draw sword against the invincible Lambabeela ? Ida, dear, no black chief would."

"Oh! then," cried Ida, clapping her hands joyfully, "they are coming, our friends are coming, Stanley and his men are coming!"

"Ida," said her father, "I both hope and fear. It is now a year and a half since those letters which you so cherish came from Stanley Grahame. He had then but a handful of followers. He was being beaten back towards the coast by a cloud of armed savages. I dread lest neither he nor Mbooma ever reached Zanzibar again. But while

I dread, I hope Archie or Stanley, one or the other, will try to rescue us.   But, darling, the moment victory should declare itself in the white man's favour might be our last. And that is why I asked you could you trust our boys."

" Father," said Ida boldly, " you mean to defend this hill."

She stood erect before him as she spoke ; she looked all a heroine then.

" I will help you, father.   Leave the boys to me."

Ross smiled and pressed her hand.

" You are a true-born American lass," he said.   " Now, dear, for years I have worked at these ramparts.   The hill is inaccessible at all parts save one or two."

" You worked, father ?"

" Ay, Ida, hour after hour, under the moon and under the stars, when you and every one were fast sleep, because I always had an idea some terrible day might come when we would have to sell our lives dearly.   Yes, nature has placed a rampart of rocks around this hill that no savage could scale.   With six good men and true I can hold the place for weeks."

" Why, children," said an aged but active-looking negress, " whateber is you about ?   Dinner 'as been ready for one, two hour an' more, and poor ole Sarah waitin' all dat time. Come, missie dear, I sartin sure you is plenty hungry. All de boys dey go to work agen, hoe, hoe, hoe ; can't you hear dem sing de hymns o' de hallelujahs ?   Come, missie, come."

There are no human beings more to be depended upon as servants to a white master than those same natives of the interior of the Dark Continent, when their savage nature has been tamed, and when they have once learned the glad tidings of salvation.   Learned, that is, to look beyond all that is sad and sorrowful here below, to that land where there shall be no more sorrow or crying.

At eventide that day, and ere the sun had gone down,

every one on Ida's Isle gathered to prayers and praise, in what Ida always called "the best room." Her father strolled out afterwards, but she beckoned to her people to stay. She sang to them the sweet songs of her far-off native land. They listened entranced. She ceased, they were silent, but in through the casement came the notes of the bulbul and the wah-moo-lee. They had taken up the chorus.

Mammie Sarah broke the silence.

"Sing to us," she said, "'By Babel's streams.'"

Ida began,

> "'By Babel's streams we sat and wept,
> When Zion we thought on,
> Amidst thereof we hung our harps
> The willow-trees upon.'"

Poor Ida! she got no further, but burst into tears.

"Oh, my lammie!" cried Sarah, fondling her as if she had been a child. "What for you cry? You catchee grief. Tell Mammie Sarah."

Ida looked about her just for a moment. She saw only sympathy in every eye. She was reassured. She stood erect, and dashed aside her tears. She was the brave American lass once more.

"God bless you all!" she cried. "I can trust you. But we are to be attacked. My father means to fight."

She repeated the words in the Somali or Makalala tongue.

"Bless Ida! bless Ida!" they cried in chorus. "We fight, we fight, we die for Ida!"

Ida, brave as she was, stood almost aghast at the storm she had raised. But she was satisfied from that hour.

All that day and all the next not a canoe came from the mainland, but signs of the coming strife were audible enough in the village of the king; tom-toms still beat, and shrieks or war-cries were heard even at that distance.

The sun went down in a sea of lurid glory that bathed hills and dales and woods.

Captain Ross and Ida sat together on the highest rampart long after the moon rose and made everything bright and clear.   No one thought of retiring.

Suddenly a shriek from Mammie Sarah.

" De black spirit on de water ! " she cried.   " Look ! "

Only Sarah's eyes could see it.   In a few minutes more, on the rampart near them and betwixt them and the moon, a tall, thin figure stood.

Next moment Mbooma was by their side.

Poor faithful boy Brown ! For more than fifty miles through the dark woods and over the hills he had come all alone, and swam the lake to carry the good tidings to Ida and her father that Stanley was coming to save them.

XXIV.

*FIGHT WITH DWARFS—STORMING OF IDA'S ISLE BY
SAVAGES—REPULSE—BOY GREEN TO THE FORE—
WAR IN LAMBABEELA'S LAND.*

CHAPTER XXIV.

THREE whole weeks and over have passed away since the night Mammie Sarah saw, as she said, "the black spirit moving" on the moonlit waters of Unga Noona —since the night the boy Mbooma dropped silently down from the ramparts and stood beside Captain Ross and Ida.

How eagerly they had questioned the lad ; how much he had to tell them ; how many messages he had to bear back to brave Stanley and his followers !

"In two day more dey come," Mbooma had said re-peatedly, holding up two yellow fingers as he spoke, and smiling. Even this was a long speech in English for Mbooma—a language that he understood, but was ever shy of using. But the occasion demanded English even from Mbooma. "In two day more dey come; plenty spear, too, plenty gun ; make plenty much bobbery, plenty much fight ; take Massa Ross 'way, 'way to good land, and poor little Missie Eeda too."

And silently as he had come, so silently went he, ere the moon had sunk in the west, and while there was still light enough for him to make his way to the northern shore of Lake Unga Noona. Ida's heart bled for the poor boy, but as she pressed his hand her soul was full of hope, though the tears were trickling down her face.

"In two day more dey come," the boy had said. But where were they all this weary time, and what had befallen the captive's would-be deliverers in the forest-land and jungle of that unknown country, where foot of white man had never before been planted ?

Mbooma had left them slowly advancing—slowly, but surely—with little to stay their progress except the difficulties that ever beset a journey through an unknown land —the intricacies of the jungle, the carrying of heavy loads over mountains and through gorges, the fording of streams, or wading through plains of grassy land far more difficult to traverse than any American prairie or wilderness.

But no sooner had Mbooma—or boy Brown, as he was called in the camp—left in order to carry the good tidings to Ida and her father than a change—and a strange one, too— came over the spirit of the adventurers' dream. They were attacked by the dwarfs. Not in open day came those hideous creatures to fight them, but by night, when, save the sentinels, the whole camp was wrapt in slumber, and poisoned arrows were showered amongst them, many being wounded at the first volley. It was in a gorge of the forest where the attack was made; out in the open they could have seen their foe, but here was no clearing; the whole space betwixt N'tooba's country and Lake Unga Noona is, or was then, a vast primeval forest.

From such a foe, in such a place, and at such a time, defence was almost impossible. Rifles were fired and charges made in the direction from which the arrows seemed to come throughout the whole night, and the hideous yells that occasionally followed the firing told that some at least of the shots had taken effect. But the unseen foe seemed to know no fear, and so the strange battle was kept up till nearly morning.

Gone ! They were gone when the sun rose, and, saving some pools of blood here and there, they had left no trace behind, and although the forest was scoured for miles around the camp, no sign of human life or habitation was visible.

Meanwhile Stanley's men had suffered severely; ten lay dead, fifteen more were wounded, but these were saved by Sambo, who found an antidote for the poison growing in the woods. Saved from death, but not from sickness, they lay as if dead, with swollen limbs and heads, rolling their eyes in agony and opening their lips only to beg for water. To Stanley's intense sorrow, Big Bill was among the wounded.

To proceed farther for some time was impossible, so the camp was removed to somewhat higher ground, axes were set to work, and a rampart built of fallen trees and earth, and before nightfall they were comparatively safe. No fires were lit, however. They were willing to risk death from the talons of wild beasts rather than at the hands of these terrible and mysterious dwarfs.

There was a strange and ominous silence throughout the forest next night. Well our poor fellows knew what it meant. The lions were far away, the forest around the camp was occupied by a more dangerous and insidious foe. Under the ramparts lay some of Stanley's best marksmen, and the crack of a rifle every now and then, followed perhaps by a short, sharp yell of pain, told its own tale. Arrows were flung into the camp, but in almost every instance they missed their aim. Daylight came at last, and the foe fled. But this time they left one of their wounded; he had fallen inside the rampart. When found his contortions were fearful to behold. Too much stricken to move off his back, he wheeled round and round, making as if defending himself with feet and hands, like a wounded wild cat. That he expected torture was evident, for on one of Stanley's men going nearer to him he sprang at his spear, which happened to be lowered, and plunged it into his heart; then, with a grin of defiance, he fell back and died.

"Poor creature!" said kind-hearted Tom.

Not much, if anything, over three feet was the creature, with hair that almost hid the face and eyes, long ape-like arms and feet, powerful joints, and a face which, when the hair was pushed aside, looked almost white but fearfully repulsive, the forehead receding and ridged, the broad nose squatting on the upper lip, and the strong lower jaw extended like that of a bull-dog.

They buried him outside the camp.

On the very day after Mbooma's visit and departure, greater stir than usual was observed in the kraal of King Lambabeela. It was beyond a doubt now that the tribe were up in arms.

"They have heard, Ida," said Captain Ross to his daughter, "by means of their scouts that an expedition is on its way to rescue us. Now let us be up and doing. Our fortress is not yet impregnable, but it is nearly so. Hope for the best, lass; there are brighter times before us."

"I do so, hope," said Ida; "indeed, father, I feel as if we were already leaving for home. Oh! think, father," she continued, clapping her little hands joyfully; "*home*, father, our dear American home!"

Only just for a moment did he press his daughter in his arms and imprint a kiss on her brow. In that kiss was a prayer and a blessing.

It was a busy day on Ida's Isle. Mammie Sarah was busier apparently than anybody else. She was here, there, and everywhere. She not only cooked the curry, but she carried stones to the ramparts as well.

"Dear Mammie Sarah," Ida remonstrated, "you'll kill yourself."

"Kill, dear lammie?" was the reply. "No, no, ole Mammie Sarah no kill. Mammie Sarah plenty much tough-tough. Byme-by we fight. Den wen de w'ite man he come, you take poor Mammie Sarah off to de 'appy land. Dat's whyfore Mammie work so. Mammie not let de curry spoil alls ame."

And the eight men of the fortress worked too, singing little nonsensical songs to themselves all the time to little nonsensical airs, so that Ida was sometimes fain to laugh, though her heart was big with fear and hope combined.

Ida's post was on the tower, the highest part of the rampart. Beside her lay the tiger, his blinking eyes following every look and movement of his well-loved mistress.

The day wore away at last, and the sun was just touching the hill-tops in the west, when—

"Oh, father, come up !" cried Ida.

He was by her side in a moment.

"It is as I thought," he said. "One, two, three war-canoes. Give me the glass. Yes, filled with warriors of the Makalala tribe. Now, dear girl, be firm. We'll have to give those murderous cannibals an American welcome."

"I'm firm, father. I have not the slightest fear," said Ida, bravely.

Now the fact is that Captain Ross was never a favourite with the medicine men of King Lambabeela's kraal. He was a rival, and from being jealous of his power over their chief they turned to hate him. As soon, therefore, as hunters of the tribe brought word to the king that an expeditionary force of white men was on its way to bring away the captives, the king called his chiefs together, and consulted his medicine men or wizards. These last could not tell what to do, or what to advise, until they had consulted their fetishes. So they got water from the magic lake and poured it on their heads; they killed cocks and goats and drank the blood; they besmeared themselves with clay and clotted gore ; and did a great many other silly things which made them look very ridiculous and smell very high. I do not think that they hurt themselves much, however, with all their mummeries, though they pretended to ; and danced, and shrieked, and lay down, and kicked, and foamed at the mouth, and grew blacker in the face than nature had made them. And all the time fat old King Lam babeela squatted among the skulls and bones in front of his wives'—he had about forty—tent and drank rum, to get which had cost him the lives of hundreds of his subjects. He drank rum and laughed, drank more and danced, drank more, clutched his spear, and stalked forth in all his majesty —not very steadily, though. He was splendidly dressed ; he wore over his shoulders a cloak of camel's hair, tasselled round with tobacco-pipes that rattled as he walked ; he had a Wellington boot on one leg and a 42nd Highlander's stocking on the other. I have not an idea where he got them, but there they were. Round his neck he had a circlet of human fingerbones, and on his head a small patent Dutch-oven, ornamented with feathers of the ostrich and red ibis—a very handy helmet indeed, because—do you not see ?—when not on the war-path one could cook one's morsel of steak in it. In his hand he held a spear surmounted by a skull.

Lambabeela cut off a head or two from the shoulders of medicine men by way of hurrying matters. Then the others gave their verdict.

"Ida Ross and her father must die."

The chiefs knew the drunken old king well. They advised the calling in of his levies of soldiers and—more rum. He entrusted the marshalling of his troops to his officers. He took charge of the rum himself. Meanwhile the rum took charge of him, he fell asleep, and for a time the curtain drops on the camp of Lambabeela.

The three war-canoes were filled with feather-adorned savages, their chief one of the most bloodthirsty of Lambabeela's cut-throat tribe. His last act before leaving the shore to attack Ida's Isle was to cast lots among the young girls of the tribe, seventy-seven of whom he imprisoned and condemned to die on that day of rejoicing when the army of the king should return to the village, bearing in front of them the heads of Stanley Grahame, Mite, and every other white man of the attacking expedition.

Now, Ross's safety depended on his being able to guard the one path that led upwards to the lovely garden in which he dwelt. Every other part of the mountain island was inaccessible to the feet of savages.

The war-canoes approached, and neared the island to the beating of the warlike tom-tom and the jack-snipe shriek of the warrior crews. They neared the island, then all was silent, and so remained till long past sunset.

Then once more that jack-snipe shriek. They were coming. Ross and his men were at their post, determined to sell their lives dearly, if sell them they must. They were armed with spears, that was all. But near to them was a cairn of boulders, each one of which would sweep the little pathway if fifty warriors were to come, each one as strong as Samson.

Upwards they rush. Ross and his gallant band can hear the crackling of the twigs and branches as they ascend. Had the path not been zig-zag, had it only been straight up the mountain's side, or had the hill not been covered with bushes and trees, then those boulders could have been brought into action while the enemy was still far away, and done greater execution than they now do; yet no sooner does the first feathered head appear than a stone is loosened and goes tumbling down. In vain is the shield of buffalo-hide elevated. The boulder does its work. Another and another follows with fearful rapidity. Breaking into fragments as they roll down the mountain-side, these stones clear the foe away, and the attack is repelled. Again and again during the night it is renewed, but with the same results, and the war-cry of the warriors is changed into yells of pain and baffled vengeance. All next day the defenders worked hard in order to get more boulders into position, and at night again the attack was renewed. More canoes have come from the mainland. Loss of life seems not to deter them from making attack after attack and rush after rush. If they could have only got to close quarters, it would soon have been all over with poor Ida and her father.

Thus night after night for many nights.

Meanwhile the moon favours the foe. It is late now before she rises, so that the ear must do the work of the eye, to tell the defenders of the approach of the foe. There must not be a hush heard above. But the enemy climb to the assault as silently as evil spirits might. .

The weary watching and constant fighting begin to tell at last on Ross and his men. Poor Ida moves around pale now and silent. Why, why does not Stanley come ?

"If it were not for these trees," says Ross one day, "I'd make it hot for these fellows, that I would."

Ida hears him. She makes a resolve, and the very next morning, while her father is snatching a few brief moments' slumber, and Mammie Sarah is busy in the house, she tells the men what she is about to do, and, although they remonstrate, she only bids them fear not for her, and, lighted torch in hand, she leaves the ramparts and steals quietly down the zigzag path towards the beach.

No one sees her, no one hears her. Now she is at the foot, and quickly fires the grass. The savages are asleep; she steals quietly past them and repeats the operation on the other side. Then flinging the torch still farther off, she springs back towards the path. Alas ! she stumbles ; a twig snaps, and next moment she finds herself pursued. Fleet as a deer is she, but fleeter of foot is that fearful savage. He is at her. He has seized her. She faints not, but shrieks. All her hopes are gone ; death only before her.

But nay, for that shriek has brought help from an unexpected quarter. Next moment the savage is writhing in the death agony in the talons of Ida's tiger.

Ida springs lightly up the path and soon is safe. Sir Stanley, the tiger, coolly follows—*with* his prey.

In a few moments the whole mountain is sheathed in

smoke and flame, and for two days, fanned by the wind that the fire had raised, it continues to smoulder. But those in the cone at the top are safe, and, for the time being, happy. At night the mountain looked like a vast cone of fire. Stanley, emerging from the forest-land after his trouble with the dwarfs, saw it, and his heart stood still with fear.

Stanley, coming to the rescue of the prisoners from the north, saw the burning mountain cone; boy Green and his merry men, coming from the south, saw it too; but boy Green simply wondered what it meant.

Archie Weir was the guide for this part of the expedition, but boy Green insisted upon being chief.

"Which it's little enough," the cheeky boy explained. "These Arab chaps are all in my pay. They're my mercenaries, and it's precious little mercy they'll have if they doesn't stick up like men, but I means to give the order on the paymaster fair and square. If he returns it marked 'No effecks,' 'tain't my look-out, is it?"

Boy Green's adventures in this expedition would fill a volume. Many a hearty laugh Archie Weir had at his daring, cool, ridiculous adventures. He was constantly getting into "scrapes," as he called them, with the lions and tigers, but he always got out of them somehow. When at last they neared the country of the Makalala, boy Green conceived and executed a piece of policy which was really not unworthy of a great warrior.

"I say, you know," he said to Weir, "we'll look rather funny marching into old Kafoozlum's camp with only twenty followers, won't we, old stick-in-the gutter?"

"Rather," said Weir, smiling; "but maybe your friends are there before us."

"But supposin' they ain't, hey? And supposin' old King Kafoozlum thinks our heads will make nice hornaments for his marble mantelpiece, hey? What then, I axes? No; I ain't a-going to risk my precious nut like that! Why, the British navy would go to the dogs without boy Green! Now, 'cross the stream 'ere, we comes to King Rumfulli's country, hey ?—so you told me."

"Umfulli's; yes."

"Well, 'Umfulli or Rumfulli, it's all the same. He doesn't like Kafoozlum, does he ? "

"Hates him like poison !"

"Well, can't yer see the game, dunderhead ? We pits *Rum*foozlum against *Kum*foozlum, and we just stands aside and sees 'em peck—hey, Scottie ? "

Scottie laughed, but he came to the conclusion, after a little cogitation, that if they could secure the alliance of Lambabeela's hereditary foe, the warlike Umfulli, they would be on the safe side. The Arabs were of the same opinion.

"But I don't know any more than the man in the moon how it's to be done," said Weir.

"No more do I," said boy Green. "You speaks the langwidge, don't yer ? "

"Yes," said Weir.

"Well, let's go in and try."   ·

Two days after this boy Green, at the head of his little troop, was marching boldly into Umfulli's camp. He would not stay a moment to listen to the palaver of the chiefs. He demanded audience of the king. He never drew a sword nor allowed his followers to do so; they mixed as freely with those fierce savages as if they had been walking in Fleet Street, and as if everybody was friendly.

They found the king squatting in the darkness of his kraal, for the day was fiercely hot.

Boy Green and Weir entered salaaming, very much to the potentate's surprise, who sprang to his feet and seized his spear.

"Don't rise," said boy Green, affably—"don't rise, Tomfooli; we permits yer to remain seated in our august presence. Weir, tell the old chap all I say."

In a few brief but pompous sentences boy Green explained what he wanted.

"Now," concluded boy Green, "I gives you a whole hour to make up yer mind; we goes and eats some curry in the meantime. If yer consents you're a made man. I'll give an order on the paymaster for all the gunpowder and all the rice and all the guns in the ship. If yer doesn't ' consent we'll go on without yer. Twenty thousand British troops, more or less, ain't far off, so just look out, for if ye refuses you'll be a insultin' of the whole might and majesty of England, and the boy Green into the bargain."

It would be difficult to say whether King Umfulli was more angry or more mystified at the audacity of boy Green. One thing is certain—that no sooner had that bold young ster retired than he summoned together all the chiefs of his tribe, and they at once laid all their wise heads together. There were many speeches made, much bluster, and much brandishing of spears. One proposed cutting the head off boy Green by way of simplifying matters, and a messenger was actually dispatched to tell the sailor lad that he had better come to the door of the king's tent and submit quietly to the operation.

"Never," was boy Green's reply. "I'll die first. Besides, tell the king that I ain't done dinner, and if I hadn't a head I couldn't write an order on the paymaster for all the rice and all the gunpowder."

Whether the thoughts of rice and guns had anything to do with the matter or not I cannot say. One thing is certain, peace prevailed in the council of the king. Umfulli thought there must be something in it; besides, Lambabeela had been very audacious of late, and if he had now a chance of paying him back he did not see why he should not take it.

The result was that next morning Umfulli ordered out his reserves, his spear-armed impis.

The din, the shrieking, the tom-tom beating, the clashing

of spears, and the hubbub generally would have confused a less bold and impudent sailor than boy Green, but he never lost his presence of mind for a moment. He was condescending to the king, .whose old white horse he borrowed, telling Umfulli, through Weir, that he would be pleased now to review the troops.

A fearfully imposing array those ten thousand savage soldiers made, but, accompanied by the king, his chiefs, Weir, and the Arabs, boy Green rode coolly past them, and returned their salaams with the air of a prince.

"I don't see no signs of a commissariat, Tomfulli. Hey?" said boy Green.

Umfulli's reply was a grim and terrible one.

"They will live well. They will eat the Makalala men."

"Oh!" said boy Green, carelessly, "is that the arrangement? Now, as far as I'm concerned, stooed rabbit, or beefsteak and honions, would suit this chicken better."

Of this great army boy Green constituted himself commandant. He stuck to Umfulli's old white horse. If he didn't bring him back, he told the king, England might see that Umfulli was no loser.

"Oh! that's the way to Lambabeela's country, is it, hey?" This is what boy Green told the chief of the Umfullis : "Well, if you please, we'll go t'other way round. We'll houtflank old Lambabeela. That's tactics, that's strategy, that's modern warfare."

A whole week of fighting ensued. Boy Green marched his men wedge-fashion into the land of the Makalala, but he encountered terrible opposition. Men fell thick and fast as leaves in Vallambrosa. It was one long battle day after day, and almost night after night, and ever at the head of the corps rode boy Green on his white charger. He seemed to bear a charmed life.

The last morning's fight was a fearful but decisive one. The Makalala men fled in utter confusion, and were more

than decimated, and before noon, still mounted on that
wonderful nag, and singing, "Britons never, never, *ne-ver*
shall be slaves," boy Green rode into the village of
Lambabeela, and at once ordered the king to be brought
into his presence.

The fat old king was terribly frightened, and seemed
to have some little difficulty in walking. But he was
"touched up in the rear," as boy Green called it. Oh!
not with a spear, only with a pin, but it was quite enough
to make Lambabeela jump along and rub.

Boy Green might have made his interview with the king
a very imposing ceremony, but I fear, from his style of
address, he somewhat detracted from the romance of the
situation. Weir laughingly handed boy Green an umbrella.

"What's this? Hey? Oh! the sceptre, is it? Well,
it isn't the sweetest o' perfoomery, at all events."

Then boy Green seized the king by the ear.

"Why 'ere's a ear for ye!" said boy Green. "I could
get a 'old of it with both 'ands easy. Stand straight, can't
yer?" Picks up a bottle. "Why, what's he been a
imbibin' of? he can't walk!" Sniffs the bottle. "Rum,
I do declare; a drop o' the very best ship's. *You* don't
know 'ow to take care o' *your* little self, *you* don't. Oh!
ye good-for-nuffin old scirmudgeon! Don't clap yer 'ands
behind yer neck; I ain't goin' to touch yer, and ye ain't
goin' to be hung afore to-morrer mornin'. Stan' straight, I
tell yer. Now what 'ave ve got to say for yourself,
hey?"

"What's the old idgit mumbling about, Weir?" continued boy Green.

"He says he wants a drop of rum," replied Weir.

"The old himbecile! Tell 'im he'll 'ave a drop to-
morrow mornin' fust thing. Six feet of a drop. I guess
he won't want more arter that. Now ax 'im where he
keeps his gold and his diamonds and sich. In his tent,
hey? Let's go there."

"Why, I do declare," continued boy Green, turning up his eyes as the treasures of the realm of the King of the Makalala were spread out before him, "there's bushels and bushels of nuggets and diamonds ! Here's war hindemnity for ye ! Here's treasure-trove ! Hurrah ! I won't have to give Tomfulli an order on the paymaster yet. Hurrah ! "

And, very much to the astonishment of the sedate Arabs and amusement of Weir, boy Green, on the spur of the moment, executed a hornpipe in front of the whole army.

"Now, Mr. Green," began Weir.

"Who're you calling *Mister* Green, if you please, hey ? King Green, that's me ! " and the boy touched his breast and drew himself up.

"Well, King Green," said Weir, "here are seventy-seven girls in this house."

" I see," said King Green ; "a very interesting sight. A kind of a girls' school, isn't it—like wot they 'as at Ramsgate, hey ? "

"No ; they were to have been executed, every one of them."

"Oh, you poor little dears ! " cried Green to the trembling girls ; "I declare I could pipe my heye. Take that old Foozles out o' here, I can't abear the sight of 'im, and tie 'im up somewheres till 'anging time to-morrer. Poor girls, then ! But they shan't be touched, then ! Now, now then, now ! "

Thus boy Green spoke soothingly to the little prisoners, prisoners now no more.

"Ha ! " cried Weir, "here is news ! A Somali lad has just come to solicit assistance for your friend Stanley Grahame ! "

It was Mbooma that had rushed breathless into the presence of the boy Green.

XXV.

THE BATTLE ON IDA'S ISLE—ARRIVAL OF BOY GREEN AND FLIGHT OF THE MAKALALAS—BACK IN N'TOOBA'S LAND.

CHAPTER XXV.

IT is no wonder that many African travellers doubt or
even deny the existence, in the far interior of that
Dark Continent, of a race of warlike dwarfs. They are
seldom seen, for few have ventured to invade the dense
and almost impenetrable forest lands where they live, and
some of those who have done so have mistaken them for
members of the gorilla tribe.

And no wonder; the war tactics of these dwarfs approxi-
mate closely to the habits of the wild beasts among which
they dwell. They never fight except at night; they seldom
move abroad till after dark. They eat to engorgement, and
their meals are often followed by long periods of sleep.
They live in caves or holes in the earth, and sometimes in
nests or small houses in the trees. Their government is a
republic, they have neither king nor laws; they are
socialists, nihilists—they are precisely what the lowest fac-
tions of politicians of our own country, France, and Russia
would fain reduce European society to; and it seems to me
a pity that those said politicians do not emigrate and live
among the dwarfs in the forest lands of the Dark Continent,
where they would have everything precisely as they wish it.

Stanley's band was composed of brave, resolute men, but
it was not a numerous one, and hemmed in by thousands
on thousands of those terrible dwarfs, it appeared all but
certain that not a man would ever leave the forest alive·

They encamped themselves, it is true; that was but changing open warfare for a state of siege, if indeed it could be called open warfare where the enemy was invisible. For the first time since the commencement of the expedition Stanley began to lose heart.

"Mite," he said one day, "I fear I'm going to sicken."

"Oh! Stan," said Mite, "don't think of that. I say," he continued, "suppose we fire the forest."

"And perish in the flames!" said Stanley, shaking his head. "No, Mite, we mustn't think of that."

Mbooma had returned. His news was far from re-assuring. The island was in a state of siege, and he feared all upon it would perish.

The dwarfs got more audacious. How long it would be before they actually stormed the camp Stanley could not of course guess. At best it could be but a few days. But one morning everybody was aroused before daylight by the beating of tom-toms, and the war shouts of an approaching army.

"Stand to guns and spears," cried Stanley, "here they come, the Makalala men. Let us sell our lives dearly, if die we must."

But here were no Makalala men, for the first to spring to the ramparts and jump into the camp was Mbooma, who had been missed for a few days.

And the next to follow was N'tooba himself—the king with the click.

It would have done your heart good to have heard the shout with which the good king was welcomed. Black as he was, Stanley didn't hesitate to press him in his arms. He was black, but the black couldn't come off, you know.

Stanley's party was escorted to the banks of Lake Unga Noona by N'tooba's soldiers. There a camp was formed, the sick were seen to, and Stanley prepared his iron boat at once, and had her launched, and manned, and armed.

The hill that was fired by Ida was still smouldering in

places, but shouts were occasionally heard that told plainly enough that the savages had recommenced their attack, and war-canoes were hieing here and there about the island.

Those shouts and war-cries were the sweetest music to Stanley's ear that ever he had listened to. They told him that Ida and her father were still alive. He shuddered as he thought of how he must have felt had he arrived and found only silence reigning on and around Ida's Isle. He lost no time now in proceeding to give battle to the foe. He was at a disadvantage, however. His boat, large as it was, could contain but few men compared to the number of savages he was called upon to face, and he dared not over-crowd it.

He left Tom Reynolds in charge of the camp, and to minister to the sick and wounded. He took with him Sool and Sambo, and Mite and Cooke, with the flower of his own little army, to say nothing of the boy Mbooma.

The savages at Ida's Isle were not long before they found out that a new danger threatened them. They desisted from the attack on the mountain, therefore, and prepared to give Stanley a warm reception. It was their last chance, and they knew it. Their army was broken up and beaten on shore, and their king a prisoner ; but with this island in their possession, this part of Lambabecla's forces had hoped to stand their ground until the enemy left the country.

All this time, it must be remembered, Stanley knew nothing of the boy Green's share in the war, and nothing of the doings on the other side of the water. But Mbooma, the clever Somali lad, had come to the conclusion that the Makalala must be at war with some tribe, and the assistance of that tribe he determined to solicit.

As soon, therefore, as the boat approached the island, he dropped quietly over the side, dived, and disappeared.

"Look, Mite, look !" cried Stanley, joyfully, pointing to the highest rock on Ida's Isle. "Yonder stands Ida herself, and her father. See, she waves her hand !"

Stanley drew his sword and waved it aloft.

"On, lads!" he cried; "pull, men, pull!"

There were no more words spoken. Deeds must now take the place of words.

Sool was steering, Stanley only waving his hand occasionally to guide him.

In a moment more they will be round the point. Both Cooke and Mite divest themselves of their jackets, look to their pistols, tighten their waistbelts, then wait.

"Down, men—down!" shouted Stanley.

Next moment a cloud of spears from the war-canoes.

Stanley replies by a volley from the rifles. His boat rushes onwards, right into the very centre of the fleet of war-canoes, several of which are sunk with their living freights. There is clashing of swords and spears, shouting and cheering, and the rattling fire of revolvers, and over all smoke. There is blood on the water; the canoes are stained with it, and Stanley's boat is splashed with the crimson flood. Many men on both sides have dropped their weapons and fallen where they stood, but in five minutes or little more the fight on the lake is virtually over. The great boat is run on the sand, and Stanley and his men, armed with drawn swords and revolvers, spring lightly on shore. Now the fight seems to begin in earnest.

Stanley and Sambo fought back to back in the midst of that yelling cloud of savages. Mite and Cooke were not far off, and tall Sool was swinging his great Arab sword to and fro with terrible effect.

There is a gash on Sambo's brow; Stanley's shirt is incrimsoned with blood.

It was soon evident that the Makalala men had had enough fighting, for a time at least. They gave way and separated into two beaten crowds, leaving a clear pass in the centre of the zig-zag path that led to the hilltop.

Mite was first on the path. Perhaps he was not sorry to get there, but then remember he was only a very little chap, and, to do him justice, he had fought well, and the sword he now waved above his head as he shouted, " Come on, Stan," gave evidence of having been used.

The savages made no further resistance at present. They retreated to the shelter of the rocks.

In a few moments more Ida, half fainting, was clasped in Stanley's arms.

" I thank you, dear boy," said old Captain Ross, with the tears streaming from his eyes, " and I thank the dear God who sent you. My little girl and I never quite lost hope ; we but prayed and prayed the more ; and the Lord has heard us. Ever blessed be His name ! "

" But you are wounded, Stanley," said Ida with alarm.

" No," said Stanley ; " it is a mere scratch on the shoulder ; but poor Sambo is."

" Oh, Sambo ! " cried Ida, taking his work-hardened hand in hers.

" Oh, Missie Ida ! dis is a happy day for poor old Sambo. He not sure wedder he should laugh or wedder he should cry ; he feels like as he wants to do boff."

Stanley's work was not yet finished. The savages were still in crowds beneath the rocks. They had fought their way through them, it is true, but the island was still, to all intents and purposes, in a state of siege. Men could have embarked in that boat and sailed away from Ida's Isle, but Stanley could not think of exposing those he had come so far to deliver to danger from the spears of the enemy. No, the Makalala men must be cleared off the island, driven into the lake.

But even while he doubted how this could be done, boats were reported to be approaching the island from Lamba-beela's side of the lake.

Canoes with white men in them !

Almost at the same time, much to the joy of our heroes, the war-canoes of the Makalalas were seen stealing away from the island and taking a north-westerly direction towards

the head of the lake. They, too, had seen the white
men coming, and, abandoning all further hope of taking
possession of Ida's Isle, had crowded into the few war-
canoes that remained, and fled away to the silent woods.

Stanley Grahame, with Ida by his side, Mite, and Captain
Ross, all stood near the rocky entrance to Ida's garden-land
at the mountain-top anxiously waiting, and wondering what
men they would have the pleasure of welcoming. Long
before a head appeared in sight up the hillside, boy Green's
well-known accents could be distinguished. He was talking loud enough to be heard a mile away, talking to Archie
Weir, and now and then bursting into a snatch of his ever-
lasting refrain,

"Britons never, never, ne-ver shall be sa-laves. Come
along, Archibald, come along, old man; don't be shy.
We've got to find 'em, if we goes to the moon for it. Mind
your feet. They're precious big uns, Archie. Nice large,
useful feet, Archie. Britons never, never, never—Yes,
Archie, you were well to the front, old man, when feet were
bein' served out. Those feet of yours ought to wear well,
Archie, and the bones would do for handspikes when you've
done wi' them. Hey? Britons never——Wonder what
Stanley'll say when he sees me. Hey! And that miserable little wision of a chap they calls Mite? Britons never,
never, ne-ver'shall be sa-laves."

"If that isn't boy Green," said Stanley, laughing, "it's
boy Green's ghost."

"A pretty way he talks about his officer," said Mite,
drawing himself up to his full height, which wasn't much,
you know, after all.

"Britons never, nev——I say, Archie, old chap, there
don't seem no end to this 'ere mountain. There don't seem
to be nary a top to the 'ill at all at all. I say, though, won't
it be a lark when we does get up and finds 'em all at home?
Shouldn't wonder if that miserable little wision of a Mite
orders me to go and get my 'air cut. If he does, boy Green

will reply in the language of Shakspeare, when he were a-crossing of the Alps at the 'cad of the Scotch Fusilier Guards, 'Britons never, never, ne-ver—shall—be—sa-laves.' Hullo! here we are at the top. My heye! 'ere is a pretty place, quite a hoasis in the desert, so to speak. Now we descends, you see, Archie, and yonder comes the 'ole crowd o' them to meet us. Wot a lovely female girl, to be sure!"

Boy Green at this moment took his cap off, not to bow—no, no—only to make a hurried toilet by putting his fingers through his hair. He even went so far as to wet the sleeve of his jacket with his tongue and rub his face therewith, just as a pussy would have done.

"I say," he said anxiously to Weir, "is my face *wery* dirty, Weir—wery, *wery* dirty? Hey! Ladies, you know, Archie, ladies. There they all come, all the lot on 'em, but I hain't got heyes for no one but Hida."

"Good morning, ladies and gentlemen," continued this audacious boy, stepping forward and lifting his cap. "Good morning—leastways, good arternoon, which it comes all to the same thing in the hend, as the pig said when he swallered a string o' sassagers. General Grahame, I salutes you; Mr. Mite, ahem!—I means Captain MacDermott, in course I does; I've come on board, Captain MacDermott; Miss Hida, I bows; the hold chap's your guvnor, I 'spects. Hey? Captain Ross, I pays my respects to you, sir; I loves to see a nice clean hold man, sir. Oh! Miss Hida, do call away that tiger, he's a-purring round my legs as if he were going to suck me in. I dessay my nerves is a kind o' upset from the priwations I'se endured in the wilderness, but I *is* afeard of 'im, and there's no use a-denyin' of it. I don't like cats o' that kidney. Do call 'im off, miss, please."

"Mammie Sarah," cried Ida, laughing, "lead poor Sir Stanley to his cage."

But when boy Green and Archie Weir "settled down,"

as the former called it, and told all their story, then indeed all knew that they had no small cause for gratitude to the strange madcap boy Green.

He finished off by excusing himself thus :

" Yer see, general, it seemed to me like a temptin' o' Providence to send the hexpiedition away 'athout a surgeon and medical hadwiser, so I determined to foller and see things right. We've made it precious 'ot for old King Kafoozlum, I can tell yer, and, as the himmortal William says, ' Hall's well as hends well.' Miss Hida, if you've a morsel o' bread and cheese in the larder, miss, or a pickin' of a 'ambone, me and my pal 'ere would be glad of it, for we 'aven't 'ad wot you'd call a square meal for more'n a week, miss."

" Oh ! mussy on me ! " cried Mammie Sarah, " de poor leetle boy must be drefful hungry. Mammie Sarah run plenty quick and make de curry for de leetle boy, and all de rest of de white folks."

Ida was thanking Weir for all his goodness.

" I assure you, Miss Ross, you have only boy Green to thank," replied Weir.   " I *might* have got up an expedition, but he took the matter entirely out of my hands. I could never have secured the services of the Sultan of Lamoo as he did. I have met many strange lads in my time, but nothing to equal the cool audacity of this boy Green." .

" Well," put in boy Green, " ye needn't begin to abuse a feller now.   Wot you calls cheek is merely tactics, and what you terms howdausity is only another name for strategy. Tactics and strategy, them's the words, Mr. Weir.   Silence, sir, when you speaks to a hofficer,—go and get your 'air cut."

Mammie Sarah determined to excel herself that day in making curry. She got Sambo to assist her to " lay de cloff " and make everything presentable for the " 'stocracy and gentry," as she called Captain Ross and his guests, and a happier party never surrounded a board than that which sat down to dinner 'in the evening in Ida's Isle. What though the plates were wood, and the forks and spoons of the same " metal"? what though the drinking utensils were but carefully fashioned cocoa-nut shells, the wine but cocoa-nut milk? all were happy—all were even merry.

But when dinner was finished and day beginning to give place to the short evening gloaming, they all assembled, both white men and black, in the bungalow parlour, and prayers were offered up to Him who had brought surcease of sorrow to the poor prisoners who had pined so long in slavery, and a blessing was begged for the successful termination of the expedition.

When the stars shone out, and were reflected in the dark waters of Unga Noona, when fireflies were dancing hither and thither among the trees in Ida's garden, Stanley and she wandered there all alone, and hand in hand as they had done at Beaumont Park when both were children.

" Yes," Stanley was saying, " I knew you would forgive me; but, dear Ida, I have never, through all these years, forgotten the cruel words—cruel, ungrateful words—I used to you that day I left Beaumont Park. But I knew I had only to ask your forgiveness in order to obtain it."

Next day was a day of exodus from Ida's Isle. All did not leave, though. Only Mammie Sarah and one or two of the others. The rest preferred to stay on the island, and look after Ida's garden and Ida's pets.

Mbooma was left. He begged to be left. He did not fear the Makalala. Perhaps, he said, he himself would soon be king, but he begged as a last favour that Captain Ross would leave his telescope with him, a favour that I need hardly say was readily granted.

Then the expedition started back through the forest on the return journey.

N'tooba's men guarded them safely past the country of the dwarfs, and in the lovely country of this good king they sojourned for many, many weeks, in order to obtain the rest they all so much needed. Here poor Big Bill breathed his last.

He never recovered the effects of the wounds he had received at the hands of those fearful dwarfs.

"I know I'm dying," he said to Stanley, who sat by his bedside in his rude grass hut. "Better me than you or Mite, Stan. I'm older, and I've nothing much to live for. Ah! there are better worlds than this, and Bill will be welcome in that far-off happy country we read of in the good Book, Stan. Good-bye. Pray for me, as you always have. Tell that dear, sweet girl, Ida, to pray—how dark the tent gets, Stan—how dark! Ah! this is death, Stan! This is——"

His honest heart had ceased to beat.

There is a great banian-tree, that grows in a green glade not far from N'tooba's village. Under the shade of that tree sleeps Big Bill—

> "Sleeps the sleep that knows no breaking,
>   Morn of toil, nor night of waking."

*   *   *   *   *

Boy Green, with his many queer ways and quaint sayings, made himself a favourite with every one. His devotion to Ida was extreme. He was ever planning some pleasant surprise for her. He roamed through the forest fearlessly and alone, and ever brought the "spoils of the chase," as he termed the contents of his shooting-bag, to her tent. Or he would angle in the river for strange fish, and bring them as a present to Ida. Failing these, he brought her flowers.

"I allers feels," he told her one day, "when I'm alongside o' you, Miss Hida, as how my hedication has been shamefully neglected. I carn't talk the Henglish langwidge in hall its native purity."

Poor boy Green! he was last seen in the jaws of a man-eating lion, being borne off towards the forest. As the lion went bounding through the camp, boy Green was seen to wave his arms, and heard to utter some words that sounded very like these :

"Good-bye—hall—Miss Hida—Sultan's boys—horder on the paymaster—Britons never, nev——"

No one heard more. But deep was the sorrow in the camp, and Ida herself was inconsolable for days and weeks thereafter. Every available soldier in N'tooba's country was turned out to scour the forest. They brought back the boy's cap, that was all."

*   *   *   *

The day for leaving N'tooba's land came round at last, and the kindly king shed tears that he took no pains to hide.

" I shall miss you all," he said, " and life to poor N'tooba will only hang now on the hopes of seeing some of you once again."

This was said with quite a large number of clicks. I think the clicks seemed in some way or other to relieve his feelings.

And so the expedition started away for the coast.

"Good-bye, and God bless you all," said Tom Reynolds. " You will say all to my people I told you. Henceforth and for years my home will be here. Here with this good people, here with this king, I have a mission to fulfil, the very thought of which fills all my soul with joy."

" Good-bye."

" Good-bye."

" Good-bye."

XXVI

HOMEWARD BOUND—THE CRYSTAL BOAT—A PLEASANT SURPRISE.

HOMEWARD BOUND—THE CRYSTAL BOAT—A
PLEASANT SURPRISE.

CHAPTER XXVI.

NOT a large ship by any means. Though only seven
hundred tons, she was nevertheless as **bonnie** a
barque as ever sailed the seas. She is moving slowly
out of Zanzibar Harbour, with every stitch of canvas set,
for the wind, although favourable, is but light. It is a
glorious day; the sea and sky are the bluest of blue, the
white houses on shore seem built of marble, and so brightly
do they stand out in the sunshine, that the shadows they
throw seem black by contrast. The *Tonitru* is lying at
anchor,—

> "As idle as a painted ship
> Upon a painted ocean."

The quarter-deck is crowded with officers in blue and white
and gold; the brass band is there too, and over the rippling
sea, with a weird tremolo born of the waves they cross,
come the sweet, sad notes of that fine old song—

> "Good-bye, sweetheart, good-bye."

Oh, dear! I must throw down my pen, seize my violin
and play it over and over again; and the music has had
this effect upon me—that I am fully *en rapport* with my
subject, and could spend a good hour describing the departure of the good ship that bore my heroine and heroes back
to their far-off homes.

> " Parting is such sweet sorrow "

Mite is not on the quarter-deck ; he is out standing there against the blue, on the very point of the flying jibboom, waving his handkerchief to his brother Stan—and, reader, I am not at all sure that the handkerchief is not somewhat damp.

Poor Mite ! he would have given anything he possessed to have been able to go home in the ship with Stanley ; but service is service—he could not.

And now a point of land hides the barque from the anchored man-o'-war, and in a few hours there is nothing around the former but the silence of the mighty deep. Ross is captain of this gallant barque ; Cooke is first lieutenant, or chief mate, as they call that officer in the merchant navy ; Stanley Grahame is second officer ; and who do you think is bo'swain ? Why, none other than our good friend Sambo.

And here is Mammie Sarah. She has been rated stewardess, but at the same time she will see after the concoction of the curry for the cabin, for I do not believe any one ever did make such delightful curry as Mammie Sarah.

Very beautiful Ida Ross looks now as she lounges in her chair, book in hand, on the snow-white quarter-deck ; very beautiful and very happy also, for now she is safe, and her father, and—yes, and Stanley is safe, and all the years of her sorrow and suffering are to her now but like the memory of some awful dream.

Not only Ida, but every soul on board, seems happy and contented, and even gay, for lo! the ship is homeward-bound. Ay, and the ship appears to know it, and to feel happy in consequence.

A sailing ship she is ; no grind and gride of terrible wheels are here, no showers of smut and sifted coal-dust to throw spot and speck on her snowy decks or disfigure the bright tablecloth that adorns the saloon table. She is clad in canvas from deck to truck stunsails low and aloft, and

HOMEWARD BOUND.

Page 342.

looks as gay as village maiden on her wedding morn ; and as she goes swinging along she seems to beck and bow and toy and coquette with the billows, as if keeping time to the song of the merry sailors, which rises time after time,

> " With a hey ! my lads, and a ho ! my men,
> For we are homeward bo—o—ound,
> For we—e—e are homeward bound."

    *   *   *   *   *

Once upon a time, my dear boy readers, there was a certain great prince who lived in a beautiful palace in one of the most romantic and lovely districts of Araby the Blest. He was not a very old prince, but he was very brave and very good, and even old men with long, long grey beards bent their heads before him and ministered to him, and told him tales and stories of all kinds, more wonderful by far than even those you read about in the Arabian Nights' Entertainments—that is to say, if anything could be more wonderful than these strange, strange tales.

But, for all this, the young prince was not happy.

" I am tired of these wild woods," he said, " tired of the splendid scenery that is everywhere around me, tired of the gardens, my pets, and my palace, tired even of you, most potent, grave, and reverend seigneurs, and even of your old-world tales. I want to go out into the world and see things myself. I want to be in the very thickest and hottest parts of the most dreadful fights. I want to see the most terrible storms that can rage and the wildest seas. I want to see adventures of every kind imaginable. I cannot stay longer in this palace ; I must go."

" But," cried the old men, " think, beloved prince, think of your kingdom, think of those you leave behind to mourn. Without the sunshine of your presence, everything that you now see around you will fade and die in the darkness of grief, and if ever you returned from your wanderings none would be left alive to welcome you back. Your gardens would be a wilderness and your splendid palace a jackal-haunted ruin."

And the boy prince did think of all this, and did, like a man, resolve, for the sake of his people, to stay at home; but, nevertheless, he often sighed to think of all the countries there were in the would that he could never see, and all the wild adventures that he could never enter into. He sighed by day, and at night he used to dream and start in his sleep, and clutch an imaginary sword, and do all kinds of antics, that simply had the effect of disarranging the bedclothes, and sending the pillow on to the floor, but did not make the prince a bit happier.

But one day there came to the palace a very, very, very old magician. He carried a long stick to keep his nose off the ground, because he was bent double by reason of his extreme age. His hair was as white as the snow on Ben Nevis, and so long that he almost trampled upon it as he walked.

He was brought into the prince's presence, for he had that to tell him which no other ear dare listen to.

"You wish to see the world?" he said to the prince. "Well, I will present you with a beautiful boat—a magic boat, with bottom and sides and masts and sails of glass purer than crystal or even diamonds! When you want to see a battle or a storm, or a fight at sea or on land, all you will have to do will be to go into this beautiful boat, and sit down in its splendid saloon, and it will sail away with you through the air wherever you wish, and you will only have to look through the crystal sides or bottom of your boat in order to see and hear everything that goes on around you!"

"And will it be safe?" asked the prince.

"Yes," said the aged magician; "it will be safe. No power on earth can injure you in your beautiful boat, for, while you will be able to see everything through its crystal sides, no creature nor thing will be able to see or injure you."

Then the young prince was exceedingly glad, and behold ! the aged magician was as good as his word. He brought the prince the crystal boat, and away sailed the prince through the air. And there was no place—not even the most remote—that he could not journey to ; nor was there anything he could not see from this wonderful crystal boat ; and whenever he was tired of sight-seeing or witnessing storms or wild adventures, he had but to wish, and lo and behold ! without even having to say, " Hey, presto !" he was back again in his own home.

Do you not envy that prince in his crystal boat, reader ? Would you not like to have such another beautiful boat ? Well, you have such a boat, for such boats are merely books, in which, while reclining in your easy-chair in the winter evenings, or out on the green grass in summer, or on the clovery leas, you can see, as through a glass, all things that are passing or have passed in the wondrous worldi n which we live. You and I for the last many months have been sailing together in this magic crystal boat, and together we have mingled in many strange and wild adventures,—I as the pilot, you as the passenger. But all things have an end. We are back once again in the dear old country,—in the land that gave us birth,—and pilot and passenger must part.

But ere we shake hands and say " good-bye," let us take one more little cruise in our crystal boat, just to see how fares it with our heroes and our heroines, about two years after the barque, homeward-bound, sailed away from Zanzibar.

I have said heroines, the plural ; well, I want to be exact, for although Ida Ross is really and truly our chief heroine, we must not altogether forget the wild woman, Weir, who first met Stanley Grahame, the boy, on the hobgoblin moor, and took pity on him in his loneliness, and kindly tended him for a night at least.

Ah ! but Jean is daft no longer now, nor does she live

among smugglers in the *cirde* house on the moor. Jean is sane and quiet. Her son has returned; she has found the lost one. Ought I to call him the prodigal son? No; for, with all his faults, Archie loved his mother, and a sweet thing is filial love.

They live now in the little cottage that erst was inhabited by Stanley's mother and sister, and Archie, the roving sailor, tills the farm by the great forest of Cairntric. He not only tills the farm,—which is a small one,—but he is one of the head keepers in the forest, and may be met there any day. But on Sundays Archie always goes to church with the old lady. She is getting frail, and Archie very dutifully gives her his arm. She always rolls her Bible up in her clean white pocket-handkerchief, and always carries on top thereof a little bit of southernwood, which keeps her awake on warm days. So we bid *them* good-bye, and, embarking once more in our crystal boat, go gliding away over the wide Atlantic Ocean.

You know whither we are bound without being told. Yes, here we are at the lovely plantation at Beaumont Park.

Well, except that yonder stalwart man who, with gun on shoulder, is just returning from the woods is Stanley Grahame, and yonder bright-faced, beautiful lady who runs to meet him is his young wife, Ida, there does not seem to be very much change about the place.

Hark! a manly voice singing a darkie song in the wood—

> " We hunt, as of old, for the 'possum and the 'coon,
>   By the meadow, the sea, and the shore ;
> We dance once more by the glimmer of the moon,
>   Near the bench by the old cottage door."

That is Sambo; there is no mistaking him. See, he goes up to an ancient darkie lady who is sitting in the sunshine among the roses and creepers, that twine around the door of her hut.

" Yah, yah !" laughs Sambo. " And so there you is, ole

Mammie Sarah ; and you does look so happy, witn your book and your glasses, that—yah, yah ! this chile must stoo and laugh !   Yah, yah, yah ! ”

“ Go ’long, do ! ” says Mammie Sarah.   “ Don’t laugh like dat ; you make your mouf ever so much bigger ! Besides, sah, you should have some ’spect for ladies, sah ! ”

And here comes old Captain Mackinlay, arm-in-arm with Captain Ross, to meet Ida and her handsome husband. They both look as hale and hearty as if they were merely the brothers of the youthful pair before them—brothers who had by some chance stayed out all night in the woods in winter and had their hair and beards turned white with hoar-frost.

“ Well, children,” says Mackinlay, “ and have you made all preparations for the coming guests ? ”

“ That we have ! ” said Ida ; “ and right glad will we be to see poor Mr. Cooke and Captain MacDermott.”

“ Oh ! ” cried Stanley, laughing, “ don’t let us ‘captain ’ him ; he must just be ‘ Mite ’ as of old ; and if he doesn’t behave himself like a good little boy, why, I shall have to pull his ears and pack him off to bed at nine o’clock.”

“ And so you are going all the way down to R—— to meet him, are you ? ” said Captain Ross.

“ Yes, we must,” replied Stanley.

“ *We* must,” said Mackinlay ; “ pray who are the *we* ? ”

“ Why, Ida and Sissy and I,” said Stanley, smiling, and putting one arm tenderly round his wife.

“ Well, well, well,” said Ross ; “ but you’ll take care of them, I know, and don’t be long away.”

“ In two days we’ll be all back again,” said Stanley, “ and then I guess you won’t have a very easy life, either of you, for a month.   We mean to turn the whole plantation upside-down.”

.“ Yah ! yah ! yah ! ” laughed Sambo ; “ and, gemlems, I is a-going too, I ’ssure you of dat fact.   I is a going wid young massa and missus to help to carry all de pretty tings dey means to buy in de pretty towns dey means to visit.   Dat is so, I 'ssure you once again, gemlems."

Captain Ross pulled out a letter with some queer-looking foreign stamps on it.

It was from Stanley's cousin, Tom Reynolds, the missionary.

It was written on very thin paper, and was fully fifteen pages long, so of course I cannot tell you all that was in it. But it was a very happy and very pleasant letter. It breathed peace and purity.

Tom sent his love to everybody, and so did the old king —the king with the click. The old king said, moreover, that he lived only in the hope of visiting his old friends at Beaumont Park. But one piece of information which he sent was very startling. It was that Mbooma, or boy Brown, was now king of the warlike Makalala, and the nation was at peace with all the tribes around.

*   *   *   *   *

The meeting of Stanley and Mite was a very happy one.

Mite was the boy all over, and he spent the whole evening in doing nothing but plan, plan, planning all the fun and sport he should have at Beaumont Park and the wild country that adjoined it.

" For don't forget, Stan," he said, " that I have six months' leave, and I mean to spend every day of it with you, old boy."

" Yah ! yah ! yah !" laughed Sambo.   " I'se so happy too."

" Shake hands again, Stan, old man. Shake hands, Sambo. Oh ! it is jolly, and so like old times."

A day or two after the meeting of the three old friends, Mite, Stanley, and Cooke, they were seated together by an old tree in the beautiful park. Presently two strangers, both very young men, sauntered along and sat them down beside the tree, with their backs to Stanley and his friends.

The seat was public property, so no notice was at first

taken of the matter, but a moment or two afterwards Stanley started, and looking at Mite, held up his forefinger.

"Listen!" he whispered—"that voice!"

And the following are the words they heard :—

"Waal, as I were a-telling you, the lion he grabbed me, and away he walks me—oh! just as easy as a cat would march off with a mouse. I guessed it were all up with me then, I assure you. I felt a kind o' wexed, too, to think I was to die so young, and wasn't good for anything else but for cat's-meat, as ye might say. But away goes the lion, and away goes I in his mouth, as in dooty bound, ye see. Waal, into the forest we goes, and just as he were a-putting me down, and a-licking of his lips, vy all at vonct——"

Stanley sprang up, and Mite sprang up, and Cooke sprang up.

"It is the boy Green!" they all cried in a breath, and round the tree they ran, and sure enough they were right, for there he sat just as self-possessed as ever, just as impudent, just as saucy.

The identical boy Green again!

www.ingramcontent.com/pod-product-compliance
Lightning Source LLC
Chambersburg PA
CBHW021718110726
47902CB00005B/1242